D0305941

THE DEATH OF ELI GOLD

Also by David Baddiel

The Secret Purposes
Whatever Love Means
Time for Bed

DAVID BADDIEL

The Death of Eli Gold

FOURTH ESTATE · London

First published in Great Britain in 2011 by
Fourth Estate
An imprint of HarperCollins*Publishers*
77–85 Fulham Palace Road
London W6 8JB
www.4thestate.co.uk

Quotation from 'No Surprises' by Thomas Edward Yorke, Jonathan Richard Guy
Greenwood, Philip James Selway, Colin Charles Greenwood and Edward John
O'Brien reproduced with permission of Warner/Chappell Music Ltd (PRS);
quotation from *Consider the Lobster* by David Foster Wallace (© 2004) reproduced
with permission of Little, Brown Book Group; quotation from *The Corrections*
by Jonathan Franzen (© 2001) reproduced with permission of
HarperCollins*Publishers*; quotation from 'I Am Woman' by Helen Reddy and Ray
Burton reproduced with permission of EMI Music Publishing Ltd.

A catalogue record for this book is
available from the British Library

HB ISBN 978-0-00-727083-5
TPB ISBN 978-0-00-736765-8

Typeset in Minion by G&M Designs Limited,
Raunds, Northamptonshire

Printed in Great Britain by Clays Ltd, St Ives plc

Mixed Sources
Product group from well-managed
forests and other controlled sources
www.fsc.org Cert no. SW-COC-001806
© 1996 Forest Stewardship Council
FSC

FSC is a non-profit international organisation established to promote the
responsible management of the world's forests. Products carrying the FSC
label are independently certified to assure consumers that they come
from forests that are managed to meet the social, economic and
ecological needs of present and future generations.

Find out more about HarperCollins and the environment at

... he persists in the bizarre adolescent idea that having sex with whomever you want whenever you want is the cure for ontological[1] despair

– David Foster Wallace,
reviewing John Updike's *Towards the End of Time*, *New York Observer* 1997

Denise at thirty-two was still beautiful

– Jonathan Franzen, *The Corrections*

I cannot live without Arthur, despite certain inner resources

– Cynthia Koestler, suicide note

PART ONE

My famous daddy is dying. Some grown-ups think I don't understand what that means, but I do. Jada doesn't. When her grandma died, Jada told me her mom said that she'd gone to heaven. OK, I said. But then, three days later, Jada told me that she'd asked her mom when she was coming back. So I asked Mommy, and she said she wasn't; that she'd gone forever. So that's why I know what it means. It means you go away and you don't come back.

Me and Mommy go to the hospital every day to see Daddy. The hospital is called Mount Sinai Hospital. Mount Sinai was the place in Israel where God spoke to Moses, and gave him the Ten Commandments. I read about this in a book Elaine gave me called *The Beginner's Bible: Timeless Children's Stories*. When I was younger – like five or something – I learnt the Ten Commandments by heart. I don't know why I did that. I didn't even know what all those words meant then. *Graven. False witness. Adultery.* But I still remember the three that really matter. Thou shall not kill. Thou shall not steal. And honour your father and your mother.

The hospital isn't much like the picture of Mount Sinai, like it looks in the book. It's just a big building. It's right on the park, and from the big window at the end of Daddy's room I can see a lake. There's a lake in the picture in *The Beginner's Bible: Timeless Children's Stories*, too, in the chapter about Moses. Moses is halfway up the mountain, holding the Ten Commandments, and looking like he's really mad about something; there's a crowd of people at the bottom and, behind them, a lake. Sometimes, when I'm looking out that window, I pretend that the lake in the park is the lake in the book, and that Daddy is Moses, even though he's always lying on his bed now, and can't stand up, or hold anything, especially not two big stones. But yesterday, Mommy came over to the window while I was pretending and told me it wasn't a lake at all, it was the Jacqueline Kennedy Onassis Reservoir. I said: what's a reservoir? She said it's a man-made body of water. I didn't understand what she meant by a body of water. How can a body be made out of water? I wanted to ask her, and also who Jacqueline Kennedy Onassis is, but then Daddy made that strange noise which is the only sound he makes now, and she rushed back to the bed.

The first time me and Elaine went to the hospital, there were loads of photographers outside. That's because my daddy is famous. Not like Katy Perry, or Justin Bieber, or any of those guys: he's famous in a different way. Mommy made me a scrapbook of bits cut out of newspapers from when I was born, and nearly all of them call him the world's 'greatest living writer'. I haven't read any of his books, because I'm still too young to understand them. But when I'm older – maybe eleven or something – I'll read them all.

Elaine told me to look down when the photographers tried to take a picture of me. Some of them shouted at me – 'Hi, Colette! Colette! This way!' – and I nearly looked up, but I didn't. I just kept looking at the shoelaces in my new Gap shoes, at the white tips of the pink strings.

'How do they know my name?' I whispered to Elaine.

'Because of Daddy,' she said, but she was walking quickly and keeping her head down, too, and didn't really explain what that meant. Then one of the photographers shouted at Elaine, 'Are you another daughter?!' and it was good that I had my head down because it made me laugh because she's my *nanny* and is, like, sixty-five or something!!

Daddy has been dying for a long time, even since before I was six. I know, because on my sixth birthday Elaine gave me *The Heavenly Express for Daddy*, which is a book to help children understand what happens when their father dies. It had a lot of pictures in it of a man who is a daddy, but much younger than mine, with black hair instead of white, and no beard; but, like mine, he gets ill and has to go to a hospital. Then, God comes and sees the man, and tells him that he's going to put him on a special train, to come up to heaven and live there with him – but then after that I don't know what happens, because Mommy took the book away, because she thinks Elaine likes God too much. She took the book away, and said she didn't believe that children, just because they were young, shouldn't be told the truth. Especially me, she said, because I'm Daddy's daughter, and Daddy doesn't believe in God, even though some of his books are sort of about Him. *Daddy*, she said – well, she called him Eli, sometimes she calls him Daddy and sometimes Eli – *Eli*, she said, *represents a touchstone of truth in this world*. I didn't know what these words meant, but Mommy closed her eyes tight when she said them and I always know that's when she really wants me to know something, so I made sure I learnt them off by heart, like my three Ten Commandments.

* * *

Coming through arrivals at JFK, Harvey Gold thinks that, these days, he would make a good immigration officer. What do they do, these guys? They look at faces. They sit in a booth and they check real face against photo-face. *Photo-face. Real face. Photo-face. Real face.* All day. And me, what do I do all day, he thinks, these days? I check faces. Every face I see, I check: I check it over helplessly, looking, examining, investigating. Harvey, of course, is checking for something else, although he wonders how different it is. The immigration officers, they're also searching for changes, for what happens to the face when it moves from stasis, from when it's *arranged*. They're checking to see how the face looks once it's not presented, face-on.

Whatever, he thinks, standing in line amongst the travellers, tired and bright and buzzing: *I'd be fucking great*. Especially – his red-eye eyes flick upwards, the pupils seeming to scratch against the back of the lids – in *this* light, this take-no-prisoners, angle-poised airport light. When eventually al-Qaeda decide it's time to smuggle Osama bin Laden into America, he could have the best fucking Afghanistani surgery his siphoned-off dirty dollars can buy, he could come to my booth cut up and dyed and pixillated, and still I'd spot him. He could come in *sex-changed*. He smiles to himself at the thought, prompting the businessman standing next to him in the queue to frown. If he had looked closely, which he does not, the businessman might have noticed that Harvey's smile is not pure, that it contains within it a lingering frond of bitterness.

Harvey's iPhone, a pocket harp, tings in his trousers: a text. He scrabbles in his jeans, which are tight around the crotch – he feels the crotch of his trousers is always shrinking these days, from the disgust that he carries eternally around with him. He knows without looking that the text will just be AT&T offering him their services, but he glances anyway – and so it is, a message of hope and welcome to America as if from the Pilgrim Fathers themselves. He is about to force the phone back through the thin slits of his front pockets when he notices another text, this one from Stella. He taps on it with his thumbnail, a thumbnail kept long as a throwback to when he used to play the guitar and imagine himself on stage with his foot up on black monitors. *Darling*, the text says, *hope the flight wasn't too tough. My love goes out to everybody who'll be there, but most to you. Be safe. XXX*

He slides the screen three windows across with his thumb, to find Deep Green. Deep Green is a chess app that Harvey is addicted to. He takes it out at the first sign of boredom or entrapment – states in which his *anxiety disorder*, as various therapists have christened it, is exacerbated. He now reaches for it instinctively in doctors' waiting rooms, illegally in traffic jams, and in all queues, because he knows that if he starts to play, the end of the wait will arrive faster. The downside is that Deep Green always beats him. He plays it on Level 4, halfway through its eight settings, and knows he should go down a level but feels that that would be pointless: that any joy there might be in defeating the computer – which for reasons unknown to Harvey has christened itself Tiny: every time he loses he has to suffer a small, smug ting, accompanied by a gloating *Checkmate! Tiny wins!* – would be undermined by the knowledge that he had to lower its game to get there.

He has only just begun the game – although his thumb is already hovering over the RESIGN button – when he senses the businessman beside him twitch with irritation. He looks up, and realizes that everyone is now waiting for him to cross the green line and approach the booth. He puts the phone away, fumbles for his passport in the bumbag strung badly across his thighs, and remembers at the last moment: the American one. Harvey is, in so many ways, a dual citizen, and US law, always keen to assert its global difference, states in the clearest of tones that all travellers in possession of an American passport must enter the country showing the Spread-eagled Eagle. The immigration officer, who is narrowing her eyes at Harvey as if already interpreting his delay as suspicious, is a woman of about thirty-five. As he approaches the bitter smile returns, and with it the memory of the sex-changed devil, Osama.

Let us be clear about this. Harvey is not smiling – and was not smiling earlier – at the idea of Osama bin Laden in women's clothes. He is smiling to himself in the manner of a man who has accepted, unhappily, something shitty about himself; who, on this issue and many, many others, has pushed the RESIGN button in his soul. He is smiling to himself because he is thinking: obviously, *obviously* I'd fucking spot him if he'd had a sex change. Because then he'd be a woman: and women get checked by his eyes a hundred-and-fourteen-fold. This woman, this immigration officer; Harvey will look at her face much more closely than she will his. Even as her eyes perform a thorough and competent scan of his face, flicking occasionally to its corollary on the page – greying, jowly, passport-stern, behind the watery eyes just a hint of teenage memory of going into those photo booths with friends and making stupid faces far too close to the lens – however microscopic her examination, it is as nothing compared to the manic burrowing of Harvey's gaze all over her skin, Photoshopping her, running her face through the Rolosex in his head, gauging, gauging, gauging: smoothness, symmetry, vulnerability of eye, fullness of cheek, of lip, of hair, thickness and tastefulness of make-up, and, most importantly, of course, resistance or otherwise to the torrent of ageing. *Who knew*, he thinks, the American phrase entering his head like a passport stamp? Who knew that the power of work, and indeed of international security, would be as nothing compared to that of sexual psychosis?

'How long have you been out of the country?' she says, startling Harvey: sometimes when he is staring at them like this he forgets that women can speak. He feels heat flush through him in response. He has hot flushes regularly – he is virtually menopausal with them – but they are not brought on by rising infertility, nor by the temperature of the June New York morning, but by fear. He has nothing to be frightened of, or at least nothing concrete, but for some time now this has been irrelevant to his physical response.

'I don't know,' he says, his voice a little strangled, and aware of its laconically flat Englishness. 'Ten years? Maybe a bit longer?'

Her eyes, which are brown, and which Harvey has already noticed have running underneath them a series of what women's magazines call 'fine lines', harden.

'That's a long time.'

She has taken it as an affront, Harvey realizes. For these sentries posted at the gates of the promised land such a length of absence is suspicious. It is suspect, the very idea that one of their own might want to be away from the mother lode for this long a stretch. What possible delights could anywhere else in the world hold for so long? He feels a movie need to say something weary and sarcastic, but quells it underneath a nod of agreement.

'Business or pleasure, this trip?'

This makes Harvey pause. He stops running the immigration officer's skin through a series of forensic sight-based (and, in his imagination, touch-based) tests. What is the answer? It's multiple choice, clearly, with not enough choices.

'My father is dying,' says Harvey, as blankly as he can: he is trying not to make it a proclamation. It is not difficult to assume the blankness: as with all information of great import, both personal and political – births, deaths, relatives, wars, injustice, all the stuff of Hallmark Cards and CNN – the fact of his father's death is taking a while to bed in. He knows it should affect him – he engages with the

8

idea that such information should shake him to the core, should easily shake down the fog of desire and depression that pumps ceaselessly from the pores of his exhausted, clumpy brain – but viscerally, *physically*, he doesn't feel it. He thinks he will, eventually, and is waiting for the moment to strike, but in the meantime remains afloat, abstracted, like a man who has been told that the plumber will arrive at some point between nine and five thirty.

But telling this to the immigration officer doesn't come out as blank as he wants: he is still trying to put across an idea of himself, the man so socked to by death that he has not known how to answer this question and therefore has told the bald truth. And he senses that there is something sexual here, something flirtatious, or at least, gender-biased: it is not a self that he would have presented to a man. He is trying to make a dent in this woman's imperviousness by doing the vulnerable thing. Of course, if he had really wanted to make a dent, he realizes, he should have said, 'My father – *Eli Gold* – is dying.'

It still works, however. Abashed, muttering sad sorries, she hands back the blue book and waves Harvey on into America. In doing so, their fingertips touch briefly above the eagle's claws, and for her it is less than nothing, but for Harvey it is a roof of the Sistine Chapel moment, divine electricity passing between their fingers. It passes immediately – Harvey is not a fool, he doesn't *believe* in his fantasies; rather, he is persecuted by them – but it leaves its scar, its never-happening scar, with all the others.

He fits the American passport awkwardly back into his overstuffed bum bag, and walks away towards the sunlit plains of the glass-roofed Arrivals terminal. Then he remembers Stella's text, and puts his fingers back through the half-opened zip, searching for the iPhone. They alight first on his house keys, and then on all the loose puddles of change that, from the outside, make this bag look like it is suffering from a terrible allergic reaction. How could the phone have gone? He was just looking at it! Did he hand it over to immigration officer with his passport? This is why he is wearing the stupid bum bag – a thing that he knows no one wears any more, and which stops him walking properly – in order not to lose stuff. He stops. His life has always been plagued by this, the everyday disintegration of absent-mindedness, especially as regards the whereabouts of vital personal objects – keys, phones, wallets, tickets, other people's address cards, documentation, jewellery, scarves, gloves – anything that can be carried about the person. But until his soul started to go bad, absent-mindedness was just something he accepted, a default fault, a thing which fucked up his life in little ways every day but wasn't worth steaming about; now, however, if he realizes he has lost something, he can't override it, he hasn't the energy, neither physical nor spiritual. He hasn't the momentum. These discoveries, these interruptions in his tiny progress, just make him want to stop. Finding out that he has left his wallet at home will make him want to sit down in the street; if he is in the car and the keys are not in the most obvious pocket, he will consider never driving away. The other day he was on the toilet and realized, too late, that he had forgotten to restock the paper roll, and felt, immediately, that there was nothing to do but stay sat on the black MDF oval forever, the shit on his anus hardening over time to a brittle crust.

He stops now, and again wants to sit, here on this faintly marbled floor scuffed with the marks of a million suitcase wheels; sit, cross-legged perhaps, until someone – God, his dying father, a woman, any woman – takes him in hand, finding for him his phone and his sanity. And then, just at the moment when the heavy hands of depression have started to push, gently, almost lovingly, on his shoulders, it rings, reminding Harvey that he put the phone back in his pocket and not in the bag at all. He pulls the iPhone out from its burial in a mini-dump of tissue dust, looks at the screen, and inwardly crumples: Freda. He considers for a moment not answering, pressing instead the DECLINE button, because his relationship with the caller is declining, because her call will only be about the decline of his father, because he, Harvey, seems to be now, perpetually, in decline. He taps ANSWER.

'Freda.' The strange thing that caller ID gives you, the need not to say *hello?*, the end of that querulous enquiry, the end, too, of the way that people can garner some small knowledge about what you think about them simply by the rise or fall in your voice when you do find out who it is: replaced instead by this, this ironic, flat certainty.

'Harvey. Hi. How are you? How was the flight?'

He shrugs, then feels a bit silly for shrugging on the phone. 'It was an overnight flight, in coach.' *Coach*: a sliver of self-disgust goes through him at having slipped so quickly into the idiom, just because he is in this land, or maybe because, reflexively, he is trying to please Freda. 'But seven hours isn't so long. And it's five times the price for Club. What hotel room would you ever pay five times over the odds to spend seven hours in?'

She doesn't answer this. The iPhone emits a mournful crackle, before Harvey asks the question he knows she is waiting for.

'So how is he?'

The pause before she replies is so long, Harvey has time to locate the Baggage Reclaim sign and begin trudging in that direction. As he does so, his gaze is routinely snagged by passing women. His neck hurts from not turning, from the urgent need to follow them as they move past, into places where he is not.

'Not much changed,' she says, after long enough for Harvey to have forgotten that she is there.

'What do the doctors –'

'Anytime. At best, two months.'

Harvey stops. He has known that his father must have roughly this amount of time left, but Freda's bald statement of it comes at him like a fist. He had not been expecting this answer so soon: in fact, he now can't quite formulate what the second half of his question was going to be – 'What do the doctors think/plan to do/give him for the pain/ look like?' He was only going to go for some general question, and work up slowly to the big Specific. He knows why Freda is speaking like this: the directness, the refusal to couch, speaks of her ownership of his father – and of his death. With Eli Gold, she must always have arrived first, even at the place of pain.

Harvey's eyes, moistened a little, more by tiredness than tears, stare into the defocusing distance.

'Right.'

'We've booked you a room at the Sangster. It's a new hotel on East 76th Street. It's very good.'

'You have?'

'Yes. I know it's a bit further away from Mount Sinai then we'd like, but it's a block from Fifth Avenue, and you can get a cab uptown from there.'

'No, I wasn't complaining. I –' He reddened. He had assumed he would be staying at their Upper East Side apartment, had already imagined sating his curiosity about his father and Freda's private life by flicking through notebooks and diaries, or perhaps just through living in their furnishings and amongst their artwork; but now he saw how much of a presumption that was, never having been there, and having seen his father only twice in the last ten years, both times in London. He saw how *un*taken for granted the idea of him staying there must be, and how clearly Freda was confirming his fringe status in the present family circle.

'We're still staying at home, but I'm thinking of staying nights at the hospital. It depends on how Eli is. I probably will at some point. But Colette will still be at home.'

'OK,' said Harvey, uncertain how to take this, wondering about the buried implication that he might be some sort of paedophile, that, obviously, he couldn't stay in the same apartment as an eight-year-old girl. He wants to protest that he is very good with children – that he has an unmolested, undamaged nine-year-old son himself – but he quells the urge, partly because Freda may have meant nothing of the sort, and partly because Jamie is, clearly, damaged.

'Well, thank you. The Sangster. That's very generous of you.'

He colours as he says it, having realized he has assumed that Freda – or, rather, the 'we' that Freda refers to, a mystical duality of her and Eli – will be paying. He wonders if he should enquire, but hesitates, not wanting to get into a detailed discussion about whether they are picking up the tab just for the room, or if minibar and hotel porn surcharges will also be included.

The iPhone crackles again, drawing attention to Freda's failure to say 'Don't mention it'.

'So shall I …? When shall I …?' says Harvey, trailing off, accepting his secondary role.

12

'Maybe go to the hotel, now … and you can come tomorrow morning?' She speaks with the American inflection, the vocal hike indicating a question, a possibility for discussion: but Harvey knows better.

'Tomorrow morning? I was hoping …' God, how much trailing off am I going to do, he thinks. He is an uncertain fellow, Harvey, in an uncertain situation – the old son returning to see the dying dad, surrounded by his new family – and now it seems as if Freda's take-no-prisoners certainty has crushed his ability to make even the smallest statement of intent. And, also, he can't match her: he can't fold back her steeliness, can't say that he thinks he should come straight away, because maybe his father might die today. His fingers reach without thought for the plane ticket in his inside pocket, with its devastatingly open return, something that had cost Harvey substantially more money when ordered – a charge which had provoked a moment of irritation, not with his father for the indefiniteness of his time left, but with the airlines, for not having a special *close relative's last days'* exemption clause. It isn't fair, he thinks, *it's not fair* that I have to pay extra because my dad is dying and I don't know when to book the flight home. Harvey's heart is heavy with such unfairnesses.

'Well,' said Freda, 'today we've already got quite a lot of people visiting … my mother's here now, and then a group of Eli's colleagues from Harvard in the afternoon – plus there was talk of Roth coming by some time this week, so … obviously he gets very tired …'

'Maybe I'll just go to the hotel and call later.' This is the best defiance Harvey can offer.

'Yes. Please do.' There is a voice off, high and insistent.

'Yes, darling, in a minute. Mom's on the phone.'

'So we'll speak later.'

'Yes. Good to have you here, Harvey. Eli will be so pleased to see you. Goodbye.'

'Goodbye.' He clicks the OK button on his phone, and forces it back into his jeans. Roth? *Philip* Roth? Harvey loves Philip Roth more than he has ever been able to admit to his watchful-for-literary-slights father. He feels intense desire to meet the dark bard of American sex and clear the decks of his depression, making him wonder, angrily, if he shouldn't just turn up unannounced at this great literary lunchtime: he is, after all, Eli Gold's son, the only one of the three adult children who has been prepared to make the journey. Then self-awareness settles like soft snow back upon him, and he realizes how far such an action is beyond him, he who has always hated confrontation anyway, and these days need only to be confronted with the smallest of obstacles for his depleted energy reserves to drain away to nothing.

Harvey moves into the Baggage Reclaim Hall, with its always palpable dynamic of tension and relief, as exhausted passengers wait nervously for their cherished belongings to be spat onto the oval belts. His conveyor, No. 4, is sparsely populated now, the phone call having slowed down his movement here. He can see his suitcase, some Samsonite-alike with pull-out handle – again, due to the particular nature of this particular journey, he didn't know which of the numerous bags piled up under the stairs to pack – forlornly beginning what looks like its twentieth or thirtieth rotation. A woman he had noticed on the plane, sitting four or five rows in front of him on the opposite side, is there, beginning to look anxious. She is in her early twenties, dirt-blonde long hair parted like that of a Woodstock girl dancing towards the crackly camera, sea-blue eyes, and, even under the whiplash Baggage Reclaim lights, skin so smooth that if Harvey were to reach out and touch it – as every cell in his hands is urging him to do – his fingers would slip.

Her bag, pink like bubble-gum, tumbles out of the conveyor hatch, the relief registering on her features, softening them even further, and making Harvey remember something one of his many more sexually opportune friends had told him once, about how, while waiting at airports for luggage, he would try and steal a furtive glance at the labels on the suitcases of any waiting attractive women, and then offer to share a taxi in that direction. As she picks up the bag, Harvey, impelled by the thought, does flick his eyes downwards and, catching sight of the zip code, thinks it might be an address near his hotel, but never has any intention of going through with all that stilted 'Hey, I see you're going my way' shite. It just tears another little track through him, the idea that it could be done, that someone else could do it.

An older woman joins her, and helps her heave her bag onto a trolley. She moves away: she hasn't registered Harvey's presence, even cursorily. He looks at his watch. He now has time, far too much time. He looks again at his iPhone and ponders the text from Stella. *I should call her back*, he thinks, *let her know I've landed*. But then the other thing grabs his heart with its cold hands, and, instead, he sits down on the edge of Conveyor Belt No. 5, to watch his suitcase travel round Conveyor Belt No. 4, round and round and round, like a lone ship on the greyest, most mundane of seas.

*   *   *

Eli Gold's first wife, Violet, is in her room just finishing lunch when she sees the item on the television news. It has been a day on which she has already veered from her normal routine. She usually watches the one o'clock news in the lounge, even though some of the other residents would always be fast asleep in there by then, and Joe Hillier's snoring, in particular, was more than loud enough to drown out the words of the newsreader. The more able residents at Redcliffe House are allowed to make their own lunch and eat it in their rooms, and Violet takes this option as often as she can, preparing it – baked beans on toast, a cheese sandwich, a tin of ravioli – in the tiny kitchenette off to the side of the room and eating at the table by the window. Lunch always reminds her of Valerie, who is forever hinting that Violet should move to somewhere more *structured*, which means, Violet knows, one of the fascist old-age homes, a place where her independence would be taken away, her privacy disregarded, and the other inmates comatose, just because Valerie couldn't bear the idea of her sister eating on her own from time to time. After lunch, she would normally get the lift down from the fourth floor, and, if it was not wet, walk the path around Redcliffe Square Gardens, which, even with a stick, would not take her more than fifteen minutes, and she was always back at Redcliffe House by five to one, ready to watch the news. She could take the lift back up to her room and watch it there, but even though Violet was a woman who liked to keep herself to herself much of the time, she felt there was no point in living in a place where so many other people lived if she never mingled with them at all: and so she always went into the lounge following her walk, and, with her cream winter coat on her knees, watched the one o'clock news.

Unless it *was* wet, as on the day she hears the news about Eli, a day on which she hadn't even bothered going downstairs to check the pavements: the rain had been hitting her window all morning, a downpour blown diagonal across the pane by the wind. Over time, an errant branch from the neighbouring hostel's enormous oak tree had grown along the walls of the house to lie pressed against her sill, and today she could count the drops on its leaves. She had just finished eating a few slices of ham and some crackers, and had already risen to take the plate into the kitchenette, when the item began.

She is shocked by seeing his face on the screen – at first some footage of him, recently giving a lecture, with the beard and the big shock of grey hair that she vaguely knew he had now, followed by an old black and white photo from round about the time they were married. For a split second, Violet thinks they might even show a photograph of her: him wearing his GI uniform, her on his arm in the white floral dress that she used to wear on their first dates.

They don't – how could they, she chided herself, when the only photos that have survived of us together are all in that shoebox under the bed? I don't suppose *he* kept any. The news moves on to a shot of a tall building in New York, which Violet gathers is a hospital. A doctor, an Indian, is standing in front of a crowd reading some sort of statement. Without her hearing aid she cannot hear what he is saying, but his name – Ghund … khali? – is subtitled below. She puts the plate down and turns away from the kitchenette, feeling her knees crack beneath her. She goes over to the television, a Hitachi ex-rental model made in 1973 which she brought with her when she left her flat in Cricklewood. Even turning the volume up full, she has to stand right beside it, bending her face to the screen to hear what is being said.

'… is said to be …' the reporter was now saying '… conscious rarely, if at all. His family are by his side. But it seems unlikely at this

16

stage that this man, considered by many to be the world's greatest living writer, will come home from hospital again. This is Rahim Khan, for BBC News, in New York.'

The screen cuts back to the main studio. The newsreader looks reverent for a second, before going on to a story about an earthquake in Sri Lanka. Violet watches for a minute, then turns it off. She sits back down by the window. The rain is easing, but even if the sun were to come out and dry the pavements, she would not go out for her walk now. Age has made Violet a creature of routine: the big surprise for her – the failing of her body – is easier to manage if she limits all other surprises. Last week, while moving the dial between her touchstones, Radios 3 and 4, she heard a plaintive voice on the wireless singing the words *no alarms and no surprises, please*, and it made her pause, thinking how true to her own desire that imprecation was now: since some irretrievable day in the past, all news – everything from finding one day that the gate to Redcliffe Square Gardens was unaccountably locked, to feeling the arrival on waking of some new bad ache in her bones, to hearing that another of the residents has died – all news seemed to have become bad news, and so she'd rather it all just stopped, that the news was all in. The only way she could make her life approach this condition was through habit.

But news would still intrude, breaking through the fragile circle of routine. Here it was: Eli in hospital; Eli, who she had not seen or heard from in over fifty years; her first and only husband; the only man to have touched the tender sections of her body except for the surgeon who must have at least held her breast for a few seconds before applying the scalpel to remove it in 1987. *The world's greatest living writer*: did that include the letters yellowing in that shoebox? If she took them out and read them now, which she has not done for many years, would the parchment-like paper mirror her skin, of which the words so sweetly sing? Violet Gold feels suddenly nauseous and stands up, heading as quickly as she can towards the bathroom, more aware than ever of the bandiness of her legs, the ridiculousness of her movement. By the time she gets there the wave has passed, and she feels relieved not to have to bend or,

17

worse, kneel in front of the white china and the tiny puddle – not so much because of the horror of having to vomit, but because of the possibility that she might not be able to get up again. She lowers the plastic seat, and sits, in reach of the red panic button on her left.

Why this? she thinks. Why this physical reaction to the news about Eli? It is not unexpected: the surprise is that he's lasted so long, what with so many wives – how many since her? Three? Four? – and his generally cavalier approach to all things healthy – although that was a long time ago, and he might have changed. And when they were young everything was different, anyway. He smoked, but so did she: so did everyone. She was smoking when they first met, she remembers; it threw off Eli's chat-up line. 'Oh, damn,' he had said, the first words she heard him speak. He had been leaning against a post in the Rainbow Corner, watching the men and women dance: it was 1944, a Friday night, and the Bill Ambrose Band were playing. Violet was with her friend Gwendoline, who was a hostess, a word Violet was never sure about – the Rainbow Corner was simply the drinking and dancing section of the Red Cross Club in Shaftesbury Avenue, where many American soldiers congregated during the war, and there were always jobs to be had for girls who wanted them, but Violet was never entirely clear what being a hostess involved. Mainly, it seemed, never saying 'no' on being asked to dance, and Gwendoline had certainly fulfilled her obligation that night: Violet had spent most of the evening on her own watching her friend's flower-patterned skirt twirling around five identical pairs of olive-brown trousers. She had just decided she was going to leave after finishing this last cigarette when Eli spoke.

'*Damn …*' he repeated.

'What?' she replied eventually, realizing he was expecting some sort of reply from her.

'You're smoking,' he said. His voice was low, a throaty rumble. Violet had met enough GIs by now to recognize it as defining him as from New York or its environs. She glanced at her own cigarette, twisting her hand to her face a little self-consciously.

'Yes …?'

'Well, that's scuppered my plan.' Violet's face remained a mask of confusion; she wondered if she'd misheard him over the music. 'To offer you a cigarette …' he added helpfully, taking a sky-blue packet of Newport cigarettes out of his breast pocket. His hands, she noticed, were large. Finally she understood; her features relaxed into gentle mockery, the face she reserved for suitors.

'You could always ask me to dance.'

He shook his head, pausing to light his cigarette. Violet remembers this pause clearly, almost more than anything else about their first meeting. He stopped his head, mid-shake, cocked his lighter, lit his cigarette, took in a deep draught of Newport smoke, and then continued the shake of his head before speaking again.

'I don't dance,' he said, fixing her in his gaze. His face was impassive, challenging: not a hint of apology.

'You don't?'

'I'm a man of words.'

'I see.'

'This lighter, for example … do you know what it is?'

Violet glanced down at the squat metal case. She had seen many of them, cupped in the crinkles of American soldiers' palms.

'What?'

'It's a Zippo. The lighter of choice for the American military. Since last year, Zippo have been producing and distributing them free to servicemen. We've all got them. But the shape …' he weighed the lighter in his palm, the back of his hand moving gently up and down on the lever of his wrist, '… is actually modelled on an *Austrian* lighter. Can't you tell? The heft of it, the dumb solidity. It's so Teutonic. So Germanic. And yet …' he patted his breast pocket '… we the Nazi-fighters keep them next to our very hearts.'

Violet felt at a loss to know how to react to this speech. She had never really heard anyone else talk like this – certainly not a soldier, certainly not a man trying to chat her up – and it seemed to leave her with nowhere to go. She understood his point, but could think of nothing to say in addition.

19

'They give off a good strong flame though, don't they?' was what she said in the end, and instantly felt the banality of it. In answer, he flipped the lid of the lighter again, stroking the wheel twice before the blue flame rose once more from the wick. He moved it closer to her face: she could feel the warmth and smell the butane, its chemical scent dizzying her a little. Through the blue she could see his eyes, what seemed sadness in them now overridden by curiosity. There was an expression Gwen used about men – she used it a lot, in order to make their attention known – saying they were *undressing her with their eyes*; Violet felt something of this now – not that he was undressing her, because his eyes did not move from her face – but that sense of feeling a man's eyes on your body, as if his sight were touch. It made her cheeks prickle. She felt, obscurely and for the first time, that when men are examining a woman's face, their method of weighing her beauty is to search for flaws.

'What's your name?' she said, because she wanted to know, but also because she wanted to be released from his gaze. He smiled, a wider grin than she expected, bringing his nose down over his mouth: he looked suddenly medieval, cartoonish.

'I shall answer that in what I believe is the customary manner.' He spoke in an exaggerated cut-glass English accent, waving his left hand in a florid eighteenth-century style. Before Violet had time to react, he stood on tiptoe, lifting the still aflame lighter above his head. It was only then that she realized he was quite a tall man: he had been slouching against the post, and bending down in order to have the conversation with her. He seemed to Violet almost to uncoil.

Her eyes went upwards, to the low ceiling of this section of the Rainbow Corner. Lifting the Zippo to the ceiling created a circle of light, revealing a messy sprawl of signatures, doodles and numbers burnt into the plaster, written by GIs keen to preserve something of themselves in this foreign country, before war or peace took them away. *Dodds, 98205D* she read, before the flame in the man's hand began to move, forming a blackening line that slowly became the upright pillar of an 'E'. Despite the general smokiness of the room, she could detect in her nostrils the acrid smell of burning plaster. A couple of other American soldiers, noticing this familiar custom being performed, clapped and cheered. The man – El someone, it seemed: was he Spanish? – seemed to be absorbed in his task. Most of the names on the ceiling were just scrawls, bearing the marks of having been written on tiptoe, in public and by drunken hands; he had the appearance, however, of deep concentration, as if he were Michelangelo on his back at the Sistine Chapel. The words were bold and clear, and he spent long enough on each letter to burn it thickly into the wood: it looked, by the end, more like an imprint, more like the International Shipbrokers company stamp that her fist had to plonk down over and over again on the envelopes at work, than letters inscribed by hand – by flame. When he had finished, he spent a little while looking up at his name, admiring his handiwork. Violet noticed that he didn't have a very protruding Adam's apple – there was no triangular skin stretch in the gullet pressing against his extended neck – which made her glad, as her previous boyfriend had done, and the feel of it pressing against her throat when they were kissing had always put her off.

'Eli Gold …' she said, intoning the words, brushing her blonde hair out of her eyes as she tilted her head back to read.

'E-*li*,' he said. He pronounced it 'lie'. She had said 'Ely', like the town.

'That's a funny name.'

'Is it? *Eli, Eli, lema sabachtani.*'

'Beg pardon?'

'It means God. Literally …' And here he raised the lighter to the ceiling again, although this time unlit, '… *Elia*, the Highest.'

'In what language?'

Eli's face creased, his smile revealing his face to be lined for his age. Somehow, it did not make him look old.

'Hebrew, of course. *Elia*'s own language.'

'Hebrew?'

'I'm Jewish. On my father's side.'

'Oh,' said Violet, who – having occasionally made the journey from her parents' house in Walthamstow to Spitalfields for meat and vegetables – had seen some Jews, but only the ones in the big black hats with the curly sideburns. 'I thought you were an American.'

Eli looked at her, his composure for the first time dented. The lines around his eyes all went upwards, as he stared at Violet's pretty, open, easy face, a face standing firmly behind the straightforwardness, the frank neutrality, of her statement. Then he laughed, loud, long peals that seemed to drown out even the brass section of the Bill Ambrose band. Violet felt frightened, but unfathomably drawn to the fear. She looked up at his name, still smoking on the ceiling. A swell hit her soul and, as can happen in moments of epiphany, she thought she saw this moment as it would be described years from now, saying to friends, perhaps to children, that it was as if he had been burning the words Eli Gold into her heart. And she did say that, to friends if not to children, and soon came to believe that such was indeed the true quality of her experience. It was only later she realized that Eli had just been writing.

✳ ✳ ✳

He is not certain he should be wearing black, in summer. It is not the heat – that is not bothering him, though he is used to the white chill of Utah – but thinks that it might, somehow, give him away. When, earlier, he had ventured into the hospital reception area, an orderly had looked at him suspiciously. This is paradoxical, as he is wearing it to fit in. Where he comes from, no one wears black: not even any of the younger, trendier Mormons, in their younger, trendier sects, the Bullaites, or Zions Order Inc., or The Restoration Church. But he is wearing it, because his third wife, Dovetta, told him that that was the first thing she noticed when she went to New York on her mission trip, *On Fire for Christ*: everyone wears black.

He wears a black jacket and a black T-shirt. Blue jeans, though. That feels self-conscious, as well, because he is fifty-five, perhaps too old for jeans. Although everyone wears jeans now, even old men; even old women. They hang off them, off their legs. This sense of himself as old, an old man in blue jeans, disturbs him. Not through vanity, even though he used to be a handsome man, and maybe still is, despite the stuck eye. It disturbs him because of the task ahead.

22

A lot of journalists and photographers are still milling about after the doctor's statement. Some of them clearly think he is one of them. He has to be a little careful not to be seen in the back of shot when the TV cameras are around. He doesn't want to be spotted by somebody, somewhere, on some Summit County TV, who might recognize him and question why on earth he is there, knowing that he could not be a well-wisher, or a mourner. Also, when the doctor was talking – when he was going on about blood cell counts and secondary infections and how the hospital was doing everything that could be done – he felt an urge to shout: to heckle. At the words 'Mount Sinai Hospital understands the responsibility it has been given in caring for this particular patient' the urge had felt almost uncontrollable; but he used the mental effort of memorizing the doctor's name – it was a long Indian one, and later he will need to know it – as a means of distracting himself. But now he has decided to leave. It is too early in the process and he is too raw with it. He feels if someone asked him what he is doing here he may just blurt it out.

Plus, he does not even have a hotel. He has not thought anything through. There has not been space for it. He does not have the *psychic energy*. That is what Janey would call it. Janey is one of his children, the oldest of fifteen, the only one born of his first wife, Leah, before she died. She is a Mormon, but does not believe, as he does, that God was once a man; she rejects the Pearl of Great Price; and, most seriously, she rejects polygamy. She no longer lives with his family.

He remembers the moment of her leaving clearly. In 1993, the Church of the Latter-day Saints, in their regular Baptism of the Dead, baptized Adolf Hitler. Despite their differences with the LDS, his own church – The Latter-day Church of the True Christ – accepted this baptism. A year later, the whole family were at Mount Timpaganos Temple, the beautiful prayer hall only just built to serve the community of American Fork, when the dictator's name came through in the list of The Endowed. Immediately, Janey got up and left. Next time he heard from her, she had moved to Independence, Missouri, to join the Community.

But he knew, even as he watched her pass through the door, under the mural of the angel Moroni, that Hitler's baptism was just the catalyst. She had grown disenchanted when he had taken Sedona, his second wife's daughter, to be his fifth wife. He had seen it when he had gathered the family around him in the living room of their then house, the one at the point in American Fork where East State Road becomes West State Road, and announced his intention. They were crammed in: the house seemed to grow smaller as the family burgeoned. Everyone else was joyful, clapping and rising to congratulate Sedona and her mother, but Janey just stayed on a chair by the window, staring straight at him. He returned her stare, blankly, neutrally, letting his good eye ask her what her problem might be; but this was hard to do, because so many of his wives and children were hugging him, and because her eyes were so full of hurt and disgust and anger. They held each other's line of vision, while the others danced between them, until at last she turned away and looked through the glass towards the white-tipped mountains of the Utah Valley.

He decides to leave the area around Mount Sinai Hospital to look for a hotel. He cannot, though, afford any of the hotels in the mid-town area. This should not be part of my story, he thinks. I am an avenging angel; I have the weight of destiny on my shoulders. But I cannot afford any of the hotels in the mid-town area.

He walks and walks. His right arm, where he has a touch of arthritis in the elbow, aches with the weight of pulling his suitcase, a blue checked bag on wheels. On his left shoulder blade, the remnants of his tattoo – a Confederate flag, removed soon after joining the Church, because the head of their Temple, Elder James LaMoine McIntyre, known to everyone as Uncle Jimmy, explained to him that the body is perfected after death – itches. To keep him going he recites in his head, for every step, the names of his family. First, the wives: step, Leah, step, Ambree, step, Lorinda, step, Angel, step, Sedona, step, RoLyne. Then, for every step, a son or daughter: step, Janey, step, Clela, step, Fallon, step, Levoy, step, Leah, step, Darlene, step, KalieJo, step, Orus, step Rustin, step, Mayna, step, Prynne, step, Dar, step, Hosietta, step, Velroy, step, Elin. Then, a final step, and a final name: Pauline. Then he begins again. After he has been doing this for a few hours, it occurs to him that three of his children – Darlene, Rustin, Levoy – are, in fact, step-children. This takes him aback for a second, makes him stop. For a moment it strikes him as funny. But he represses the urge to laugh, and reorders it in his head as a sign, a small sign, that there is a pattern to all things. He walks on.

The list allows him to resist New York. He has never been here before – he has never been out of Utah – but he knows enough about it from when he was young, and from what he has seen on the inter-net, to understand that the City will distract him from his destiny. He keeps his head down, focusing on his feet, on hitting a new name with each foot, and refuses the City – he refuses Park Avenue, even as he walks all the way down it; he refuses the Chrysler Building and the Empire State and the Waldorf-Astoria and Grand Central Station and One And Eleven Madison and all the other temptations of the Kingdom of Man. He refuses even the yellow taxis and the steam rising from the street gratings and the hotdog sellers and the WALK/DON'T WALK signs, the things about Manhattan that might chime with its movie self, and which might draw him in through living up to its mythology, revealing its icons like a peacock its feathers.

Just as he is getting too hot and tired to continue – the sun has been stoking the air all afternoon, and underneath his clothes his sacred white undergarments are heavy with sweat – he finds a cheap place, on East 25th Street, called the Condesa Inn. The Condesa Inn is a hippy hotel. He likes that. He was a hippy himself, once. He was a Mormon then, too, but a regular one, just born into the Church of the Latter-day Saints, and not too fussed about it neither. Him and his sister used to smoke a lot of dope together, and listen to a band called The Outlaws. He loved her most then. It was at an Outlaws gig when he first saw Jesus – the Azteca in Salt Lake, in 1975. Hughie Thomasson was really going for it, on 'Searching', their greatest song, their 'Free Bird'. Hughie had just sung: *Searching through the seven skies/for some place your soul can fly*, and hit the strings of his Stratocaster, when he saw him: Jesu, the Lamb, rising from behind the drum kit, arms

25

outstretched, smiling a smile that widened further as Hughie and Billy Jones dug into their guitar battle like the out-there Confederate heroes they were. It filled his heart with joy. When he told Pauline afterwards she was so pleased for him, even though she made a joke about how good the dope must have been that they smoked before they went into the club. He didn't mind that joke. He knew she knew it was true: and that she would accept, in time, that he had to forsake Salt Lake City for American Fork, and the Church of the Latter-day Saints for the greater truth of the Latter Day Church of the True Christ.

He knows that the Condesa Inn is the hotel he should be staying in, because every room is painted in a different way, each by a different artist. The woman on reception, who looks like she may have been a hippy as well once, shows him photographs of the rooms that are available, and there is one with a picture of Jesus across the wall. The woman says it is not Jesus – she says it is the lead singer of the Flaming Lips – but he knows that it is, because the bearded half-naked figure is enveloped by an angel. Then the woman says:

– Well, if you want it to be Jesus, I guess it's Jesus. It's eighty dollars a night, shared bathroom.

He smiles a little, a smile the woman would not be able to read. At home, he shares one bathroom with twenty-one other family members. Most days, the waiting to get into it is so long he ends up going to the bathroom outside, behind the privet hedge that surrounds their small patch of land.

– Is it a smoking room?

– No. We don't have any rooms you can smoke in any more. You have to go stand outside. Sorry.

– OK. Do you have wi-fi internet access?

– We do. It comes and goes a bit, but, yeah.

– How much does it cost?

– On the house. When you can get it, that is.

– Is there a password?

She picks up a card with the Condesa Inn logo on it, and a pen, and scribbles on the back: H98BCARL. She hands it over, smiling. He looks at it and feels disappointed. He had thought that this word might speak to him: he had thought it would be a word connected with his destiny, or maybe at least with their shared hippiness, OUTLAWS1, or something.

OK, he says, and goes up to the room, with his suitcase. They do have a porter in the Condesa Inn, but he does not want the porter to carry his suitcase, because he only has a small amount of money and cannot afford tips. It contains, along with two changes of outer clothes and five of sacred underclothes, his own copy of *The Book of Mormon: An Account Written By The Hand of Mormon Upon Plates Taken From The Plates of Nephi*, his Dell PC laptop computer, the photograph of his sister, before she was raped by The Great Satan, wearing her favourite red-check dress, smiling and waving, looking so fine, and his gun. It is the gun, an Armscor 206 .38, which he bought online from GunsAmerica.com, for $308, as new, that has meant that he has to travel all the way from Utah by bus; the gun that has meant he cannot travel by airplane. There are ways of getting a gun on an airplane – he has learnt this from surfing the web, from reading the posts of some of the jihadis – but the ways are difficult and he decided against it. He goes up to the room alone.

Inside the room, the picture of Jesus is bigger than it looks in the photograph. The only window looks out onto the back of some kind of kitchen, and the picture itself is not that brightly painted – Jesus is in a sharp profile, like he might appear on a playing card, and wears a dark red toga, in sharp contrast to the bright blue of the angels' dress – but still, when he turns to face the mural, it nearly blinds him with light. This is proof for him that it is the Lamb of God, Lucifer's spirit brother, again. He has to shield his eyes, which hurt like staring at the sun, something he did once when he was a kid during an eclipse, even though his father had told him not to. He did that because he didn't understand why, if the sun was covered by the moon, you couldn't look at it. He looked at that eclipse for five minutes, and it was beautiful, so beautiful he didn't feel the burn in his right eye that would leave the pupil fixed in the middle of the socket, and working always at no more than 20 per cent effectiveness. He thinks of it now as his first intimation that knowing God, really knowing God, always involves pain.

The light fades. He sits on the bed. He takes a deep breath. The room is dusty. He feels as if he can feel the motes in his nostrils. He should change, but there is a comfort in the sweat of his sacred underclothes drying on him, as if warmed by the heat and light coming off this Christ. He takes out his Dell, and waits patiently as it boots up, and then more patiently as it finds the Condesa Inn wireless signal. *Poor*, it says, red bars flickering into green. There is something that has been bothering him, bothering him all the way here on the Greyhound, looking out of the window as the landscape flattened towards the east. Google has been key for his destiny – Earth has shown him New York, Street View the area around 1176 Fifth Avenue, Images the internal layout of Mount Sinai, and it was the main search box which led him to The Material, there on unsolved.com – so he has feared being without it. To test it, he types the words 'death penalty states united states'. It takes a while, but then it comes. He goes to Wikipedia first, an entry: *The Death Penalty in the United States*. A map comes up, in which most of the states of the country are red, but along the top, blue, a geographical clustering of mercy. The colour of New York, though, is confusing – half yellow, half orange. He goes back to the search box, and replaces the words 'states united states' with the words 'New York' and presses return again. The sixth entry is called Death Penalty FAQs. Scrolling down, the question appears, in bold: **Does New York have the death penalty?** And the answer: The death penalty was reinstated in 1995.

Nineteen ninety-five. Two years after his sister died: was killed. He could have done it any time over those two years. And he didn't. A voice that seems not his speaks in his head: does he regret it? That's what people are often asked about on TV: regret. And this voice is like a TV interviewer's voice: polite, friendly, softly spoken. He knows this is not 'voices in his head'. It is just something a lot of people do, imagine themselves being interviewed on the TV.

– No, he says, speaking out loud. I don't regret it. He continues in his head: *because then I was grieving, and because I thought Janey might come back then and she didn't, and because I didn't know until I heard*

28

the news that he was dying that I understood what it was that I had to do. It was only then that I knew my destiny. And besides, he is expecting to be caught, and imprisoned, and executed. He is not trying to commit the perfect crime. He is trying to avenge it.

   – I don't regret it, he says again out loud. He raises his chin while saying it, in an act of untargeted defiance, and as he does he catches Jesus' eye, which looks down upon him with love.

On arrival at the Sangster, Harvey Gold finds it difficult not to feel a tiny bit disappointed. He was not a man used to staying in five-star hotels if his father (or his estate) were not paying, and it might perhaps have been expected that he would only be grateful; or, if not actually grateful, at least so unaccustomed to this level of luxury as to be mollified by it. There are, however, a number of problems:

1. The Sangster, although a very beautiful hotel, is not what Harvey had pictured in his mind when, in the taxi from the airport – as a check and balance in his head to the oncoming deathbed visit – he had mused expectantly about the prospect of staying in a Manhattan hotel. For Harvey, although himself born on that island and technically a citizen of it, a stay in Manhattan still required a certain amount of cliché: that is, a room at least seventy storeys up, with floor-to-ceiling windows, giving out on a glittering nightscape of Koyaanisqatsi skyscrapers. The lift at the Sangster, however, travels to a maximum only of twenty-two floors, fourteen of which were extraneous to Harvey anyway, as his room was No. 824. It is perfectly comfortable – more than perfectly comfortable – but has a view only of the internal courtyard of the hotel, and is furnished in a faintly European style. Harvey's entrance into the room, once he'd got over the initial flummox of American tippage – *such* a pain in the arse, he thinks, handing over a five to a somewhat unsmiling, virtually fancy-dressed porter – is accompanied by a small sinking of the heart, that once again he'd come to America and wasn't staying with Kojak.

2. He is still not sure who is paying for the room. At reception, he had been asked for his credit card, along, once again, with his passport, but knew that this was standard procedure. Then again, it may have meant that the room was paid for, but he had to provide a surety for any extras. On handing over his HSBC Visa, Harvey had puffed up the courage in his rather pigeon-like chest, and said, to the autumnally suited man behind the desk: 'Sorry … can I just ask: has my room been paid for in advance?'

It was a question he didn't feel entirely comfortable asking, since it clearly indicated a hope on his part that it *had* been, and therefore was likely to generate a sense in the autumnally suited man that this particular resident may not easily be able to pay for the room should the answer be 'no'. Harvey knew this was the case from the way he raised the tiniest eyebrow and drummed some code out on the keyboard of his computer.

'It's been reserved on an AmEx card, sir … yours?'

'No, I don't have American Express. Well, I do, but I don't use it.' This was true: a lot of shops in Britain didn't take it, and long, long ago, Harvey had forgotten the PIN. He sensed, on saying this, a suspicion from the receptionist, a resentment not unlike that he had felt at the airport from the immigration official when it had become clear that he owned an American passport but had chosen not to use it: why would you possess such a jewel and not offer it in your palm to demonstrate your kingliness? Harvey felt he could hear the resentment in the way the man went back to his computer, in the heavy dents his fingers made on the keys.

'I'm afraid I can't quite make out from the reservation whether or not all charges are to be drawn on the AmEx card, sir. This may be because the booking seems to be open-ended …?'

He phrased the surmise as a question. Harvey felt moved to answer with the information that his father was dying, but sadly not to a nailed-down schedule, hence his room would indeed have been booked for an open length of time. But instead he just nodded and moved away to the lifts.

3. He doesn't have a suite. On arriving in the room, his first action – before even opening the heavy oak doors of the TV cabinet to check if the pornography channel was hard- or soft-core – had been to take his Sony Vaio laptop out of its silver case, connect it to the Plug and Play wire, and go straight to www.theSangster.com in order to torment himself with what he did not have. Fourteen suites, he had discovered, feature Steinway or Baldwin grand pianos ('in keeping', said the unctuously written website, 'with the hotel's musical heritage') tuned twice a week. Harvey didn't play the piano (although he still had a faint sense of the absurd needlessness of tuning any piano *twice a fucking week*) but nonetheless felt, on reading this, the deep, deep deprivation of not having one in his room. Further picking away at the scab of his envy, he read about the 'legendary' New York suite, on the twenty-second floor, with its sizeable dining room, kitchen, traditional living room, fireplace with faux-quartz logs, antique books, sunburst clocks, Lars Bolanger lacquered boxes, sage velvet seating area, another fucking piano (Steinway – tuned, no doubt, every fifteen seconds), wall-mounted plasmas, state-of-the-art Bang & Olufsen acoustic system and, of course, a 'two-storey view of the Manhattan skyline'. He closed the computer, wondering, if he *had* been certain his dad was paying for it, whether or not he would have demanded an upgrade.

These three reasons finesse his dissatisfaction, each one rising and falling at different times on the graphic equalizer of his anxiety. What would his present therapist – No. 8 – tell him to tell himself? *I would really like to be in a better room, with a view and a set of Lars Bolanger-lacquered boxes, but the fact that I'm not is not the end of the world.* Something like that. He gets up from the leather-topped desk and flops down on one of the two twin beds in his room. Harvey doesn't much like that either. No matter how posh the Sangster is, the presence of the twin doubles makes it feel like a room at a Travellers' Rest somewhere on the A41. Against his overhanging gut, he feels the dig of what should have been – according to the décor – an antique silver cigarette case, but is in fact his iPhone. He takes it out, noticing that another text has come in from Stella: *Darling, hope you landed safely. Call me when you have a moment.*

He remembers then that the phone had trilled again halfway through the journey from JFK, where he had ignored it, because it had arrived just as the taxi set wheel on the Brooklyn Bridge, allowing him to take in his first view for ten years of Manhattan Island. However much the overall idea of this journey has upped Harvey's already monstrous anxiety levels, he had at least been looking forward to this: this packed vertical Oz, rust-brown and silver, rising from the sea in the limpid light of the morning. It always made him catch his breath, that such an urban sight could be so beautiful. He held the view, sliced across by the cables of the bridge, for some seconds, allowing its splendour to work some small massage on his migranous soul. Then he had caught sight of the gap where the Twin Towers of the World Trade Center used to be, and the view became the mouth of a prize-fighter with two teeth knocked out.

Harvey wonders about calling home. Assuming that extras above and beyond the cost of the room are definitely going to be charged to him, he worries about the cost of the phone bill. He knows that phone calls from a five-star hotel are likely to be charged at an absurd number of dollars per minute. He considers using his mobile but then thinks that that too would be very expensive internationally. There is another option: one of the many bills that arrive daily on Harvey's brown-as-dead-grass welcome mat at home, one of the many direct debits signed years ago and eating away at his solvency ever since, is for some company, who offer – for a small monthly payment – to provide a four-digit phone number that their customers can dial while staying at hotels, especially hotels abroad, before the number of their actual call, and which fix that call at a standard local rate. Which would now be marvellously useful for Harvey if at any point on any trip since signing up to this direct debit he had remembered to write down the fucking four-digit number and bring it with him.

Putting off the decision, he decides to check his email. Harvey gets anxious if cut off from the internet. He hears about writers – he just about considers himself one, even though collating the Dictaphonic outpourings of celebrities rarely seems to qualify him as such – who, as soon as they sit down to write, unplug the modem. Not Harvey: if his home modem freezes, as it periodically does, he panics, diving immediately down on his knees amidst the wires and discarded newspapers and sweet wrappers of his study floor in order to unplug and replug it. While waiting for it to restart, he cannot work – it is as if he himself has frozen. There is no rationale for this – occasionally he needs to Google some fact, but most of the information he needs is already provided by his subjects – but the possibility of exclusion on this worldwide scale is too much. He needs to feel he is in there, one of the myriad upturned mouths sucking on the global InfoMother's billion teats.

The Sony Vaio rumbles for while, worrying him, and then Windows Mail opens: he hits Send and Receive, and watches the bar fill to a solid blue. He has nine messages. Eight of them are Spam – Ebony Anastasia Does Interracial Dicking Time, MILF Celestine Opens Her Sweet Ass Do You Want Some?, Superhot Trannies Notwithstanding, PlayPoker UK Exclusive Promotion, Hard Erecttion in 20 Minutes, Erectile Dysfunction?, ChitChatBingo, and one which makes him feel a bit weepy entitled Let Us Protect You, Harvey (from an insurance company) – and one from his agent, Alan. He knows what Alan's email is going to say – he knows it will be delicately poised between expressing condolences for his father's condition and wanting to know when Harvey is going to deliver the pitch for Lark's autobiography – but still opens it with a tiny hope, as he opens all emails, that they will carry news of something stupendously positive. It is a message delicately poised between expressing condolence for his father's condition and wanting to know when Harvey is going to deliver the pitch for Lark's autobiography.

Harvey pitches for a lot of autobiographies these days, many more than he actually writes. Lark, though, is a tough one, as she has done, as far as he can make out, absolutely nothing. Lark is a pop star, but Harvey, like everyone else, has never heard any of her songs, nor even seen a picture of her. This is because Lark is being kept under wraps. Her record company, her management and her PR agency – who

34

have decided, the way these people can now, that she is going to be huge – have created a new marketing strategy around Lark, whereby she is going to burst forth fully-formed onto the public, Athena from their combined Zeus-like forehead. On some so far unspecified date in the future, Lark will be brought forth to the world – her single, her video, her MySpace page will all be let out at the same time, followed closely by her album, and her autobiography. This is what Harvey is supposed to pitch for. He does have some information about her – Alan keeps on sending it, as attachments to his increasingly urgent emails – but every time Harvey remembers the only fact he does know about Lark – that she is nineteen – he cannot face opening any of them.

He shuts down Mail and opens a document file entitled IdeasJune. Harvey has many places in which he writes down ideas. In his hand luggage, along with a newly purchased copy of *Solomon's Testament* – he had wanted, because she was pretty, to blurt out to the girl behind the till at WHSmith in Terminal Four at Heathrow, that he was Eli's son, and had a first edition inscribed to him at home with the words 'To Harvey, may you read it when you're ready …' and was only buying this one because he hadn't read it for years and, well, he didn't really know why he was buying it now but thought he should maybe read it again on the plane over because he was going to see his father on his deathbed – along with that, his father's masterpiece, sits a Dictaphone, and two notebooks, one covered in gold leather, and one in moleskin. Harvey fetishizes notebooks. He has a drawerful of them at home in his study desk – covered in so many materials (velvet, cloth, zebra print, PVC); large hardbound ones and small; policeman-flicking-it-open-in-the-dock ones – and in all of them he has written thoughts for novels, films, plays, even – in one of them – business ideas. They are not empty. But they are not full either; each one has a series of scrawls, written in Harvey's lazy script, which end after about five pages. It is partly the act of writing – that is, handwriting – that fails. Harvey likes the idea of opening the gilded notebook, and mark-ing its embossed paper with the varied scents of his mind, but when it comes to it, writing with a pen has become a bit of a faff. More than that: writing with a pen doesn't feel significant. It feels the preserve, now, of telephone numbers and email addresses hurriedly scribbled on stickies that he knows he's going to lose. For his words to mean something, they have to be written on a computer. He knows this, yet continues to buy notebooks.

The document IdeasJune has a number of sentences already in it. Some are fully-formed pitches: 'Reality TV Idea: convince someone they've died and gone to heaven.' Others just phrases, pending novels yet unwritten: 'Her breasts spilled out of her bra like muscle rain.' On a new page, Harvey writes:

Film Idea
Title: SHALLOW
John Shallow is obsessed with looks. He is also an immigration officer at JFK. His obsession serves him well in his job because he always checks people's – especially women's – faces very thoroughly. But it doesn't serve him so well in his marriage, which is falling apart.

However, through a long and difficult process, involving much therapy and various epiphanies (? don't know what these are – something profound/life-changing) he comes to terms with it, and saves his marriage. Just at that point, though, while at work, he spots – because he's still got the skill (the skill at looking) even though he's sorted out the problems that come with it – someone coming through immigration who turns out to be Osama bin Laden, incredibly well-disguised, using plastic surgery etc (a woman?). Osama is arrested and overnight Shallow becomes a national hero and a major celebrity.

This leads to loads of sexual opportunities and wrecks his marriage.

Harvey leans back. Something's not right about it. He highlights the main body of the prose, and then opens the Formatting Palette, and clicks on I. This happens:

Film Idea

Title: SHALLOW

John Shallow is obsessed with looks. He is also an immigration officer at JFK. His obsession serves him well in his job because he always checks people's – especially women's – faces very thoroughly. But it doesn't serve him so well in his marriage, which is falling apart.

However, through a long and difficult process, involving much therapy and various epiphanies (? don't know what these are – something profound/life-changing) he comes to terms with it, and saves his marriage. Just at that point, though, while at work, he spots – because he's still got the skill (the skill at looking) even though he's sorted out the problems that come with it – someone coming through immigration who turns out to be Osama bin Laden, incredibly well-disguised, using plastic surgery etc (a woman?). Osama is arrested and overnight Shallow becomes a national hero and a major celebrity.

This leads to loads of sexual opportunities and wrecks his marriage.

Yes, that feels better. But now – as ever, when he has done a bit of work – Harvey must grant himself some small reward. He turns away from the computer and takes from his pocket a small bottle of blue liquid. However bleak the journey, there were always consolations on coming to America: the Manhattan view was one, and here was another. While pushing his baggage, ill balanced on the trolley, through JFK's anywhere-in-the-world airport mall, saliva had gathered in the corners of his mouth, sent up from his forever inflamed throat glands, and Harvey had realized that he was hungry. Not straightforwardly for food; there was something specific which was making his mouth water at that moment, something specific that his system was reminding him can only properly be got hold of in America, reminding him a split second before the words formed inside his damp, sleepless skull: *sour sweets.* Harvey loves sour sweets; he loves the taste contradiction, the sugar fighting the acid, his tongue a pair of apothecary's scales holding these opposites in perfect balance. He loves the *dialectic.* And he loves the fact that all things are postponed during the sucking of a sour sweet; that, while the conflict between sweet and

37

sour remains unresolved, Harvey can float, his soul buoyed up by the sensual striving towards that equilibrium, and nothing matters until it's over. If he could only get hold of enough of the right kind of sour sweets in the UK, he thinks he may never be depressed; instead, he would be happily addicted to them, despite the terrible stomach cramps that eating them always eventually induces. But in the UK, none of the sweets – not Sour Haribos, not TongueBubbler, not even Toxic Waste – were anything like sour enough for him.

Here, however, in this land where contradiction was possibility, there were sour sweets, Harvey knew, that took the concept of sour-sweetness into a whole new dimension. He had seen on the internet, available from various US confectionery sites, boxes of brightly coloured jelly beans, emblazoned with the promises Extra Sour, Extremely Sour, Very Sour Sours. Yes: Harvey has Googled the phrases 'sour sweets', 'sour candy', and 'sour confectionery', wrapping them in inverted commas so as to allow the computer to make no mistakes about his intention. He had Goo-ogled them, in fact, bringing up multiple images of boxes and wrappers to lasciviously stare at. Unbelievably, perhaps, for a forty-four-year-old man, he had even read *reviews* of some of these sweets. Zours Incredibly Sour Tangerines had got a unanimous five stars on cybercandy.com, and Harvey had been on the verge of getting them to ship a box out when he remembered he was soon to visit his native land – which, at that moment, figured in his head as Willy Wonka's factory to Charlie.

Half mad with the craving, and once through the small hiccup in customs, he had dashed inside the first available confectionery containing store, leaving his baggage on the trolley outside, aching to be control-exploded by security. The shop had stocked no Zours, leading Harvey into a mad twenty seconds of uncertainty, his eyes riffling through the Hersheys and the Oreos, until finally asking, in a voice hoarse with desire, 'Do you have any sour sweets?' The store assistant, a ginger-haired, fuzzy-faced woman, looked blank, so Harvey looked down, ashamed, feeling that her blankness must contain a condemnation, a deadpan amazement that a man of his age should have such adolescent needs; at which stage he noticed that her

38

index finger had stirred from its fellows, and was indicating downwards and to the left. Harvey's eyes followed, past the brown and green and pinks, and nearly missed it, because it wasn't in a wrapper: it wasn't even a sweet as such, in the boiled, solid, chewable and/or biteable sense. But then his eyes did a double-take, and returned to the words emblazoned on the labels of three small bottles perched above a bright rack of bubblegum: *Extra Tart Sour Blast Spray*.

Harvey could hardly believe it. Even in all his research he hadn't come across this: a spray, a *concentrate*. The sour-sweet sensation, literally bottled, distilled, injectable directly onto the tongue like morphine into the pain receptors of the brain. He bought all three bottles for what seemed at that moment like the incredible bargain price of $2.25 dollars apiece. He had intended to wait until he got to the hotel before trying them, in order to savour the moment. Unfortunately, self-control of this order – or, rather, the lack of it – lies at the very heart of Harvey Gold. This was why various lucky travellers who happened to be passing through the gates of Terminal One of JFK that day were treated to the sight of the middle-aged son of the world's greatest living author standing in the queue for the airport taxis, mouth open and eyes closed in some small ecstasy, spraying what appeared to be a sample bottle of cheap perfume onto his stretched-out thirsty-dog tongue, gradually coating it blue.

Now, in the hotel room, lying prone on one of his two quilted boats of bedding, he offers that same tongue up for another spray. The wardrobe door opposite has swung open from a bizarre attempt he made soon after entering the room to pack his clothes away, giving up almost instantly on the realization that – even if his father should survive longer than Freda's projected six weeks – Harvey will continue, while here, to live out of his suitcase, like he has always done on every other trip that necessitated a suitcase. On the inner right-hand door of the wardrobe is a mirror, where Harvey can see himself, or, rather, where he can see all those parts of himself that are not hidden by the solid explosion of his stomach rising from the bed like a termite mound from the ground. His tongue is out of his mouth, and looks, blue and upside-down, like a football shirt drying on the washing line of his lower lip. He undergoes a visual epiphany, not unlike when a mirror on the bathroom door swings your toilet seat image into view, making you think: *is man but this?* This is a thought Harvey has about himself around five times a minute, however, and so he overrides it with a gust of Extra Tart Sour Blast Spray, flooding his aching taste buds with soursweet rain.

After the hit, trying to avoid the aspartame comedown, Harvey shifts his bulk around to the side of the bed and dials his home number on the telephone on the side table.

'Mr Gold, how can I help you?' a smooth, sonorous voice says. Harvey wonders, at first, if it is God, finally asking the requisite question, but then realizes his mistake.

'Sorry, I forgot to dial ...'

'It's nine for an outside number, sir.'

'Yes. OK.'

'Is there anything else I can help you with?'

Harvey thinks: *everything?*

'No. Thanks.'

'Thank you, sir.'

He clicks off, and dials again, adding the magic nine. And then at the last minute he remembers: five hours behind. His eyes flick to the hands of the faux-antique set on the bedside table: quarter to eleven. In England it will be just gone six – and then she picks up. He hears an airy silence, the rustling of sheets and blankets, before Stella's 'Hello?' comes down the line, alarm penetrating her tone even though her throat is husky and clotted with sleep.

'Sorry, darling ... sorry. I forgot about the time difference. Go back to sleep.'

'Harvey? Are you OK?'

'Yes. Yes.' He knows this is never true, but – not just with her, with everyone that asks it – you can't go through it all, not every time, can you? *No, I'm overweight, exhausted, I get these weird pains in my legs, I have constant low-level nausea, I have prostituted what tiny talent I have ghostwriting the lives of idiots, every woman I pass fills me with despair, my child has Asperger's Syndrome, my father is dying and I deeply, deeply love my wife but can't bear the idea that she is starting to grow old. And yourself?*

'Your dad … is he …?'

'I haven't seen him yet. No change, as far as I know. But look – what time is it there …?'

A shuffling sound. He sees the scene, familiar in his mind, the safety of the half-light, the day not started, her profile shifting towards the digital clock on her bedside draw.

'Five forty-five.'

'Yes. So sorry. Go back to sleep.' He can feel, even across the wide swathe of water, how it's too late, how his phone call has rushed consciousness up to her surface, like an air bubble floating from the deep.

'No, it's OK. I needed to get up early anyway. Jamie's got the Montgomery Clinic …'

'I thought that wasn't until nine thirty.'

'Yes. Well, I've got to wash my hair.' In his mind's eye, Harvey sees the process: her lying back in a full, scalding bath, her face surrounded by water, her curls spiralling away like sea snakes, the whole image a benign Medusa. When she rises out of the steam to work on her hair, her fingers on her scalp move with some precise feminine alchemy, so distinct from his soapy plonk and rub. Every so often, she rotates her head from side to side to prevent the liquid pooling in her ears. The intimacy of watching her wash her hair can feel at times overwhelming. And afterwards, when her hair is wet, falling across her face, before she lifts it into a towel – he does not know where to look. She feels too vulnerable, and his eyes too searching.

'And I've got a lot of work stuff to do, as well, so it's probably a good idea to get started …'

'Stop trying to make it better for me.'

'I'm not. I won't get back to sleep now anyway. And however pissed off I am about that – which is, yeah, a bit – I'm also pleased, Harvey. To hear from you. I thought your plane must have crashed.'

He laughs, but knows she means it. Every time Harvey flies anywhere, Stella assumes his plane will crash. Her kisses, when he leaves, always have a force to them, impelled by a sense that this could be the last time.

'That would have been on the news.'

'The CIA might have been keeping it quiet.'

'Why?'

'I don't know. They might have imposed a security blanket.'

'I think the word you're after is blackout.'

'Oh, yeah. But it's quarter to six in the morning. I can confuse blanket and blackout. Because I'd like both.'

'How's Jamie?'

He hears her rearranging the pillows.

'He's OK. He was happy enough after school yesterday. Only got upset at bedtime that you weren't here. Did you read his note?'

'Note?'

'His picture. I put it in your suitcase.'

He gets up off the bed, still holding the phone. 'What, as a surprise?'

A soft beat, her patience diffusing. 'No, I told you it was in there, yesterday.'

'Oh sorry, I –'

'It's OK. You were in one of your nervous flaps when you were leaving. I knew you weren't really listening.'

'Hold on, I'll go and have a look.'

'It's in the zip-up pocket. In the top bit.'

He goes over to the suitcase. It is there, a white envelope with the word 'DAD' written on it, in Jamie's painfully immature handwriting. Inside is a piece of asymmetrically folded A4 paper, on one half of which Jamie has drawn a chess set. The figures are not arranged on the board, but around it. They are not rendered exactly, as they would be if Jamie was an extraordinary Asperger's child, but randomly: it is difficult to make out which are pawns, and which are major pieces. They look like chess figures in the wind.

Jamie has not written anything to go with his drawing, but on the facing half, in Stella's looping hand, it says: 'Have a good trip, even though it's for a sad thing. I love you. J xxx.' Harvey holds the note in his hand, and feels his heart crack with love.

He comes back to the phone. Before he speaks, having heard him pick the receiver up, she says:

'That's exactly what he told me to write.'

'It's really nice. Did you suggest the chess thing?'

He says this knowing that both of them would rather their son had chosen the subject himself, thereby indicating that he has, of his own volition, noticed something about his father's interests.

'I may have done,' she says.

She yawns. He sees their bedroom, dark and warm: Stella makes everywhere cosy. They live in Kent, in a cottage on the North Downs, which would be idyllic were it not for the proximity of the M2. Wooed by the oldness, the Englishness, of the place, Harvey had succumbed easily to the previous owner's trick of enclosing the front garden with a series of tall hedges, obscuring the surrounding countryside. On a final visit before completion, while visiting the upstairs toilet, he had noticed a somewhat busy road in the middle distance, but, infatuated with the place, and too frightened to disturb at this late stage the serious business of property transaction, had put it out of his mind. Now he spends much time in the garden, trying to gauge exactly how loud that muffled roar is, trying to work out how he couldn't have heard it before, and trying to think himself into Stella's method of imagining it's the sound of the sea.

'I still think you should go back to sleep.'

'I said: I'm awake now. Look, don't worry about me. Did you sleep on the plane?'

'No. You know I can never sleep on a plane.'

'You should have flown business …'

'That's what Freda said …' A momentary silence follows this: Harvey assumes she has taken the comparison with his father's wife as an implicit rebuke, which he had not meant, at least consciously. There is an awkward pause, such as can happen even between couples who have been together for fourteen years, and for whom blips of silence are not generally registered. He waits, wondering if it might be possible over the phone, in another country, to hear the sound of the M2.

'Well, anyway, darling …' says Harvey, eventually, feeling the spasticity of words said to break such silences, '… I'll call you later.'

'OK. I love you.'

'I love you, too.'

It is the truth, however fast it makes his heart dip.

⋆   ⋆   ⋆

My daddy seemed a bit better today. The nurses sat him up in bed, and they took off that see-through mask he usually has to wear over his mouth and nose. He didn't have it on for ages (later on Mommy told me it was over *five minutes*!). He still didn't say anything – the nurse had to put the tube back into his neck while he had the mask off, so that probably didn't help – but Mommy told me to come over and hold his hand. It made me feel a bit funny, because I haven't held Daddy's hand before for so long. After a while I started to notice some of the weird things about it: how he's got loads of these big brown patches (and some black spots) on the top side and how the bones seemed to be poking through the skin, so that it was a bit like holding a skeleton's hand. The tops of his fingers (around the nails) look sort of yellow, like he's bruised them or something, and his nails are really long too – I remember Mommy telling me that Daddy's nails grow really quickly, and he always forgets to cut them – especially the thumb ones, which were so long they were kind of gross. You might think that nails wouldn't grow when you're asleep all the time, but they do.

Sometimes this happens, that Daddy's skin and stuff makes me feel weird. I've noticed before that his skin isn't like mine – obviously! – or Jada's, or even Mommy's, but I guess I've kind of gotten used to it. I didn't really notice it at all until Jada said to me that time that thing about how my daddy's skin looked like it had lots of little holes in it. I said shut up, stupid, like I always do when she says something like that, something just meant to be nasty, but afterwards I couldn't help looking and it made it hard to forget because I could see what she meant, sort of. His skin looks more like a net than skin; it kind of looks like bits of skin knitted together around all these tiny holes, like wool looks like close up.

His skin looks even more like wool now, because he's got all these little white hairs coming out of it. Mommy told me it's difficult for Daddy to shave now – well, it's impossible for him to shave, but it's not even easy for anyone else to do it! They're so worried about cutting him. But he has lots of little white hairs coming out of the tops of his hands, too, even on his fingers, and he never shaved those even when he wasn't in hospital. I suppose you would need a special kind of tiny shaver to do them, and I don't know if you can even get them in any store. I got this really funny idea in my head, that I wanted to turn his hand around, and play round and round the garden with it, even though I haven't played that for years, not since I was a really tiny baby – but still, when I thought about it, I remembered how I used to like it so much, the tickly feeling so nice, as the grown-up's finger goes round and round, watching it and feeling it at the same time, and waiting, waiting, waiting for the bigger tickle up the arm. I didn't do it with Daddy's hand – I mean, I knew it'd be a stupid thing to do – and, besides, I don't know if he can actually feel a tickle when he's so ill and dying and everything.

After Mommy told me to hold Daddy's hand, her cellphone rang, and she was on it for quite a while (you aren't really meant to have your cellphone on in the hospital, but I think it's OK for Mommy to keep hers on because Daddy's so famous). I held his hand and tried not to think about how weird the skin on it was: I tried to look at his face instead, but that's even weirder really, because Daddy's cheeks hang really low, and his ears are so big (especially the bottom bit, the soft bit), and his nose is so long, that now because his skin is all grey his face reminded me of an elephant's face. Which made me want to laugh at first, but I kept it inside, by holding my breath, which I can do for nearly a minute. Anyway, then I started talking, just saying stuff, things that were in my head: I said, 'I love you Daddy' and 'I hope you get better soon, Daddy' even though I know he's not going to get better, he's going to die, but I didn't know what else to say – it would have sounded *really* weird to talk about him dying – but it doesn't matter anyway, it's just good to say stuff. He can hear me. Mommy always says he can, even though he never says anything, or even nods his head or whatever. Sometimes she tells me to look in his eyes – *Look deep into his eyes*, she always says, *because that's where he still lives* – and where you can see, she says, that he still understands everything. But his eyes were only half open, and what you can see of the inside bit looks really red – I don't mean just at the bottom of the eyes, that bit's always been really red on my daddy's eyes, and kind of wet, and sometimes I used to think his eyes were bleeding, or that maybe, because he's a genius, when he cries, it's blood – God! *So* mad! That's like something from *Twilight* (which Mommy doesn't know I've watched – Jada showed me it at her house, her mom never cares what she sees on TV and stuff).

So then I just kept going, saying whatever came out of my head. Mommy was still on the phone and the nurses were moving around the room and that machine that Daddy is hooked up to all the time with the green lines on it kept on beeping, so no one was really noticing. I told him about Aristotle, my cat, about how he's started to get really fat because while we haven't been at home the whole time Noda – that's our housekeeper; she's from the Philippines – just leaves food out for him, like a whole tin at once!! And then he just goes over and nibbles on it all day like a cow eating the grass. I told Daddy about how last time me and Elaine took him to the vet, the vet said that he needed to lose weight otherwise he might get ill, and so we bought him this cat food they only sell at the vet called Seniors, which is meant for older cats – which he kind of is, too, even though he's younger than me, six and a half, but you have to times it by ten, so that makes him sixty-five (which is *way* old, but still quite a lot younger than Daddy) – but it's good for fat cats because it's got less protein and stuff in it and that helps to make them thin. But all that's like a waste of time now because Noda just opens the tin of FancyFeast and pours it all out for him to nosh at all day.

I felt a bit silly talking about Aristotle like this, because I didn't know if it was the right kind of thing to talk about. I thought maybe I should be talking about something more grown up, but I couldn't think of anything. I started to feel sad, because I haven't seen Aristotle that much since we've been going to the hospital all the time, and I really miss him. He's a really sweet cat, with black and white fur and a really cute little pink nose, who always purrs when you stroke him. I think he misses me, too, because he always comes right up to me when we do get to go home, and nuzzles my leg for ages. So because I was thinking about him and about how he wasn't getting to eat the Seniors that he's supposed to, I started to cry. Then, I felt really silly, standing there, getting that funny tickle between the corner of your eye and your nose when the tear comes out – I mean not like blubbing crazy, not even sniffling, just one or two tears coming out – but Mommy quickly stopped her phone call and came over, knelt down and gave me the biggest hug, squeezing me so, so tight.

'Colette! Darling! It's OK …' she said. 'Cry if you want to. Cry. It's OK.' She was patting me on the back at the same time, like Elaine sometimes used to do when I was little and had swallowed something bad. 'It's OK.' I was still holding Daddy's hand. Mommy was smiling, that smile she does when she looks at Daddy sleeping in his bed, or sometimes when she picks up one of his books. Sort of sad and pleased at the same time. 'We all feel like crying at the moment.'

'But you don't cry …' I said.

She did one of her smiles. 'I want to. Really. But sometimes when you're grown up you have to be strong.' She pulled a tissue from her sleeve and wiped my eyes. 'Do you need to blow your nose?'

I shook my head. 'When I say strong I don't mean like when some-one who lifts something really heavy.' I knew she didn't mean that. 'I mean when bad things happen – when the worst things happen – you have to try and keep going. With a smile on your face. To make sure everyone else doesn't get more upset.' She touched my cheek. 'I have to be strong for you.'

I thought about this for a bit.

'OK. But if you *want* to cry it's OK, too, Mommy,' I said. 'Maybe when you cry, I can be strong for you.'

Mommy looked so pleased that I said this. But she also looked a bit like she was going to cry there and then. She gave me another really big hug, and then said, in her softest voice:

'Thank you, Colette. Thank you.'

I wasn't sure whether or not to say anything about how much I missed Aristotle. Instead I said: 'Mommy. Is Daddy in a comma?'

She blinked, and moved her head back a bit. 'I'm sorry, darling?'

'I heard Dr Ghundkhali say that that's what Daddy is in. A comma. At first I thought they meant like that little thing you write in a sentence when you want the person reading it to stop, but not for as long as when you do a full stop – I thought maybe it was something to do with Daddy being a writer? – but then I realized it must be a word that sounds the same but means two different things. Like *pair*. Or *been*.'

Mommy looked at me. She was making a weird face, all frowny. Then, behind me, I heard one of the nurses – I think it was the one with the curly hair and the banana nose – laugh. I could feel my face going red, because I knew straight away that I must have said something stupid or kid-like, and I hate doing that – I hate doing it in front of *anyone*, and I especially *hate* doing it in front of Mommy. I am Colette Gold, and I do not *say* stupid eight-year-old kiddie things that grown-ups laugh at because they're so cute. I got so cross that I started to feel another little tear come out, which only made it worse.

'Colette, darling,' said Mommy. 'Don't get upset. That's a very good question. You just slightly misheard Dr Gundkhali. He would have said that Daddy was in a "coma". You see, it sounds a bit like *comma*, doesn't it? But it has an extended – like a longer – "o". *Coama*.'

'Oh,' I said. Then, like I was saying it in slow motion: 'Coa … ma.' She nodded, one of her slow nods which makes her fringe move like a little curtain in front of her eyes. No one said anything for a bit. So then I said: 'Yes, but what does it *mean*?'

Mommy opened her mouth to speak, but then the hospital door banged really loudly, and a man came in. He was fat, and sweaty, and his suit was too tight for him. Mommy got up, and looked at him for quite a long time without saying anything.

'Hello, Freda,' he said.

'Colette,' she said. 'Come and meet your half-brother Harvey.'

★ ★ ★

This is too much rain, thinks Violet. She means too much rain to go for her walk, but is aware as she thinks it of a sense that, for some summers now, there has been too much rain. It used to be funny, the unpredictability of British summer, something that she might have commented on with a resigned shrug to her neighbours if they bumped into each other buttoned-up in July, and the neighbours would nod and smile resignedly back, and it was a nice, reassuring, confirmation that they shared the same mock-weary national expectation. But that was just about the way the sun used to stand the country up. It was not about rain like this, like a monsoon, hitting the pavement so hard that filthy fat globules of dust-water fly up from the cracks.

She has opened the frosted fire-glass front door, and is standing on the top step, looking out at Redcliffe Square. She already knows from looking out of her room window – and from the way the stuck branch trembled, like it was freezing – that the weather was probably too bad to venture outside, but she thought it might look better at ground level. It does not. If anything, standing here brings home the problem more clearly, which is not so much the weather as the ground itself, transformed by the rain into an assault course for her and her stick. She does not mind the weather, really: she does not mind getting a bit wet, or having her hair blown into a mess, even though she had only last week been to the hairdressers and had it styled and coloured (plus a root perm to give her some body and to cover the small bald spot just below the crown). But she does mind being attacked by the ground; she minds slipping on a puddle or being blown over by the wind and crashing to the concrete and becoming in an instant one of the residents who has *had a fall* – the three most dreaded words at Redcliffe House, heard only in whispers, the care home equivalent of Auschwitz's *chosen for selection*.

She shuts the door: the cold street air in her nostrils mingles for a second with the sickly overheated scent of the hallway. She had hoped to buy a paper, to see if there was any more news about Eli. Three newspapers – the *Mail*, the *Telegraph* and the *Express* – are delivered daily to the house, but when Violet enters the living room, she sees that, as ever, they have been snapped up by those (mainly male) residents keen to demonstrate their lack of senility. Joe Hillier, she notices, is busy consolidating this demonstration using the *Telegraph*, the paper which best allows for the requisite amount of page-flapping and harrumphing. Luckily, for Violet's purposes, Pat Cadogan collars her immediately to give her a long report on the condition of her shingles, allowing her to feign concern while standing at the back of Joe's chair looking over his shoulder.

Sure enough, Joe turns the page out of the front few pages and all their pressing seriousness about politicians she can no longer remember the names of, and there he is – her ex-husband (the phrase sounds ridiculous, even inside her head), centred on the page, the same black-and-white photograph that had been on television the day before.

'What is it?' says Pat, a grimace of irritation breaking though her seen-it-all implacability: she had noticed Violet's lack of concentration, her failure to nod at her retelling of the last two castigations of the house doctors.

'Sorry Pat ... I ... Joe?'

Joe Hillier looks up, but, as Violet is behind him, he simply scans the room, shrugs his shoulders, and puts it down – in a rather matter-of-fact way – to voices in his head.

'Joe!' She taps him on the shoulder. He tries to look round, but the turning circle of his neck fails him, and he has to shift his body sideways to see her.

'What is it?'

'Would you mind if I had the paper?'

He looks at it, folded now on his lap. 'This one?'

'Yes ...'

'Well, I haven't finished reading it yet.'

He stares at her, with all the truculence that old men reserve for old women.

'OK. Can I have it when you have?'

'Well, I think Frank ...' Joe raises an arthritic, yellowing finger towards another resident, a man wearing thick-lens glasses rimmed with heavy, 1960s black frames whom Violet has never spoken to '... was next in the queue for the *Telegraph*.'

'Well, fine. Just whenever everyone's finished with it, I'd like the page with that photograph.'

Violet's natural instinct is diplomatic, and she had been smiling, but her voice, raised by the betrayal within it of a tiny level of frustration, causes a number of men and women in the room – at least, the ones with their hearing aids on – to turn round. Violet had never raised her voice before in three years at Redcliffe House, and it is clear from the uncertainty on some of the residents' faces that they have no idea who had been speaking.

'Have it? You mean, keep it?' says the man who Joe had referred to as Frank.

'I don't think that's House policy, is it?'

He takes his glasses off, in the manner of a board member at an important meeting, dealing with a thorny issue someone else has brought up. Behind them, red threads creep in from all sides of his eyes towards the cataract-white centres, like blood dropped in milk. With a sinking heart, Violet realizes that the two men are going to use her request as a means of pretending they still exist in the world of the living.

'Absolutely correct, Frank,' says Joe. 'The rules state that all newspapers and magazines put out in the communal area for use of the residents must be left in the communal area at the end of the day for recycling.'

'Oh, for crying out loud Joe Hillier,' says Norma Miller, one of the more lively residents. She is Welsh – so always addresses people by both their names – and her hair is dyed shockingly blonde for a woman in her eighties. Her face is so engraved with lines it looks, Violet always thinks, like crazy paving: she has smoked her whole life, and is furious that she is not allowed to continue to do so inside Redcliffe House. 'Don't be such a stupid old stickler. Let her have the bloody paper if she wants it.'

'Why *do* you want it, anyway?'

Violet turns; it is Pat Cadogan who had spoken, her eyes squinting with suspicion. Violet had dreaded someone asking this. She had hoped the newspaper would just be handed over, and she could squirrel it away to her room, but now, as always, events had run out of control. It was why she never spoke up; why she chose, often, not to say anything at all.

'Oh, no reason, really. I know – I used to know …' she doesn't want to say his name; it would just lead further away from the straight line back to her room, '… him. The man in the photograph. A long time ago.'

Joe Hillier picks up the paper and shakes the pages out. 'Barack Obama?'

'No! Him. On the facing page.'

Joe scans the print. A piece about the arts, about books – worse, a writer of fiction: she could hear in the snort of breath through his solidly packed nostrils that this was an article that he, a man from the north of England, would normally disregard.

'Eli … Gold. Yes, I've heard of him.'

'Didn't he kill one of his wives?' says Frank.

'No!' says Violet. 'It was a suicide pact that went wrong.'

Joe Hillier frowns, though it is unclear whether this is from disbelief, or because the idea of disposing of one's wife in that way – Joe had lived for fifty-two years with a woman dedicated to making his life a disappointment – suddenly occurs to him as brilliant.

'Gold …' says Pat, menacingly; she looks over Joe's shoulder at the picture. 'Is he a relative of yours?'

Violet seizes on it. 'Yes! Yes, he is. A distant … cousin.'

Pat stares at her, her tiny eyes – had they shrunk with age? Weren't eyes the only part of the body that didn't do that? – narrowed to slits. *Don't you lie to me* is so clearly etched into her expression, it seems to be written on a comic-book balloon attached to her mouth. Violet turns away: she does not want to lie – she is naturally no good at it – but it is so much easier than the truth, which in this case, she thinks, would not be believed. It seems so unlikely, really, even to her, that *she*, as she sees herself in the big gilt-edge mirror over the living-room fireplace, an ancient husk of femininity, could ever have been loved by *him*, as he is pictured in the newspaper, so pert and sharp-suited and – a word the young people used to use: or did they still? – *cool*. She may even be put down as showing the first signs of senility. And even if it were believed, in the unlikely event that someone were to check the information and discover its truth, she knows she would only emerge from her cocoon of anonymity as an object of resentment. It was impossible for such worlds to meet; the one in the paper, even though it was past and dead – the world of fame, and worldliness, and glamour – and this one, Redcliffe House, this apex of mundanity. It was like trying to push together the wrong ends of two magnets; she would be held responsible for forcing such a bad conjunction.

'All right, then,' says Joe, shrugging. 'I'll ask one of the nurses to hold onto that page for you at the end of the day ...'

'Thank you, Joe. That's very good of you.'

But of course he forgets, and when she asks the next day all the newspapers have already been sent off for recycling.

*   *   *

Where were all these women in winter? thinks Harvey, viewing the teeming Manhattan sidewalks from the back windows of another cab. It is not the first time he has had the thought: it seems it comes to him earlier every year, his own deeply dysfunctional first cuckoo of spring. He knows the argument: it's just the clothes, with their dizzying gaps between belt and top and neck and bra strap, giving onto the soft planes of caramelizing flesh. But that makes no sense to Harvey, because, looking round, he knows for certain that the women who snag his gaze in these clothes would snag his gaze were they dressed head to foot in straw.

Fifth Avenue, the boulevard his driver has chosen to take in order to bring him back from Mount Sinai to the Sangster, is full of shoppers. Harvey is glad he isn't driving, as looking out onto the fecund streets at this time of year from a vantage point above a steering wheel – whether in London or New York or anywhere – is lethal. Not lethal as in 'God, man, that's *lethal*', said, say, with a wipe across the mouth on putting back down on the bar a high-alcohol cocktail. Lethal as in looking so hard and so long back over his shoulder, at this woman or that woman or this woman or that woman or this woman or that woman, in order to check out whether her face and front fulfils or undoes the promise of her hair and back, that Harvey drives headlong into the truck/car/bus/building in front. Many is the time, in London, from April to September, that Harvey has had to apply the brake split seconds faster than his leaping heart in order to prevent an imminent body flight through the smeary glass of his Toyota Avensis windscreen. And many is also the time – about one in four, Harvey reckons – that a clear sight of said woman would, he thinks, have been just about worth, if not actual death, at least being cut screaming from the molten Toyota/truck conjunction with oxyacetylene.

This is a somewhat contradictory thought for Harvey Gold – which is OK, contradiction being his air, his water – seeing as he knows that much of his trouble comes from this type of looking. This looking isn't pleasure, it isn't contemplation: like the rest of Harvey's stuff, it's symptomatic, pathological, obsessive compulsive. It is desire rendered only as pain, unrequited even in Harvey's imagination. He is not interested in what he knows he can never have. He is only troubled by it.

There are male friends he has spoken to about this issue who love the streets at this time, including one who, despite having three cars and more than enough money for taxis, always, on travelling into central London in spring and summer, will get the bus, in order to sit on the top deck and leer. Harvey does not understand his friend. Harvey does not understand the idea of the enjoyment of looking. Very early on in their time together, Therapist 4, the Kleinian, had suggested the possibility that Harvey could contain the anxiety looking at women on the street caused him by comparing them to beautiful paintings.

'You can look at beautiful paintings without being overcome with anxiety – you can in fact look at beautiful paintings and enjoy them …' she had said, with an air of *this'll sort him out*, 'why don't you try and think of these women as beautiful paintings?'

'Because,' he had replied instantly – always at his quickest when pressed on his own neuroses: the nearest Harvey comes to his father's speed of mind is his ability always to have an answer for why this or that suggestion *will not* cure him – 'when I see a beautiful painting, I have no desire to touch or kiss or lick or fuck the canvas.'

Harvey remembers the face of Therapist 4 at this moment. She was his first woman – chosen deliberately, in the hope that that would be the key – and sixty-three, also a deliberate choice, and had had a minor stroke that caused one side of her mouth to fall faintly out of symmetry with the other. Physiotherapy had got her facial muscles back to about 80 per cent of their pre-stroke strength, but her lips still had something of the look of a falling graph and, in response to this particular remark, seemed to fall just a millidegree further. Harvey took this to mean that he had stumped her, and felt, despite the fact that he was paying her to cure him and therefore not to be stumped, a small thrill of triumph.

'Are you OK, sir?' says the taxi driver, a Sikh. Harvey looks away from the window; again he has the impulse to delineate the thousand ways in which he is not. But he says:

'Fine. Yes. Why do you ask?'

'You were sighing?' His accent is Bengali, but the intonation, going up at the end of the sentence to make the observation a question, is American.

Harvey looks at the ID card in the right-hand corner of the glass partition that separates passenger from driver: the words Jasvant Kirtia Singh and a face, most of it covered by turban and beard.

'Sorry, I didn't realize …'

'It is someone you're seeing at the hospital?'

Harvey looks at Jasvant Kirtia Singh's eyes in the rear-view mirror. Animated from their I'm-Not-A-Terrorist impassivity on his ID, they are small black beads, birdlike, but framed by eyebrows gently suggesting both enquiry and a willingness to retreat if the passenger does not wish to talk.

'My father.'

'He is unwell?'

'Yes.'

'I hope he gets better soon …?'

Harvey wonders what to say to this. It has happened a few times, particularly early on, before the obituary writers began sharpening their pencils (or, rather, Googling 'Eli Gold'): he would tell someone that his father was ill, and they would offer some encouraging words indicating hope of a return to health, and Harvey would have to face saying, *No. He isn't going to get better.* The next stage of the conversation would then be stunted, and Harvey would feel at some level rude for having burdened them with this information. It crosses his mind, therefore, just to tell the taxi driver that his father is indeed on the mend – after all, he is not someone who needs to know the truth, nor is ever likely to find out that he has been lied to anyway. But Harvey doesn't: even the tiniest lies will up his already heightened anxiety levels.

'I don't think so …' he says, and the Sikh's eyes hold his for a second, then move up and down as the back of his turbaned head nods in sad understanding.

'I am sorry,' he says, for the first time not framing the statement as a question.

Harvey is grateful, however, to have his mind brought back to his father. He feels, with his gratitude, a stab of guilt that he should be thinking about his sense of exclusion from the huge variety of female flesh out there so soon after seeing his father on his deathbed for the first time. Harvey knows what the world demands: there are certain things, of which the death of your father is certainly one, that must drive all other thoughts from your head, filling your sky as effortlessly as a wide-winged black eagle, but the truth – Harvey's truth, yes, but he senses that here, for once, he is not alone – is that the widower at his wife's funeral is for a second snagged by the breasts of the female mourner standing on the other side of the grave, straining against her tight black jacket; that the father at his son's hospital bed is distracted, against all his will, by the curving back view the nurse creates as she reaches up to change the little boy's drip. It is the source of men's deepest shame, the ever-presence of the penis; or, to be more exact, the *incongruity* of the penis, its continued presence on those occasions when it would be so clearly in accordance with every idea of human dignity for it to be absent.

Harvey tries his best, though. He attempts to use his short-term memory – the pictures in his head of where he has just been – to drive himself into mental propriety. He thinks hard: he *focuses*. But not in that modern self-help, how-to-improve-your-golf-swing way – he actually does his best to make his mind's eye like a camera lens, closing telescopically on the world around him to see only the immediate past.

Eli's room had been in Geriatrics, at the end of a long, bright corridor, on whose walls were hung a number of photographs commemorating the opening of the new Geriatric Medicine Facility, by Martha Stewart, in 2007. Outside the room itself stood a hulking security man, both black and dressed in black. He held one huge finger, his index, to his ear, pressed against a Bluetooth cellphone earpiece. 'ID, sir,' he said, managing to pack into those two words all his adamantine non-negotiability on this requirement

Harvey's stomach fell. He hadn't, of course, considered that access to his father's hospital room might be controlled: a stab of resentment towards Freda for not mentioning it went through him. He could have brought one of his two passports, but they were both in his bum bag, presently in his hotel room, flung over the twin bed he had chosen not to sleep in – a decision he had remained uncertain about throughout the long jet-lagged night, even swapping beds for twenty minutes at around 5 a.m., hoping that the other mattress might be soft enough to grasp what little oblivion the dark still offered.

'I don't …' he began, and saw the security man's wide face settle into stone. 'Look. I'm his son. I'm Eli Gold's son.'

'Can you prove that, sir?'

This took Harvey aback. He realized that without some kind of documentation, he could not. He did look a bit like his father – they shared fleshy, porous noses, and skin that looked as if it might need shaving four times a day – but not having seen him as he was at present he could not even confidently claim a resemblance. And as for any other inheritance: well, Harvey possessed neither the genius nor the charisma, although he wondered why he was thinking this, as he was not sure how he would demonstrate either in the hospital corridor, and even if he could, doubted they would count as an access-all-areas code.

'I've got a credit card …'

'I'll need a photo-ID, sir. There's a lot of journalists and crazy people might want to get into this room.'

'Yes,' Harvey said, and then remembered that he did have his driving licence on him. He unbuttoned his jacket – because, despite it being forty degrees in Manhattan, he was wearing a dark blue, buttoned jacket; uncertain and jet-lagged this morning he had decided that the occasion of going to see his dying father necessitated some formality – and reached into the inside pocket for his wallet. He scrabbled through the variety of useless cards in the leather slits – how many fucking membership cards for defunct DVD rentals did he own? – until he spotted his shrunken head on the pink picture card. Handing it to the security guard, Harvey felt nervous, under pressure; the moment came into his mind when Jimmy Voller, the swarthy Brooklyn hero of Eli's brutal third novel *Cometh the Wolf*, has to produce his passport at the door of an East Berlin brothel to persuade the madam that he is neither Turkish nor Moroccan, the two nationalities she has decided to bar entry to.

The security guy removed his finger from the earpiece – Harvey noticed that he was not, in fact, in telephone communication with anyone, and wondered if the finger-in-the-ear stance had just been to make him look more like security guys always do – and took his time scanning the details of the licence. Harvey had never spotted the parade of weird tiny vehicles on the back of it before – what is that, he thought, a VW Beetle? And that looks like the silhouette of the van in *Scooby-Doo*. They seemed tinier than ever, perched in the security guy's mighty hand. He produced a clipboard, which, also being black, had remained invisible before, camouflaged against his enormous black puffa jacket. Harvey wondered who was paying for this guy: the hospital? His father? The government? Waiting for what seemed a stupid amount of time for his name to be checked against the names on the clipboard, Harvey felt absurdly like he was trying to get into some sort of exclusive nightclub.

Eventually, the security man looked up, scrutinizing Harvey's face as if it were another card. He gave him his licence back.

'Just stay here a second, please, sir …' He turned, with a slow movement not unreminiscent of an oil tanker listing to port, and went into the room. Harvey dropped his head to look through the recessed glass window in the door. The room was spacious, and well furnished in a hospital way, but oddly windowless. In the foreground, he could see Freda on her knees, talking to a girl – Colette? – a doctor, a nurse and, in an alcove off to one side, the bottom edge of what must be his father's bed. An image flashed through his mind of the comedy medical clipboard that should be hanging there, marked in black with a zigzag graph hurtling downwards, but all he could see were chrome bars and white sheeting.

The security guy hovered behind Freda, waiting for her conversation with the child to end. His finger had returned to his ear. Harvey had a moment of wondering if the security guy's finger, so wide it completely obscured the earpiece, was bigger than his own penis, and then immediately feared that such a thought might be racist. He took out a bottle of Extra Tart Sour Blast Spray and gave his tongue a quick atomize. He removed his iPhone from his other pocket and tapped a few moves into Deep Green, but could see straight away that he was heading for a quick *Checkmate! Tiny wins!* so put it back. He considered, not for the first time, how quickly he panicked, while waiting: how quickly he needed to distract himself, before his mind and body went somewhere bad. Thinking about his body makes him suddenly feel a need to piss. Micturation, or the urge to do so, comes upon him like this these days, with no build-up, no gradual turning of the tap. He knows it is something to do with his battered and bruised prostate, the internal organ he has always been most conscious of: it will be, he knows, swollen or shrunken or just generally giving up its hanging walnut ghost, but he cannot bring himself to go to the doctor to check it out. Not because he is embarrassed about it, but because his GP in Kent is a young and pretty Pakistani woman, and there is no way he can go to the surgery and ask her about his prostate without it looking as if it's a ruse to get her to put her finger up his anus. Even as he makes the appointment he will feel the receptionist suspecting his motivation. He needs to get over this concern, he knows, partly because Eli's first brush with cancer was of the prostate, and partly because he actually would quite like the GP to put her finger up his anus.

The security guy was still hovering over Freda like the alien ship in *Independence Day* over earth as she talked. 'Fuck it,' Harvey said to himself, and walked quickly down the corridor, and found the rest room. *Rest room.* It could be restful in the toilet, Harvey felt, although only if you were sitting down – something he chose to do more and more these days, whatever the character of the ablution – but even then only really in your own private toilet, where any anxiety about sharing intimate information with strangers could not intrude. The door was locked. Harvey tried it a few times, as if under the impression that perhaps there was something wrong with the lock, but really to make it clear, to the present user, that someone was outside waiting. Eventually, the door opened, and Harvey drew back: the person exiting was a woman – Korean? Chinese? Malaysian? he felt bad about not being able to tell the difference – with tired eyes. There was no reason why it should not be a woman – the rest room door had no trousered or skirted hieroglyphic on it – but Harvey instantly wished to withdraw his aggressive shaking of the handle, somehow more acceptable had the occupant been male. It flashed through his mind to say – 'Oh sorry, I thought you were a man' but he quashed it. Instead, a glance passed between them, a glance he has – this is the word, guilty though he feels about it – *enjoyed* before. If Harvey is waiting to use a unisex toilet, on a train, say, or in a private house at a party, and a woman comes out, Harvey *enjoys* (he knows it's wrong but still allows himself the minute, tawdry thrill) the moment in which their eyes meet. He thinks the glance means that, for a second, they have both shared an image of her sitting on the seat with her pants down and the sound of liquid on china, or metal. This is the glance that passed between him and the nurse. As ever, he felt bad about enjoying it, but still. He noticed, though, that she squinted at him uncertainly, as if catching that something about Harvey's look was not accidental, so he looked away, covering his shame by moving quickly into the cabin.

When he came back to the door to Eli's room, the security guy was waiting, finger in ear. He looked Harvey up and down once more, and then stepped aside. Harvey chanced a friendly nod at him, which was met with a blank stare, making Harvey worried that his friendly nod may have been misinterpreted as 'see?', but continued on past his gravitational presence and through the door.

The first thing he noticed on entering was that the room was not windowless. In fact, the bed faced a floor-to-ceiling glass rectangle, looking onto exactly the view of Manhattan – across Central Park, towards downtown – that Harvey so covets. He drank it in – or, rather, since what hit him with a rush is not beauty but envy – he sucked it up, the sweep of sky and skyscrapers, before turning and saying, 'Hello, Freda.' His *stepmother* looked up – it had never occurred to him with the same force before; two years younger than him, that was still, technically, what she was. She stared at Harvey for so long – the oddity of their interaction reinforced by her being on her knees – that he started to wonder if she was trying to remember who he was.

'Colette,' she said eventually, 'come and meet your half-brother, Harvey.'

When the girl looked up, her face under her curls was set in a tight frown. She may have been crying, although not, Harvey thought, out of sadness: her expression contained that classic mix of rage and self-pity that children's faces emit when they have just been told off. She did not do as she was told; she did not come and meet him, but stayed where she was, raising her chin defiantly and staring as if he was complicit in – perhaps even the mastermind of – whatever slight had just been perpetrated against her.

Or maybe she *was* sad, about her – their – dad dying, and this was just what she looked like when she was sad. After all, Harvey had never met her before. He had been sent a photograph soon after her birth of the three of them at their New England lodge (not by Eli: the accompanying note, including the statement, 'Eli is so overjoyed about his new child' was all in Freda's hand). Eli, in a big fisherman's jumper, grinning beneficently, his arms around Freda, her trademark proprietorial smile cross-fertilized with an element of self-conscious sheepishness, as if to say, 'Can you believe what little me has ended up with?!', and in her lap, the baby. Harvey wondered who had taken it, as it was too professional – the light too dappled, the wood-panelled walls of the lodge too burnished, the composition of the threesome too perfectly arranged – to have been done on a self-timer. It looked, he thought, like something from *OK!* magazine. But he could not relate his memory of that infant, looking out at him from the photograph with something of the complacent gaze of a cow, to this fierce child with the thermonuclear stare.

'Hello,' he said: the word felt stupid in his mouth. Colette just nodded at him, and Harvey felt suddenly furious at Freda for spiking his route to his father's bedside with this introduction, impossible as it was to brush off because of the absurd and irreducible fact of him and this thirty-six-years-younger girl being siblings. Freda must have known that his first thought would be to get to Eli's bedside – and Harvey *had* really wanted to do this, although not so much because he just wanted to see his dad, more that he wanted to get the first sight of him over with. He was scared about it. Approaching the door, he had felt much like he had as a kid watching *Dr Who*, knowing that a new monster was about to appear. The ten-year-old Harvey, trembling beside his mother (who let *Dr Who* under her steel bar of what Harvey was allowed to watch, although in later series changed her mind, deciding that the Time Lord's always-female assistants were becoming oversexualized) in his blue, bi-planed pyjamas, would not hide behind the sofa. He would, rather, watch intently, wanting the monster to appear as soon as possible; the worst thing was not knowing. He wanted to face it, so that he could know the fear, hold it and calibrate exactly how bad it was going to be.

'Last time I saw you, you were a tiny baby,' he said, his voice sounding astringent against the sentiment, holding down his rage at having to have this conversation now. Surreptitiously, he flicked his eyes over towards his father's bed, more of which was visible from this angle. The movement of his eyes sideways reminded him of the painful glancing action always prompted by an attractive woman across a room. He could see the thin hump of a wasting body underneath bedding, but still not the face. It was facing the face that filled him with dread.

'You saw me when I was a baby?' said Colette.

'No. I saw a photo …'

'Oh. OK.' She looked at him. Her frown deepened, producing little lines on her forehead. 'Why is your tongue blue?'

The awkward stalemate this response induced was broken by the sudden appearance of Freda with her arms outstretched. Harvey, opening his to accept the hug, looked at her frame, spread like a net in front of him, and thanked the Lord again that he didn't find her attractive. Although younger than him, and a woman – normally enough for his needs – there was something about Freda that inhibited Harvey's reflex interest. She had that parched-face look so common to female humanist academics that Harvey felt they should try their utmost to avoid, thinking that they had fallen into the exact trap – unfemininity – which Victorian patriarchy had predicted for women should they become learned. This particular intellectual conundrum was a hangover not from his father but his mother, who, despite being herself a female humanist academic, and an arch-feminist, never emerged from her bedroom without a cosmetic face mask three inches thick.

It had occurred to Harvey many times that, physically, Freda was the opposite of everything Eli usually went for in women – except in respect of her youth, relative to him. It did not go unnoticed by Harvey that that was, as it were, the last thing to go – that all the other staples of Eli's desire could be sacrificed, but not this one, not even in his dotage.

The hug went on for some time. Harvey, who had been hugged by Freda before, felt in it, as ever, no particular love or affection for him: but much love and affection for the idea of hugging. This one was tighter and longer than usual, but still somehow failed to convey any sense that she was pleased to see him. Uncomfortably, however, it did give him time to feel the full length of her body against his – the emotional distance between them allowed him, in a bleak, detached way, to take stock of her body in a way that he never had before – and, then, much to his consternation, come away from the hug, in spite of his long-held notions about her mannishness, with a hard-on.

'Go …' said Freda, pulling back from him, Harvey hoping against hope not because she had noticed it. She was speaking in what sounded to him like a stage whisper. 'Go to him. Speak to him.'

'Speak?'

'He understands. He hears.'

Harvey nodded, not wanting to say anything that might disturb her reverence. The tumescence in his pants subsided. He choked down an urge – with him most days, although undoubtedly charged up by the situation – to shout an obscenity at the top of his voice. He walked towards his father's bed, his feet padding against the quality carpet of the room.

Glancing back, he saw that Freda had crouched down again to whisper to Colette. The doctor and nurse in the room were busying themselves with notes and drips and bleepers: none of them offered to guide him – neither geographically nor spiritually nor even educationally – through the scene. Harvey felt again like a nonentity in some exclusive club, unable to make his presence felt. It even flashed through his mind to say *Don't you know who I am?* He wished Stella were here, to hold his hand, even though Harvey was uncomfortable with hand-holding, because it made him feel more aware of the fact of fear, and because, sometimes, he could feel the small bones in her hands.

These thoughts were halted by the interruption into his vision, finally, of his father. Even then it wasn't as Harvey had imagined it, a kind of naked confrontation with mortality. Eli's head was propped up against the pillow, and covered nose to mouth with an oxygen mask. Attached to various intravenous ports, six or seven different tubes curled around his bed and into his body, like he was being gently cradled by an octopus. Machines, humming and bleeping and oscillating with sine waves, surrounded him in a stately circle, as if his father were whatever invisible deity lurks in the centre of Stonehenge. It felt to Harvey that all this apparatus was designed not just to keep Eli from death, but also his visitors: that it formed a buffer zone between them and the reality of his condition. So much so, in fact, that the sight of his father was almost an anti-climax after all the girding of his loins. *Where is he?* he wanted to say, and not in a metaphorical way – not in a *This shrunken shell of a human being cannot be My Father!* way – but physically: he wanted to rummage through all this stuff, all the sheeting and the wires and the plastic, chucking it over his head like a man sorting through the trash, to find him.

He also felt he couldn't see him because of the things that were not there. People assume that the way to reveal an object is to remove its external trappings, but that doesn't hold true for the human object. Glasses, for example: Eli had for Harvey's whole life worn thick black beatnik spectacles, and without them, as now, he was somehow not Eli. The lack of glasses, along with the lack of a cigarette in his mouth – something Harvey had also grown up conditioned to see, although Eli had finally given them up two years ago – was not an unmasking. It just made him look like someone else.

But then Harvey looked more closely – having realized that he had been focusing on all the last-days' paraphernalia exactly to avoid doing that – and, indeed, there he was: in the wet, grey clumps of hair stuck to his temples, wisps curling away from his skin like they always did; in the deep trench-like lines on his forehead – the same ones that he has just seen reproduced in miniature on his half-sister's brow – whose up or down state the child Harvey had desperately relied upon to monitor his father's otherwise unguessable moods; in the remnants of his beard, its close trimming evocative of his decline like some upside-down Samson, but bringing back to Harvey a distant memory of Eli scraping his emery stubble against the virgin cheek of his son, who would protest, but laughingly, finding the touch both abrasive and delightful, redolent of the rough promise of the adult world; and perhaps most of all in his hands, which were still, despite the pulse meters and the blood clots and the mountainous veinscape rising angrily from their backs, sheathed in the same skin, brown and rough as bark, and still incongruously large, still, even here, suggesting strength, the hands of a labourer, on the end of arms which had avoided heavy lifting their whole life. Harvey, a sucker for comparisons, found himself looking at his own hands by contrast – he'd done this before, of course, but the OCD lizard king in his brain always required new checks – raising his right one a Reiki hover away from his dad's. It looked small, but Harvey has always known he has small hands, girl's hands, easy prey for 'you-know-what-they-say-about' jokers. He wondered how the DNA divides it up – what fall it is of the cellular dice that has given him his father's nose, mouth and skin, but his mother's eyes and hands.

He did not know what to do. He felt that the correct – the polite – thing to do was to speak, as Freda had advised. But looking at his father again – less like his father, and more like a mad scientist had given up halfway through making a robot version of his father – the idea of speaking was clearly ridiculous. He felt not unlike he always did in church or synagogue, fighting an urge, during the endless roll call of praise and plea, to shout 'No one's listening! No one's even there to listen!!' And what was he supposed to say? *Dad: it's me*? Since even those keeping the faith in Eli's ability to hear did not believe, presumably, that the dying man could see as well, this would then require him to say, in explanation – '*Um … Harvey*' – like he was on the phone. And then what? *How are you?* Oh my God, it *would* just be a fucking phone call. Something more supportive? *I've just come to say I'm going to be here for you …* oh no. No. I am a dual citizen, he thought, but I will never become that American. He didn't know what to say. He wondered who the people were who did, in this situation. He looked round, as if, at any minute, they might come into the room and tutor him.

Even the first word he might say – *Dad* – felt weird. It was a word he'd always had problems with. Eli had left Harvey's mother at a time when his son – six, after all – called him Daddy. There was then a period of some years when Harvey hardly saw his father at all, but still referred to him, in his absence, as Daddy. Thus, when he began to see him again, at increasingly irregular intervals in his teens, he found he had missed out on that poignant slide from Daddy into Dad that marks out children's first maturity. He addressed him as Dad at this point, but it felt somehow wrong, and he found himself wanting to say Daddy: not in the front of his head – like any other post-pubescent boy, he was keen to avoid any word or deed that might make him seem childish – but in his gut, in the reflex part of his linguistic centre. When he saw Eli, the word that formed in his mind was *Daddy*. Latterly, a number of different titles for his father were attempted, knowable as the word Harvey used following 'Hello' when seeing his father or hearing his voice on the phone – Father; Eli (never comfortable); Dad (still not right); an attempt at irony, Pater. Now, by his deathbed, his mind was saying, again, *Daddy*.

He decided not to think about it, and just trust what might come out. He coughed, something of a stage *ahem*. It emerged from his mouth much louder than he had expected, in a weird croak-grunt, shattering the quiet of the room. Freda had taken Colette outside for some form of pep talk, and the doctor had been whispering to one of the nurses, no doubt detailing some complex medical issue, although Harvey had been unable not to wonder if it was flirtation. Both of them looked over, surprised for a moment, before going back to their huddle. And then, at that point, almost as if he *had* heard, Eli stirred. His hands, one of which was still just underneath Harvey's, stiffened, the long fingers – whose nails had, Harvey noticed, been neatly trimmed – extending like sickles. His eyes even opened, although the pupils were long gone, high up into his head, revealing just two grey-white ovals, slivers cut from an English sky. Under the oxygen mask, his mouth, previously lopsided into a shape, ironically, like a speech balloon, opened further on that side, and from the weird aperture came a sound that was part-howl and part-yawn, with something oddly synthetic in it as well, not unlike the note produced by a theramin. It was loud, and deeply disturbing: a noise that knew and did not know, like a cow makes at the touch on its temple of the stun gun, a distress call back to this world from the black country.

Immediately, the doctor and the nurse rushed over, in their long coats. Freda burst back through the door, trailing Colette, still sulky. Harvey stared at the blind, raging stump of his father, guilt-stricken, convinced that somehow this atrocious convulsion must be his fault. 'What's happening?' he said. 'Is he waking up?'

'No,' said the doctor – Indian, Harvey guesses, with short, tufty hair combed forward to cover a receding hairline – 'he does this from time to time.'

He does? thought Harvey. Over the last few weeks, Freda had somehow implied to him that Eli's unconsciousness was serene – even, perhaps, that the coma was itself a work of art, a kind of late period ripeness-is-all evocation of tranquillity. Not this – this roaring zombie, this Eli Agonistes.

Freda had taken hold of his hand, clutching it with both of hers. 'He's still so strong,' she said, looking up at Harvey. 'So strong.'

Freda's face, constipated with hope, forcing out the positive from this indigestible horror – something pitiful in that, Harvey realized: this woman, for whom it was such a prize, capturing Eli, never quite realizing how much she would have to pay for it, and how soon – it is Freda's face which seems to reflect back to Harvey from the window of the cab as the light of the Sangster forecourt creates of its glass a mirror. It dissolves like aspirin in water as men in autumnal uniforms come gliding towards the passenger door in order to smooth his passage to the lobby.

*   *   *

He has spent two days now in his room at the Condesa Inn, going over The Material. He has gone over The Material many times before but he thinks that now, so close to the act, it has a different force. It feels shaping and controlling: it feels as if it's making clearer what he has to do. The why helps the how, he thinks.

He has not contacted his wives. It has crossed his mind often on his journey to do so. He would prefer to write to them than to telephone. He feels that he could Lie for the Lord – lying to preserve a greater spiritual truth, a Mormon practice that Uncle Jimmy explained to him once – easier that way. But none of his wives are allowed to have a computer, or use email, and, at any rate, the only computer in the family house is the Dell, which sits at this moment on the white sheet of his bed, cradled underneath by his crossed legs. He knows what his absence will have occasioned. Ambree, as the

68

most senior now that Leah is dead, will have called a meeting. It will have been held in the kitchen, because, although the living room is bigger, the kitchen is the enclave of the wives, and they will have found it easier to shut the door to the children, although RoLyne would still probably have brought in Elin, his youngest, to breast-feed her. He is confident that Ambree, the most virtuous of his wives, will have led the meeting to the correct decision – despite protests from, he suspects, Angel and maybe even Sedona – that he was their husband, and he knew best: that if he had taken it upon himself to disappear for days without explanation, why, that was no different from Our Lord deciding to enter the desert for forty days in order truly to understand Himself and His Mission. Our job, he was sure she would say, our job as his celestial wives, is in the meantime to care for his house and his children, and be ready to welcome him on his return.

Having thought this through, the urge to communicate with his loved ones recedes, and he turns back to The Material. The intermittent wireless connection at the Condesa Inn troubles him, but also helps. It helps because it makes it harder to watch streaming internet pornography, tube8, or pornhub, or keez, which he normally watches a lot. Thus the intermittent connection is a good thing, as he would feel ashamed of watching these in front of Jesus, and, also, they distract him from his destiny.

The ones that don't distract him are GunAmerica, and Justice Coalition, and Unsolved, and Restless Sleep, and the jihadi ones. A part of him likes them best. He is even enrolled on the forum at al-jinan.org under the name Pbuh53. Pbuh – he found this out on another website – is the Islamic name for Jesus. He wasn't sure about this: he was worried it might be seen by God as saying that he himself was Pbuh, was Jesus – writing it into the electronic login form, he felt the butterflies in his stomach that he always feels when he thinks he might be doing something wrong by the Lord – but he went ahead, because it was surely a way of spreading His Name amongst the heathen. And then the site told him he had to add some numbers too, so he wrote his age, as well. That was two years ago.

He enrolled on al-jinan because, when he hears the jihadis speak, something in him stirs. He likes the fierce commitment to God; he likes the language, the poetry of rage, purged of all the trivial inflections of modernity; and he likes the belief in – no, the *knowledge* of – destiny. To know absolutely both the nature and the quality of destiny – to know what role God has chosen for you and exactly how heroic that role is – that is what he would want for himself. He watches some of the videos that suicide bombers make before they embark on their missions, and he sees in their eyes no sway, no diversion, and it inspires him, even as he knows that the Jesus-less path they have chosen is wrong. He sees how only revenge inspires true religiosity.

And, of course, like him, they are fundamentalists. That is why he calls Eli Gold The Great Satan. It is sort of a joke – a joke he tells only himself – but it is a joke with a purpose. It inspires him to hate him more; to remind him of what the writer stands for; and also to help him to think like the jihadis do, about destiny.

He opens the Dell lid: the square light of the screen shines in the dimness of the room, a hot, white beacon showing him the way. He is not on al-jinan. He is looking, for perhaps the hundredth, or the two hundredth, time at the transcript on www.unsolved.com. Unsolved has a lot of these transcripts which purport to relate to unsolved crimes. The one he reads, over and over again, is an interview between Police Commissioner Raymond Webb and The Great Satan. The interview took place on 15 June 1993. His third and index fingers caress the mouse tracking pad expertly, bringing the transcript into plain view:

RW: So, Mr Gold, I'm sorry to have to make you do this …
EG: How sorry are you exactly? Not sorry enough to not want to bring me down here at a time of deep personal grief.

[inaudible]

EG: Yes, well … how long will this take?
RW: Not long, sir. We just need to go over some of the facts.

70

EG: Facts …

RW: Sir?

EG: May I have some coffee?

RW: Er … yes, I guess.

[inaudible]

RW: Showing Mr Gold case document R45/100 … do you recognize
this?

EG: Yes.

RW: Mrs Gold showed it to you before she took the pills …?

EG: Yes.

RW: And then sealed it in this … showing Mr Gold case document
R45/101 … envelope?

EG: Well, I didn't watch her lick the glue.

[pause]

RW: What did you make of it?

EG: What did I make of it? For fuck's sake, Commissioner …

RW: Webb.

EG: … Webb, it wasn't a *seminar* …

RW: But she had been one of your students. When you met.

[pause]

EG: I really don't see –

RW: 'I have no desire left for life. Surrender is preferable to despair. I
go, to the soft quiet land: and I thank my love for leading me there.'

[pause]

RW: Are you OK?

EG: I shall be.

RW: Sorry to … I know it's upsetting.

EG: It's beautiful. I think.

RW: Yes. Yes, it is. But –

EG: Yes?

RW: *I thank my love for leading me there.* What did she mean by that?

[pause]

EG: You are asking a question of the dead, Commissioner.

RW: No, Mr Gold, with the greatest respect, I'm asking it of the living. Because you, of course, despite also writing a suicide note, are still alive.

He hears some shuffling in the corridor outside of his room. It could be the cleaner, a Filipino woman, who has tried to get into his room to clean six or seven times over the course of the last two days, or it could be the man next door, who caused him to wake up in terror last night with the sound of what seemed to be nails scratching against the other side of the wall. He shuts the lid of the Dell as if caught looking at something he should not be.

I didn't want to go in and see Daddy today. Aristotle is *definitely* missing me. When I sit in my bed at night reading my story, he comes and sits on my chest, right up by my face. I can feel his whiskers tickling my nose. And then he purrs, really loudly, much louder than he normally does, like he's like so, so happy that I'm there. Then he usually goes away, but this morning he was *still there* in the morning! I told Jada this and she said he probably went away during the night and came back just before I woke up but I think he was there all night, 'cos I felt this big weight on my chest where he'd been sitting, and like I said before he's gotten really fat while we've been at the hospital every day so it was really something, like even after I got up it was like he was still sitting there, or like his ghost was still sitting there or whatever.

Also Jada has got the DVD of *Marmaduke* and she wanted to come round after school and have a movie night. She said she'd bring popcorn and everything. So after Noda had done serving us our breakfast, I asked her – Mommy – that is.

'Mommy? Can I stay home today?' I said.

She didn't say anything at first, just carried on cutting up her eggwhite omelette into little slices, like she likes to. I don't know why she likes to do that. It's like what people do for a baby who can't cut stuff himself yet. I hate it when she does that.

'Mom?' I said, 'cos I wasn't sure she'd even heard. But then she put her knife and fork down.

'Yes, darling,' she said, in that voice she has which means she's cross with me but won't admit it, 'I heard you. I'm just wondering why you don't want to come to the hospital with me.'

'I didn't *say* I didn't want to come to the hospital! I just asked if I could stay home!'

'Well, staying at home means you won't come to the hospital. Doesn't it?'

I took a drink of water. I only drink mineral water. I like Volvic, Evian, and a fizzy one from Europe called San Pellegrino. This one was Evian.

'Yes,' I said, when I put my cup down, which has a picture of Aristotle on it – I mean the real Greek guy, not my cat! Mommy bought it for me when we went to the Metropolitan Museum, 'but it doesn't mean I don't *want* to come. It just means I just want to stay at home today *more*.'

Mommy got out of her chair and came and crouched down really near me, so that her eyes were the same height as my eyes. Her eyes, which are greeny-brown, were all watery, and the white bits had little lines of red in them, those kind of tiny strings of red you get in your eyes when you rub them a lot. Mom took hold of my hand.

'Colette … I really think you should come …' she said. With her other hand, she brushed my fringe, kind of like she was brushing it out of my eyes, but it was never in my eyes. This made me shiver a bit. I could feel lots of stuff inside me that I wanted to say. I could feel it wanting to come out like I was going to throw up, like the words were food or maybe something that wasn't food that I shouldn't have eaten, like when Jada told me she once swallowed an earbud.

'But it's so *boring* in the hospital! They don't have anything for me to *do* there, and the TV is just on CNN all the time, and the only toys they have are for babies! And no one who's my age ever comes there and I have to meet lots of creepy people like that fat guy Harvey – and he's like my brother and I haven't even met him before!'

I didn't think I was screaming or anything when I said this, although I knew it must have been quite loud, because Noda came out of the kitchen making that face that she makes when she thinks something's wrong, but Mom just shook her head and did a little wave of her hand, and she went back in again.

'Colette. Firstly, could you not raise your voice to me like that? And secondly, could you not talk in that stupid way you've just learnt off the TV?'

I didn't say anything. I looked down at my plate. My pancakes had gone cold. I could see the syrup on top of one of the cranberries had gone all hard. I heard her breathe really deeply. I was so annoyed by then that even that annoyed me, hearing her breathe really deeply. It was like it was louder than it needed to be, like she was making sure I heard her breathe.

'Darling,' she said after a bit – her voice had gone softer, because she wasn't telling me off any more – 'you always knew that you had half-brothers and sisters that you've never met. Harvey's just one of them.'

'Well, I don't like him. He's fat and sweaty and he smelt funny.' She opened her mouth to tell me off then, but before she could speak, I said: 'And he upset Daddy.'

Her mouth stuck open at that for a bit, like a fish. Her face went different.

'Do you think so?'

'God, *yeah*! He was really upset when he saw him. It was like he was saying *Could someone please get that guy out of here!*'

She smiled, that stupid smile that means *Oh darling you don't understand.* 'I don't think so, darling.'

'Who are the others?' I said.

'What others?'

'The other brothers and sisters.'

Her forehead went all lined. '*Colette.* I've told you all this before.'

'I know but that was *ages* ago.'

Mommy tutted, and looked at her watch. It was a present from Daddy. It's got diamonds in it and everything.

'Apart from Harvey, there's Simone, who lives in France. And Jules, who lives in Los Angeles …'

'Is that a boy or a girl?'

'It's a boy. A man.'

'Has he got any children?'

'No, he's gay.'

I know what this means. Mommy told me this when I was little. It means he can have sex with men, even though he is a man. Women can do it, too, with women. I don't know about girls and boys. When I was little, Mommy used to say it means a man can fall in love with a man, or a woman with a woman, but now I know it means they can have sex, too.

'How old are they?'

'Uh … Jules is about fifty, I think. Simone is … I don't know. She never tells anyone her age, Daddy says.'

'Why not?'

Mom just shook her head. 'I guess she's fifty-something, too.'

'Are they coming to see Daddy, too?'

Mommy made a bit of a weird face when I said this, like she'd hurt her tongue or something.

'I don't think so, darling. That's all a bit complicated.'

'You're doing that thing.'

'What thing?'

'Of not telling me something because you think I won't understand.'

She did a big sigh and tucked her hair behind her ears. There are red veins on the top of her ears.

'So why do I have to go every day, when they aren't even coming at all!'

'Col …'

'They're Daddy's children, too!'

She looked a bit surprised when I said this. I guess I did say it pretty loud again. Although I don't know if that was why she was surprised. It was more like I was saying something she didn't know. She didn't say anything for a bit, just stared at me. Then she did another big breath.

'Listen, Colette, I know how hard it must be for you, seeing Daddy like he is now …'

76

'Yes,' I said, because I could tell that this was the best thing to say to get her to let me stay home. But when I said it, I felt really sad inside, like it was just true.

'… but – you know how we've talked about how – how Daddy's not coming back from the hospital?'

'Yes. He's going to die there.'

'… yes.'

'But he *is* going to come back.'

Mommy kept on looking at me, doing that thing she does of really looking at me, like she can see right behind my eyes into my brain or something. 'No, darling, he isn't …'

'Well, how are we going to have the funeral then?'

'Oh. Well. Yes. His body will come back. Well, not to here exactly, but …' She stopped speaking and turned to look out of the window.

'Daddy wants to be cremated, doesn't he?' I said. *Cremated* was a word I got taught by Elaine just before Daddy went into his hospital. Mommy told her to teach me all the death words, *cremated, coffin, undertaker, postmortem, bereavement, funeral* (although I knew that one already) and *mourning*, which although it sounds the same is different from morning. After I had learnt all these, I went and found out a few others by putting the word 'Death' into Google onto Daddy's computer: *decomposition, decay, rigor mortis,* and *putrefaction.*

'Yes, darling … but the point is: he isn't coming back, not really. And I know it's hard but I think it's important that you come to the hospital because – here's the thing – nobody knows when Daddy is going to die. And I think it's really important that you are there when that happens.'

'But why?'

'Colette …' She put her hand on top of mine. I was looking away. I didn't want to look at her because I was cross and I kind of knew that what I was saying was wrong but I didn't really know why, and I knew that she would be doing that thing with her eyes again and if I looked at her doing that it would maybe make me cry proper or be more mad. 'I don't expect you to understand. Maybe if I was Daddy – maybe if I had his words – I could explain it to you. But for now, you'll just have to trust me. Because you have to be there not just for him, but for you. I know that if you're not there when Daddy dies, when you're older, you'll regret it. You know what *regret* means, don't you?'

I nodded, but without turning round to look at her. 'It means when you do something and then you think you shouldn't have.'

'Yes. Or in this case, when you don't do something and then you think – maybe for your whole life – that you should have.' She took my chin in her hand and moved my face back so that she could look at me. I thought about holding my neck stiff so she couldn't do that, but then I thought that might hurt, and also I wasn't so cross by this time.

'But won't Simone or Jules regret it that they won't be there?'

Mommy's lips went all tight. 'That is their decision. Which they will have to live with. So, Colette …' she said. 'Of course, it's up to you. I don't want you to be there if you don't want to be there. But I just want you to think about what I've said. And while you're thinking about it, I'm going to go and get ready to go. And if you still don't want to come with me when I come back, that's fine.'

And then she got up and went out of the dining room. I sat there for a bit, eating little bits of my cold pancake with my fingers. Then I started rubbing the bits before I put them in my mouth and they went all spongy. Aristotle came up and rubbed the side of his face on my leg. He was purring, and it was like he was saying, *It's OK: you can go. I'm OK.* So I thought, OK, I'll go. I kind of knew that that was what I was going to do all along.

But when I got down from the table and picked up my knapsack – the one shaped like a rabbit – I had a weird thought, which was: I wonder what Daddy would do. I don't mean what he would do *really*, because Daddy wouldn't want to watch *Marmaduke*, he never even watches any films, but I just meant if he was like me or if I was more like him or whatever. Because Mommy sometimes says to me when I don't know what to do about something – she says: *OK. What would Daddy do?* And I thought: he wouldn't go. He'd stay in and do movie night.

* * *

Eli and Violet were married quickly, in the manner of wartime romances. Eli was one of many American soldiers stationed in the UK in preparation for the D-Day landings, and the possibility that he might not return from Europe propelled their engagement almost as fast as the Nazi bullets over the dunes of Normandy. This possibility – that Eli might be killed in action – was what defined their love in its early stages. It was a possibility that Eli seemed to hold, Violet felt, ironically: he would talk about his chances of dying with a smirk and a raised eyebrow, his voice slowing to that Geiger-counter drawl it always did when he wanted to signal that nothing of what he was saying was serious. She had never met anyone so infused with irony, so unable to present any statement as the thing itself, always implying that nothing was truly meant. This applied across the board to Eli's discourse, whether in the matter of their love, his death, or who they should invite to their wedding.

The one picture Violet still owns of their wedding day lies in the same shoebox that contains Eli's love letters. Her back cracks like an ice cube tray as she bends to pick it up from underneath her single bed, laid as ever with too much bedding – her bed seems to have a belly, Violet always thinks, reminiscent of those on the malnourished African children she sometimes sees on the television news. She once mentioned this to one of the maids, Mandy, but then felt anxious that it might have been a wrong thing to say, as Mandy, like all the maids and most of the nurses, is black. The presence of so many coloured people makes Violet anxious. She is not intrinsically racist: like most of her generation, it is more that the presence of black people around her, existing in a taken-for-granted, unremarked-on manner, serves as a constant reminder that the world is no longer the one she knows.

The box, however, is too far under the mattress for her to reach just by bending, and getting down on her knees is out of the question – she imagines the joints turning to powder at the first touch of the hard, dark lino. Bewildered, she sits down on her one armchair, a high-backed plum-red reproduction antique, last reupholstered in 1973, but still plush enough to look faintly outrageous in this setting. Violet knows that if she sits long enough, she will forget what it was she was concerned about, anyway: when this first started to happen it was intensely worrying, but lately she has begun to think of it as a comfort.

Before her memory has a chance to erase the issue of the shoebox, though, she remembers her walking stick, waiting for her at the door like a faithful dog. Getting out of the chair, with its relatively deep cushion, is difficult; halfway up, her elbows lock and her arms tremble – making her look for a second like a gymnast straining on the parallel bars – before she pushes herself off.

She retrieves the stick from the door. Violet's walking stick was a present from her sister: as Valerie didn't forbear to mention, it cost over £40. Violet likes it, likes the feel of the silver-plated handle, and knows the stout brown wood of the shaft will not easily break, but has enough of a sense of irony herself to feel the sad absurdity of a walking stick being her one luxury item. She goes back to the bed – not a long walk: her room, kitchenette included, is something of a shoebox itself – and, bending again, flails the stick back and forth under the bed, knocking out first her crocheted slippers, before hitting something heavier with a clang: it is her chamber pot, thankfully empty. She breathes heavily, and tries again: this time, her stick alights on something that feels right. She drags it towards her and, sure enough, eventually, the edge of the shoebox, its top askew, appears by her feet.

Another difficult bend to pick it up: the box is heavier than she had imagined. When she sits back down with it on her lap, she realizes why this is – having thought the shoebox contained only her letters from Eli and her wedding photo, it has over the years become a more general repository. Inside are crinkled black-and-white photos of her nephews and nieces as children, less crinkled, colour photos of their children, a random brooch, an old purse, and the letter from Redcliffe House saying how pleased they were to accept her application for a room. There are also photographs of her, eerie images of her girlhood, so po-faced it seems as if she must have grown up in a much earlier era, before people understood that the thing to do on camera was smile, plus one fragment of her as a young adult on a beach, waving and grinning and holding her coat around herself for warmth. And then there it is, sepia as a cell from a silent film: her wedding photograph. It has a strange, lopsided composition: she is standing flanked by her family, her mother and father and Valerie, their smiles tight with self-consciousness, but there is no one except Eli on his side, because he didn't invite any relatives.

Violet remembers the day. It was April, and spitting with rain. She had wanted to wait until later in the summer so as to guarantee the weather but the shadow of Eli's imminent dispatch to France made that impossible. In the photograph, the rain has polished the steps of Streatham Town Hall, on which they are standing, black. Violet had always imagined a church wedding, but Eli hadn't been keen.

'Why not?' Violet had said, already feeling the clench of anxiety in her stomach that always accompanied any attempt to challenge him. This discussion took place in the Piccolo, a café near Liverpool Street station: he had only time for a short meeting before catching a train back to his barracks near Colchester. It was January, and the radiators were on full blast, steaming up the windows – though the one they were sitting by produced more noise than heat, for which Violet, in her woollen winter coat, was grateful.

'Oh, come on, Birdy,' he said, his eyes fixed on his spoon, idling in the froth of his coffee, 'let's not fight.'

Birdy was a name he had started calling her one night coming back from the pictures. They used to go every Friday to the Streatham Astoria, a place Violet loved. It was like an Egyptian palace, she thought, with its columns and murals and friezes in red, green and gold; even in the ladies' toilets there was a wall-painting of a figure bathing in a lotus pool. They'd seen a movie about a female internment camp in France, in which the prisoners put aside all their differences to help hide a group of shot-down British airmen from the Nazis: it was called *Two Thousand Women*. One of the women was played by Jean Kent, who Eli always said Violet looked like. In the film, this character was called Bridie, and Eli said, on exiting the Streatham Astoria, that he was more convinced than ever that Violet looked like her, so he swapped round the I and the R and started calling her Birdy. It made no real sense, but formed part of a happy memory, and so had stuck.

She looked away, hurt by the implication that they were a couple who regularly fought, the truth being that their relationship – or, at least, what sense of their relationship she could garner from an engagement conducted so far mainly in letters and snatched meetings – ran very smooth, certainly compared to what she had seen in other couples. Gwendoline and her husband rowed so much that Violet sometimes wondered if Henry, a conscientious objector, wasn't trying to fight his own war within the confines of their tiny flat in Shoreditch.

She also knew, however, that their freedom from fighting depended on her assumed complicity; so felt the fist in her stomach tighten, even before she decided to continue:

'Is it … is it because you're Jewish?'

He looked up, his face set behind the shield of his trademark grin, the one that brought his nose over his mouth, making him look, Violet thought, Jewish. 'Of course it's because I'm Jewish.'

'But your mother wasn't. Was she? Catholic, you said. So it doesn't matter, anyway.'

Eli lit a cigarette. He still had the Zippo. There was too much petrol in it, and the flame seemed to cover half his face, making Violet back off.

'And you've told me you don't believe in religion, anyway.'

'I don't.'

'So what difference does it make?'

He frowned. The lines on his face, very pronounced in the grey light falling through the window, joined up to form circles, like contours around a mapped hill. She had noticed now many times how Eli's facial lines served to exaggerate – to underline – his every mood.

'Well, when I say I don't believe in religion, what I mean is: I don't believe in it. Any of it. So getting married in a church – a building which only exists because one thousand nine hundred years ago the Jews got so fiddly about the pissy little dos and don'ts of God-bothering that a whole new mutant religion had to be born out of its already exhausted old womb – that seems to me even more hypocritical than doing it in a synagogue …'

The radiator between them coughed and shook violently, like an old smoker waking up. Eli looked at it with interest.

'What about me?' Violet said. 'What about what I want?'

He glanced at her, surprised. She felt her own eyebrows forming virtually the same expression: the idea of Violet introducing her desires into their conversation – indeed, the idea that Violet had desires, or, at least, desires that could be put up in conflict with Eli's – was as startling to her as it was to him.

'Birdy,' he said, putting his two hands on the one of hers that was resting on the table: she felt their enveloping weight and warmth. 'What's more important? Getting married, or *where* we get married?'

She looked at his eyes, scanning them for insincerity. In this instant, their deep brown seemed to her the opposite: the substantial brown of leather book covers and panelled walls. And if eyes are the windows to the soul, like her mother was always saying, then substance, tangibility, something in Eli's soul to hang on to, was what she needed to see in those windows. She knew that his words could as easily have been said by her to him – he was the one who didn't want to get married in a church – but this fleeting moment of Eli being serious – serious, for once, about them – was more important.

'You're right, of course,' she said, adding her other hand to the hand pile on the table. Their four hands together, his two in between hers, looked like a sandwich in which the dark meat filling could not be contained by the two small slices of white bread. The radiator croaked again, and then gushed, as the hot water inside forced its way along the cast-iron coils.

'It must be like a coral reef,' said Eli, looking away from her towards the sound.

'Sorry?'

'Inside the radiator. The water's having such a hard time getting through it, heating it up – inside, it must be studded with rocks of fur and scale, sprouting off the sides and up off the bottom, like a coral reef.'

Violet looked towards the heating implement. 'Yes,' she said.

'Have you got a pen?'

She shook her head.

'What, nowhere? Not in amongst all the God knows what you carry in your handbag?' Underneath its normal New York insouciance, his voice betrayed, a hint of petulance.

'I don't think so,' she said, picking her handbag up off the floor and starting to file through it anyway. 'You're the one who wants to be a writer.'

'I know.' He opened his palm. 'But I'm also the one who can't keep hold of anything.'

She tutted, although smiled at the same time, pleased at the notion of coupledom – you're this, I'm that, my weaknesses, your strengths – that this declaration assumed.

'Why don't …?' Violet began, about to suggest asking the waitress, but before she could finish he had leant across the table, his pinched waist awkwardly angled against the Formica edge, and extended his long index finger towards the window. On the fogged-up glass, he wrote: *Inside the radiator, a coral reef.*

'What use is that?' she said, as he sat back in his chair, surveying his handiwork with a satisfied air. Various other diners in the Piccolo were looking round from their tea and cakes and staring. Violet felt annoyed by this action. When he had written on the ceiling in the Eagle it had felt spontaneous, a sheer outpouring of self, but this had an element of self-consciousness about it, of deeply considered writerliness. It felt contrived. 'Are you going to telephone a glazier? To cut the window out for you?'

She noticed you could now see through the window, or at least through the bits of window revealed by his letters. This fractional view obscured the daily commotion of the Liverpool Street forecourt, lending its towers and turrets something of the collegiate calm the architect must have intended.

Eli, however, was still looking entirely *at* the window. 'I don't need to take it away,' he said. 'I'm sure that'll do as an *aide-mémoire.*'

*   *   *

How many therapists, then, has Harvey Gold been through? The answer, leaving aside the many friends and minor acquaintances who he has, in his more frantic moments, forced to listen to his troubles, is eight. They are:

1. Prof. Stephen J. Wilson, professor of child psychology at the University of New York 1957–78, a Winnicottian (trained, in fact, under the man himself), writer of numerous significant case studies and one commercial work, *Neither Angels nor Monsters*, bought in its millions in 1966 by young American family-starters desperate to escape the parenting traps of their parents. Eli met Wilson at a party in 1974 thrown by Susan Sontag, just after splitting with Harvey's mother, his third wife: Joan, the pale-faced postgraduate student he had settled upon as the prospective third way between Violet's artlessness and Isabelle's sophistication. Joan was always a feminist, but had become, immediately following Eli's desertion, arch; he mainly switched off during her recriminations, but had managed to catch '*and no doubt you haven't even stopped to think about what your fucking selfish fucking behaviour will do to our child* …' On meeting the professor, therefore, it occurred to him he could kill two birds with one stone: rebut at least one section of his ex-wife's rants, and gain a further bit of cachet with the New York literary salon, enamoured as it was at the time with psychoanalysis, by putting his six-year-old son into therapy. This, at least, is how Harvey now reads the fact of his having had a short series of sessions with Professor Wilson. Of the sessions, and of Professor Wilson himself, he has very little memory, although, once in a while, in his dreams, an image of his father seems to merge with that of a smiley, kindly, white-haired benevolent, who emerges from behind a plain white door to say: '*Now Harvey – do you remember when the bed-wetting started?*'

2. Donovan ('Donny') Lanes, a counsellor, really, rather than a proper therapist, who Harvey saw once a week while an English student at Leicester Polytechnic in the mid- to late 1980s. This was during a period, Harvey knows now, when he was not depressed. He thought he was depressed, but in fact he was simply attracted by the idea of depression, in order to cement some sense of his own seriousness.

Actual depression, Harvey knows now, is quite different, being a condition much less like the student Harvey imagined – something gaunt and brooding and gravitas-gaining while at the same time sexy; Socrates crossed with Robert Smith of The Cure – and more like a continual panic attack crossed with severe influenza.

Donny's main focus was Harvey's mother, which struck Harvey at the time, even before he was an old hand at therapy, as a little route one. It being the mid- to late eighties, however, it may have been less about his counsellor adopting a crude Freudianism than a fascination Donny developed with Joan, the proto-feminist. When Harvey talked of Joan – of her bookish, pinned-back beauty, of her endless fury with Eli, of her insistence on keeping him always informed, even as a child, of her agonizing and infinitely various menstrual issues, of her aggressive intelligence, of her ongoing project to write a feminocentric response to *Solomon's Testament* called *The Solo Woman's Testament* – he could see in his counsellor's eyes an excitement, a love even, growing at this picture he was painting of an undiscovered English Gloria Steinem. Harvey could almost see the book cover forming in Donny's mind – *Joan Gold* (she had kept the name, despite everything): *A Woman's Struggle* by Donovan Lanes – even as he once again took her side on another instance of what Harvey had previously thought of as a clear infliction of maternal damage.

Donny was particularly energized by Harvey's revelation that Joan had, in her late thirties, become a lesbian. Harvey had known, even at the time, even in the confusion of puberty, that his mother had made this choice politically. All Joan's choices were political, and, at the same time – in Harvey's opinion – psychological: motivated, that is, by a need to enact some kind of revenge on Eli. Because this revenge was ongoing – Joan never seemed able to find the emotional or sexual act that could completely cancel out the outrage of his leaving – it had to conform to the changing political tapestry of the times. The politics of the mid-seventies necessitated that her revenge take the form of sleeping with – and dismissing from her life immediately afterwards – an enormous number of unsuitable men; the politics of the late seventies and early eighties required becoming a lesbian. As he grew into adolescence, Harvey found it hard to believe that, ten years after their divorce, the anger inside his mother towards her ex-husband could still be powerful enough to impel her towards a completely new sexuality. In truth, the teenage Harvey, already the person he is now, already astounded, flabbergasted, by the pin-down force of desire, simply could not accept that sexuality could be shepherded in this way. Sexuality, Harvey thought and thinks, directs you, not the other way round. He feels guilty about this; it makes him, in his mother's language, a reactionary.

The sessions – and particularly any attempts to talk freely on this subject, of sexuality and its discontents – were hampered a little by Harvey's growing suspicion that Donny was gay. This was not something which Donny proffered, but he did, Harvey noticed, have a tendency to draw any conversation towards the subject of safe sex. Moreover, he was, when not counselling, the singer in a local electronic duo, and Harvey had noticed that all the singers in the electronic duos of the time, The Pet Shop Boys, Soft Cell, Erasure, all had something in common. He wasn't sure about Sparks.

Harvey tried very hard, in a very mid-1980s way, to think himself into a space during the sessions where it didn't matter that Donny might be gay, but it was problematic. Firstly, because Harvey assumed, despite his possession at the time of hair so stiff with Studioline it made him look like a permanently alerted porcupine, that Donny found him attractive; and secondly, because, even though Harvey was not then depressed, from the tiny acorns of his faux-depression the enormous black leafless tree of his real depression would still grow, and it was women, obviously, and the tension between his desire for every other pixie-booted one he saw on campus, and his fractured and difficult relationship with his girlfriend-from-home, Alison, a timid, passive aggressor with a sharply cut bob, which formed the basis of much of his emotional complaint. Suspecting that Donny might be gay, and therefore not subject either to the desire for, nor the demands of, women, made Harvey feel like talking about it all to him was, as it were, preaching to the never-going-to-be-converted: too alone, even in the distinct separation of the therapy room. When he spoke of his terror, for example, of the prospect of splitting up with Alison, Donny would nod sympathetically, but Harvey thought he could detect a certain blankness in his slightly bulbous blue eyes, and attributed this – despite Harvey's complete ignorance of the lifestyle – to Donny living within a world where sexual traffic was always free-moving, and the idea of desire becoming bogged down in the dull pull of attachment was anathema.

Two months before he left college, however, Alison left Harvey: for Donovan Lanes, who was neither, it turned out, gay, nor entirely ethical about passing on revelations from his sessions to the partners of some of the students he was counselling. There was then a period of fifteen years, during which Harvey disavowed therapy.

3. Laurence Green, a straightforward no-nonsense Freudian. He even had a white beard and glasses. The now genuinely depressed Harvey – clinically depressed, to give it the term that separates the illness from the everyday experience – did the sessions on a couch and everything. He used to face Laurence's formidable bookshelf and wonder, since Laurence used to say virtually nothing, whether the solution to how he felt could be found in any of them. His hot flushes: could they be sorted by Bruno Bettelheim's *The Art of the Obvious*? The suffocating tightness in his throat: would there be something on that in *Separated Attachments and Sexual Aliveness* by Susie Orbach? The raised, banging heartbeat: any joy in *Self in Relationships: Perspectives on Family Therapy From Developmental Psychology*, edited by Astri Johnsen and Vigdis Wie Torsteinsson? When, having given up on prompting a response from Laurence, the sessions would fall into silence, the name Vigdis Wie Torsteinsson would sometimes rotate at high speed in Harvey's head – *Vigdis Wie Torsteinsson Vigdis Wie Torsteinsson Vigdis Wie Torsteinsson Vigdis Wie* – until he wanted to scream. This tic had also happened to him on other occasions with the names Benedict

Cumberbatch, Barack Obama, Tiscali broadband and the phrase 'Apples, hazelnuts, sultanas, raisins, coconut, bananas'.

4. Adrienne Samson, the sixty-three-year-old Kleinian. Their sessions were somewhat overshadowed by the death, halfway through their time together, of Harvey's mother. Joan had always been powered by rage, a magnificent, sometimes inspiring rage, but then came the great forgetting, the neurological airbrushing, of Alzheimer's, which meant that she forgot what it was she was angry about. Harvey never quite realized how much he felt for his mother until she got ill. When the time came to move her to a residential nursing home in Ashford, and the manageress of the Day Care Centre in London that she had been attending said to him: 'We'll miss her: she's so sparky and fun and interesting – she really perked things up here …', he found his throat closing and tears of sadness and pride welling in his eyes.

As the disease worsened, Joan imagined that she was still married, and that Harvey, on his visits to the nursing home, was Eli. Eventually, Harvey found it easier just to go along with this idea. The more Harvey accepted the role of Eli, the more Joan was placated: he even bought a pair of glasses exactly like Eli used to wear in the 1960s in order to avoid his mother asking where his glasses had got to. He saw, at these times, even if only through the distorted lens of dementia, a version of something he had no memory of, which perhaps only existed before he was born or when he was very young: his mother happy and in love. He got a sense of what marriage to Eli might have been like before it went bad; he saw peace on her face. He wondered how it would have been – what it would have done, or not done, to him – to have been brought up by a mother like this. The visits were, in a bleak way, blissful.

The leaving of them, however, was not. Every time he said goodbye, Joan would die more than a little. She would panic; then she would get angry. For Harvey, these moments were a weekly microcosm of his parents' divorce. There was comfort in that at least – that by the time he reached the door of her tiny room, Joan, shouting at him to fuck off and not come back ever, was recognizable once more as the mother he knew. Towards the end, though, this pattern changed. Then, when he left she would only get sad. Once, she asked, with great clarity, 'Which wife am I again?' To which it occurred to Harvey to say, *the only one, my love*, but he found that it felt wrong to lie within the lie, and so simply answered, truthfully, 'The third.' Another time, Harvey turned back to say goodbye and she had taken all her clothes off. She did not pose for him in some grotesque sexual way. She simply stood there. It seemed to Harvey a statement of self, of wanting to strip all things away in the hope of being re-seen and re-found. It seemed to him like that for a moment, before he closed his eyes.

Adrienne found much to chew on here. She suggested, more than once, that Harvey taking on the role of Eli in these visits was not something he was doing just to keep his demented mother calm, but that it had an oedipal motivation. She pointed out that he had referred, often, to his mother's singular beauty when she was young. Harvey, who had only been talking about his mother's beauty because he thought it might relate to his general over-investment in beauty, and therefore to his wider issues with women, and who found the basic idea that all men unconsciously want to fuck their mother absurd, countered that if the Eli-acting was serving a buried need, it was more likely to be a desire to be like his father, the Great Man he so clearly had not grown up to be. But he didn't truly believe that either. It was just something he said in therapy, used as he was by now to playing the game. In his heart, he really, really thought he was just doing it to help his dying mother have the version of reality she wanted.

5. Zoe Slater, an EMDR specialist. EMDR, which stands for Eye Movement Desensitization and Reprocessing, involves a therapist moving his or her finger backwards and forwards while the person with the problem watches it and thinks about their problem. It's based on the idea that a state similar to REM-sleep is induced by the eye movement, which mollifies the memory of whatever it is that causes the watcher anxiety. It was designed for people with serious post-traumatic stress – rape victims, shell-shocked soldiers

– and Harvey, knowing this, felt bad, trying, while following Zoe's finger, to focus on his narcissistic, ignoble little sexual pain. Plus Zoe was reasonably attractive – certainly for a therapist, who, on both sides of the gender divide, tend to think that facial hair and elasticated waistbands are the very dab – and looking for a long time at her finger would tend to lead Harvey's mind the wrong way.

6. Dr Anthony Salter. A proper psychiatrist, Harvey's only one. A very small man – Harvey often wondered if he could legally be classified a midget – Dr Salter seemed to be mainly interested in a tiny, idio-syncratic memory, which was that when Harvey was a young child, and started crying, or being upset about anything, Eli used to say to him: *stop hacking a chanik*. Harvey had only mentioned this in passing, and explained to his psychiatrist that it was just his father speaking, as he often would, in nonsense language, but Dr Salter came back to it again, and again, as if *stop hacking a chanik* might be the primary cause of Harvey's psychic ills; so much so that after a while Harvey felt moved to say to him – although never did – *stop hacking a chanik*. Dr Salter's other main proffered solution was to prescribe antidepressants. Harvey would come back after a few weeks, to tell him how the antidepressant hadn't worked, and he would prescribe another one.

7. Dr Xu. Dr Xu was not an actual psychotherapist, but an acupunc-turist and specialist in Chinese massage. Harvey went to him because his depression had become by this time so bodily, so located in his chest and his legs and his skin that he thought only manipulation of his frame could help. He still often thinks that the way to peace is for him to be touched: that if he could have some-one permanently stroking him – on his back; on his feet; wherever it is on the body that the reassurance centres lie – his anxiety would be brought under control.

Dr Xu did his best to pull and prick Harvey's depression out. Harvey wasn't sure about the underlying ideas of acupuncture – the meridians, the yin and yang organs – but he knew that Karl Marx had said that 'the only antidote to mental suffering is physical pain' and, not being prepared to flagellate himself with thorns, wondered if pins in his skin might do the trick. And it worked: in the room. Lying on his back, looking not unlike the bloke out of *Hellraiser*, he would find himself distracted by the pain out of depression. The skips and jumps of electrical current induced along his muscles by connecting needles did seem to be clearing his system of something; or maybe the cold evidence they presented, that the body is simply a machine, made him feel more positive than usual about the prospect of finding a fix.

It only worked, however, while it was happening. It only worked when the needles were in his flesh. By the time he returned to his house from Dr Xu's practice in Sevenoaks, a journey of some thirty-five minutes, Harvey would be feeling as anxious as ever. To try and extend the life of the treatment effects, Dr Xu prescribed Harvey some extraordinarily foul-smelling herbs, the drinking of which as tea made him more depressed than ever. Dr Xu did also offer him the odd piece of psychotherapeutic advice, consisting mainly of the not unheard-before imprecation that he should *live in the moment*. It would be proper to report that Dr Xu did not fall into the stereotype here and tell Harvey that he should *rive in the moment*: it would be proper but it would not be true. Harvey felt, for a whole host of reasons, that he should not laugh at this, but since Dr Xu, when offering this homily, himself always laughed, as he also did while applying needles, prescribing herbs, walking on Harvey's back, or offering him the buttons of the Visa machine for payment, it seemed almost rude not to.

Even without the Chinese pronunciation, Harvey has never been keen on the live-in-the-moment thing. He knows people think it is the key to happiness, but it seems to him that he, driven by his physical impulses, lives always in the moment. If he buys a sandwich at 10 a.m., intending to eat it for lunch, he will eat it as soon as he gets back to his house at 10.15. If he feels tired, wherever he is, he falls asleep. If he sits down at his computer intending to spend four hours writing ghost-biography, he will spend three hours and forty-five minutes of that allotted time watching internet pornography. That is what living in his particular moment is: and it has brought him to a depression so severe it feels as if large weights have been sewn onto the inside of his skin.

8. See below.

'But obviously, I *can't* get back in time for the session,' says Harvey, frantically looking at his watch. The phone call to Dizzy Harris has gone on for over five minutes, and he knows, since he is still unable to remember the *fucking* pre-dialling number, that it is costing him a fortune in hotel charges. 'I'm in New York. I can't leave because my father might die any day. You're my *therapist*. Have a fucking heart.'

There was a silence on the other end of the line, a silence that Harvey took to be judgemental. This made him feel furious in two ways: first, because he *was* being judged – in that particularly infuriating non-reactive therapist's way – and secondly, because those five seconds of silence just cost him, he reckoned, ten dollars.

'As you know, Harvey, I'm entirely sympathetic to your situation,' said Dizzy in his measured burr: Dizzy speaks posh Scottish, an accent that modulates very easily into patronizing. Harvey hates that tone, especially now, when he feels that it is being measured out in small Dickensian piles of his coins. 'But most of my clients, if not all of them, are in difficult situations emotionally. And they all have to work with me according to the same rules. Which I did explain to you at the beginning.'

Why, thinks Harvey, did I go with this *twat*? I should have known straight away from the name: what kind of therapist – no, what kind of *twat* – calls himself *Dizzy*? Not even as a nickname – *Dizzy* is his name, or at least he's made it his name, it's on his books, the ones forever lined up prominently on his shelves: *Psychological Dysfunction and Mental Wellness*, by Dizzy Harris. *Overcoming Bad Belief* by Dizzy Harris. *Beyond Anxiety Disorder* by Dizzy Yes That's Right You Heard Me *Dizzy* Harris. Dizzy calling himself Dizzy is all part of what's wrong with Dizzy, which is that he is a self-styled colourful character, the type of person who might wear a multi-coloured waistcoat, although in his case he announces his colourfulness by wearing, for

the sessions, a velvet smoking jacket and bow tie. For the first session
the bow tie was at least matching; but latterly he has greeted Harvey
at the door of his west London consulting rooms wearing one that has
been striped, and another polka-dotted.

'While you are working with me, I'm afraid I have to charge for
missed sessions.'

'A hundred and thirty pounds.'

'That's what I charge, yes. The point is that I keep the session open
– it is, as you know, standard therapeutic practice. On Tuesdays, at
eleven, I come here and I sit here, whatever. Even if you have told me
that you are not coming.'

Harvey does know this, but has always hesitated to believe it. Partly
because the image of Dizzy, in his bow tie, sitting on his own in his
self-styled colourful character red leather chair resembles nothing so
much as the man who used to read out Odd Odes on *That's Life*, and
partly because he does not believe in the compassion that Dizzy doing
so would imply.

'Do you really do that? For fifty minutes?'

'Yes.'

'What do you do?'

There is a pause at the other end of the line: Harvey wants to say,
Watch TV? Wank? Flick through a bow-tie catalogue? Think about
me? Or do you just count your fucking cash? Dizzy does not answer
the question.

'I offered the possibility of telephone sessions …'

'Yes.' You haven't offered the possibility of *paying* for the telephone
session, though, have you, Dizzy? The *transatlantic fifty-minute* telephone session?

Harvey hears Dizzy exhale. He feels, almost as clearly as if the smiling jpg of Dizzy on his iPhone screen were moving, his therapist's
head slowly shaking.

'We should have discussed this before you left, Harvey. What we
were going to do about your sessions while you were … away.'

'Yes,' says Harvey, weakly. He knows that he should have done
that. But somehow, last week, standing by the door of Dizzy's

consulting room, the idea that he, Harvey, was going off to New York later that night, to begin a vigil by his father's deathbed, seemed utterly unreal. A different type of therapist might have said that by not discussing what to do about the missed sessions, Harvey was in denial about his father's impending death, but Dizzy is a Cognitive Behaviouralist, and therefore uninterested in such subtextual hoodoo.

What Harvey wants to say – what he wants to shout down the dark well of this telephone – was that a better therapist – or, rather, a *nicer* therapist, a nicer *person* – might have suggested it themselves. He doesn't say this; instead, he begins coughing, the dry retch that always accompanies a rise in his anxiety levels.

'Look, here's what I suggest …' says Dizzy, cutting through Harvey's hacking throat with an air of munificence, '… if, in the next …' – Harvey senses a checking of watch – '… forty-five hours, you can find someone else to take the session, then, obviously, I can charge them instead.'

'But I'm in New York!'

'The telephone?'

Oh more fucking hotel-rate international calls, thanks very much.

'So – what? I'm supposed to ring around my friends in London, and say "Hi – haven't spoken to you for a bit – but anyway, how mental are you feeling? How depressed? How wrung out by existential despair? Because I've got just the man for you."'

'Sounds perfect,' says Dizzy, with a chuckle. 'Look, I must go – client waiting.'

Suddenly, Harvey can't be bothered with it: with all of it. With Dizzy, with being in therapy, with being on the phone, with being in New York, with trying to battle how he feels. 'OK.'

'So, let me know …'

'OK. I'll call you.'

'Bye … send my best to your father.'

'Bye, Dizzy.'

'And remember the mantra.'

'I will. Bye.'

He puts the phone down, imagining in his mind a meter stopping somewhere in four figures. He settles back onto the too-many pillows of his hotel bed, and looks out of the window at his lack of a classic view of New York.

The mantra: he can vaguely remember it, but the wording is so unwieldy he can't quite believe he's got the order right; and seeing as it is a mantra, a spell of sorts, Harvey feels he needs to say it correctly for it to have any power. He actually has it written down on a piece of paper, hidden in the bottom of his bum bag. With a grunt (when did *that* – the overdone old-man exhalation that now accompanies all his bending, sitting, and standing – start happening?) he forces himself out of the pillow nest and towards his case, which is resting open and overflowing on a chrome and black elastic suitcase holder by the door. Yesterday he actually had a go at unpacking, but gave up after twenty minutes of furiously stuffing too many items of clothing into a drawer and trying, unsuccessfully, to force it shut, which led to forty-five minutes of sitting on his bed staring into space.

His bum bag has been laid, rather tenderly, over the spilling mound of those clothes still left in his suitcase by some maid. The cliché rushes into his mind: young, French, apron skirt, puff sleeves, stockings, feather duster, bent over the suitcase holder, blushing perhaps as she notices his underpants. He picks up the belt, and rummages inside the sack, his fingers brushing first his passports, then, underneath the usual bureau de change of irrelevant currency, the piece of paper. He takes it out. Paper, at least, he can fold: this small square looks, he realizes, remarkably like a cocaine wrap, and blanches inside at the thought that he had taken it through customs. His brain chases the idea as he opens it: for a second, he is one of the JFK customs officers and his image in the wardrobe mirror is himself, trembling in waiting fear. This is not a big leap for Harvey's imagination. Although he had got through unquestioned this time, the wobbly onrush of self-consciousness that always hits him while passing through the Nothing to Declare channel – despite carrying no contraband, he always feels an urgent need to appear nonchalant; nonchalance not being a consciously strikeable attitude, what he appears to adopt, from the point of view of the customs officers, is the bearing and gait of a Colombian crack baron – has often led to his being stopped, interrogated, and, on one occasion, strip-searched.

He imagines himself as the customs officer, excited at having caught a class A smuggler, his fingers feverishly worrying at the folded square; and then that excitement draining away as, crestfallen, he discovers that the wrap is not a wrap – it is actually just a piece of paper, containing all that paper usually does: some words. These words:

> I would much prefer it if Stella was not becoming less beautiful with time; but the fact that she is becoming less beautiful with time (like we all do) is not the end of the world.

He imagines the customs officer, in a booming American baritone, reading out the words. He doesn't just imagine it: he does, on his own in his hotel room, an impression of this customs officer. He reads the words out loud, in a terrible hammy borscht belt New York accent – accents are not Harvey's strong point; to do an accent, you have to move away from yourself, and Harvey, however much he hates himself, hates not being himself even more – adding, at the end, a question mark, and not just because of the American intonation. Because the customs officer would be confused, as well he might be.

It is a proclamation that Dizzy Harris has tailored to Harvey's needs (there had been a previous version, which had attempted, along the way, to subvert the whole idea that the lessening of beauty with time is inevitable – it had used phrases like 'what is considered beautiful' and 'in conventional terms' and 'gender-specific' – but this had proved even more unwieldy and harder to memorise). Dizzy's theory and practice as a psychotherapist boils down to something quite simple, which is: *you must change your must-haves to a preference.* His branch of cognitive behavioural therapy has realized (correctly: for all Dizzy's appalling manner, he is not wrong) that the dysfunctional mind is urgent. That it says: I want I want I want I want. I must have must have must have must have. Or, alternatively, I want that gone or

97

I must have that out. The way to sanity is not, Dizzy says, to block this urge entirely. That way – for desire, sensing a block, will implode – madness lies. Instead, one must negotiate with desire, even though we are told we must never do that with terrorists. And the negotiation is this: this shift to the laid-back, to the laissez-faire. If one's problem is alcohol, rather than thinking 'I must have a drink' one must think 'I'd really like to have a drink, but if I don't, it's no big deal …'; if it is continually being overlooked for a promotion, rather than constantly saying to yourself 'Why didn't I get that job? I need to get it!' think 'I'd really like to have got that job, but the fact that I didn't is not a disaster …' And thus anxiety, depression and manic despair are coaxed and massaged – tricked, perhaps – into *feeling just a bit unsatisfied by life*, which is, as it turns out, the true, the median experience.

So this is what is at the heart of Harvey's depression. He is forty-four. Stella is forty-two. They have been together for fourteen years, twelve of them married. Harvey's twenties, post the drear university relationship with Alison, were a long slog through the backwaters of love. Every two years or so, Harvey would fall rabidly in love with a new woman. When in love, he would be lifted out of himself; his natural – and, in the normal run of things, disabling – sense of consequence would evaporate, and he would dive as deeply as possible into the whirlpool of his own emotions, helplessly swooning in the swirl. Every phone call, every look, every scrawled message from the beloved would fuel his heart with God's own petroleum, while the absence of these was as a match to his aorta, turning the entire organ to dust. This state of affairs would last, every time, three months. And then, every time, there would come a morning when Harvey would wake and – without her saying anything, without him even looking over at her sleeping form: this news would be carried on the wind, the small wind blown up from the settling sheet – know instantly that the feeling had gone. It was shocking, always, even though it had happened before, but love, like, supposedly, childbirth, comes with its own built-in amnesia, which airbrushes any pain from the memory when the time arrives for the next episode. When starting up his heart again, he always believed that this time it would last. And then when, every time it faded, came this mixture of deadness and panic, his cold turkey, his comedown from the heroin of love.

He would hold out for a while, chasing the feeling, hoping that it might come back, but knowing in his heart that you cannot chase love, any more than you can think yourself into nonchalance in the Nothing to Declare channel. Then he would give up, and settle into a relationship with the object of his recently flown love, which would function with varying degrees of success but remain always haunted by the lost utopia of those first three months. Not that this meant that the relationship would easily peter out. The grey Sunday polytechnic afternoons with Alison had set the template: splitting up with a woman was always, for Harvey, an unimaginable terror. He could carry the dread of it around with him for months or even years. He wondered how many men and women lived their lives like this, nervously, always on the brink of saying the terrible thing, holding the bad words down like a Tourette's sufferer. He would see his everyday domestic dialogue as on a computer screen, where what he wanted to say would be rendered in faint type, words unclickable-on by his soul's mouse:

GIRLFRIEND: Would do you want for dinner?
HARVEY: Look we have to talk.
HARVEY: What about getting a takeaway?
GIRLFRIEND: I dunno. We had one on Monday.
HARVEY: It's not you it's me.
HARVEY: Oh come on let's go crazy.
GIRLFRIEND: Indian or Chinese?
HARVEY: Sometimes I think I'd rather be in prison than with you. Sometimes I wish you had died. None of this means I don't love you. I'm just not *in* –
HARVEY: Indian.

And, meanwhile, somewhere out there, in the world or on TV, people moved in and out of relationships with ease, treating love as if it were weightless. Harvey didn't know how you got to this world. He was barred from it, by fear and, more importantly, by friendship.

Friendship: what a problem it was. Men of his father's generation, in most cases, had gone one of two ways: they either married someone who they grew to hate for life, or they left women in stages when their sexual interest waned (his father, obviously, the latter: King of the Latter). In neither scenario would they and their women become friends; it was never even on the emotional map. Harvey, however, always became friends with his girlfriends. Sometimes he became best friends with his girlfriends.

So this is what breaking-up with them meant, something it never meant for his father or his father's friends, who were all men: destroying a close friend. All the work of the seventies and eighties, which did so much to make men like Harvey lose their *fear of intimacy* and their *commitmentphobia* – those olive branches laid across what used to be called, so quaintly, the sex war – all that work had this dreadful unforeseen consequence, the laying waste of so many friendships. Harvey came to realize that fucking and friendship are actually incompatible at some level. Not in the *When Harry Met Sally* way, that you cannot be friends with a woman without wanting to fuck them. Just the opposite: because you *can* be friends – you can become really close friends – with the woman you fuck. You cannot, however, *remain* friends with them – certainly not the same sort of friend – once you are forced to tell them that you no longer want to fuck them.

Eventually they would leave him. The words that Harvey was always holding just the other side of the mirror had an imprint. They came through the screen. And so the women would go, sometimes to other men, sometimes not, but always away from Harvey and his unspoken constant goodbye. The break-up would still be awful, but Harvey could at least hold on through the hours of emotional hanging, drawing and quartering to the rope of his innocence: they were leaving; it was not his fault; Love had handed him a pass. They would go and Harvey would mourn, he would feel the absence of his friend, he would maybe write a long letter to his ex where some small shards of writing talent would show through the self-consciously tortured lyricism, he would lie in whichever double bed they had bought together unsleeping in its sudden width, and then, after a week or so, he would embark on a short sexual rampage.

His hit rate, even in the AIDS-soaked eighties, was not bad: he was not then unattractive physically – he still had some of his mother's dark prettiness, and his tendency to fat remained at this point a tendency, like Militant, never quite taking over the entire body – and, more importantly, he found out then that his Gold status actually had some currency. It's a peculiar thing, sexually, being linked to the famous: at what point, Harvey sometimes wondered, did the line of desire run out? In a band, groupies who want to sleep with the front man will accept the drummer – some may accept the roadie – but probably not the front man's brother, unless he's in his own at least moderately successful band. However, if the object of desire is a writer, and an older writer, and on his way to being named as the world's greatest living writer – and if you can claim to be a novelist, too, as Harvey could, at least in this stage of his career, before the slow slide down into ghost-writing – then being Eli Gold's son was indeed a short cut to the sheets of – well, a handful of women working in publishing in Thatcher's Britain.

The young Harvey also had some success, weirdly, with exactly those women who round about this time cast Eli Gold as their object of hate. It was a strange but, from his point of view, not unuseful paradox that his father's placement in the hall of sexist shame along with Norman Mailer and Kingsley Amis and Philip Larkin and all the other misogynist behemoths, led various militant young feminists between 1982 and 1987 to think that having sex with Harvey was some sort of strike for their cause. Particularly if Harvey was prepared to express guilt or regret over his father's deeply flawed representation of women: as indeed he was, and, it should be said, not just in order to, in the common parlance, get his end away. Already well schooled by his mother in sexual politics, Harvey in the mid-eighties was a ball of shame, all the information coming at him all the time from remembered lectures at the polytechnic and songs by the Au Pairs and every woman around him in their berets and DMs convincing him that everything he felt, especially everything sexual, was wrong: wrong not just in the sense of not correct, but evil. It was a relief, therefore, a great blanket to cover his wrong and evil head, to place much of his guilt and regret and uncertainty and shame and ignorance and despair of ever getting it right about gender at the feet of his father.

But Harvey could not keep casual sex up for long. One, or, if he was lucky, two women might pass through his hands, and then the third would snag. It could be her skin, or her hair, or her eyes, or, most likely, some abstract sense of promise made concrete by sex. And so it went, his twenties, the same pattern, the all-consuming love, the patter down into a relationship, the soul-melting break-up, the charge into casual sex, the starting again with the snag. Until Stella, who arrived in his early thirties, just at the point when it was beginning to dawn on Harvey that he couldn't carry on living this way forever.

It would be helpful at this stage to be able to say that what drew Harvey out of the relationship cycle – what made him choose Stella to be his life-station – was her soul. And, certainly, there was much to get snagged on in Stella Marsten's soul. She was, Harvey was to come to realize, one of – he estimated – three people, none of them family members, he had ever met in his life who was deep down good. This was a stranger and more complicated thing to encounter than he at first realized: true goodness is a forceful challenge to the standard self, and to be able to bask in it without resentment takes a fair amount of goodness of one's own, more than Harvey assumed to be in his reserves. The Good are a minority (being modest, as they must be, perhaps the *most* silent minority) and prey to the same abuse as any other, the carping and cat-calling of the deeply flawed majority, who would prefer to link the state to easy adjectival negatives: boring, goody-goody, Pollyannaish, and – that most unsexy of conditions – nice. Before Stella, Harvey had often told himself and his friends and his various therapists that he was not interested in women who were good, precisely because of these associations.

But Stella was none of these things: she was not Ned Flanders nice. The propaganda that the deeply flawed majority wish to ply about The Good – that they are no fun, that goodness equates to no sense of humour – was not true of Stella. She managed somehow to demonstrate a facility for and understanding of a critical component of humour – cruelty – without compromising her essential goodness. She was many things not normally ascribed to her type: maverick, and complex, and stylish, and capable of vice, and flighty, and confident, and passionate, and still fucking good. It beat Harvey, at some level, how it was possible.

Perhaps the key was that at the core of her was not what people lazily assume to be the DNA of goodness – giving a lot of money to charity or spending all your time in a hospice – but empathy. This was what really took Harvey's breath away, Stella's endless empathy. She always seemed to know how other people were feeling, or, if she didn't know, had a deep awareness of how they might be, and that awareness was what ruled her behaviour. This is what goodness actually is: being possessed of an unforced, unmediated engagement with the desires of others. It was the unforced and unmediated part, Harvey realized, that really mattered. Although sometimes feeling close to it, he was not a sociopath; he knew he was supposed to factor other people's desires into the everyday progress of his own. But this knowledge was never reflex or natural: it was always learnt. For Stella it was existential. It was like breathing.

And Harvey was to feel the greatest benefit from it. If you become emotionally linked with someone who breathes empathy, then, quite quickly, they offer something which, after all is said and done, may be the only hope for love in the long term: true knowledge of who you are. The Hollywood notion of Love, the myth of it that has replaced God for us, is wrong. We do not search for someone to complete us. We search for someone to know us completely – to reflect us back to ourselves. We look for someone who will never get us wrong. Harvey was lost – at some level he would always be lost – because he had grown up with a father who was himself widely known but who had chosen not to know him. To be found, for Harvey, was to be known – like a child playing hide and seek, only not where you were, but who. Stella was his finder. In animation, the artist often works with a sketchy black and white outline of a character, and only when it's finished does he or she superimpose on this image, using a plastic transparency, a replica outline of the same character, filled in with colour. This is what Harvey felt when his relationship with Stella began to bloom: she was his animator. She knew, to an exact degree, his real outline, his true colours, and she had laid them softly and gently over what used to be his shadowy self. She had matched him up with himself.

And yet it wasn't all these things that made him choose Stella, or which held her for him. It was – depressingly, at some level; unoriginally, of course; but as hard and true as arithmetic – her beauty. For she was also beautiful. Her inner matched her outer, in the classical, the fairy-tale, model. When Harvey first set eyes on her, in a small independent bookshop in Canterbury, he was reminded of a passage of his father's:

Her face had impact: I felt it not in my eyes, but in my stomach.

It was from one of Eli's lesser known novels, *Reluctance*. Harvey was on the short reading tour which followed the publication of his only novel, *Blah Blah Blah*, a melancholy piece of ladlit which hardly attempted to disguise its *roman à clef* trails through the romantic badlands of his twenties. He knew the form of the evening, or thought he did: a flat, dull train ride out to a provincial bookshop, an awkward conversation with a taxi-driver about who exactly he was, a cup of tea, or, if they were pushing the boat out, a glass of Jacob's Creek, with the tired store manager and his or her unimpressed staff barely restraining themselves, normally unsuccessfully, from asking questions about his father; a couple of nervous glances towards the front of shop, where, with a few minutes to go, someone would be rearranging four rows of chairs into three; and then, finally, show time, in front of the fourteen people who had turned up, in order to sit through his reading so that they could ask some questions about his father. It had all been proceeding as normal – he was in a back room, and, indeed, the manager of Ex Libris, a grey-haired stick of a man keen to tell Harvey that he was a bit of a celebrity himself, having once played bass in The Subway Sect, had just handed him a glass of sickeningly fruity Merlot

– when the door opened, and in she came. Harvey turned, and the line from *Reluctance* flicked into his head like a pop-up. The store manager was saying her name and something about her working for the publisher's lawyer, but Harvey wasn't listening. She was red-haired, and grey-eyed, and her face, full of soft symmetries, seemed to hit him, only not in the stomach, but in the heart. Her beauty was like a punch in the heart, expelling love.

Harvey fell, as he always did, like a sky-diver, like those people you see buffeted by winds on helmet cameras, screaming and gurning in a mash of adrenaline and abandon. Except this time, when the free-fall of infatuation opened into the parachute of relationship, the eventual landing wasn't, for once, a crash. There was still a bump, but he held on to the rope, the safety harness, of her beauty.

Later on, of course – with marriage, and a house, and a child, and time, and full exposure to her goodness – Stella's beauty was not the only thing. They became, of course, best friends: the bestest, in fact. She was the first woman he had ever been with who was not angry. This was one difference between the friends who were his girlfriends and his friends who were just friends. Harvey didn't row with his friends. He might disagree with them – he might even get pissed off with them – but he never got into a proper fight with them. His girlfriends, however, were friends who could switch at will from being friends to being girlfriends – which meant the licence, suddenly, to become possessed by fury at something he had said that he had imagined innocuous, or by his glance pausing for longer than two seconds on another woman, or by failing to understand the directions to a weekend cottage.

It was only when he began seeing Stella that he realized that these constant flares away from friendship were not incidental: rather, they were indicative of the truth that every woman he had ever been with was deep-down angry. Harvey was not sure why this was. The man reared by Joan, and fostered by the 1980s into a New One, assumed that these women were deep-down angry with him – deep-down angry with the knowledge that the all-consuming love he had presented them with early on had died, and that they were just now carrying on until the exit was found: angry, in other words, because they were friends. Another part of him – not exactly a new part, more an older one, always there, just unopened – thought that perhaps all women were deep-down angry, because of men.

Except for Stella. He had found the Holy Grail, it seemed (much more so for his generation than the Zipless Fuck): The Unangry Girlfriend. They never rowed. What this meant was that they became even closer, even more the model of lover-friends. Harvey, who had always pushed his relationships towards a notional condition of maximum intimacy, was astonished that there was a level of closeness beyond that achieved with anyone else, and here it was. They were married eighteen months after the reading at Ex Libris, a small civic ceremony in a hotel in Canterbury, which defied the presence of the looming cathedral down the street with its lightly-worn irreligious-ness, poems – 'An Arundel Tomb,' 'Aire and Angels,' 'Sonnet 116' – replacing prayers. Three years later their son was born, and Harvey found himself astonished again, how despite everything he had read in Parents sections of broadsheet newspapers about how difficult marriage became once a child split the love three ways, that he and Stella bonded more rather than less over Jamie. Even when the blissful bath of babyhood ran dry, and they realized that all was not quite right with Jamie – that when they smiled at him, he failed to smile back; that although his hearing was unimpaired, he wouldn't respond to his name; that he played obsessively only with one toy, a rainbow-coloured spinning top, to the exclusion of all others – his condition, rather than alienating them from themselves, drove them deeper into the bunker of each other, the three of them against the world.

And then, one day, seven years into their marriage – when Jamie was four and Stella thirty-seven – they went for Sunday lunch at a restaurant on the Thames. It was a beautiful afternoon: London rose from the river like it used to on the television, on the Thames TV trailer. Harvey and Stella sat at a table outside. Jamie was being rela-tively easy, entranced by the boats and the potential opening power of Tower Bridge. Harvey had ordered a spicy Bloody Mary: it was his concession to alcohol, something his taste buds, hardly changed since childhood, otherwise had little truck with. It was just as he liked, where the vodka wasn't actually discernible on the tongue, but provided an insensible tang of adulthood within the sweet and sour gazpacho mix. It spoke to him of brunch, of Greenwich Village, of glossy, cosmopolitan presentations of the urban life. Stella looked fantastic. Despite being from Ashford, and knowing of no other genetic antecedents for her outside of Kent, Harvey often projected onto her features something Celtic, especially, as then, when framed by water – an image of her standing in front of a loch, red curls blowing across her merciful face. He knew this was sentimental, linked to the goose pimples that always rose on his flesh when he heard 'Danny Boy' or 'I Wish I Was In Carrickfergus', but it touched him in any case.

She was talking, and Harvey was laughing. She was saying:

'… Bumblebee have offered us a Disneyland trip.' Bumblebee was an autism charity. Jamie sometimes got invited to Bumblebee events, although when they participated Harvey felt he could always detect from the organizers a slight froideur that they'd got in basically under the wire – that Asperger's was a pretty diluted form of the disorder and not, therefore, necessarily a qualifying pass for the consolatory goodies. The word Bumblebee was whispered, so as not to set Jamie off.

'Disneyland?'

'Yeah. Paris.'

Harvey took another sip of his Bloody Mary. The ice was beginning to melt, thinning the tomato juice halfway down the glass.

'Would he like that?'

Stella looked at their son. He had his eyes fixed on the bridge. Harvey had told him that it was due to open in three hours and forty-seven minutes; a lie, but Jamie had asked incessantly on the car journey over. *His face is so memorable*, Harvey thought – with its nose larger than a kid of four should have, sandwiched between his still-pillowy cheeks, blown out now, indicating concentration. Ironically memorable, as Jamie suffered from almost complete face-blindness, only just about able to recognize Harvey and Stella: all others moved in a blur to him, teachers and relatives and the small group of children who Harvey suspected of being forced by their well-meaning parents

107

to be his friends. His mouth was not moving, as it sometimes did when faced with this kind of calculation, but Harvey knew he was still counting the three hours and forty-seven minutes down in seconds, even though they would be gone long before the spurious set time arrived.

'I don't know,' said Stella.

'He likes Winnie the Pooh,' replied Harvey. She was nodding, raising her eyebrows in sarcastic agreement: Jamie's liking of their *The Magic of Pooh* DVD meant putting it on normally a minimum of nine times a day.

'Yes. But I think it might frighten him.'

'Frighten him?'

'Yes. You know Muna, Khalil's mum …'

'Yes,' said Harvey, his nod self-consciously weary, knowing that Stella assumed he had no idea who anyone was at Jamie's school. This was essentially true, but Harvey always disavowed it with this weary nod.

'She said they went last Easter, and Khalil cried throughout. Terrified. Especially at the beavers.'

'The …?'

'Leave it.'

'What?'

'That face. Yes: the beavers. They hang around with Snow White. Or someone.'

'I think they might be squirrels …'

'Well, whatever cuddly vermin they are, the point is – I reckon – that they're too big.'

'Big? But they have to be that size so that people can get in the costumes.'

'I know that. I know that they're not actually giant beavers stroke squirrels. But my point is – do the kids know that? No. Because the one thing you're not allowed to tell children on their way to Disneyland is "By the way, darling, just in case you were wondering – someone lives in Mickey Mouse. Most likely a bald out-of-work dwarf who might also be a paedo."'

Harvey laughed. Her observation was made somewhat more absurd because she was semi-whispering, so as to avoid Jamie hearing it.

'So I know it might seem obvious to us, but the kids, I think, are expecting Mickey and Donald and Goofy and Winnie and the beavers to be kind of the size they are on the TV. *Their* size, in other words, or maybe smaller.'

'You said it was a dwarf!'

'Well, that was just a thing I said. I don't mean a dwarf. I mean a big midget. The point is I think most kids when they walk into Disneyland are thinking: *Shit! What's happened to Mickey? When did he get elephantiasis?* Or the equivalent in four-year-old terms.' Harvey laughed again. 'I'm serious. This is an even bigger problem if your child happens to be …' she glanced at Jamie again, lowering her voice still further, '… very committed, psychologically, to a specific idea of, say, Winnie the Pooh.'

Harvey sat back in his chair. He looked at Stella, her face settling into a not unfamiliar seriousness, held back from being too earnest by a tinge of irony playing around the edges of her mouth. He smiled at her, signalling that he had enjoyed her rant, but understood too that here was something they needed to think about. But he didn't worry about it: he didn't worry about whether or not they should accept the invitation to Disneyland. He looked at her face and felt a soft arresting, like a blanket being laid on trembling shoulders: in his gut, he felt his digestive organs settle, and faint sounds played in his ears – just London sounds, the plash of the river as a motorboat went by, the murmur of couples walking on the towpath, bells in the distance from some church the name of which he would never know but assumed to be something to do with Hawksmoor or Wren – and, for a second, it felt as if the world was harmonizing. What Harvey felt in that second was contentment, but he would not have recognized it.

And then the light changed. A cloud settled over the sun like a kidnapper's hand over his mouth. Stella frowned, and – always more affected by the cold – picked up her cardigan from the back of her chair and wrapped it around her arms. As she frowned, Harvey noticed something he had never really spotted before. She had lines on her face. And to Harvey, suddenly, these lines looked not like tiny infolds of skin, but like slashes, like her face was one of those portraits by Leonardo or Raphael that mad men so can't bear the beauty of they have to rip it with a carving knife: except these slashes had been done by a tiny madman, who simply couldn't bear the beauty of her eyes, and had poured out his criss-cross violence only around them.

Harvey felt mad. He felt it must be some kind of terrible optical illusion. *What the fuck?* A voice started whispering in his head, underneath all the other sounds, but more insistent, more audible: *You've just never noticed before that she's growing old.* Frightened though he was of the voice, he wanted it to enlarge, to explain and clarify how this could have happened, how he could have missed it, but it didn't. It just repeated the phrase over and over again. It was his voice, of course, or whatever passes for one's own voice when the mind, as it does at times of crisis, speaks thought out loud, but looped and shrill and scratched and tampered with. It was his own voice played backwards on vinyl by a teenage death-metal fan looking for Satan.

Immediately, a counter-voice – a counter-voice that came from a place of love, of love under attack – and, also, from Harvey's reflex knowledge of what was good and right and proper when it came to men and women – parried: *So? Everyone gets old. And when you love someone, such things do not matter.* Words read out at their wedding – LOVE IS NOT LOVE WHICH ALTERS WHEN IT ALTERATION FINDS – flashed up in his mind, in capitals, and he reached for them, as the truth, as his truth, but found that the sentiment only exacerbated this anxiety. Because this was the law, the iron-clad, first law of love, and of course what he was doing, presently, was breaking it; LOVE IS NOT LOVE WHICH ALTERS WHEN IT ALTERATION FINDS operated in this moment like the hand on his shoulder of an arresting policeman.

An image came back to Harvey from childhood. When he and his mother first came back from America, the young Harvey was clearly lonely, disorientated by being brought back from their enormous apartment on the Upper West side of Manhattan with a battery of childminders, to a two-bedroom flat in Wembley (Joan, of all Eli's discarded wives, reacted with the most fury at his desertion: but her fury was allied to an immense pride, and a certain self-flagellating stoicism, which led, in contravention to most furiously deserted wives, and much to her ex-husband's delight, to a refusal to take a cent of Eli's money). So his mother bought him a cat. The idea of a dog, the more obviously companionable animal, was impossible, seeing as Joan very quickly got a job in the English department of the newly established North London Polytechnic and the six-year-old Harvey even then, even by six-year-old standards, gave off a sense of being unable to cope with responsibility. Joan had also decreed that they should not have a kitten, partly because she didn't want to deal with house training, but also, with her fierce sense of rectitude, because she felt that there was something improving about making Harvey look after an animal that was already somewhat infirm.

Harvey loved the cat, who he called Luffa, a diminutive of Fluffy; years later, he would discover this to be the name of a homeopathic nasal spray. His ability to love had spaticised with his parents' split, but not his reserves of it. The young Harvey was desperate for a recep-tacle to catch the overspill of love endlessly pouring from his heart, and that was Luffa. Harvey was transfixed by the tabby mongrel's deadpan feline beauty. He would look at her face for hours, and silently beg her to grace his lap with her warm, soft form. He would come home from school, tight with the small trauma of the day, and run to wherever she was for release, sometimes burying his face in her fur. Every day for three years he would do this, until one day he saw her from their living-room window sitting under a tree in the small communal garden behind their flat. He ran as excitedly towards her as ever – the run even more purposeful now that Luffa was getting old – until he got close enough to bend down and kiss her: but then, just before his lips made contact, across the side of her sleepy face crawled a large spider. Harvey was terrified of spiders: as a child, and indeed as a grown man, they flooded his body with horror, exploding his senses into a whiteout of fear and revulsion. If, for the pre-women-worshipping Harvey, cats were Beauty, then spiders were anti-Beauty.

He literally recoiled, like a spring had come out of Luffa's head, knocking him backwards about four foot onto the grass. Even as he fell he knew immediately that he was scarred, if not physically, then psychologically; that here was a memory which would come back to him at some bad time in the future, death crawling over the face of love.

So here it was, returning in middle age: the spider on Luffa's face. As he stared at his wife's altered features, a mixture of emotions coursed through him: disbelief, uncertainty, profound existential terror. These coalesced into a form of intense psychic discomfort, as if a sadistic dwarf – the one, perhaps, in the Mickey Mouse costume – was scraping its fingernails down a blackboard in his soul. Stella, her empathy antennae immediately twitching, said:

'What's the matter?'

He looked at her. They had no secrets. She was his best friend. He had found what he was supposed to find, his soulmate, and the mating of their souls had happened without censorship. But here: here was something unsayable. She was his *friend*. He *loved* her: fiercely. How could he say words which would break that love in two? He couldn't: and not just to Stella. He saw, in his imagination, not just her face, but the faces of all the women he had ever known, and all the women he had learnt from when younger, and all the women who had written and were writing in all the books and all the newspapers, about men and their shallowness and cruelty and objectifying and body fascism and misogyny. They seemed to crowd around his wife, challenging Harvey to tell the truth: he saw them, an infinity of women, arms folded, tapping their heelless shoes, drumming their unvarnished nails. He heard them chorus in unison: *Well?* And in amongst all the women, nodding and raising their eyebrows, he saw as well many men; men in glasses and suede jackets and well-cut hair, men who looked very like himself, carrying copies of the *Guardian* and the *New Statesman*, men who had accepted and internalized all the arguments about the dark truths of patriarchy, and now held them as unblinkingly – if not more unblinkingly – as the women. It was a huge right-thinking congregation, as unshallow as the river it stood beside. And then he saw their reaction should he offer the real answer – a wave of disgust, disappointment and outrage, passing all the way from Stella to the massed ranks watching on Tower Bridge, ready to open in three hours and forty-seven minutes like all the legs in all the pornography the watching of which had clearly led Harvey to this pretty pass.

It was unsayable, what he felt. The only thing was that it also felt – despite being horrible and awful and a source of great self-loathing that it should be felt at all – natural. It didn't feel like it should, a symptom of a false consciousness. It felt as natural as vomiting.

So Harvey did what he often did, with people he didn't really know, or with previous partners: he half said it.

'Have you changed your make-up?'

She burst out laughing. 'Have I *what*?'

'Sorry, I …'

Then she stopped laughing, abruptly: 'What is this, now?' she said. Harvey felt chased, then, by her empathy. She knew him too well. He wanted immediately to pass it off as nothing; but her understanding of him was like a prison searchlight.

'Really, it's nothing. I just wondered – I was thinking about Bumblebee …'

Stella raised her palms but it was too late.

'Bumblebee, stumblebee, buzz, buzz, buzz. Bumblebee, Stumblebee, buzz, buzz, buzz,' said Jamie.

'Sorry,' said Harvey, 'I forgot.'

She shook her head at him, with some irritation, and began searching in her knapsack for something to distract the boy. Harvey had not forgotten, although he knew that her general acceptance of his absent-mindedness would cover him: he had deliberately said a word he knew Jamie fetishized in order to switch focus. It was a trump card, but one which he had never thought to play before, and, as soon as he had, realized that doing so was mildly abusive.

'Zubb, zubb, bzzzzz, beebumble …'

Jamie would continue echolaliaing around Bumblebee now for at least ten minutes, unless Stella managed to shift his attention onto one of the various action figures she had brought to lunch with them, prepared for such an eventuality. She took one out of her bag.

'Jamie! Jim-Jam! Look!!'

She bent down to jiggle the plastic monster in front of Jamie's face. The boy was frowning now with something between concentration and possession.

'Beeblebum, busy busy bee, bee bum-bum …'

With her attention directed towards Jamie, Harvey was able to stare at Stella's face unhindered. Looking at her directly while in the grip of this sudden neurosis had been too much, like staring into some black sun, and, besides, she could see his eyes that way round: she could read him. In profile, he could be a voyeur. He could project all his anxiety onto her face in unpeace. At this moment he began a process that was to be repeated endlessly in the coming years, a type of feverish checking, a hypervigilant, furtive scanning for more lines and for anything else that might proclaim a falling away from youth: roughness and/or falling of skin, open pores, neck slackness, grey hairs, spider veins, spiders themselves. *Why*, he thought, *would I look so hard for something I don't want to find?* But the urge felt unstoppable: his gaze moved across her face, sifting and microscopic, powered by negative hope like those rows of people searching in fields for clues that will only tell them that the lost child is already dead.

Then the sun burst back through the clouds, just as Stella looked back up towards Harvey from Jamie, and the feeling was gone. She looked beautiful again. Harvey shuddered, as if waking from a bad dream, and immediately resolved that this experience had been some kind of hallucination. He knew, instantly – or at least, desperate to locate an explanation which placed the responsibility outside of himself, felt it as hard fact – what had brought it on: it was his father, the father who had fled from every woman he had ever loved the minute they had begun to age. It was his father's voice that he had heard whispering frantically inside his head. There was stuff embedded in him by his father, which he clearly was not even aware of: dysfunction, misogyny, fear and loathing of women. He determined immediately not to succumb to it, to Eli: he could give this basket of bad feelings that name.

114

Later on he would realize that this both was and wasn't true. Or at least that knowing this made it no easier to fight. He would come to realize many things: that the handmaiden of this phobia was light, and that light plays many tricks, one of which is that bright light reflects off skin, making, outdoors, the effects of ageing *less* visible in the sun; that the worst days are the cloudy ones, when grey light picks out grey skin; that once you've noticed that someone has aged, you can't not notice it, there is no deactivation switch; that parts of the body which he might have thought irrelevant to the beauty-policing-eye (elbows, armpits, feet) can all become sites of this anxiety; that every woman would soon be scanned in this way; that the way he would look at young smooth-skinned women in the street would become no longer straightforwardly sexual but, rather, medical, as unreachable antidotes; and that the point about the lines on Stella's face was not that he doesn't love her because of them, but, rather, that when they seem magnified on her face, Harvey fears that he may not be able to make his love work. Her beauty is not the only thing he loves about her, by any means, but it is the key that unlocks his love, that makes him think of her softly, that makes him appreciate all the other attributes more keenly. He has swallowed the beauty myth so deeply – the propaganda, force-fed to us from the fairy tales onward, that beauty is goodness – that he needs to see her beauty to see every-thing else – to see all the things that are beautiful about Stella that are nothing to do with her beauty.

He has lived with all this for so long now that he is no longer sure that the responsibility lies with Eli, living inside him and directing his eyes like a malevolent oompaloompa. He has come to New York to watch his father die, but also perhaps to find out for himself at last how much of what Therapist No. 3, in one of his rare moments of speech, referred to as his particular version of *body dysmorphic disor-der by proxy* was inherited, and how much it was just intrinsic to him, Harvey Gold, who had, after all, not lived in daily contact with his father since he was six. On the day Eli actually left, the day he walked out of their East Side apartment, he gave Harvey a present: a chemis-try set. It was summer. The previous Christmas his father had given him a chess set – he had been waiting ever since for Eli to teach him how to play – and Harvey can remember thinking that because this box was also emblazoned with the word 'set' that this present must be something similar: and he was correct, insofar as both presents implied, in his father's mind, a misplaced idea of Harvey as intellectually precocious.

The chemistry set was a wooden case, with a lockable hinge on the side. On the front was a drawing, of a man and a boy, in silhouette, looking towards a mountainous horizon: the man had his arm around the boy's shoulder. They were dwarfed in the frame by an enormous triangular beaker, in which an orange liquid was bubbling. Above the beaker were the words Lionel Porter Chemcraft Lab Chemistry Set, and a sticker warning that the set should not be used by children except under the supervision of adults, that it should be handled with caution, and that it should be kept away from children under eight years old. As a result, the Lionel Porter Chemcraft Lab Chemistry Set was never opened by the young Harvey, instead becoming, first, an instrument of outrage for his mother to berate his father with, and, second, something that she decided to leave behind, very deliberately, when they sailed for London on the QE2 a month later.

Nonetheless, it is this chemistry set that Harvey finds himself imagining when he considers his psychological project here in New York. He imagines that big beaker full of whatever toxic, corrosive compound it is that makes him feel as he does about Stella; he sees it bubbling, and he sees it distilling into its constituent elements, allowing him, the man who still feels like the boy in silhouette, to find out once and for all what part of this is Eli, what part Harvey, and what part just default fucking maleness.

Of course, most of the therapists and all of the few friends that Harvey has confided in about this anxiety have gone for the obvious conclusion: that it is simply a projection of his own fear of ageing. Looking at himself now in the wardrobe mirror at the Sangster Hotel, he knows, as ever, that this isn't true. He doesn't deflect his own ageing. He sees it happening every day, in the ever-thinning of his hair, the ever-fattening of his frame, the ever-froggying of his features.

It gives him no joy; he isn't pleased about it; but he isn't pathological about it. It makes him sad; it does not make him despair.

But then Harvey has never thought of himself as beautiful. He has always relied on others to provide him with beauty. And so that is why, when he looks back down from his froggy face and tries to read out his unfolded mantra – *I would much prefer it if Stella was not becoming less beautiful with time; but the fact that she is becoming less beautiful with time (like we all do) is not the end of the world* – he can't. The words freeze in his throat, and even if he does manage to croak them out, they sound thin and racked and stuttery. They sound like a lie told by a bad liar. Because Harvey knows that it is the end of the world.

He sits in the restaurant waiting for his brunch. He would rather the restaurant was a diner, and he would rather brunch was just called breakfast, but the nearest diner that might serve a real American breakfast is six or seven blocks away, and when he is on one of his hospital days he doesn't like to go too far from Mount Sinai. The restaurant is called Hanratty's.

The brunch menu has some stuff on it he doesn't much like the sound of, but it does have steak and eggs, which he doesn't eat that often but his mom used to make it at home sometimes when they could afford it, and she said it was the best way to start the day, the thing that would keep you going whatever happened, and so he orders it, even though he is not planning on doing much more than watching today. He remembers that Janey used to talk about *focus* a lot, about how that was what you needed to achieve your goals. Her goals, in the end, were to leave Salt Lake City and join the Community, but that was OK, now. He had been angry with her at the time, but now he realizes that it is all part of his destiny, and that if Janey hadn't left that maybe he wouldn't be here, and even if he doesn't like being here that doesn't matter. You don't get to like your destiny.

So he thinks that, even though she is not here and he hasn't heard from her in three years, he should listen to his daughter. He is listening to Janey. He is *focusing*. However long it takes, he will find his focus by continuing to look at The Material. Hanratty's has broadband for its customers, so he has brought the Dell with him. This means that he can keep working while he is in the restaurant. It also means that he does not have to sit in the restaurant on his own doing nothing waiting for his food. He is a loner, yes, but he doesn't want people thinking he is a loser.

He is hungry and the smells from the kitchen are making him hungrier, but he needs to focus, so while he waits for his food to arrive he works. He Googles 'Eli Gold trainscript Commisioner Webb 1993 Pauline Gray suicide genuine?'. Google comes back with *Did you mean 'Eli Gold' transcript Commissioner Webb 1993 Pauline Gray suicide genuine?* He clicks on it. The key word in his selection – genuine – goes nowhere, never appears in the context he wants, which is: is the transcript on Unsolved real? He has always assumed so, but recently, certainly since he has been in New York, he has begun to question it, almost as if the city, with all its willed confusion, has crept into his understanding of things. Would The Great Satan not have brought a lawyer with him (an issue he raises in the text, but seems not to follow up on)? Would the interview have been recorded at all? Wouldn't there have been another policeman in the room? Would they not have been too worried about The Great Satan's status to subject him to this?

But there is no discussion anywhere else on the web of the transcript's authenticity. It's all just taken as read, evidence from which a thousand bloggers can link to other pages, along with whatever other conspiracy shit they're into. Eventually, he clicks on Unsolved again, and then on the thumbnail of The Great Satan and his sister, to get to www.unsolved.goldwebbtrans.html, and reads it again:

EG: I have no obligation to answer this. If I had known the tone of these questions in advance, I would not have agreed to be brought down here. Certainly not without legal representation.

[pause]

RW: I apologize, Mr Gold, for my tone. I'm a police officer, not a great writer, and perhaps not such a judge of my own words.
EG: Yes, well –

RW: I have here a copy of your own note. Showing Mr Gold case document R45/103.

[pause]

EG: What about it?

RW: Sorry, I was just thinking about the fact that it's a copy.

EG: So?

RW: Well, we have your wife's suicide note. But I understand you didn't want us to have yours.

EG: I didn't want you to have my wife's! It was taken from my – from our – apartment while I was still in hospital. The only reason you don't have mine is that Larry picked it up.

RW: Yes. Record to show: Larry that is – correct me if I'm wrong – Larry Barnett, your literary agent.

EG: Yes.

RW: Who found yourself and Mrs Gold.

EG: I believe so, yes. Obviously, I was unconscious.

RW: He has a key to your apartment, does he? Larry.

EG: Not always. But I had lent him one, recently. During the last days of our marriage, when we were trying to work things out, we spent a lot of time in our lodge in New England.

RW: And on the occasion of the ... on the evening in question, 3 June 1993 ... Larry Barnett was ... coming round to see the two of you? That had been arranged?

[pause]

EG: Commissioner Webb. I have won the Pulitzer Prize. I have won the National Book Award twice. I have been offered the Nobel.

RW: Wow. I knew your work was admired but, no, I didn't know all that.

EG: So: do you think I'm an idiot?

RW: No, sir.

EG: Well, what sort of idiot would invite a close friend round to their house on the night that he and his wife were planning to commit suicide?

RW: Someone who wanted to be found?

EG: Found …?

RW: After death. No one wants to rot there for days.

[unheard]

RW: Or possibly someone who wanted to be stopped. Suicide is often a cry for help.

EG: Not in our case, Commissioner.

RW: No. Of course not. Anyway, this note – why did Larry Barnett insist on keeping the original?

[pause]

RW: Does he think it may be valuable? It's an original piece of writing, after all. By a Pulitzer Prize-winner.

EG: How long is this going to continue, Commissioner? I'm still recuperating and all these questions are making me tired.

RW: Not much longer, sir. Let's move on from the notes for the moment. We'll come back to them later. Showing Mr Gold document R45/107.

[pause]

EG: This is an autopsy report?

RW: Yes.

EG: I'd really rather not see this if you don't mind.

RW: I know it's painful, but I'm keen to … [unheard] … so if you check the following page, it concludes that she died from taking a combination of Demerol and Naproxen. The doctors estimate about thirty pills of the former and twenty of the latter. Plus they found traces of … hold on … Paroxetine Hydrochloride? Is that right? In her bloodstream. But not in yours.

EG: It's Paxil. An antidepressant.

RW: Right, right.

EG: She was on it. But had come off recently.

RW: She'd come off antidepressants recently?

EG: Yes.

RW: Why would you come off antidepressants if you were suicidal ...?

[pause]

EG: I'm really not certain that psycho-pharmacology is all that simple,
Commissioner. But you would have to ask an expert.

RW: You were not on antidepressants?

EG: No.

RW: Have you ever been?

[pause]

EG: No.

[pause: sound of writing]

RW: Not even when you became, as your medical records show, chron-
ically depressed? Or during the period leading up to this – suicide
attempt?

EG: ... No.

[pause]

RW: OK. So let's discount, for the moment, the Paxil as being involved
in the death of Mrs Gold. The doctors also estimate, from your time
in hospital, that that's what you took. Thirty Demerol and twenty
Naproxen. Would you say that was correct?

EG: More or less.

RW: More or less? You didn't count them out? That's what suicides
tend to do.

EG: I took one pill and she took one pill. One at a time, until we'd finished both bottles. We fed them to each other. We looked into each other's eyes as we did it. It was what we both wanted: a perfect, peaceful symmetry. Are you satisfied now, Commissioner? Now that you've broken into our final intimacy?

RW: That is not my intention, sir.

[pause]

RW: You're what – six-foot one? Two?

EG: Six-foot two.

RW: And what do you weigh, Mr Gold?

EG: What do I weigh?

RW: Yes.

EG: At the moment, about a hundred and eighty pounds.

RW: You lost a little weight following your ordeal.

EG: I believe so.

RW: So you weighed, on 3 June, maybe … a hundred and ninety pounds?

[pause]

EG: I didn't, on the night that me and my wife planned to exit this universe, spend much time on the scales.

RW: Your wife, on that night, according to this report, weighed a hundred and ten pounds. She was five foot two. Would you say that the amount of Xanax and Vicodin needed to kill a hundred-and-ten-pound, five-foot-two woman would be the same as that required to kill a six-foot, hundred-and-ninety-pound man?

[pause]

RW: Would you not say, in fact, that, pharmaceutically, the one thing required to make sure that both of you exited this universe as planned, was *asymmetry*?

123

He feels a sudden pressing need to urinate. This comes over him these days much quicker than it used to. There is no gradual build-up of pressure any more, just a switch in his bladder that flicks to urgent. He makes a mental note to make sure he doesn't drink too much water and goes to the bathroom in good time before the day of his destiny. It would not help his focus to be thinking about that.

He makes sure to put the Dell to sleep before he gets up, not wanting any passing nosy waiters to look at his screen. The waiter points him the way downstairs to the rest rooms.

Inside the men's room there are framed newspapers above the urinals, mainly the *New York Post*, although there is one old copy of the *National Enquirer* with a gory front-page photo and headline that says 'I CUT OUT HER HEART AND STOMPED ON IT'. He does not read the one above his basin at first, as all his energy is concentrated on getting his penis out of his flies quickly. Once past the swoon of relief he can breathe normally again, and notices that the framed paper in front of his face has a picture on it of Hanratty's, with the words *Rudy and Judy's Hideaway* underneath. He peers at it. When he and his sister were children they had a hideaway. It was a small natural clearing, hidden within the overgrown hedge that ran along the side of the back garden of their house near the airport in Salt Lake City. Pauline hung a series of blankets over the branches around it; once you were in there it felt like a tepee. They even tried to light a fire in the hideaway once, with some twigs and a lighter he had found in the graveyard behind the City Temple: their dad caught him and beat him hard for that. They called their hideaway by their names, too, though by their nicknames, not their real ones. Because she had protruding front teeth at the time, he called her Bugs, and she called him Swish, the noise his corduroy pants made when he ran. *Swish and Bugs' Hideaway*. They got up to all sorts in there.

His piss takes a long time, long enough to read the first paragraph of the attached article, which he is pleased about, as sometimes now he needs to go really badly and yet when he does out comes nothing but a small dribble.

– Busted, eh? says a voice next to him. He looks over. His relief had been so full, he had not noticed that a man had come and stood by the adjacent urinal. He is pleased that he did not notice this, as close proximity with other men inhibits his bladder in public toilets.

He does not say anything. He looks over at the cubicles. They are a good size, he thinks. There would be room in there.

– I remember that, says the man, unperturbed. Giuliani. What a guy. All that zero-tolerance shit, and then he's fucking some cunt on the side. And not even that on the side, he brings her here every Sunday for brunch!! Sings her fucking Italian love songs! Over waffles and eggs fucking Benedict!'

He nods. He shakes himself off, carefully – he has issues there, too – grateful to move away. But the man continues, looking over his shoulder at him, even though now he is at the washbasins.

– Still – everyone's got some shit going on, haven't they? And there's always a woman at the heart of it. Isn't there?

He feels that he should answer – the man's questions, although rhetorical, seem to demand some gesture of agreement.

– I guess … he says.

– Zero fucking tolerance.

He feels the cold water run over his hands and watches in the mirror as the man turns, doing himself up. The man is balding, and fat enough to struggle with his fly. He sees himself, his sharp, white face, one of those faces that still looks somehow boyish even though it is old, and feels an urge to rush over and tell this man everything about his sister, about The Great Satan, about the long hard road to his destiny: and he wants the man to approve of it, to nod and purse his mouth and shake his head and say *too fucking right*. He doesn't know why he so wants this man's approval, but senses, as with the jihadis, that it is something to do with certainty.

When he gets back to the table, his steak and eggs are waiting, going cold.

* * *

I read one of Daddy's books today. Well, Mummy read it to me. Then she had to go back to the hospital so she let Elaine carry on until it was time for me to turn my light off. I can read, of course, but Mommy didn't want me to read it by myself. I think she wanted to read it to me. Also I worked out she wanted to check there were no bits in it that were too grown up for me to hear, about sex and stuff. When she was reading it sometimes she'd stop for a second and then the lines on her forehead would come out like they do when she's thinking hard about something and then she'd carry on and I reckoned she was maybe missing a bit out.

It's the first time I've been allowed to see any of Daddy's work. Although I did see the Butter Mountain. That was a thing he did before I was born. Daddy stopped writing for a bit then – Mommy says he had 'writer's block' which is when you're a writer and you can't think of anything – so he became an artist, just for a little while. Mommy and Elaine took me to see it because Daddy doesn't like it any more. It's in a big gallery downtown. It is actually a mountain made out of butter. It's not the same size as a real mountain but it is really big, bigger than me, and it looks exactly like a mountain, except made of butter. The gallery has to keep it in a special cold room to stop it melting. I said to Mommy, did Daddy really make this? Didn't his hands get really greasy? Stupid questions like that, because I was only four. She said no he didn't make it himself, but it was his idea: and that artists didn't have to make their own things any more. I didn't really understand that but I really loved the Butter Mountain. I wanted to tell Daddy how much I loved it when we got back but Mommy said not to, because he hates it now.

Anyway, Mommy said it was time. She said it kind of slowly, with that very serious face she sometimes puts on.

'Time for what?' I said.

'Time that we introduce you to Daddy's writing. It's time you got to know why Daddy is such a great man.'

'Before he dies,' I said.

She nodded, and breathed in, without saying anything: it looked for a minute like she was holding her breath. She always does this

126

when I say anything about Daddy dying. I don't know if I'm not meant to talk about it. But in *The Heavenly Express for Daddy* they tell you that you should talk about it if you want to.

Before she started Mommy explained to me that Daddy didn't write books for children (like I didn't know *that*) but that this book was maybe the nearest thing: 'It's something of a latter-day fairy tale,' she said.

'Like café latte?' I said.

'What?' she said.

'A latte day. Is that a day when you only drink café latte?' This is what she always orders in Starbucks (there's one downstairs in the hospital): grande, skinny, extra-hot. When I was little I always used to be frightened that extra-hot would be *so* hot that she'd get burnt when she picked it up or that maybe she'd go 'Ow!' and then throw it up in the air and it would all land on my head or something.

She smiled that smile which means that I've got something wrong, again. When she does it her front lip goes up quicker than her bottom one, so she looks a bit like a rabbit, about to bite on a juicy lettuce.

'Latter-day, darling, not latte day ...' she said, kissing me on the cheek. She smelt of wine, though not much, just a little. I liked it. 'It means ... it means today. *Mirror, Mirror* is like a fairy tale for today. Except it was written over thirty years ago. We'll just read the first chapter for now, and see how far we get.'

Mirror, Mirror was what the book was called. Daddy wrote it in 1978. It is his seventh novel. Mummy told me that when it came out it didn't get such good reviews – that's when people in the newspapers tell you if stuff is good or bad – but that now everyone realizes it is a classic. I put my head onto the pillow and held onto Cuddles. He was cold and I wanted to get him warmed up but Mummy had already started reading.

In this land of ours, which inspires gratitude in some and resentment in others, there was born at the start of the century a boy, whose given name was Herbert Aloysius Morris, but who would come to be known

127

to all his friends as Herb, and to his parents *[and here Mummy did that frowny forehead thing]* as Herbie.

She carried on, but it was quite hard to understand, not that much like a fairy tale at all. There were no fairies, and no castles, and no witches, and no princes or princesses. I thought that Herbie was supposed to be the hero, but he was just a boy with really bad asthma like that kid Patrice at my school has got. It made me wonder how long I was going to be away from school. Mom took me out when Daddy went into hospital. Elaine does some more home teaching now: a 'top-up' Mommy calls it. At first I was really pleased, like I'd been given a special holiday all of my own, but when Mommy said the thing about asthma it made me think of Patrice and his funny blue inhaler thing and I realized I kind of missed it. School, I mean, not Patrice's inhaler!

When I started thinking about school I thought that maybe I wasn't listening hard enough so I tried to listen really hard, although then I thought I don't know how you listen hard. Jada can make her ears move and I thought if I could do that I could maybe make them go like towards Mommy's mouth or the book and that would be a way of listening hard.

> … a nose so prominent and genuinely beak-like the boys playing stick-ball in the gutter outside Olinskys on Pelham Parkway would stop and flap their arms at him. Herbie didn't mind that so much; he wouldn't have minded at all if his nose, with its huge oval tunnels designed to maximise breathing, actually worked. But every morning, he awoke with a palate so dry it felt like he'd been sleeping open-mouthed on the dead soil of the Great Plains at the height of the Dust Bowl.

Mommy stopped here and started to explain to me what the dust bowl was, but it was even harder to listen to her explaining it than it was listening to the story. As she was talking, the pages of the book flicked back to the start, and – I know I should've been listening but I just got bored – I had a look at the bit at the start again.

I was right. She had a missed a bit out, when she did the frowny forehead thing. She'd even underlined in pencil the bit she'd missed out, and put a little question mark by the side of the line. In the book, what it *actually* said was:

… but who would come to be know to all his friends as Herb, and to his parents – and wives – as Herbie.

I didn't really understand why she'd missed that bit out. It just meant that all his wives had called him Herbie. What's wrong with that?

So I said: 'Mommy? Can you warm up Cuddles?'

She did that face where her eyes go all hard.

'Darling. I'm trying to explain to you about the Dust Bowl. Have you been listening?'

'Yes, but Cuddles is cold,' I said.

'Well, I'm warm him up in a minute, when we've finished reading.'

'Her.'

'*Her.*'

'Please do it now, Mommy, please. I want Cuddles to hear the story, too, and she only comes alive when she's warmed up …' Mommy made a face at this, but it wasn't a bad face: it had a bit of a smile in it.

'Really. When she's cold, she's dead,' I said.

'Yes, all right,' she said, and took him, and went out.

'One and a half minutes …' I said.

'I know!' she said from outside the door. That's how long she has to put Cuddles into the microwave for. She's got lavender pebbles in her tummy, and if you put her into the microwave for one and a half minutes they warm up, and it's a lovely smell. While she was gone I grabbed the book and started flicking through the pages. There were loads of little marks she'd made in pencil. I didn't get to see all of them. I saw this bit first:

… rather than cleaning them off, he would rub the sticky drops into his chest, convinced that the pleasure invoked by their release was contained somehow within them, and that such pleasure must promote good effects in the body. His sperm was medicinal, revitaliz-ing and cheaper than Vicks VapoRub, which his mother bought in three packs from Bigelows and insisted on rubbing into his torso every night so vigorously he thought his ribs might break.

I tried to remember all the words: *promote*, *sperm*, *invoked*, *medicinal*, *VapoRub*, to ask Jada tomorrow. She always knows what grown-up words means. I got to see some more pencil-marked bits – just little bits of them, flicking through quickly, because I could hear Mommy coming back:

> … the long dark progress towards marriage's moribund centre …
> … his ice skates, blades sharpened like bayonets …
> … 'They've raped that neighbourhood, the Italians …'
> … the architecture of the dead …
> … her ass raised, hovering, almost politely …

It was exciting, like watching grown-ups when they can't see that you're there and they start saying stuff you're not meant to hear. I really wanted to read more but she was nearly in the room. I put it back down on the sheet where she left it just in time.

'Here he – she – is!' she said, holding out Cuddles. 'She's more than warm enough.'

I took Cuddles. 'God,' I said. 'She *is* warm. It's like she's got a fever or something.'

Mommy laughed and shook her head. 'A fever! I don't know. You must have inherited your father's black sense of humour.'

I smiled.

'Are we going to read the rest of the chapter?'

She looked at her watch. 'Well, what with warming up Cuddles and everything I'm not sure I've got time now. I said I'd be back in the hospital by nine.'

'Oh, please, Mommy,' I said.

She reached out and touched my hair, rubbing it. She looked really pleased.

'Well, OK. I'll get Elaine to read you the rest of it. Till the end of the chapter.'

I nodded. When I was younger, like five or whatever, I sometimes did this thing of nodding when I wanted something. Nodding a lot, over and over again. I guess I thought it was cute, like a puppy or something. I did it again now. It made Mommy smile even more.

She went out and called Elaine. I could hear her slow steps on the floor outside. She always sounds like she's got a limp when you hear her, but when you see her, she hasn't. I hoped that Mommy would leave the book on the bed again, but she hadn't, she'd gone outside with it. I could hear Mommy whispering stuff to her. She was telling her about the pencil marks, about not reading me those bits. I guess she was showing Elaine them, too.

But Mommy didn't tell her about Cuddles. I touched her. She was already going cold.

*　*　*

The news that Meg Antopolski has had a fall goes round Redcliffe House like – not exactly wildfire, given that the actual information had to be conveyed from geriatric mouth to geriatric ear, with a fair amount of mishearing and drifting off halfway through sentences – but certainly very quickly. Because the nature of the days is so static, any news is exciting, even bad news. And, in fact, bad news happening to someone else is, as it is in any other human environment, particularly choice: one shouldn't imagine that the inhabitants of an old-age home are any less prone to *schadenfreude* than anywhere else. One perhaps thinks they should be, because of the supposition of wisdom, which is, in the conventional imagination, harnessed to selflessness, but also because it's all going to happen to them very soon: there's no point in luxuriating in a peer's downfall if you're quite so imminently in line for the very same downfall – that very same fall down, in fact, to the same bone-shattering parquet.

But then again, the bad things befalling the inmates of Redcliffe House are the bad things that will befall us all, eventually, so certain residents are entirely happy to indulge in the delicious frisson afforded to them by the realization that their hip bones, however arthritic, are not at present fractured, unlike both of Meg Antopolski's. Pat Cadogan in particular luxuriates in the telling; or so it seems to Violet, as she listens to her in full flow at teatime.

'Both gone; smashed to smithereens. She'll not walk again,' she says, her thick Yorkshire accent painting her prurience over with a patina of common sense. It must be nice, thinks Violet, to possess vowels which make everything you say sound like it must simply be the most natural response.

Mandy puts their plates brusquely down in front of them. Violet has ordered the soup, tomato and basil; Pat a cream cheese and cucumber sandwich, sliced neatly into triangles, with a small handful of crisps on the side. Teatime at Redcliffe House is at five thirty, and the last meal of the day. Like lunch, residents can make their own in their rooms, but Violet, like most, is always too tired this late in the day to cook.

Violet remembers when she first arrived, realizing that teatime did not mean actual tea, with perhaps some cake or scones, at three, but rather a kind of early supper (but never with very much food, designed to facilitate an expected bedtime of nine, and minimize digestive issues); it made her feel like repacking her bags and going back to her flat in Cricklewood, re-rented though it was. So many things go with age, but it was the ones that slipped through the net without notice – or, rather, that were slipped through the net by others who, in their idea of your best interests, tried to make it seem as if nothing had been lost – that induced not just sadness, but rage.

'I mean, to be honest, she never looked where she was going, did she? Meg.' Pat was continuing. 'Always barging about. No one could ever tell that woman anything, let alone to look out. You know what she was like, always thinking she knew best.'

'Did she trip?' Violet knows that Pat will have the details. She chooses to ignore her use of the past tense.

'Slipped getting out of the shower. She had one of those rooms with the sit-down showers. She reached up to hold onto the rod and it was all soapy, wasn't it – her hand slips off, and then ...' Pat makes a small exploding noise, inducing her lips, with their thin coating of cream cheese, to tremble.

'So she was found …'

'Completely starkers. Yes. Got to the panic button but couldn't get to the towel rail.'

'Poor love,' says Violet. Pat raises an eyebrow, as if to say, *that's what happens if you go barging about without looking where you're going your whole life.*

Norma Miller comes into the dining room, unseen by Pat. She makes a face to Violet, indicative of the awfulness of having to eat with Pat. Violet suppresses a smile, which becomes harder when Norma approaches Pat's chair from behind with an invisible dagger, bringing it down on her back over and over again.

'What?' says Pat and turns round.

'Hello, Pat …' says Norma, having recomposed her features. Her hand, however, is still raised above her head in a fist.

'What on earth are you doing?'

Norma looks up at her hand. 'Well. The nurses made an announce-ment: apparently a sexy young man is coming into the house and is looking for a dinner date for tonight. So I said …' she gestures to her raised hand, 'Me! Me! Me!' She shakes her head. 'And then I just couldn't get it down. Arthritis, you know.'

Violet laughs, engendering a sour glance from Pat. She has seen Norma do this before: she is one of those old ladies who likes to draw attention to the absurdity of their sexlessness. Pat is not. With a wink to Violet, Norma moves off towards another table. Violet wishes she could go and eat with her and listen to more of her incongruous raunchiness, even to the point where it might become too much, as she knows it would.

'Where is Meg?' says Violet. 'At the Royal?'

'Yes.' Pat sniffs, and pats her mouth with a napkin. She looks Violet square in the face. 'She won't be coming back.'

Violet blinks, knowing that the way Pat has presented this informa-tion is intended to be demonstrative of her straightforwardness, and, in particular, her straightforwardness in the face of death. It says something about herself, more than about poor Meg: it says, *and of course, when* my *time comes, I shall be ready for it. I shall not lark about.* Violet's hand hesitates, holding her spoon, and Pat glances towards the small red puddle within, daring her to prove her own no-nonsense acceptance of death by carrying on the journey of spoon to mouth.

But Violet does put her soup spoon down and smoothes her hands over her lap, the rucked-up flowers on her dress regaining their equidistance from each other. She wonders about hips: about why so many people of her age break them, and why this so often represents the opening of the morbid door, the first step down to the darkness. Her bones are good, she thinks, a consequence of her mother always insisting that she begin the day with a glass of milk, even when it was difficult to get hold of. But feeling the tips of her hip bones now, tiny, jagged mounds grazing across her palms, it is hard not to gauge their fragility.

She has only ever broken two bones in her life. When she was nine or ten she had a skipping accident and broke her wrist. Like many of her distant recollections, the tones and colours of this memory seem clearer and more real now than events and conversations that happened yesterday: sometimes even than the meandering, shiftless present itself. She remembers the rope tied to a fence post, her sister twirling it faster and faster at the other end, telling her she could skip as fast as her if she tried, and then the touch of the rope, hairy, spidery, tangling on her naked ankle. She remembers the fall, crashing to the cobbles. She remembers the particular cobble, the small brown dome rising up out of the road to meet her right wrist smack in the centre of the bone. She remembers screaming, remembers her father charging out from their backyard, remonstrating with her sister, and the rush of air as he picked her whole body up in one clean movement. His chest was heaving with the effort of running so quickly out of the house, and each expansion of it squeezed her more tightly, but the pain seemed to counteract the pain in her wrist, the good fire chasing out the bad, and she wanted to be squeezed harder. She remembers him saying, *Vi, Vi, where does it hurt,* his normally raucous Cockney voice whispering, full of the knowledge that even though the accident was not his doing it had happened on his watch.

The other time was when she was with Eli, when they were living together in one room above a bakery in Walthamstow just after the war. She broke her nose. It was soon after the war – eighteen months into their marriage – and at first there was no convincing Gwendoline that Eli had not punched her. Gwendoline was by this time living apart from Henry, and had herself sustained a number of black eyes and bloody noses on her way out of the door: thus she had already, in her mid-twenties, become the sort of woman whose most unshakeable convictions are built upon an assumption of the evil of men.

'You may as well tell me,' she said, as they walked through Walthamstow's post-war streets, searching for somewhere that would sell them sugar. Gwendoline wanted to bake a cake, but she had baked two this week already – she had filled out a lot, Violet had noticed, since leaving Henry – and her ration limit was up. 'I know when you're lying.'

'I'm not lying,' said Violet. 'I fell out of bed and hit my face on the chest of drawers. It's Eli's fault, in a way, because our room's so small and I've told him to shut that drawer before, but he stuffs it with his clothes, and it sticks a bit …'

'And he's lazy.'

Violet looked down at her feet, moving over the dust-filled pavement cracks. This was true, as regards shutting drawers, or, indeed, any domestic duty; it was not true in other respects, but it was too difficult – and not worth it on this point – to challenge Gwendoline.

'But why did you fall out of bed? What on earth was he making you do?'

Violet looked up. Gwendoline's mouth had curved along a line poised halfway between prurience and disgust.

Violet wondered what to say. The truth, on this occasion, was nothing. But there had been many times when the violence and strangeness of Eli's desires had made her think she was not just going to fall out of bed, but out of herself. Violet had been a virgin on their wedding night, and nothing Eli had told her about himself had led her

135

to believe otherwise about him, but there was a purpose and resolve to the way he moved sexually which disorientated and at times frightened her. Any sense she may have had of sexual understanding being a joint process – each overcoming the other's nervousness, holding hands as they took their first paddling steps into the sea of love – vanished. Instead, she often felt, in bed, like a spectator, even as she herself was made into spectacle. For example: she had expected that this aspect of their marriage would be conducted in the dark, but Eli insisted on the light always being on. And then he would look at her: but really look, peering, studying, all the time frowning and rapt as if the answer to whatever question burnt away at the centre of his soul lay somewhere in her secreted self.

On one level, Violet relished this – sex allowed her to feel that here at last she was Eli's focus, that she held his gaze at night in a way she could never do during the day. It allowed her to imagine herself as the rarest of diamonds, examined through an eyeglass by this most studious of jewellers. At other times, it simply emphasized the stern, unyielding fact of their separateness. Eli's lovemaking, then, she knew, was not a dialogue; it was entirely rhetorical.

'Well?' said Gwendoline. She had stopped, ostensibly to look inside the window of Percival's Toy Shop, but mainly to emphasize her need to know.

The truth was that Violet had been pregnant for two and a half months, unbeknownst to anyone. She had no one to confide in – her mother by this time was insensible with alcoholism, and Gwendoline herself, with her entrenched hatred of men and deep cynicism about Eli in particular, would only have been negative about the prospect. And not Eli: she had no idea what Eli would think about having a child. It was a period of time when he was squeezing every second between the end of work and bedtime – he had got a job in the sorting office for the local branch of the Royal Mail – to write. He had written a set of short stories, and was two-thirds of the way towards the completion of *Solomon's Testament*, the manuscript of which lay on the floor at the end of the bed, there not being enough room on Eli's tiny desk to accommodate both its towering pages and the fat black

wedge of his Remington typewriter. It sat there, day and night, growing as he wrote, a totem pole of paper, around which they tiptoed in
silent reverence.

Would a child disturb him too much? Or would he be pleased?
Would it help him in some way? She had been convinced, always, that
she would have children, and never would have imagined that the
announcement of the imminent arrival of one could have elicited an
ambiguous response from her husband, but there it was: she had not
been sure how he would take it.

Then a week ago she had woken up in the middle of the night with
a piercing pain in her stomach. One of her many uncertainties about
her condition was whether or not it was all right for them to continue
to make love while she was pregnant, but since she was not the kind of
woman who could withhold her body against her husband's demands
for enigmatic, undisclosed reasons, they had carried on as normal.
And she did not think, on waking and feeling this pain, that it was her
husband's fault. She blamed herself, in fact, for not saying anything;
for having wriggled underneath him during sex in a vain attempt to
move the clutching life out from under his weight; for not knowing
– for never knowing – what the best thing was to do. Her hand went
between her legs and she could feel a mix of liquids. She lifted her
hand to her face, but was too frightened to switch on the light – the
same light that had been left so resolutely on a few hours before.
Quickly and quietly, not wanting to wake her husband, she scrambled
out of bed, trying to get towards the tiny bathroom – shared, on the
landing, with the flat next door: it crossed her fevered mind that she
might be found on the floor by the neighbours – but in her haste, and
in the dark, she fell, her face coming directly into contact with the edge
of a drawer left open by Eli. It was, as she had said to Gwendoline,
always too close, that chest of drawers – dark and huge, it loomed over
their single bed in a way that would have convinced a child that it was
a monster – but there was nowhere else in the room it could go.

She cried out, falling back onto the bed, and then rolling off onto
the floor. Blood seemed to be flowing from all ends of her. As she
toppled she became aware in the dark of a fluttering in front of her

face, and, at first, thought it was something brought on by the blow, like the stars that circled round the skulls of head-injured characters in *The Beano*; but then the light came on, and she saw that it was a page of *Solomon's Testament*, one of a few that had risen up from the pile on the floor following her fall. Some more were strewn about the threadbare carpet, but the majority had remained in a block – the block that she had fallen on directly, and that she could feel still underneath her. At the edge of her vision she could see some of the words – words that Eli had forbidden her from reading while he was writing – but only the unfinished end of a page: *and then turns, on his broad heels, into Times Square, where the ailing hues of a thousand different.* She rolled a foot further, off the main block of paper, and looked round to see, as she had feared, the cover page and numerous other sheaves of Eli's masterpiece-in-waiting streaked with red, some of it still dripping down the white sides like the daring strawberry icing she had once seen on an enormous wedding cake in the pages of *Ladies' Home Journal.* Her mind filled with blood: she didn't know whether the blood on the pages was from her nose or between her legs, and she wondered how that could be found out; wondered, too, how it was that paper could cut, and why it was that, when it did, it produced from fingers virtually no blood. She felt Eli's shoeless steps behind her resonating up from the floorboards: it was him who had turned on the light. He would pick her up in his arms, now, just like her father; he would squeeze her, and, even though the squeezing of her in bed earlier in the night had been bad, this would be a good squeeze, a healing squeeze, like her father's. It would stop the bleeding: his arms would be a tourniquet. Violet waited for the small rush of wind, and then indeed it came, wafting up her nightdress, but she did not come up with it. Instead, Eli crouched down and lifted the block of paper into his arms. He stood over her, naked, clutching the soiled *Solomon's Testament* to his chest like a child: and it was, in fact, in its blend of her blood and his words, his brain and her body, the nearest they would get.

Violet lay there for some small time, listening to him breathing, not wanting to do so herself: wondering if it would have been better if she was dead. Then he knelt down and whispered, in a voice hoarse with relief: 'It's OK …' and put his hand on her hair, stroking it away from her coldly sweating forehead. 'Vi … It's OK.' Violet looked round to him. His face was compassionate – there seemed to be tears in his eyes – but even though she nodded, accepting his touch, she wasn't sure. She wasn't sure what he meant. It was an imprecation that she would continue to wonder about, much later, even into the time when these kind of things were no longer shrouded in mystery and you could read articles in newspapers, for heaven's sake, insisting that sex during pregnancy was fine, and there was only a very small chance of a miscarriage from it – even then she would sometimes wonder whether Eli had been reassuring her, or forgiving her.

* * *

Harvey is in his hotel room looking for the optimum YouTube clip of Linda Ronstadt. This doesn't mean, necessarily, the *best* YouTube clip of Linda Ronstadt: her performance of 'It Doesn't Matter Anymore' on *The Don Kirshner Rock Concert*, for example; her beautiful – if, on the tiny Sony travel speakers he has attached to his Vaio, acoustically challenging – version of 'Blowing Away' at a Lowell George tribute concert in 1979; or her 1969 appearance on *The Johnny Cash Show*, which, though clearly far too early for Harvey's purposes, does distract him for a while, partly because Linda is so astonishingly gorgeous on it, and partly due to this dialogue she has while sitting on stage with Johnny:

JOHNNY: Where you from Linda?
LINDA: I'm from Tucson, Arizona.
JOHNNY: That's wonderful country, I like to go out there and jack-rabbit hunt. Do you ever go rabbit hunting?
LINDA: I never could pull the trigger, you know?
JOHNNY: Well, I didn't like to shoot 'em, I just liked to hunt 'em.
LINDA: It's OK to shoot them.
JOHNNY: If you're hungry, I guess.
LINDA: If you're hungry, right.
JOHNNY: Hey, let's do a song.

139

None of these are right, although the 1979 appearance is close. What Harvey is searching through the YouTube image wall for – as he has done in the past with Brigitte Bardot, and Debbie Harry, and Jane Fonda, and Audrey Hepburn, and Raquel Welch, and, more latterly, Meg Ryan, Joanna Lumley, and Felicity Kendal – even, once, Tessa Wyatt (from the ITV sitcom *Robin's Nest*; used to be married to Tony Blackburn; unbelievably lovely to look at in 1983) but could find no matches for her – is the point at which this beautiful woman's beauty peaked. And by peaked, Harvey isn't thinking so much as maximized, although that's sort of in the mix, as *reached its tipping point*: peak beauty as in peak oil.

With all these women – whose beauty at its height dismantles him; there is a clip of Jane Fonda from a black-and-white movie called *Catfight* that he cannot watch without holding his breath – he wants to find the point at which they lose it. This is not sadistic. He does not want, like some middle-aged male version of the Queen in *Snow White*, to revel in the downfall of their looks. What he wants is to see how far he can push his desire: how far down the line.

So the truer description would be to say that Harvey is looking for the point *just before* Linda Ronstadt became – in his eyes – no longer a great beauty. He is presently convinced that this point is an appearance on *The Leo Sayer Show* that Harvey estimates to be early 1980s, therefore making Linda, who Wikipedia dates as having been born in 1946, mid- to late thirties. In the clip, she undoubtedly still carries herself as an attractive woman, and is quite clearly fancied by Leo Sayer (a fancy, Harvey surmises, not obviously reciprocated by Linda, who can hardly bear to look at the gyrating Isro-haired monkey). They sing 'Tumbling Dice', and, in an eighties BBC kind of way, it's meant to be sexy. All this helps, as Harvey can be influenced in this matter; if other men regard a woman as being sexually attractive, Harvey will take notice.

The point of all this is to train – retrain – his eyes. The novel thing that YouTube has given the voyeuristic billions – the ability to trace change in a person by seeing them in gobbets young and then old – is being used by Harvey to discover if desire is, as some of his therapists have insisted it is, malleable. This is not something he instinctively believes. Desire for Harvey is adamantine. Or, perhaps more precisely, it is fast: too fast to steer. The sight of female beauty makes Harvey a mirror. Beauty reaches his eyes and is returned as desire, at the speed of light.

But despite this Harvey tries. What else can he do? He will not leave Stella because her beauty has passed some imagined optimum, however much his father's ghost may be pouring that poison continually into his ear. He will not read this anxiety as a mandate, forcing him away from his life. So he has bought into the possibility that you *can* consciously shift the coordinates of your own desire: you *can* lead it to where it's best for everybody, to a place where it causes no trouble. And if one way of doing this might be to watch Linda Ronstadt in her late thirties singing with Leo Sayer on YouTube, in the hope of discovering that, although her face no longer makes him hold his breath like it does when she is on the cover of *Rolling Stone* in 1978, he still finds her attractive – then he will watch it and watch it again.

There are other ways in which Harvey uses the internet for self-medication. Pornography, for example: Harvey feels that, for him, it has a use beyond the obvious. It can be incorporated into the same Neuro Linguistic Erotic Reprogramming that might result from extended looking at mid-life clips of iconic female beauties. He feels that there is a political dimension to this. Harvey, still Joan Gold's son, has made internet porn right in his head. Or, at least, while being aware of all the arguments against it, has come up with one in its favour, through remembering that one of the big no-nos of porn is that it fosters the idea that only one type of woman – young, slim, smooth-skinned – is erotically acceptable. Well, Harvey thinks, say what you like about the internet, but it has fucking subverted *that* hegemony. Now women can be erotically objectified whatever state they are in: morbidly obese, mutant, severely disabled and, yes, old. This bar has been raised and raised again, in cyberspace. It has taken apart the whole under-twenty-six, under-120 pounds stranglehold on the erotic that pornography used to insist upon. Harvey has even put this argument to some women, and some of them have even listened.

Beyond the multitude of MILF sites and www.over50.com, however, lies the slightly more troubling area of granny porn. Harvey's argument falters, he knows, in the face of www.oldgoats. com, www.uglyancientsluts.com, www.isitmymom.com. The other thing comes out, the possibility that the finding of the old and the crippled and the deformed erotic is just another form of degradation: that what the masturbating viewer is enjoying is the pure and final humiliation of decay. But *fuck that*, thinks Harvey: he never imagined that you can crack the egg of what men find erotic and find only goodness. Besides, his central project is not intellectual, but self-improving: he thinks that looking at these sites may be a type of familiarization therapy for him, acclimatizing him slowly to the ineluctable fact that women do age. Or, rather: that women who age can still be women you might want to fuck. He knows, obviously, that the idea that female fuckability lessens with age is shameful, but his first instinct is that it is true at least for his libido; what he is hoping for is that watching some of this stuff might lead him to a second instinct. It is a strange world, of course, where watching granny porn can be construed as being in the cause of love.

Trouble is, though, these sites don't do it for him; not at all. He finds them disturbing psychologically, physically and, for all his intellectual sophistry, politically; the images of these ladies – he wants to use the word, ladies; that's what their faces, age conferring its quiet dignity, still seem to inspire, even as the way their bodies are arranged violently rejects the word – invoke in him a seemingly impossible mix, an oil and water mix, of repulsion and compassion. They don't stimulate Harvey's erotic centre; at best, what they produce there is confusion – a kind of start-stop thing, whereby he can feel his libido responding initially to the basic coordinates of the image – it is a woman, she is in lingerie, she is opening her legs – but then halt, uncertain, distraught – when her age becomes, a split-second later, apparent. These sites profoundly disorientate his sexual self; and, for that, he is sometimes grateful, because what he wants most of all is to think that that self can be shifted.

Other times, he just endlessly Googles the problem. Ageing; 'sex and ageing'; age partner anxiety getting older sex psychological; wife skin age time; on and on and on, desperately thinking that the right combination of words will unlock the cure. And what he has discovered is this. There is what he has come to think of as a Great Silence on this issue. That in all the billions of words on the millions of subjects that the web contains, no one has said anything on the subject of what it is like to fear the sight of your loved one growing old. There are sites – many – about how age doesn't matter in love; discussion forums for people whose partners are fifty or sixty years older than they are, full of contributors making the point over and over again that 'age is just a number'. There are sites for older women with much younger men, and vice versa; there are sites where women complain to other women about being dumped for younger women; and there are endless, endless sites about how to make yourself – if you're a woman – look younger, all full of imprecations about how this, of course, is not important to one's inner self but we all want to make the best of ourselves and hey why not and let's do it but do it responsibly and look at this photo of this woman and how much younger she looks now and so therefore everything is now right with her world. But there are no sites that say: *Are you like me? Do you love your wife/husband/partner but cannot bear the sight, or even the thought, of them growing old? Is their beauty so important to you, that for reasons that you don't even understand, the loss of it from your gaze feels terrifying? And do you hate yourself for having these thoughts and these feelings but can't stop them?* That's what Harvey wants, a site that says that. And then: Well, I can help you. Or at least: you are not alone.

He clicks off YouTube, glancing past a video grab of Linda Ronstadt as she is now. He doesn't want any more self-help from the screen, but other temptations rear up from the empty Google box. Harvey can't help himself, the rich colours of the word call to him: the bright blue Gs, the sapling-green l, the red and yellow Os like deliciously over-made-up eyes. He types it in. *Harvey Gold.* Twenty-eight thousand and two hundred entries. The same stuff as always, in the same order as always, starting with the Wikipedia entry for the other one. Harvey doesn't understand why his entry doesn't come up on the search page. Instead, he has to click on this other Harvey Gold, the one who, he knows only too well by now, is an American guitarist, bassist and organist turned keyboardist for the avant-garde rock/New Wave band Tin Huey. I really must download some Tin Huey at some point, Harvey thinks, before clicking on *For other persons named Harvey Gold, see Harvey Gold (disambiguation)*.

His short entry comes up; not, at least, a stub:

Harvey Gold
From Wikipedia, the free encyclopedia
Harvey Gold (born 2 March 1966) is a British-American writer. He is the son of the world-famous novelist Eli Gold. In 1996 he himself wrote a novel; *Blah Blah Blah*, which was neither a commercial nor a critical success. He has ghost-written a number of celebrity autobiographies. His name does not appear in any of these but it has been suggested that the celebrities may include Ian Anderson of Jethro Tull, Jeremy Vine, Chris Noth, Glen Campbell, Simon Cowell, Jocky Wilson, Nicole Richie, Benedict Cumberbatch, and Natascha Kampusch.

Natascha Kampusch? That was a new one. The only biography Harvey has actually ghosted in this list is Chris Noth's (of *Sex and the City*) *Bigger Than Big*: Harvey's main memory of writing it now is the number of times he had to correct himself after writing his subject's name as North, or Moth – but some Wikipedia-editing wag seems to take delight in adding to this list every time he looks at it. He had originally edited all the names out – he had thought about putting some whose autobiographies he *had* written, but knew it was against his contract – but they keep on coming back, different every time, and now he has given up.

He clicks back to Google, and then slides his fingers around the mouse square to bring the cursor to the bookmark Amazon, for the second stop on his daily cyber-round of self-immolation. The page comes up: http://www.amazon.co.uk/exec/obidos/ASIN/0349117462/ref=ed_ra_of_dp/026-8296630-3788113. It is the page for *Blah Blah*

Blah (paperback edition), currently standing at 239,767 in the bestsellers' chart. He scrolls down. Two stars: seven customer reviews. They have shifted the order of these reviews around for some rebranding reason, so the first one is now gangstero (Isle of Man), who says:

** **not a chip off the old block**, 23 Jun 2002

By *gangstero* (Isle of Man, UK) – *See all my reviews*
TOP 1000 REVIEWER
Harvey Gold has got a lot to live up to, and if I hadn't been expecting something at least in the ballpark of *Solomon's Testament* and *Criminality and The Compliance of Women*, then maybe I'd have given it a few more stars. But even without the expectation set up by the Gold name, I'm not sure it ever really works. I just didn't really like any of the characters. Especially the hero (?) and narrator, Jake, a self-obsessed and obnoxious character who, at the end of the day, just wasn't a very pleasant person to spend all that time with. I finished it but only because I never give up books halfway through.

Although he's read gangstero's review a number of times before, it still makes Harvey furious. Like? You didn't *like* him? Do you think you're supposed to *like* Raskolnikov? Humbert Humbert? Portnoy? Solomon Wolff? Odysseus? He thinks these things, trying to absorb his basic hurt that gangstero has not liked Jake, who is, in virtually every respect, him.

His eye glances down the other Amazon reviews, all bad, searching for the comfort of the one good one. It has been removed from the page itself, but he finds a link to it on the right-hand side:

***** **Amazingly funny and well written; could almost be by his dad**, 17 Jan 2003

By *chill*
I don't know what most of the other reviewers on this site are going on about. I loved this book. The characters, especially Jake, are

really well-drawn, and, yes, they push the envelope a bit in terms of behaviour, but that just makes it all the more interesting. The story maybe droops a bit in the last third, but it stays funny and moving all the way through. The bit where Jake and Ella split up made me cry, too.

He wonders if there's a way of getting this one shifted onto the main page. He wonders, too, if he should have added a bit about how clever the end plot twist is, to counteract the thing about it drooping in the last third, which he'd only put in so that no one suspected his authorship. Adding a drop of something negative hadn't caused him as much pain, however, as the reference to his father. He knew, of course, that every single review of his book would begin by name-checking his father – he knew, too, that even good ones (had there been any) would have adopted a the-bar's-been-set-pretty-high-for-this-guy tone – but he would've liked, he really would, just one review, even on Amazon, even written and click-posted, slightly sweatily, by his own hand, not to have mentioned Eli. He knew, however, that since all the others did, he had to.

It's not in stock new, he notices, but there are twenty-three available used, starting at £0.01. Homonculus, adele1, and bookzone_uk are all selling them for that price. Harvey thinks: who the fuck sells a book for £0.01? How the fuck are they making any money? How many books do these people need to sell to break even? New, on Amazon, *Blah Blah Blah* is available at the reduced price of £6.99: so Homonculus needs to sell 699 copies of *Blah Blah Blah* just to buy one new one.

He shakes his head. Unable to resist another, equally masochistic, impulse, he goes back to Google and types in 'Eli Gold'. The screen shows Results 1–10 of 1,947,000. None of them about a different Eli Gold. Above the standard search results are the News results, seven or eight different entries all told, but linking onto hundreds of others, saying 'Doctors uncertain about great novelist's health', 'Literary world fears for Eli Gold', 'Gold's publishers promise reprinted posthumous collected works', 'Eli Gold: the last Great Man?' He ignores them and clicks on the first main entry:

Eli Gold

From Wikipedia, the free encyclopedia

Eli Gold, born Eli Goldblatt (born 25 May 1923 in Troy, New York) is an American novelist, poet, screenplay and short story writer, essayist, conceptual artist and literary critic. His most famous works include his first novel, *Solomon's Testament* (for which he won the Pulitzer Prize), and his dissection of the state of American marriage, *The Compliance of Women*. He is the recipient of the Pulitzer Prize, the Flannery O'Connor Award for Short Fiction, the Frost Medal, the National Book Critics Circle Award, and the Neustadt International Prize for Literature. He is the only person ever to have turned down the Nobel Prize for Literature, offered to him in the mid-eighties. He has had five wives, the fourth of whom, Pauline Gray, committed suicide, apparently as part of a pact with Gold, which he survived. Despite the scandal surrounding this, he is widely considered – particularly since the death of Saul Bellow in 2005 – to be the world's greatest living writer.

Contents [hide]

1. Biography
    1.1 Early life
    1.2 Early career
    1.3 Success
    1.4 Late work
2. Themes and influences
3. Criticism and controversy
    3.1 Plagiarism
    3.2 Refusal to accept Nobel Prize
4. Pauline Gray's suicide
    4.1 Details
    4.2 Scandal
    4.3 Exoneration of Eli Gold
5. List of works
    5.1 Fiction
    5.2 Essays

Biography

Early Life

The eldest son of Ernst August Goldblatt, a Jewish-American immigrant from East Prussia, and Helen Harris, a Catholic of Irish extraction from Boston, Eli Gold was born on 25 May 1923 after the family had settled in Troy, a city in New York state.

Yeah, yeah, he thinks. He clicks back to Google from the Wikipedia entry. Two video thumbnails sit at the top of the search results. One, on Veoh, entitled *Eli G, Gore Vidal, Germaine Greer arguing on Dick Cavett, 1970*, he hasn't seen before. He clicks on it. It is a middle section of the interview. The camera is on Greer and Vidal, listening. Harvey notes that she was gorgeous, then, and considers searching for some other footage in order to run her through the Linda Ronstadt mill. It cuts from her and Vidal – their faces wear the same archly amused expression – to Eli, who sits opposite, next to the central figure of Cavett. The set is very brown. A book sits on a beige table. There is the sound of scattered laughter, some applause. Eli is leaning back in his chair with the face of a man whose last bon mot went well. He is smoking.

His hair is full and dark and his eyes are alive. He is in a black suit and black glasses and white shirt and black tie. He looks like the famous sometimes do: like Elvis in 1956, or Jagger in 1969, or Margaret Thatcher in 1981 – someone who is not just living in the moment, but living in their moment. The moment *is* them. Harvey looks at his father, last viewed white-eyed and screaming in a hospital

148

bed, and realizes that he is seeing, here, his father's apex, his point of peak beauty.

CAVETT: But seriously, Eli – can we address … I mean we have Germaine here. She's been, well, some would say, stringent in her criticisms of your work.

GERMAINE: I called him a misogynist.

CAVETT: That's a strong word.

ELI: You know, Dick … fame is like starlight.

GERMAINE: Oh, here we go.

ELI: It is. Whatever you were first seen as, that's what people still see, years later. And that's what Germaine, or at least, her – as it were – foremothers, decided I was when I first started out and so now there's no going back. It's fixed, from that point way back in time.

CAVETT: You're saying that's not a fair description of you, any more? Misogynist?

GERMAINE: Oh come on. [picking up a copy from the table] This is your new book, right? *The Compliance of Women*?

[Audience laughs]

GERMAINE: Yes, exactly. That says it all, doesn't it? But there's more, inside. [she opens it, starts to read] 'Anyone can fall in love at first sight, thought Willard. It's whether you can stay in love at second sight. Or third sight. Or five hundredth thousand sight, when the sight may not be quite what it was to boot …' [to audience] Don't laugh!

CAVETT: It's not often I let a guest say that!

ELI: That's true for both genders, that sentiment, isn't it Germaine?

GERMAINE: It's a man speaking.

ELI: But not me.

GERMAINE: What's your point?

ELI: Is it a misogynist book? Or is it a book *about* misogyny?

There is some applause, and some sneering from the audience. Greer sits back, shaking her head. Vidal laughs. The camera cuts back to Eli, smiling and blinking slowly. Harvey's email pings. He pauses the screen, glad to stop scratching this over-scratched itch, and clicks onto Mail, some part of him expecting, as always, redemption.

The email is notifying him about a message to his Facebook page. Harvey doesn't look at his Facebook page much any more, after the first flurry, the Facebook frenzy, of a couple of years ago. He clicks on the link: it is from Ron Bunce. He sees Ron's tiny jpg come up by his message – blond, lantern-jawed, the 1950s marine face slightly betrayed by something mental in the staring blue eyes – and then reads what he has written in the message box:

Hi Harv! How goes it! Listen, really pissed to hear about your dad. I'm a fan, too – may have mentioned this – but mainly of the short stories, which are corking. Still he is like, what, 100? And had a fucking good innings, money and fame-wise but more importantly chick-wise. On the bright side – does that mean you're in the Land of the Free? If so, let me know. You know how much I fucking hate Hymie-Town (no disrespect: although you're only like one quarter Yid, yes? So scale the disrespect down three-quarters anyways) but I have to come up to Connecticut anyway to hang out with the cops there who arrested a pedo we apprehended in New Haven, on the run from Toledo, before we put the cunt down for many many years of rasping lubricated-only-by-AIDS-infected-spit anal rape.

I'm coming up next week, so if the old man's still breathing then, let's have a drink and score some stripper pussy. Or I will and you can watch, if you still insist on taking marriage seriously.

Harvey rubs his eyes. He has not heard from Bunce for over five years. They became friendly at college – Bunce was over for one year from Michigan State University doing a course in, of all things, theology. Actually, this may not have seemed so unlikely on a first meeting with Bunce: his absurdly American looks could be interpreted as respectable – he sometimes wore a tie, his hair remained cropped in a rectilinear blond block at a time when most was gummed and backcombed up to look like enormous sea anemones – and, with those he didn't know, he was shy, even to the point of stammering. But in private – and this is where the student Harvey, at the time hardly able to breathe for fear of getting the politics of breathing wrong, fell for him – Bunce was absurdly unrestrained: obscene, expressive, ridiculously sure of himself, able, uniquely at the time, to say whatever he wanted, about whoever he wanted, without first checking the utterance with some internal policing mechanism. In later life, Harvey would come to realize that the reason Bunce so fascinated him was that he combined being funny and clever with illiberality, a combination which in 1986 he would have considered impossible.

But lately they had had no contact. Harvey knew from email round robins that he now worked as an assistant prosecutor for some DA's office in the Detroit area, but that was all. Harvey wasn't sure whether to respond. When younger, he had been a social optimist: happy to meet new people, or re-meet old people, and to shift his personality around to suit the situation. Now, he only really wanted to see the people with whom he could be entirely himself: the thought of preparing a face to meet the faces that he might have to meet exhausted him. Thus, at home, he only really wanted to see Stella, and perhaps one or two other close friends.

But he was not at home. He was, in truth, a little lonely. He was prepared to risk a small amount of awkwardness: or, more precisely, he was prepared to force himself to be a bit more male than he was actually comfortable being, in order to fit in with Bunce's idea of him as his friend.

Bunce,

he wrote,

Great to hear from you. Yeah, a night out would be fun: and a relief. It is pretty grim, the whole Dad dying thing. I'm staying at a place called

the Sangster. Not in a suite, so if we're going to be carting a lorryload
of hookers back, we'll probably have to find somewhere bigger. Give a
call here when you get to Connecticut, or on my cell, 00447835 381449.
cheers
Harvey.

He gets up from the antique reproduction desk tastefully positioned
in an alcove in the room, and wanders over to the window to look out
at the elegant internal courtyard of the Sangster Hotel. The climate
control system, humming at a discreet level just beneath his sonic
notice, protects him from the apparent mugginess of the thickening
sky. He wonders again if he is here for business or pleasure: he wonders
if the Sangster is a *business* hotel. He is almost certain that it would
describe itself as that, among many other things, but not a *pleasure*
hotel, which sounds to Harvey like a euphemism for a live-in brothel.
He wonders how much it would cost – in both dollars and shame – to
move into a pleasure hotel and employ the staff to take away all
the pain.

His phone rings, shaking him out of his thoughts like an alarm
jolting him from deep sleep. The contact glowing on the screen says
Alan Agent. Harvey has often wondered why his agent, who is eight
years younger than him, is called Alan, a name he thought became
extinct in 1971.

'Alan,' he says.

'Harvey! How are you?'

Well … Harvey thinks. *Let's not go into that.*

'I'm OK.'

'How's your dad?'

Alan's tone is sympathetic, but on the edge of efficient. Harvey
knows a long description of his father's medical condition is not actually being asked for. He glances at Eli's frozen, smiling image on his
computer, which has become warped by the video grab. It looks like
a Francis Bacon portrait of Eli. It looks, in fact, like *the* Francis Bacon
portrait of Eli.

'He's … y'know.'

'Yes, of course. I feel for you.'

Back when he still thought of himself as a writer, rather than a ghostwriter, Harvey used to have another agent, called David. He and David were friends, sort of. He used to enjoy his calls. He didn't feel that when David said pleasantries to him not about the matter in hand, it was just stuff that he had to get through before arriving at the matter in hand.

'Thanks, Alan. I appreciate it.'

'Did you get the Lark material?'

'Yeah.'

'Have you had a chance to read it yet?'

'Well – you know, I've got a lot on my plate at the moment ...'

'She's in New York.'

At the words, Harvey looks out of the window, expecting to see it – New York; perhaps expecting to see Lark dancing amongst the skyscrapers. Instead, there is the sedate internal courtyard of the hotel.

'Oh, right ...'

'Her people are taking her round to meet all the American music moneymen now – so that when she releases in the UK, they can coordinate it all simultaneously stateside.'

People? Stateside?

'Anyway, I've had a word with her people, and they're keen. They think – and so do I – that it's fortuitous that you happen to be in the city at the moment. I really think you should read that material I sent you on her, work up the pitch, and then we can set up a meet? OK?'

Meet?

'Well, OK, Alan. But I can't promise anything. You know, with my dad being the way he is and everything ...'

'Where are you staying?'

'Where am I ...? The Sangster.'

'Fuck. Really?'

'Yes. My dad is paying. Well, he might be.'

'That's where *she*'s staying.'

153

'Fuck. Really?'

'That's what I said!'

This is the nearest Alan has ever come to a joke with Harvey.

'Yes …'

'But that's brilliant. That makes everything so easy. Listen, Harvey, I have to go but do have a look at that material. It's only a couple of pages from the PR company …'

'OK, OK.'

'And once you've read it, and had some thoughts, I'll get back on to her people.'

But who are my *people? Alan? Are you?*

'This is great news, Harvey. I'm sure this is the one you're going to get!'

Harvey feels, for a minute, that Alan is going to say 'Laters!' But he doesn't. He just puts the phone down, too busy, clearly, to say goodbye: pleasantries only at the start, never the end.

The one you're going to get? Is that what it's come to? An assumption at the agency that Harvey Gold is the client who never gets the gig? He searches on his email and finds the one Alan sent before. He sees the attachment, a PDF: Lark1resend. He becomes filled with a terrible ennui, the sort of thing that used to hit him sometimes during work, but these days before work, at the thought of work: he may be the only person in history to suffer from ghostwriter's block. With what feels to him like a superhuman effort, he overcomes his disinclination and clicks on Lark1resend. It takes a few seconds to open, the Vaio doing that thing it sometimes does of looking like a very simple operation has caused it to die. In the pause, he wonders if Dizzy's mantras could work for stuff that you don't want as well as stuff you do want. They are designed for curbing desire, or at least preventing it from curdling into depression – *change your must-haves to preferences* – but could it work the other way round? Change your must-nots to oh all right thens? *I do not want to have to fucking pitch for this fucking autobiography of this done-nothing fuckwit, but if I do have to, it's not the end of the world.* Something like that. With a whirr and a click, the PDF opens. Oh no, he thinks. Not her.

154

– Hi, says the blonde woman.

She is maybe twenty years younger than him. He has seen her here before, hanging around the sidewalk outside Mount Sinai. She always carries an enormous shoulder bag, with the strap across her like a sash, and wears a woollen beanie hat, rows of green and purple and orange. Sure enough, she is wearing it now, even though the temperature, when he checked on www.weatheroutthere.com this morning, is going to be in the eighties.

– Hi, he says, although he prickles at the approach. *What does she want?*

– I've seen you here a couple of times, she says, brightly. He nods, but is uncomfortable with the thought that he has been noticed.

– You're not a journalist, are you?

– No. I'm not.

She smiles, like she knew that.

– I guess you're here for the same reason as me, then, huh?

He does not know what to say to this. She is acting like some people do, all familiar, like she has seen his face and decided that they are friends.

– What's that? he says, eventually.

She smiles again. Her teeth are discoloured, not yellow or grey but just not quite white. She raises herself on tippytoes, and moves her face towards his. He backs off, instinctively, but still her mouth is close enough for her to whisper; he feels her breath in his ear.

– *You love Eli Gold.*

She hits every word of the whisper, like there's a full stop between each. She moves back down again and looks at him, wanting to find his eye.

His first instinct is to tell the truth: to say, *No, I hate Eli Gold, and have come to bring him justice.* However, he knows this would be a bad idea. It is time to Lie for the Lord.

– Yes. You're right. I'm his biggest fan.

She opens her eyes wide, and waves her index finger this way and that, like he has sometimes seen black women doing on *Jerry Springer*.

– No way, baby. *That* ... would be me.

He knows how to play along now, so he smiles, which feels strange on his face, like he can feel every little muscle doing it.

– I think not.

She makes a face like she is sucking a lemon.

– Ur ... OK.

She puts both hands into her bag. She takes out a photograph and holds it in his face.

– Do you have one of these?

He squints at it. It is a photograph of her, smiling, in a bathroom – he can see the edge of the toilet behind her – holding an old book, hardback, with some red and black old-style modern-art image on the front. Above the image are the words: *The Teriblo Conspiracy.* Her finger appears around the frame of the photo. Her nail, which has a neat line of dark under the pale crescent, points to the book.

– It's a first edition.

Another photo appears in front of his face. It is the book again, but shot close up. It is held open at the title page, on which there is a scrawl of some sort.

– *Signed.*

She takes the photos away from his face, revealing her face, triumphant. She puts the photos back in her bag.

– Why photographs? Why don't you just carry the book around with you?

Her face screws up.

– Are you mad? What if it got stolen? Or damaged? It's an old book – published in 1961, as I'm sure you know – and just exposure to the air will yellow the pages. I keep it in a humidor.

– A what?

– A humidor. It's a box to store cigars in. I got it on eBay. Keeps them at a constant temperature. And humidity.

– Cigars …

– And books. Obviously. Anything you put in it.

– Why is it in a bathroom?

– The humidor? It's not.

– No. That photograph. You're standing in a bathroom.

– Oh. The light. I don't have much light in my flat. The bathroom has the brightest bulbs.

He nods. He looks up from the photograph to her. He makes a defeated face.

– Well, no, I don't have one of those.

She raises her chin proudly. She rummages in her bag again, getting out some cards. She holds them up in a fan in front of his face. All of them are photographs of The Great Satan, relaxing, smiling, looking jaunty, looking wise.

– All signed. I have others at home.

– Did he sign these for you?

She snorts with laughter. The wings of her nostrils contract into a V-shape. He imagines it raw and red in the base of that V, maybe even eczema-spotted, when she has a cold.

– Of course not. I got them on eBay, too. I've never *met* Eli Gold.

He notices how she always refers to The Great Satan by his full name. Then her eyes, which are a pale green, narrow at him.

– Why? Have you?

He thinks about how to answer this for a second, and then decides to tell the truth. He does not like lying, Lying for the Lord aside. He will not go on to tell her the whole truth, of course, but it is good, when he can, to minimize lying.

– Yes.

It was just the once. He – although none of his wives or children – had been invited to the blessing of his sister's marriage. It was in 1986. Her and The Great Satan had married in secret, but she wanted some kind of event afterwards, so they had a blessing on Martha's Vineyard, in New England. Later, he would come to see this as ironic, because of Chappaquiddick. But at the time, he had been happy enough for her. He knew she was gone from his life – she had been gone for a long time, ever since she moved to New York and went to college – but on that day, it didn't matter. He forgave Eli – he still would call him that then – for taking his sister away from him, because she looked so blissful and beautiful.

He only spoke to him once. The blessing, which was non-denominational, took place in the grounds of a lodge, which Eli owned. Like most of Martha's Vineyard, it overlooked water, not the sea but one of the island's many small internal lakes. In the evening, there was dinner and speeches and dancing in a marquee. His sister and Eli danced the first dance – to 'Just One Of Those Things' – but then Eli, already in his sixties, was too tired, and sat down, not on the top table but right next to him, in a chair vacated by a woman who had spoken no words throughout dinner and who had now stood up to dance.

– Hi, he said.

This was a time when he would still address people before being spoken to. Eli carried on just breathing, looking down at the floor, which was made of wood even though they were in a tent. It was spring: cold enough at night on the Vineyard for the older man's breath to steam in the soft marquee light.

– Hello, said Eli, eventually. He looked up at him. Eli's face, close up, was a crazy mess of lines.

– Are you OK? he said.

– Never better.

– Really?

– Hey. I've been tested. I have the blood pressure of a man half my age. And the *sexual* capability of one a third of it.

– Oh, he said, great. But then felt a little silly responding seriously to this when he looked into Eli's eyes and they were laughing; not telling him that that was a joke, that what he had said was not true: just laughing.

– And, you know what? Even if I have, it's true, felt a little winded by the dance, hey … I'll soon be up again, buoyed, energized – made *young* again by the sight of, and here his eyes turned to face the dance floor, my wife! Look at her, would you? I mean: just *look* at her!

He looked round. Other couples were joining the floor now, but Pauline was still dancing on her own, like she used to when they were kids, except that wild jerky child movement had all gone into grace, a sweet, swinging grace, like a blade of grass on a summer breeze. She was in a trance, brought on by joy and music, and, for a second, the two men just watched and drank in her dancing.

– Already you see, Eli said, I'm reborn. She's like vitamins for me. She's intravenous! He leapt up, indeed like a man half his age, and almost skipped towards her, opening his arms as he went.

– I'm her brother, he said, her twin brother: but he was long gone.

He doesn't tell the blonde woman any of this. He says, into her wide, insecure stare:

– At a reading.

– What? Where? He stopped giving public readings thirty years ago!

He looks at her. She looks a little like she might cry. He does not know what she wants: whether to be told it is a lie, that he was only trying to best her and has never met her idol; or that he has, and that he therefore holds within him whatever great secret she has always assumed such a meeting would unearth.

– Yeah, he says, I'm older than I look.

* * *

We went into the Maternity Unit today in the hospital. I was just looking at the sign in the elevator, and Elaine annoyed me because she saw and she said, 'That means the place where the babies are born' and I said, 'I *know*.' I mean I hadn't been completely sure but I sort of did know.

Anyway, I love babies: they're *so* funny. So I said can we stop and have a look. And Mommy said she wanted to go straight up to Daddy's room, but that it was OK for me and Elaine to go in and join her upstairs later. It's all part of me knowing about what she calls the facts of life. It's a funny phrase, that, isn't it? *The facts of life.* When Mommy says it she means sex and stuff, but it should mean loads of other things as well.

It was nice in the Maternity Unit. There were lots of drawings and photos up on the walls, and even some balloons. It felt really different from Daddy's floor. I guess it would. When we came in there was a nurse at a desk who asked us which mother we were visiting, but then Elaine told her who we were, and even though she didn't know another nurse came over and said that was all right. When we were walking away I heard the first nurse say, 'Are you sure?' and the other one say, 'Yeah, it's the famous writer's daughter' and the first one said, 'So what?' and the other one said, 'Oh I don't know. Anyway, it's an old lady and a little girl. It's not like it's a man come in creeping around.' There were loads of babies in there. There were some being fed milk from boobies, and some from bottles and some who were asleep in cots. Elaine always asked the mommies if it was OK for me to go and look at them. One of them – he was called Alexie – looked really like a little old man. He had a little woolly cap on and when I put my finger in his cot he held onto it really tightly. His face screwed up and I couldn't get my finger out at all. 'Look at him,' said Elaine. 'He's holding on for dear life.'

As we went out we passed somewhere called the Labour Ward. I heard someone screaming in there. It was really frightening.

'What's that?' I said.

'That's someone having a baby,' said Elaine.

'Why are they screaming?' I said.

'Well,' she said, 'because it hurts.'

'Hurts? How?'

Elaine went a bit red and carried on walking.

'Elaine?' I said. I could tell from her being quiet that this was one of those times when she didn't agree with Mommy about me and the facts of life.

'It's a birthing pool,' she said, when I caught up with her, which didn't answer my question at all.

'What's that?'

'It's a little round pool of warm water that ladies sit in when they give birth. It's supposed to be a nice, natural place to do it in.'

I nodded, and looked back. There was another big, horrible scream, and some bad swear words.

'Do they have a dying pool?' I said.

*　*　*

Harvey doesn't believe in God. He knows that God does not exist. He knows it as pure fact, like he knows that stone is hard and that his room does not have a panoramic view of New York City. And yet he carries with him a completely contradictory sense that life is, in fact, patterned. These patterns are godless, but they are patterns. Harvey cannot quite articulate how, intellectually, he contains this contradiction, but in *Spasms of the Soul*, the collection of essays that first moved Eli away from fiction into metaphysics, resuscitating his writing career at the turn of this century, his father says:

> When faced with the regular argument that a divine being could not possibly allow *bad things* – war, cancer, famine – to exist in the world, believers in God should say – instead of going on at length about free will – that God is interested in neither good nor evil but simply in his greatest act, creation. He is an artist. He is, in truth, a post-modern artist: unconcerned by morality or balance or even narrative.

This gets quite close to how Harvey feels about it, although he does not know if, when his father wrote this, he was an atheist. He knows that Eli was very committed to unbelief when he was young, but he did turn, in later life, a bit mystical. There's a fair amount about religion in the later philosophical essays (including the famous pronouncement on Israel – 'The Jews have enough people who dislike them already without actually being in the wrong' – which led to an official condemnation by the Anti-Defamation League) and much

161

mulling over the subject of God, although often in ways which seems to equate Him, more or less, with Eli Gold.

Anyway, it's things like this – like Lark turning out to be a) staying in the same hotel and b) the woman he had seen waiting for her luggage at JFK – that make him sense the acute presence of these patterns. It doesn't bring him any closer to God. He feels that they are malevolent, these patterns, that they contain synchronicities designed to destabilize his small chance of peace – and he knows that for them to *be* malevolent, for him to ascribe to these patterns a moral condition, is to accept an idea of intelligent design to the universe. Which completely fucks up his atheism. He sometimes likes to think, assuming in his head a raffish, Oscar Wilde-like air, *I don't believe in God; but I do believe in the Devil.* He never actually says this out loud, however, which is probably for the best.

He knows Lark is this woman because of the jpg on the front cover of the PR PDF, Alan's attachment Lark1resend. He hadn't been absolutely sure it was her at first – however much not in need of airbrushing, and good lighting, and extra make-up she had been in the airport baggage hall, all this had obviously been added to her publicity picture, distorting her away from his memory – but applying to the picture his usual face-searching skills, zooming in on it until the pixels blurred, had convinced him. The girl with the Woodstock hair, who stabbed Harvey with her beauty at the airport, is Lark.

So Harvey has begun to work on a pitch for her autobiography. It is stupid, he knows, that this is how he has got over his ghostwriter's block. After all, he would have been able to guess, without opening Lark1resend, that Lark would be attractive – either straightforwardly beautiful, or, at the very least, quirkily sexy. Why it makes a difference that he happens to have seen this particular beautiful young woman before he does not know. He does not know why that coincidence impels him on to pitch for writing the story of her short life more than if he had opened the attachment and she'd just been any beautiful young woman.

He has begun work on her autobiography even though thinking about meeting her makes him anxious. Harvey knows he is a beauty addict. He knows he craves beauty like a junkie craves crack. And like a junkie trying to stay clean, he tries therefore to avoid beauty. This is, unfortunately, much harder to do. It's much harder to come off beauty than crack. You don't see crack walking down every street; you don't see it constantly glorified and celebrated on the TV, in magazines, at the cinema, in song; you don't see it on billboards imbued with the message YOU NEED THIS. His method – his way of getting by – is to accept the ambush but not the trap; to fix but not to fixate. His eyes, he knows, will be caught, his life every day hit by a series of little stops, but that aside, he will not dwell there. He will not sit down with beauty – other than Stella's, of course: a beauty he is not so much sitting down with as chasing into tunnels.

So the idea of spending time, of actually being with Lark, disturbs him, but he blanks it out as best he can, thinking that he can always shield himself with a Dizzy-style mantra – *I would love to kiss or lick or fuck Lark – all the things, in fact, that I do not want to do to beautiful paintings – but the fact that I can't is not the end of the world.* Something like that. He can cope with her, he tells himself: it is just work. Work-wise, though, there is very little to go on in the PR PDF. It just talks hazily about Lark in the usual modern myth-making ways: about her *relevance,* her *unique personal style,* her *status as a contemporary artist,* her *quirky and subversive sense of humour,* and her *amazing connection to her audience.* Trying to come up with a genuine angle, a real way into her, is like trying to hold water in his hands. For a start, there is absolutely no indication, in the tiny précis of her life given in the press release, of the thing that, as a biographer, he would normally look for first: struggle. Her parents were themselves in show business – father an actor, mother a model – and she seems to have been groomed, from a very early age, for stardom. He realizes the way forward – the way most likely to get him the job – is simply to rewrite the press release: to give back to the people in control of Lark what they have already decided to hear.

In terms of his own integrity – which he surprises himself by thinking about – Harvey has squared it by deciding that whatever he writes doesn't matter anyway, not once Lark becomes, as she clearly will, famous. Harvey, although not famous, has spent long enough around fame to know that the version of the person it presents is always wrong. Once they are out there, stuff about them gets around that is all just hearsay, but somehow, because it is written down in newspapers, on autocue scripts, on the internet, it becomes truth: not just the half-truths, but the quarter-truths, the eighth-truths, the absolute zero-truths. It all becomes, somehow, gospel: like the Gospels.

So he has started work. He has just written the first words of his pitch – *a lark is a bird; but it can also mean a merry prank, a joke, a thing of laughter and joy* – and is about to highlight/delete when his iPhone rings. He looks at the lit-up micro-window: Stella.

'Hi,' he says.

'Hi, darling,' her voice responds. She sounds alert, upbeat, through the transatlantic crackle. 'How are you?' Her voice modulates easily, with no crunching self-conscious gear change into concern.

'I'm fine. Yeah.' He pauses. 'Working.'

'Really?'

'Yes. Don't sound so surprised …'

'OK, I won't. And Eli?'

'Yes, he's … well, no, not fine. I don't know. I'm not aware of any change. I've still only seem him the once.'

'You haven't been back?'

'Stell … I've only been here a couple of days.'

'Three. Three days.'

'It's still two days here. Two days and a bit. It's still only the morning of the third day, I mean.'

'Yes, I know what you mean … Hi?' A man's voice rumbles in the background. 'Oh, thanks. Brilliant. Yeah, I'll be off in a minute.'

Harvey waits a requisite amount a time, before saying: 'Was that Godard?'

'It was Geoff.'

Stella works – three days a week – as a solicitor, in Maidstone. Her office, which he has been in twice, had been a challenge even for Stella to cosy up, but she has made a good fist of it, bringing in lamps so as to negate the flickering downlight, placing a furry rug under her desk, changing the regulation blinds for an old pair of red curtains. He is always amazed at how much her surroundings matter to her.

'Was he trying it on?'

'No, he wants to show me this new people-finding software we've had put in to the system.'

'People-finding?'

'Yeah, it's linked to government databases. Allows you to access the whereabouts of anyone, anywhere. Anyone who might know something about one of our cases …'

'I see. And does he perhaps want to show you this software, while leaning over you – looking down your office blouse? I don't know why I don't come in and punch Mr Goddard's lights out.'

She laughs. 'Yeah, yeah. Stop pretending.'

'I'm not pretending.'

'Yes, you are. You love it, Harvey. You love it if any man burns any kind of tiny candle for me. Makes you feel all puffed up and proud.'

'Like a peacock.'

'Exactly. Even if that man is a fifty-eight-year-old conveyancing specialist with psoriasis.' Harvey laughs: but then she continues: 'It helps you believe that I may not be such a dried-up old skank, after all.'

Harvey doesn't reply. 'How's Jamie?' he says, after a while.

'He's fine. Good,' replies Stella. 'I'm going to have a chat with Mrs Irshad when I pick him up – he seemed a bit worried this morning about his eight and his nine times tables – but otherwise – you know how it is …'

Harvey does. Jamie goes to Blue Hill, a special school in Rochester. It is a brilliant school, specifically designed for children with dyslexia, dyspraxia and what the brochure describes as 'specific learning and language difficulties' – which would include Asperger's. He had gone to various schools in London before, and never settled: at Blue Hill, he seems to be approaching something like happiness.

Stella's mention of Jamie's multiplication problem nags at Harvey, reminding him of his secret issue with his son's Asperger's. Jamie is not a movie Asperger's kid. He is, as far as his condition will allow him to be, sweet-natured, but he has no special talent: he cannot sketch St Paul's Cathedral in charcoal from one viewing, he cannot in a flash tell you what day of the week 21 May 3080 is, cannot look at a confectionery jar and instantly guess how many pear drops are in there, and cannot go into a casino and win millions on blackjack because of a computer-like card-counting ability. Although Harvey loves his son, he can't help feeling that this is at some level unfair: that the sheer slog that he and Stella have had to go through to deal with Jamie's condition – the lack of speech for years, the shutting down for no apparent reason, the tantrums, the obsessive itemization of every Pokémon card ever made – should have some kind of payback. And underneath this secret issue, another one, even more secret: a notion that Jamie's condition represents a trickle-down degradation of Eli's genius. That he, Harvey, with all his neuroses and anxieties and depression, has inherited only the backside of genius: and that he has passed on this shredded gene to his son in the form of Asperger's, this particular form of Asperger's, all idiot and no savant.

'When are you seeing him again?' says Stella.

'Who?' says Harvey, thinking she means their son, and wondering if this is the beginning of some kind of pressure to come home.

'Who do you think?'

'Eli? Oh, I don't know.'

'You don't know?'

'Well … the whole visiting Dad thing is kind of regimented – lots of people wanting to get in there – and Freda, she seems to be in control of it all, and you know I've always had a weird relationship with her.'

'So?'

'Well, she hasn't told me when I can come again.'

'Harvey. You're his son. The only one of his adult children who's bothered to turn up to visit him on his deathbed. You don't have to get an OK from his fourth –'

'Fifth.'

'Fifth wife, in order to get to his hospital bed.' There is a beat. 'Five? Is it really five?'

'Yes.'

'Who am I forgetting?'

Harvey, glad of the small respite from the scratchy subject of his access to Eli, puts out his fingers for counting.

'Violet. That was his first one. Then Isabelle, the French film star.'

'Mother of Simone and Jules. Who didn't bother to come.'

'They didn't not bother. They fell out with Dad. Years ago.'

'At least they had enough contact to fall out with him.'

'Yes, anyway: then, there's Mum. Then the one we don't really talk about ...'

'Pauline Gray.'

'Shh. For us Golds that's like saying Voldemort.'

'Us Golds. Of course.'

'Then Freda. Obviously.'

'So which one did I forget? Violet, I think. The first one. Do we know anything about her?'

'No. I've never heard Dad talk about her.'

'So that's *two* wives us Golds don't talk about. Is she still alive?'

'No idea. Maybe it's in one of the biographies? I should read one.'

He hears a tsk sound over the line. He knows it portends his wife getting back down to business, having enough with distraction. 'Anyway, Harvey, you must get over there. Your father's very ill. He might die at any moment.'

'Stella, Freda's his wife ...'

'And I'm *your* wife. Who let you go to America at a really difficult and inconvenient time.'

'Oh, come on: don't make me feel guilty about going to see my dying dad.'

'So go and see your dying dad!!'

Harvey pauses: then starts to laugh. After a beat, he can hear Stella joining in.

'Sorry … sorry, darling … I shouldn't have shouted …' she says, through her laughter. 'And you told me you were working, which is really great, so …'

'No,' he says, 'you're right. It's idiotic.' He is relieved; she has let him off, for the moment, the anxiety about Lark. 'I'm gonna go for a run, and then go right there.'

'Why don't you run there?'

'What?'

'Well, it's only about – what is it – about five blocks away? You could run along the park.'

Harvey tosses this around in his mind. 'But then I'll be in my running gear. And all sweaty.'

'So?'

'Well …' he feels a hot shoot of embarrassment, the prescience of having got something wrong: but this is not painful. Harvey likes the transformation of embarrassing moments into anecdotes for Stella, presenting himself as a naïf, an unfortunate, who, hoping only for the best, seems cursed with wondering into social discomfort – these stories make her laugh, and sometimes hug him. He wonders, occasionally, if perhaps he seeks out embarrassment – for he seems to find himself confronted with the sensation often – as material to make his wife look upon him fondly.

'I went quite smart last time.'

She doesn't laugh, but he can hear the smile. 'Did you? Oh, darling, that's so sweet.' Another pause. 'How smart?'

'A jacket.'

'Not a tie? Your suit?'

'No.'

'Thank Christ for that. If he'd have woken up he'd have thought it was his funeral.'

Harvey laughs at this joke, although it is not so ridiculous an idea. He hates wearing suits, and has only brought one for this trip: a black one.

'Sorry, Harvey, I can hear my other phone ringing. Listen, darling: seriously. It doesn't matter what you wear. It doesn't matter if you're

168

a bit sweaty. Go and see your dad. If it was me, I'd be running there every day. Like the wind.'

Harvey looks out the window once more. He wishes he did have the view he always covets, because that might show him the way: the way across Central Park, to his father.

'I love you, Stella.' It is not difficult to say: it is not as ash in his mouth.

'I love you too, darling.' And she is gone.

✴   ✴   ✴

Valerie, Violet's sister, stands in her room at Redcliffe House looking out of the window. She has been standing there for the last fifteen minutes, talking. Violet has not heard everything she has said, and certainly would not have been able to remember it all anyway: but she has noticed the standing. Valerie is only three years younger than her, but never misses an opportunity to make clear to Violet her greater level of health and fortitude. She has always found ways of making clear to Violet how much better her life is than her sister's – particularly since Eli became famous. Eli was not long in staying with Violet after the hail of praise that rained down on him following the publication of *Solomon's Testament*, propelling him through the high windows of celebrity and genius, but still, it was Violet who was with him when he was writing it, Violet who could say (although she almost never did), *my ex-husband Eli Gold* and people would instantly be impressed; therefore it was Violet who had made the better match, trumping at a stroke Valerie's certainty that that would always be her, with her marriage to Michael, a chartered surveyor from Bexley Heath. Deeply, without ever admitting it to herself, Valerie felt that there was something unfair – something not in the rules – about Violet bringing into play (however unwittingly) *fame*: one's husband's career, money, houses, children, number and intensity of close personal friendships with local dignitaries – these were the categories on which she could rank their status. Fame, or an association with it, blew all these away: it didn't belong in her intricate calibrations of social standing, but made those calibrations seem faintly ridiculous, and for this Valerie could never forgive her sister.

So here she was – after years of demonstratively mentioning to Violet Michael's progress to partnership, and the success at various redbrick universities of her two sons, Jeremy and David, and the whole family's movement upwards to bigger and better houses in Bushey, and many other signifiers of small-world success – here she was, deliberately standing in Violet's room for fifteen minutes. Michael was dead, of what Violet always imagined was a blessed heart attack four years ago; the sons were middle-aged and married with their own children, who Valerie did often mention, Violet being childless, but not that often, seeing as Jeremy would not let her see her grandchildren and David had moved to Australia; the biggest house, the one she and Michael had continued to live in long after their children had left, had been sold, replaced by a one-bedroom flat in Stanmore. Valerie had one card left to play and she played it with a firm and extremely well-moisturized hand: her relative youth. She was saying a lot of things, but, really, Violet knew she was only saying one thing, over and over: *You'd have probably had to sit down by now.*

'... I mean surely it could be a little bigger. And the view! That tree is just in the way. Couldn't they get the council to trim the branches?'

Violet nodded, understanding that this was just a sub-section of Valerie's triumphalism, meaning *of course I don't have to live in an old-age home.* The problem with Valerie, Violet found, was not so much her pettiness, or passive aggression, but her transparency. Her motivation shone so clearly through every action that it was all Violet could do sometimes not to shout 'I know! I know why you're saying this! I get it!'

But then, so much of the world seemed obvious after Eli. Valerie didn't like to mention Eli at all (when telephoning Redcliffe House, she would always make a point of asking for her sister by the name they once shared, Evans – *Hello there: can I speak to Violet Evans, please* – even though, since Violet called herself Gold, and was registered as such, this would always lead to confusion); but when forced to, she would talk about Violet's experience with him as if it had been a form of abuse. But what exactly, Violet wondered, was the nature of the abuse? It wasn't physical, not in the straightforward sense: he never hit her. Nor was it sexual, exactly – she was an adult, and she consented to everything, and even, sometimes, enjoyed it. Psychological, then. Well, yes, she was unhappy much of the time; he neglected her, first for his work and later for other women; she had a miscarriage. But this was so par for the course for women of her generation, before feminism forced both genders to recast marital behaviour previously thought of as standard as unacceptable.

It was complexity: that was the abuse. Being with Eli was like being hit over and over again with complexity, more dizzying and disorientating to the young Violet than a cosh. *A simple soul* – that was how, through the misty glasses of self-pity, she sometimes saw her pre-Eli self. She had believed the world was as it was. Even as the bombs rained down on London, and in Wannsee Reinhard Heydrich was outlining how a half-Aryan might be exempt from extermination unless he were possessed of a 'racially especially undesirable appearance that marks him outwardly as a Jew', still, the young Violet had no reason to doubt that the universe was essentially as suggested by the slogan 'A Nice Hot Bovril Is Better Than A Nasty Cold'.

Eli, though, presented her with a version of the world in which everything she knew was wrong. At first that was exciting: Eli seemed to be able to display all sorts of secret, new knowledge. Not just about things of which she knew nothing, but in combinations that she had not thought possible. He was a Jew and a Catholic; a God-hater who could quote the Gospels by heart; he liked classical music and jazz – Louis Armstrong and Mahler; he loved all sorts of books, philosophy and fiction and poetry, and if there was one thing Violet had learnt from her time at school it was that if a man loved books he wasn't that bothered about girls, but the opposite was true of Eli (he also really liked and knew about sport, or sports as he called it, something else which didn't fit with liking books).

Physically, too, he confounded her. His nose was too long and more bulbous at the end than it should be; the skin on his cheeks was over-crowded with hair follicles, each one so marked and ringed sometimes when he fell asleep – as he did often, in the middle of the day, stretched out on the floor even though the bed was just there – she would start counting them; the lobes on his ears were long and hanging, like those of a much older man – but taken together his features seemed to work. Or, rather: Eli's absurdly heightened sense of self, his sheer power of identity, seemed to manage his essentially unharmonious features into a taken-for-granted version of male beauty. His face challenged you to find it unattractive.

And he was thin enough for her to imagine, if it was anyone else, that given the wrong sort of contact he might snap like tinder, but there was something sinewy and contained about his skeletal frame, as if it held much greater power than his weight would suggest. But then he ate like a horse, as her mother said on one of the few occasions that she fed him. Violet remembers her mother saying it, and thinking immediately that Eli would hate the cliché. Cliché was a word that Eli had taught her. He didn't take her that far into his intellectual lair, but this much he had uncompromisingly imparted: cliché covered the waterfront of everything he despised. It had taken her a while to understand what the word actually meant – to understand that it covered more than just proverbs, more than just *a stitch in time saves nine*; and that although it was a French word, it was English, too – but by the time of this meal she knew, if only by the hot pinch of anxiety that accompanied her mother's words.

As it was, he only smiled between mouthfuls and said, 'No, Doris: I eat like a ravenous dog.' Her mum pursed her lips a little and stirred her stew with her fork, uncertain about being contradicted, but perceptive enough to know that his analogy was the more correct: put food down in front of Eli, and it would be gone so quickly, Violet sometimes wondered if it were not a magic trick. Sometimes, she would put plates down for the two of them, go back for the salt and pepper, and by the time she returned he had finished. Another contradiction – a thin man who ate like a fat one; a cerebral man, but a man of great appetite.

Once, late at night in bed, Violet brought up the subject of living with her parents. She had imagined that after their marriage they might live for a small time in the house in which she had grown up, as most of her friends had done, but Eli had insisted on finding somewhere independent for them, even if all they could afford was a room the size of two cupboards suffused with the thick smell of dough. It was a speech she had carefully rehearsed: she knew Eli had wanted them to be together, by themselves, but – seeing as, so far, his work at the post office and her job in the typing pool at International Shipbrokers Ltd wasn't putting enough in the bank for them to rent somewhere better – maybe they should just move back in with her mum and dad? Just for a little while? It would mean – and this, she thought, was her trump card – that maybe Eli wouldn't have to work so hard at his job and would have more time to write.

Eli just carried on reading – some book by some American writer whose recent acclaim she knew just made him angry – and said, without looking up: 'I couldn't take the chewing, Birdy.'

'It's not that bad,' Violet said, pleased at least that he had been jokey about it, and pleased in a deeper way that he had noticed this idiosyncrasy of her mother's.

'Anything is bad that involves the mouth which goes on that long. Apart from …'

She leant over and put her hand over his lips. His eyes, locked with hers, laughed. It was true enough. Her mother had a habit of chewing every morsel of food for an inordinately long time.

'It's because when she grew up they didn't have much food. Even less than we have now. So that's what Nana – that's what her mum told her to do.'

She took her hand off, having felt his lips curve upwards on the soft skin of her palm. It was a mild night: her hands and feet were not cold in bed like they sometimes were. They had a coal fire in the room, but Eli could never be bothered to light it.

'Hmm … OK,' he said, a word she had found herself using recently, even though Gwendoline would chastise her for trying to sound American. 'But did Nana take into account the fact that your mother would one day wear *dentures*? What the fuck do Mom's false teeth

173

look like? Don't tell me she leaves them in a glass of water at night – to clean the food off those gnashers she'd need some battery acid. Or maybe a machine gun.'

Violet laughed, a bit louder than she might have done, to cover up feeling guilty: there was something sacrilegious about the idea of joking like this – this *violently* – about her parents.

'I could probably still get one from my old unit. A gun. What do you think?' The book fell out of his hands and off the bed, as he mimed, with surprising grace and certainty, holding an invisible M917 Browning and spraying a round of bullets towards the offensive dentures. 'Rat-a-tat-tat-tat-tat. Rat-a-tat-tat-tat!!'

'Shh,' she said, worried that he might wake the neighbours. The walls of the house were very thin: Mrs Black from the bedsit below had already knocked on their door three times to complain about the sound of Eli typing at all hours, visits which Violet had kept from her husband, partly so as not to disturb him, but also because he might respond to the news by going downstairs and shouting at the old woman about being bourgeois, whatever that meant.

He sat back in bed and placed his hand on her breast. She could feel the hair on his knuckles brushing her other one. She knew this meant that the talk of moving back in with her family was over.

'What about your parents?' she said, with just an edge of resentment.

'What?'

'Your parents. We never talk about them.'

He took his hand off. 'That's because they're cunts.'

Violet winced: the word was like a little lash.

'You shouldn't talk about them like that.'

'Why not? They're my parents. And you've never met them. You wouldn't know if they were cunts or not.'

'Stop saying that.'

'My father in particular. He is a terrible cunt. He used to hit me with his belt. And he's a fat cunt, too, always has been, so it's a long belt, which he would swing high above his fat head before bringing it down with all his fat weight on my tiny ass.' He shifted his pillow matter-of-factly, plumping it so that he could sit back comfortably against the wall. Violet felt him settling into his subject. 'That's when I was lucky enough to get it on the ass, as opposed to around the face.'

She turned round and put her hand on his shoulder.

'That's terrible, love.' *Love* felt slightly wrong in this context: it often did when she said it to Eli, not just the verb but also the noun.

'And here's the kicker. He doesn't even drink.'

'Like you.'

'Like me.'

She had noticed this. All the men she knew before Eli drank. All the men she knew before Eli met and lived and gave of themselves in the pub: it was their place. It was one of the many confusions for her about their marriage, one of the many *practical* confusions: what were they supposed to do in the evening if they were not to go to the pub? Many evenings Eli would just stay in and write, and as she did not want to go to the pub by herself, more often than not she would end up spending all night staring at the unlit fireplace.

'So he didn't even have that excuse: he's just a pure sadist. Or he just really hated me.'

'Eli, I'm sure that's not true.'

He looked at her, and in his eyes there was contempt – another word that she would not have used before Eli, but she knew it now.

'How can you be sure of that?' She didn't answer. 'Come on, Birdy, I'd really like to know? How can you be sure?'

'Because …'

'He's my father? My dad? My old man? My *parent*?'

Violet didn't answer. She felt the pressure of water pooling behind her eyes.

'He cheats on my mother all the time, do you know that?' Eli continued, picking up a cigarette packet – Benson and Hedges: he had given up Newports after the war – by the side of the bed.

'Cheats?'

'Unfaithful, Birdy. He fucks other women.'

She had known what it meant: had just been repeating the word. 'How do you know?'

175

His lighter flashed bright in the room, dark except for Eli's tiny table lamp on top of the chest of drawers. The inside of its orange flower-patterned shade was burnt in three places, three brown-black blobs backlit by the 40-watt bulb. The tip of the cigarette glowed red. Violet saw a small cloud swirl from his mouth before Eli sucked it into his lungs, sharp and fast, the same way he consumed food.

'He boasts about it.'

'To his son?'

Eli nodded. 'And to his wife.'

There was a silence. Eli reached up, over the drawer that a few months earlier had killed Violet's baby, and clicked the light off. It was always up to him when the light went off in their room. Most nights, Violet went to sleep straight away. It was like the switch on the light was a switch on her that Eli controlled, on to look at her naked form, off when he was finished. But this time she stayed awake, aware that, as usual, he did not go straight to sleep, but smoked for a while longer in the dark. She knew that sleep was difficult for him, which was another new complexity; before Eli, she had never heard of the word *insomnia*, having not imagined sleep to be a condition any more difficult to achieve than waking.

She wondered about what Eli had told her. She wondered why, despite these good reasons to hate, she still felt so uncomfortable with his hatred. She had been brought up with love. Her mother and father existed as concrete blocks of herself. To imagine them so negatively – to imagine them as available for critical analysis of any kind – was to make of one's parents separate beings, and this felt like untangling the genetic code itself.

But also she wondered if it were true. She had realized this about Eli – that he never quite told the truth. It was the most complicated of his contradictions. He was obsessed with the truth – he would go on and on about how all the writers who everyone else thought were great didn't tell the truth: the truth about men, and the truth about life, and this was the big thing that Eli Gold's novels, when they were published, were going to do. And yet, whenever he told a story about something that had happened to the two of them – either back to her, or on the rare occasions where they were in company – the bare facts were always changed and embellished. Violet always told people stuff unvarnished – it never occurred to her to add bits and pieces to make life more interesting. Eli didn't just add bits and pieces: he pushed events around, he made people say things they hadn't said, he brought in people who weren't there – sometimes he would add a whole new ending, changing the entire point of the story. His motive in those cases was clear: to make mundane stories funnier or more entertaining. But here – with this thing about his father – why would anyone do that? Change facts to make things more horrible, more awful than the truth? She felt, obscurely, that Eli would want to do that; but she wouldn't have been able to articulate why.

'And your mother,' she said eventually, the darkness making her feel more exposed, drawing attention to her speech, 'why is she a …?'

'Cunt?'

'Yes.'

Eli drew the sheet over himself, and turned away. She reached out and stroked his back for a few seconds, knowing for sure at least this about her husband, that he liked to be touched. Between his shoulder blades the skin was taut and furred.

'For not leaving him,' he said, quietly.

Violet's stomach rumbles, shaking her from her reverie. The smell of food, or, rather, of cooking – of boiling and fat and elephantine pans – is a constant in Redcliffe House, but normally the body only tunes into it at mealtimes. The noise of her guts is loud enough to make Valerie, proudly unpossessed of a hearing aid, turn. Violet blushes, feeling the heat on her face. She wonders how her skin looks, how the blush will colour around the topology of her face, whether the red will go orange and pink in the whorls on her cheeks. She wonders how it is that she still blushes over this, or any, exhibition of her bodily function, here in this world where involuntary rumbling and farting and pissing and shitting are part of the texture of everyday life. She wonders how strange it is that as the body fails it shows itself more, turning itself inside out and amplifying all its doings. One thing she knows, however, is that all this wondering – it didn't happen before Eli.

∗   ∗   ∗

Harvey hates running. He doesn't understand what people who like running say about running. People who like running say: 'It's hard at first, but then you really get into it.' *No*, he thinks, as he watches yet another jogger power effortlessly past him on the running track surrounding Central Park's Jacqueline Kennedy Onassis Reservoir, *quite the opposite*. It's OK for about twenty-five seconds when you start, and then it becomes an awful, sweat-soaked miasma of pain, and the more you run, the worse it gets. People who like running say: 'It's meditative: I get to think about so many things while I run.' Harvey thinks about one thing: running. How much it hurts, and how soon it's going to stop.

Nonetheless, he runs. He runs to lose weight – although that would not seem to be working, seeing as his weight has remained on a steady upward trajectory since 1994 – and he runs to pay lip service to the idea of keeping fit, but, much more, he runs because it is the only thing that really works for depression. There is a terrible, typical irony in this, in that the major symptom of depression is stasis: depression means exactly that, to be pressed down, and therefore not to want to move; to sit or lie with that weight, in bed, or on a chair, or on the floor. It's a struggle every time to put on his baggy tracksuit bottoms, but running's capability of combating depression is – just – worth the depression induced by the idea of running.

Harvey has come to this conclusion after many years of combining therapy with antidepressants. He has tried every antidepressant on the market. Of the standard SSRIs, Prozac made him woozy and insomniac; Paroxetine made him more anxious than before; Citalopram had no effect; Zoloft made him fat. All of them made him anorgasmic. All those teenage years of wishing there was something you could take to hold off orgasm, but it turns out, he would think during the long drawn-out Stella-obviously-bored-and-wishing-it-was-over pumping, it's hell: who wants to be endlessly tickled once someone has amputated your ability to laugh? The tricy-clics were worse: Amitriptyline he'd taken when younger as a sleep-ing pill, and thus had built up an immunity to, and Imipramine – well – Imipramine just appeared to melt his brain. He would be sitting at his computer and wondering if the radiation from the screen had somehow got inside his head it was so hot. He'd tried a number of newer drugs, including Venlafaxine, an SNRI (Harvey often wondered when they were going to produce a category of anti-depressants called INRI; or perhaps RNLI), which, just out of curios-ity – and maybe out of a desire to make it seem like the taking of these drugs was recreational – he used to snort. He would take the two tiny plastic domes apart, like two halves of a Russian doll, spread the powder into a line, and sniff it up through a rolled-up tenner. This had the effect neither of making it more fun, nor of helping it to work. The last one he remembers taking was Buspirin, a cocktail antidepressant – part anxiolytic, part serotonin reuptake inhibitor – which may have been good, but by then he'd taken so many it was impossible to tell: he had no memory of what his default chemical balance was any more.

He stopped taking them, partly because he realized that they did fuck all and partly because he discovered, following one particular incident, that coming off them is worse than coming off crystal meth. He had been in Hong Kong, pitching for Jackie Chan's autobiography, when his hotel room was broken into, and all his belongings, includ-ing his toiletries, stolen. He had three days left before his flight home, and no means of getting hold of a new packet of Buspar or Zoloft or whatever it was. He spent the three days – one of which was supposed to be in the company of Jackie – in his bare hotel room, unsleeping, throwing up, shaking violently and convinced that a colony of ants were burrowing a series of tunnels into his bones. He never got the Jackie Chan gig.

So now he runs. And often, five minutes into a run, he can feel the moment when depression lifts – or, rather, when it *bursts*. It's a painful release, similar to that when dabbing Bonjela on his mouth ulcers, like the pain has to maximize before it will go away. He feels the depression in combination, all physical symptoms – hot flushes, pins and needles, anxiety shoots in the stomach – all coming together as one, like when dying people revive for one last time before they vanish. He didn't always know that running could temporarily relieve depression; he remembers sitting in a Jacuzzi at his local gym after twenty-five minutes on the treadmill and thinking, almost in tears, *God, Paroxetine really works.*

Another runner, a woman, goes past him along the line of the water. Harvey wonders about trying to catch up with her to see what she looks like. Sometimes he does this while running, justifying it to himself as physically advantageous, a kind of fitness-aiding, less precarious version of his need to get in front of female pedestrians when in his car. *Use her unknown beauty as a pacemaker*, he tells himself, and starts to move faster, but it turns out that sexual curiosity, even though it may seem to Harvey the most powerful force in the world, isn't quite enough to take him up to the requisite speed. As her back disappears into the distance, the sun begins to punch its way through the clouds, and a shaft of light moves across the reservoir, making the rhythm of her feet seem in tune with nature.

Harvey takes his iPhone out of the front pocket of his hooded top, and slides a sweaty thumb across the screen in search of the iPod function. He is wearing Bose Noise-Reducing headphones, and has created a new playlist specifically for this run. Harvey cannot just run: he needs to have a number of things in place, things that make it bearable, and the most important is music. He sometimes spends so long creating playlists in order to carry him through his runs that there is no longer any time left to run. When he got his first iPod, he thought: this is the answer, the way through to fitness (music had always been his preferred palliative to the pain of running, but occasional attempts to jog with CD Walkmans and battery-powered radios had proved abortive). And for a while it was: he must have run more often in the first six months after Apple introduced the iPod than at any other time in his life. But then he begun to realize that digital music, so far from improving his listening experience, was destroying it. The thing about pleasure, Harvey has come to realize, after much time not realizing this, is that it has to be rationed or it becomes meaningless. When he was young, music was important to him in ways he knows it will never be again, not simply because only the young truly engage, in an identity franking way, with music, but also because in order to listen to a favourite track, he had to go to his record collection, select the album by hand, clean the vinyl, and position the needle precisely over the correct circular groove. This meant that Harvey – lazy even when young, even before laziness transmuted into the stasis of depression – never did that thing that some of his friends would of listening to the same track over and over again. But it wasn't just laziness. When he found a song that raised the goose pimples on his flesh – an important sign: Harvey has always looked to his body for evidence of what he does and doesn't like – he would decide immediately not to play it again for some time, because he knew that the song's power would have a half-life; that there would come a moment where he would fall out of love with the song, just as he would fall out of love with the various women he attached himself to, and that that moment needed to be deferred as long as possible.

Digital music had screwed all that up. Now, songs that he loves – songs that he thought he might always love, that might keep the goose pimples coming indefinitely – bore him. He does still love these songs, but, because of the ease of access to them which iTunes has provided, he loves them like he still loved the women he continued to be with after the passion had gone. He loves them but the love is underpinned not by desire but nostalgia: by the *memory* of what they once did to him. He loves them but they do not move him any more: they raise no goose pimples on his flesh. Sometimes he looks for them on his arms, but they never come, and he knows, anyway, that goose pimples are something you feel and then look at, never the other way round. One song – Radiohead's 'Fake Plastic Trees' – is actually now undergoing the painful process of goose-pimple death. During the refrain at the end – Thom Yorke plaintively repeating, over and over, 'If I could be who you wanted …' Harvey can almost feel them coming – there is still the slightest stiffening of the hairs on at least one arm – but it's fleeting, comparable to the movement that might be caused by a light breeze. Once, the ending of 'Fake Plastic Trees' could make his arms feel like they were made to brush horses.

It doesn't make the playlist for this run, which Harvey has put together – even writing the songs down, in his gold leather notebook – with one eye to stiffening his resolve in regards to turning up at his father's deathbed unsanctioned by Freda:

'Father, Son', Peter Gabriel
'Someday Never Comes', Creedence Clearwater Revival
'A Little Soul', Pulp
'Everyone Says Hi', David Bowie
'Son of Hickory Holler's Tramp', O. C. Smith
'Never Went To Church', The Streets
'I am Woman', Helen Reddy
'Not Pretty Enough', Kasey Chambers
'Let Me Be Your Yoko Ono', Bare Naked Ladies

The first five songs are the ones he can find in his library that are actually about fathers and sons. 'Son of Hickory Holler's Tramp', which is about a mother who turns to prostitution in order to feed her fourteen children following her husband's desertion, is not strictly relevant, but Harvey was reckoning on the run taking at least half an hour, and he had to fill up the playlist somehow. Thinking laterally, he then moved away from the parental idea and towards trying to find something self-bolstering, something that would take away the anxiety – not the big anxiety, not his umbrella anxiety, but the local anxiety about feeling that he isn't really allowed to just turn up at the hospital. The sort of song that had come to mind was one of those big reach-for-the-skies ballads that *X Factor* and *American Idol* hopefuls are so keen on – singing out, they imagine, their stellar destiny: all those songs with the word *hero* in them, 'Search For The Hero Inside Yourself', or 'A Hero Lies In You', or 'Holding Out For A Fucking Hero'. However, he doesn't like these songs, which means that, rather than searching for the hero inside himself, Harvey has had to search for a song that might make him feel a bit heroic within

can make him suddenly take off, his feet and lungs made exuberant by song, powered by music. Reddy's jaunty feminist anthem, though, has an apparent lyrics problem: she's not, he thinks, really speaking to me, is she? But then, as he runs on the spot, waiting for the WALK sign to contradict the DON'T WALK sign and allow him to cross Fifth Avenue, the music swells, and Reddy starts singing about how she might be bent, but she can't broke, it all just makes her more determined etc etc, and it sort of all becomes relevant, to him, to Harvey Gold. Simplistic, yes; imbued with that tinpot heroic defiance that Americans so love, yes; but sometimes when you are running and exhausted and on the edge of collapse both physically and psychologically that stuff doesn't really matter: and so, he can feel the music do its trick, raising him up to the higher ground, and, because he is running on the spot, it feels like it's actually winding him up, so that when the green WALK light does eventually come on, he's off like a rocket, his feet sweeping over first tarmac and then sidewalk in double time, triple time, as the backing singers and the brass take it to the bridge. It's what he needs to hear, as he powers up Museum Mile, seeing pedestrians swerve in anticipation of his approach. Lost in music, unembarrassed for the moment about his voice, made more tone-deaf than ever because he can't hear it above Helen Reddy's, he joins in: singing about how strong he is, how invincible – and there it is, the looming grey-black central tower of Mount Sinai, from whose top floor he can imagine his father's sightless eyes looking out. He reaches the reassuring blue canopy of the Madison entrance, and, feeling his soul swell, he shout-sings: *I am woman*! It doesn't halt him – if anything it makes him feel more lifted – but at the same time it makes him laugh, and then, the laughter breaks up his breathing and forces him to cough, and he deflates, all the air and energy rushing out of him like a flying balloon, holding onto the side of the revolving doors while doctors come in and out, one or two of them looking as if they might ask him whether or not he needs to be admitted. He shakes his head, but at the same time can't breathe: no sound comes out of his mouth. He takes out his iPhone to halt the doctors looking at him, to avoid embarrassment, to stop the music which now is making him feel mad, but also because he thinks of the iPhone as something of a mother box, the sentient mini-computer worn by Mister Miracle and Orion and Metron in Jack Kirby's *New Gods* series, comics he remembers reading as a very little boy still living in America. The mother box always saved them when they were at their most vulnerable. He knows that thinking this in terms of his own present predicament is completely ridiculous, but still, getting out the iPhone does in fact work – yes, it is his mother box: just holding it in his hand and looking at the still blue earth on its screen calms him down, and jump-starts his lungs, allowing him to breath normally, stopping him from having to think about which songs on the machine might be picked out to form a suitable playlist for dying.

Although, in hindsight, Harvey agrees with Stella that the jacket he wore last time he came to see Eli was overdoing it, he wishes now, watching the enormous brick head of the security guard shake slowly from side to side, that he was wearing it again. It probably wouldn't make any difference, but the edge might be taken off the unauthorized nature of his showing up here if he was wearing … he doesn't know: anything, rather than this sweat-soaked hoody and falling-down tracksuit pants complete with has-he-shat-himself? gusset and oversize headphones. However much he doesn't feel unlike one, at least he wouldn't actually *look* like a homeless nutter.

'Oh come *on*,' he says, knowing that one thing that never changes these blokes' minds is an irritated tone of peevish entitlement, but finding it coming out of his mouth nonetheless, 'you know who I am. You let me in on Monday.'

The guard breathes heavily out of his nose: the exhale, to Harvey, had just a tiny element of a snarl.

'I let a number of people in on Monday, sir.'

'And you remember me?'

The guard raises an eyebrow, as if to say, *Don't try and get into my head. Mind games cut no ice with me.* His hand goes to his earphoned ear.

185

'I let a number of people in on Monday, sir, and I would let any of those people in again today, were their names on the list. Your name is not on my list. For today.'

Harvey feels his anxiety symptoms, damped down by the run, starting up again, one by one: throat constriction, heaviness in his legs, hot flushes, nausea.

'Am I on the list for tomorrow?'

'Would you like me to check, sir?'

'Well, if you could tell me the day when my father is going to die, and then the day my name is under, and persuade me that the former day is after the latter, that would be most reassuring.'

The snarling exhale again, followed by a flicking up of the black clipboard to his chest: Harvey sees the small indentation the plastic makes in the puffy satin of the jacket. He decides to try a different tack.

'Look, mate,' Harvey is never comfortable with *mate*, neither as a jocular, friendly form of address nor as a stressed grace note of aggression, but he finds it coming out of his mouth here nonetheless, 'what's your name?'

'My name?'

'Yes, your name.'

The security guard looks at him for what seems to Harvey an inordinately long time before answering: 'John.'

'OK, John, the thing is … is it really John?'

'What?' For a moment, the security guard looks genuinely angry, possibly because he is thinking *What did you assume my name was? Leroy? Winston? MC Secure?*

'No, I just thought – y'know – *John*. It's a bit obvious. Like I'm not saying you *are* – but when you are – I don't mean you, specifically, I mean one – when one is lying – about one's name, John's like the first name you think of.'

The blank look again: then, very Americanly:

'Sir: my name is John.'

Harvey nods. 'OK, John.' What to do here? Harvey sometimes tries, when faced with irrationality, to become, in response, over-rational:

to outflank the person blocking him or arguing with him or shouting at him by a detached deconstruction of the situation. It is a strategy learnt from his father. It is worth a go, he thinks.

'The thing is, John, though, when someone dies – especially when that person is important or famous and stuff – people can kind of go into a sort of competition over them. Over who controls their death. Who owns it. Because nothing says *this person is the one that really matters in my life* more than being the one who owns your death. Right?'

John blinks rapidly at him, drawing Harvey's notice to his eyelashes, which are long and womanly. Have I gone so far, Harvey thinks, that I am now unable not to notice female features, even when they are on male faces?

'And here's the thing: Freda's great, of course, but she is …' he says, intending to open out his thoughts, to touch on the uselessness of such competition, the speciousness of the idea that death can be owned, the family harmony and openness that would surely be preferable at this time, and other, attendant, thoughts, but John interrupts.

'Someone has to be in control, sir,' he says, 'in every circumstance. Even death. And in this case …' and here he jerks his anvil neck backwards to gesture inside the room: Harvey follows the movement towards a quarter-view of Freda's back bent over the bed, ministrating, '… it is Mrs Gold.'

Harvey's soul sinks. He remembers, too late, how this strategy learnt from his father only ever works for his father.

'Excuse me,' says a voice beside him. Harvey looks round. A man is waiting, hovering, almost as if he is waiting in line to speak to the security guard, but not quite: something about him suggests that he would be able to walk straight into the room, with perhaps no more than a passing nod at the gatekeeper, but is too polite to do that while Harvey is stuck. Harvey looks at him, at the springy, receding grey hair and the black eyes, and the air, despite his age, of muscularity, of contained power, and then they come, goose pimples so large and fat it feels as if a layer of clothes have moved away from his body.

'Mr Roth … I'm Harvey … Eli's son …'

'Well, pleased to meet you, Harvey, even at such a sorry time. Please …' he says – and there it is, the passing nod: it is returned by the security guard with an accepting shift to the side – grasping the door handle and opening the door slightly, 'let me follow you in.'

* * *

So some more people came to see Daddy today. Some new doctors I hadn't seen before, and my weirdo half-brother and Uncle Philip, who's another really famous writer. He's like the No. 2 best writer in the world after Daddy. I call him Uncle Philip but he's not really my uncle he's just a really old friend of Daddy. When I heard he was coming I said to Mommy maybe Uncle Philip'll be pleased that Daddy is dying 'cos then he'll be the No. 1 writer in the world, but she said no, because him and Daddy were such friends – 'notwithstanding,' she said, 'Philip's terrible review of *Absent in Body* in the *New Yorker*, which Eli was of course good enough to forgive him for – eventually …' I have *no* idea what she was talking about; she does that sometimes, and when you say *What?* or *Sorry?* or *I don't understand* she does that breathy laugh and that little wave of her hand in front of her face, which means that she's kind of forgotten that you're there.

So there was him and the doctors and The Larvae – that's what I'm calling him – it wasn't my idea, it was Jada's, I was telling her on the phone about how creepy my half-brother was and how he my makes my skin crawl a bit like it does when I know there's a scary bug in the room, and she said, 'Harvey the Larvae'. I didn't know what larvae was but they've just done it in science class. She told me – urggh – and I felt a bit tickly inside about calling him that – it seemed a bit too horrible, but it made me laugh and she said it again and before you knew it that's what we were calling him.

So, anyway, I don't know what it is about The Larvae that makes me feel weird about him, but I didn't feel so bad about calling him that after what happened today. He came in following Uncle Philip – and Philip was really nice: he came right up to me and said hi and shook my hand and said how sorry he was that Daddy was 'poorly'

– that was the word he used, 'poorly': I liked it – but The Larvae came in just looking at the floor and not looking at me and Mommy like he wasn't even supposed to be there even though he is Daddy's son. He was wearing this horrible running top and trousers and he looked all red. Mommy smiled at him and gave him a kiss on the cheek but I was watching and I could see that her lips didn't touch his skin and I knew that meant that she wasn't really pleased to see him. She gave Philip a proper hug, one of her specials that go on for like over a minute. He kissed her. I couldn't see his lips from where I was standing but I'm sure they touched her skin. Mommy's got lovely skin, especially for a Mommy. Some of the mommies at my school are the same age but look a load older.

The Larvae didn't say much to me – he smiled but the sort of smile when you don't mean it, like when you don't really want to have to your picture taken. I could tell all he was interested in was Uncle Philip. It was like he sort of couldn't believe that Philip was there. I saw him when Philip was talking to Mommy or one of the doctors, just staring at him with his mouth open and his eyes all wide like Philip was a magical king or Robert Pattinson or someone.

Anyway then – like ALWAYS – all the grown-ups went and stood around Daddy's bed like meerkats looking at him and looking at each other and I went and sat in my chair in the corner with my Nintendo DS Lite. Mommy didn't want me to have a DS Lite at first – she doesn't approve of video games, so we haven't got an Xbox or a Nintendo Wii or anything. I have got a computer – a Macbook – but Mommy got them to set it at the shop so I can only look at websites that she likes, like kbears.com or learnit.org. There's something called Stardoll that Jada's a member of, where you get to make your own girl who you can dress up and buy make-up for, which she's showed me once at her house, and I really liked it, and tried to get Mommy to join me (you have to pay, like, ten dollars a month for it) but when I showed her she said I couldn't. I said why but she wouldn't explain; but later I got up in the night after they put me to bed to go the bathroom and I heard her talking to Daddy (this was before he got properly sick) about it, and she said all this stuff about sex, and children, and abuse, which I

189

know is a really bad thing. I didn't know how Stardoll could be that. Then she stopped speaking suddenly and I thought that maybe she'd worked out I was listening so I went back to bed.

But then when Daddy got really sick and we started to have to spend so much time in the hospital that Dr Chang (who works with Dr Ghundkhali) said to her that maybe she could get me a DS Lite, because otherwise, he said, 'it could just get too boring for a kid'. Mommy got a bit angry at that, because I don't think she thinks it's at all boring in the hospital, but then he said quickly – maybe because he could see that she was angry – that you can get Brain Training. Mommy didn't know what that was, but Dr Chang explained, and I could see she still wasn't sure, but I said I would like one, and then just at that point Daddy made a small moan so she kind of just said oh all right yes, because I think she didn't want to think about it any more.

So now I play on it a lot of the time we're at the hospital. I have Brain Training and Dr Kawashima – who looks a bit like Dr Chang, only older – has put me up to Level 4 on the writing and Level 3 on the math. Jada gave me her copy of Purr Pals, and sometimes I play that as well. I have three kittens I look after. One of them is just like Aristotle and of course I named him Aristotle. I was feeding him with the stylus, when Uncle Philip said he had to go. He said goodbye to Daddy first – well, he didn't say anything, he just held Daddy's hand for quite a long time – and then Mommy. She gave him another big, big hug, and then moved away from him but still holding his hands a bit like they used to dance in the olden days. She was smiling at him but crying at the same time: not big crying – just one or two tears coming out of her eyes. I went back to feeding Aristotle and then started him off playing with the ball of wool and when I looked up they were still holding hands. Then he came over to me and bent down and I showed him Purr Pals and he pretended to be interested in it for a bit like grown-ups do, and then said, 'It was lovely to see you, Colette: I hope I see you again soon' and stroked my hair which I don't really like people doing but he had such a nice face and big, strong old man hands that I didn't mind.

Then he got up and I think he was looking around for The Larvae to say goodbye to him, but then he popped up, from behind him, with a really worried look on his face and said:

'Mr Roth … I just wanted to say … something I've been wanting to say to you for ever …'

And then he stopped and looked over his shoulder back towards Mommy like he was checking whether or not she was listening or something but she wasn't, she was in one of her huddles with all the doctors, and straight away I knew what he wanted to do. I don't know how this happens to me sometimes. Maybe it's to do with being the daughter of the world's greatest living writer or something, but sometimes I can just tell what people are going to say before they say it. Ages ago, when I was like, seven, Jada was going to tell me that she thought maybe she liked *Hairspray* more than she liked *High School Musical* now, but all she got to say was 'Colette' and I said, 'I know. Me too …' and that was it, we both just *knew* what it was she'd been going to say. It's amazing.

Anyway, I knew he wanted to tell Uncle Philip that he thought he was a really great writer. Not just that: I knew he wanted to tell Uncle Philip that he was the best writer in the world. Already. Like before Daddy was even dead. That he thought *that even before Daddy was even dead, Uncle Philip was the No. 1 writer in the world.* I wasn't going to let that happen. So when he turned his head back round again, I stood up and said, really loudly:

'Daddy can hear everything that is said in this room. He might look like he can't, but he can. *He can hear everything!*'

They both turned to look at me. Uncle Philip just looked a bit confused, but I knew I was right because The Larvae looked really, really frightened, and kind of caught out, like Leo from the next door apartment looked when Mommy came into my room and caught him showing me his winky-wonk.

'He can hear *everything* and he can understand *everything*!'

Everyone was looking at me now, all the doctors and nurses as well, and I thought about telling them. I thought about saying, 'Harvey was about to tell Uncle Philip that *he* was the best writer in the world!' but instead I just stared and stared at him, letting him know that *I* knew. And then Mommy rushed over and gave me a hug, and said, over and over again, *You're right darling he can, you're so right, he can hear everything.*

Then no one said anything: and then Philip turned back to The Larvae and said, 'Sorry, Harvey, what was it you wanted to tell me?' But he just shrugged his shoulders and looked down and mumbled something about hoping to see him another time and so Philip smiled and nodded and put his coat on and left.

I carried on just staring at The Larvae. He stared back at me. He looked sort of sad but sort of furious as well. Then Mommy, who was still holding onto me, turned round, and then we were both staring at him.

RW: What would you say your relationship with your wife was like?

[pause]

EG: It was very beautiful.

RW: ... OK.

EG: What is your relationship with *your* wife like, Commissioner Webb?

RW: I'm not married, Mr Gold.

EG: Oh?

RW: Divorced.

EG: I see.

RW: She was a Mormon, wasn't she?

[pause]

RW: Pauline ...

EG: She came from that background, yes.

RW: But no longer believed?

EG: She had her own belief system. It was longer dependent on the teachings of Joseph Smith, no.

[pause]

RW: In my experience, someone brought up in that environment never entirely loses their faith. Or at least, their need to believe.

EG: Is that right …

RW: My sense is that they simply find something else to worship. Instead of God.

EG: Uh-huh.

[pause: shuffling of papers]

RW: Showing Mr Gold case document R45/110, a testimony from Mrs Gold's psychoanalyst …

EG: This is from Rosynski?

RW: Yes.

EG: But surely this is unethical?

RW: What is?

EG: Revealing information divested during analysis.

RW: We interviewed him. He gave it freely. But if he hadn't, we would in a case like this have been able to impose a –

EG: He gave it freely?

RW: Yes.

[pause]

EG: Well, I shan't be recommending him to any of my friends again.

RW: What do you make of his testimony?

[shuffling of papers]

RW: Mr Gold has handed back document R45/110.

EG: I don't think it's ethical for me to see this.

RW: I beg your pardon?

EG: It's Pauline's intimate stuff. For me to see it breaks every code that should exist between analyst and analysand.

RW: Are you suggesting – what? – that you reading this might screw up the transference, between Pauline and her analyst?

EG: No. You mistake me –

RW: Hey, I know that there's a lot of debate in psychoanalytic circles as to when analysis ends – that some people think that it never ends, it's an ongoing, open-ended process – but you know what: I think death kind of draws a line under it, don't you?

[pause]

EG: You're a wit, aren't you, Commissioner Webb? I bet you really wow them at the annual NYPD dinner. Why did your wife leave you? It couldn't possibly have been because of your lack of sense of humour.

RW: My wife didn't leave me.

EG: Oh. You left her? Some younger snatch catch your eye over the doughnuts? Someone with bigger tits and smoother skin who giggled and mooned over how clever and funny you are, how not like a normal cop at all? 'Oh Commissioner Webb, no one else in the department knows anything about Freud, please do let me put your cock in my mouth while you talk to me some more about *transference*.'

[pause]

RW: Well, since you won't read it, let me summarize for you. Arnold Rosynski, who had been Mrs Gold's therapist for the last four years – her entry into therapy having been suggested by you, Mr Gold: we have no record of your wife ever having any previous psychological issues – he concludes that Mrs Gold was not what he calls an endogenous depressive. That is, he does not think that she was either psychologically or genetically given to depression. That therefore she was a reactive depressive: that is …

EG: I know what a reactive depressive is, Commissioner.

RW: That is, that the depression which Mrs Gold was clearly suffering from, particularly in the last year, was a result of some stress in her life. Only Arnold Rosynski doesn't think that Mrs Gold's depression

195

was straightforwardly produced by stress. He describes it as being linked, and he's clear about this, to *your* depression.

EG: So she became depressed from living with a depressive. What's new?

RW: You were depressed because …?

EG: Now you see you've revealed yourself as not quite as up to speed with psychoanalysis as you pretend to be. If you were, you would perhaps know that finishing the sentence 'I am depressed because …' in no more than fifteen words is not that simple.

RW: No. I see that. Perhaps you could help me out then? You haven't written anything for three years. You have a number of children from previous marriages who I believe you've lost contact with. Reviews of your attempts to enter the art world were, to the say the least, mixed. You have prostate cancer.

EG: Well, thanks very much for detailing those things …

RW: … although I believe the cancer is now in remission, yes?

EG: 'On hold' I think would be a better way of putting it.

RW: So it was … the depression …?

[pause]

RW: Let's put that to one side for the moment. Rosynski goes on to say that what seemed unique to him about Mrs Gold's depression is it wasn't just caused by your depression – which he admits is not uncommon, it being, as you say, stressful to live with a depressive. He says that he thinks that 'Pauline Gold felt in some way that to be *not* depressed while her husband was so depressed was, in some way, a failure: a failure both marital and intellectual. For her to be happy – for her even to be unhappy, but not pathologically or clinically so – while her husband was depressed would indicate a disjunction between the two of them that she was not willing to contemplate. A better description of her condition than reactive depression would be copycat depression.'

196

[pause]

RW: How is your depression at the moment, Mr Gold?

He stops reading. His face is washed in the white backlight of the screen. He is tired. He shuts the computer down. Feeling himself invisible in the dark, he decides to chance a cigarette. He feels for the packet and lighter and puts a stick in his mouth and lights it. He lies back on the thin pillow of his bed and lets his lungs absorb the kick. Each time the tip glows, he sees, dimly, the face of Jesus.

* * *

The other channels, Violet thinks: how would I get them on my television? She only really understands three channels, BBC1, BBC2 and ITV; and even ITV she never used to watch when she properly watched TV, when she lived in Cricklewood. It wasn't snobbery – it wasn't that middle-class 1970s English thing of drawing a horrified line in the cultural sand, on one side of which was *Play for Today*, *Panorama*, *Face the Music*, and on the other *Benny Hill*. It was choice: she had grown up in a world where there wasn't that much choice, in any realm – food, husbands, leisure activities – and there was a comfort in that. Lack of choice was a safe place: you just worked with what was at hand, and didn't fret all the time about getting it wrong. So the idea that, at any given viewing moment, she was at liberty to choose one of *three* options – it was too much: two was enough.

But now she wanted more: she didn't just want the three terrestrial channels, or four or five or whatever it was: she wanted Sky and Virgin and Bloomberg and Living and Bravo and TCM and UK Gold. She didn't know what kind of programmes they showed on these channels, but she had seen their names come up when the nurses flicked through the numbers on the big television in the living room, and assumed that all must have news programmes, like the ordinary channels did. That was what she wanted, news, news like she had read could be found on the television now, 'rolling' news broadcasts, the constant giving out of the world's stories to the world. She had seen something of that on the downstairs TV when it was left on BBC News 24, but that wasn't quite it. Violet doesn't know it but what she wants is CNN: she wants the world refracted through America.

She wants news about Eli. Since that first item, caught by chance last week, she has heard his name a couple of times: a discussion on some BBC2 review programme, concentrating mainly on who might next be crowned 'the world's greatest living writer', and an update on his condition on Channel 4's breakfast news. She was surprised there wasn't more, as long-drawn-out demises of the famous seemed to provide a good story for TV these days: she remembers that when the footballer George Best went into hospital for the last time, there seemed to be reports on the TV every five minutes charting his worsening condition. Surely Eli's more important than a footballer? Surely there should be more information about how he is than there was about George Best? But the calibration of fame has not been clear to her for years: she doesn't know who most of the people who are famous now are, or why they are well known. All she knows is that they are all young. When she herself was young, the famous – a small group: film stars, major politicians, the royal family – were not. So perhaps now that you have to be young to be famous, to be famous and dying is, in most cases, oxymoronic.

She could sit downstairs in the living room but the nurses do not keep the communal television on the news programmes for very long. She has noticed from the way they frown and flick forward whenever a newsreader appears that they are concerned, presumably, that the news might disturb the inmates: all that death, too near the arthritic, liver-spotted knuckle. This presents a problem, though, as the news could sometimes seem the only programme on the television now designed for people over twenty-two, and they have to flick even more quickly through swearing men on panel shows and topless women on reality ones before settling, thumbs aching, on whichever shopping or travel show might provide the requisite reassuring wallpaper. This goes against the mission statement of Redcliffe House to 'allow residents the highest level of independence their health permits', but most people had their own televisions anyway, and it meant that at least there weren't geriatrics rowing over the remote control.

Violet bends down, her back cracking, and looks at the eight buttons to the side of the Hitachi's bulging green screen. Eight: that had seemed so many, so outlandishly futuristic, when she bought it. Also the buttons – at the time; now two of them don't work at all – were touch-sensitive, the merest stroke lighting them up red and changing the channel. There had been something sensual in that. Valerie hated this television, Violet remembers: partly because she saw it as an outrageous encroachment on her territory that her sister should have purchased something sophisticated (something with *all mod cons*), and partly because while watching it for the first time, on a family visit with the young Jeremy and David, Valerie had sneezed, and a split-second later, the channel changed, from BBC2 to ITV. There had been a moment of uncertainty, then Jeremy had started laughing and then David, although he was only four and was mainly laughing because his brother was, and finally Violet herself. Valerie sniffed and adjusted her flower-patterned skirt and looked away, saying, 'Obviously, there's something wrong with it', but the laughter continued, racking up into hysteria at the idea of an invisible bullet of mucus shooting from Valerie's pinched, oval nostril in a perfect parabola all the way to the touch-sensitive button. Shaking, tears running down her cheeks, Violet remembers feeling stupid and not a little bit scared of her sister's glowering detachment, but unable to stop, at one with the children and their mad hilarity and unable to get over the invisible fence back to sedate adulthood.

Eight buttons: it wasn't anywhere near enough now to cover the waterfront of television, even if she knew how to tune them in, if tune them in was what you still did: maybe now you just picked up the channels – what was the word? – *wirelessly* or whatever. The word made her remember that, of course, she did have a radio – she called it a wireless – a Phillips portable bought she couldn't remember when: she had stuck a small piece of black gaffer tape, cut into a thin arrowhead, over the wavelength meter where Radio 4 could be found. But even Radio 4 didn't seem to be mentioning Eli that much: she had heard an item about him on the *Today* programme the morning after she had seen the television report about his hospitalization but nothing since. Although she didn't listen as much as she used to now, because of her hearing – most of the time she couldn't hear it, and turning up the volume made the sound reverberate uncomfortably through the metallic filter of her hearing aid, making her feel as if her head were inside the tinny, tiny speaker.

Perhaps she could ask Gordon, the handyman at Redcliffe House, about how to retune the TV; but she felt she would be wasting his time, or, worse, he might say that she needed to buy some piece of equipment. That was the problem, starting a chain of events that would lead inevitably to her being placed out of her depth, holding out a pathetic piece of paper with some Japanese name scrawled on it to a young man with terrifying hair in a shop full of minuscule plastic gadgets with screens on them so small she couldn't imagine how they could be viewed without a magnifying glass. Violet often ruminated on scenarios like this, everyday places, everyday errands, where just being the age she was laid her open to extreme humiliation. Lately, her imagination of such scenarios was becoming darker. Thinking on this one she sees herself, once ignored – once the young man has shrugged at the piece of paper and turned away to another customer – screaming and pulling her skirt up and defecating on the grey carpeted floor, between the rows of devices and the rows of cables designed to plug them into each other.

Turn it on, then, she thinks. But she doesn't: she just stares at the television, at its heft, its wood, its obsolescence; at its eight buttons, two of them not working, and then at the screen. She has the big light on in her room – it was another dark, soaking day – and she can see, in the screen, her room reflected. Violet likes her room – she likes the floral wallpaper, and the little Persian rug, and the dark brown wardrobe, and the neatly made single bed, and the small folding table by the window on which she sometimes ate – but in this reflection, foreshortened and misted by the opaque television glass, it looks nightmarish. And then, unexpectedly, she sees her face. The only place she sees herself, these days, is in the one mirror in her bathroom, and she tends not to stop and look there: it is too much to see herself naked, to take in all the crumpling and the falling and the folding in of the flesh. It is a job of work.

But here she is, on the television: Violet Gold, on the television. She doesn't, she thinks, look too bad. She has learnt to expect the worst from shock appearances of herself, in shop windows or taxicab mirrors. She is familiar with the confusion, the moment of uncertainty about who exactly this buttoned-up and snowy-haired old dear hobbling through the puddles might be. But she remembers from when she was younger, from when she used deliberately to look at herself, that some mirrors were better than others. The mirror she particularly liked to see herself in was not a mirror at all: she remembers the one good thing about her journey to work every day, on the tube, was her reflection in the train glass. She first noticed it when she was still with Eli, when her daily route took her down on the Bakerloo line into town, before getting the Drain across to Monument, the stop for International Shipbrokers Ltd. If she could get a seat, and there wasn't a wall of pinstriped trousers in the way, as the train moved out of the light of the platform and into the darkness of the tunnel, an image would appear, behind the head of the passenger opposite: herself.

She could hold this reflection – given commuter comings and goings, and its disappearance in stations – for most of the journey. Violet had never thought of herself as beautiful, despite her awareness when young that attracting men came easy enough to her; but there was something beautiful about this ghost of her, fading and reappearing against black. She had read in *Everywoman* that sometimes starlets and models adjusted lights or put Vaseline on lenses in order to disguise skin flaws, and maybe it was just a subway version of this, but there was something else, something more than just the taking away of bad detail. Marriage to Eli had removed most of her sense of self, and when she looked in one of the two mirrors they owned in their tiny flat, she knew that she wasn't looking at herself for herself, but only for him. He often seemed to be lurking behind her when she looked at her reflection, smiling in the knowledge that he had compiled the checklist she was mentally ticking off. This, though, this foggy angel of the tube, was hers.

And so was this face in the television. She moved closer to it, closer and closer, feeling the wide green static like a force field on her skin. She had read somewhere in some women's magazine once of electricity being passed through the skin to remove wrinkles. *How many million volts would I need*, she thinks, not grimly: it just passes through her mind, like any other thought. The ticklish charge was welcoming, like many tiny fingers touching her face. She shuts her eyes, submitting to the fantasy that the static was stroking her, unborn children, reaching up to touch her skin.

She only stays in this position for a second; her back hurts too much to bend for so long. She moves away from the screen, and pushes a finger, bent by arthritis into an arrowhead, against the first button. The machine takes its time, but a second or two later a newsreader appears, a black man – Violet feels that mild jolt of surprise she always feels on seeing one on the television wearing a suit and tie – but, no, it is nothing to do with Eli. Something about bigger taxes on cars that pollute the environment, another of the many, many daily stories that do not involve or concern her. It goes to footage of roads and traffic; she switches it off before one of the people, the Green people, says *what kind of world are we leaving for our children?* They often say this, and she always wants to say, directly to the television, *I haven't got any children.*

There is no news about Eli. But she knows what the ultimate news about her ex-husband is going to be. *One day, soon, he will die.* So why, she thinks to herself as the rain hits her window hard, do I need to know how he is now? It's all just – what was the word? The opposite to sequel? It was fine not to be able to remember that one, it was not like forgetting the word for curtains or teapot. Prequel. It's all just prequel.

The truth, though, was that Violet did not want news. Her craving for it was simply a distortion of her real need, which was to be in advance of the news. Violet knew she was a long way away, in time and space and experience and celebrity, from Eli, but if there was one small shred of her life with him that still counted now it was this: she wanted someone to tell her of his death before the world was told; someone kind, someone nice; someone connected. Her never large sense of self, miniaturized now by age, had only this desire: that she should not stumble upon it in the television or in the papers like everybody else. She had no idea who this person might be, and no real hope of their intervention. But just someone who cared enough to say: *Look, I'm really sorry* or *I hate to have to bring you this information* or *Violet, I think you should perhaps sit down*. Because however much she knew that the news about Eli was coming, she still didn't want to be surprised, or alarmed, by it.

* * *

'So what have you got for me?' says Michaela. The question shakes Harvey, as once again he has been staring. He blinks and looks away, to suggest that he has not been. This looking that he does, at these women – women like Michaela – is different from the usual. It's not the pressing his nose to the window of Eden that young women inspire, nor the frenzied, scuttling battle of desire and despair his vision fights out every day across the face of Stella. It is a confused looking. He can see that Michaela was once beautiful, but this realization does not inspire the consequent pity – is this patronizing, this pity, Harvey wonders? Would the feminists think so? – that lost beauty usually does. This is because someone has gone into Michaela's face and rerouted its arc towards decay: someone with knives and syringes and chemicals. The confusing thing for Harvey, however, is that he (Harvey imagines it must be a he – the people who do this, for women, are almost always men) has not exactly rerouted it back to beauty. He has made her face airbrush-smooth, eradicating all the lines and flaps and tiny tree-like veins that connect his eyes directly to darkness. But it is an angular, hard smoothness, like polished wood: it has none of the softness and give and butteriness that causes the young female face to arouse in men like Harvey feelings of hope and wonder – and also, of course, feelings of exclusion and outraged, furious loss.

Michaela's face, specifically, has, despite strong resemblances – despite, in fact, looking like a polished wood carving of the same face

203

– none of the softness and give and butteriness of the features of her daughter, Lark. This contrast is heightened – *the morning sun, when it's in your face*, thinks Harvey – by the thick New York light streaming in from the Sangster's restaurant window. He is on one side of the table, and on the other sit Lark and Michaela, who, as well as being her mother, is her manager. Next to them sits Josh, her American PR, a large suit of a man with an incongruous shock of black curly hair. They are having tea.

'Well, I don't know if my agent told you, but I'm not in the city to work – I'm here because my father is very ill …'

'No, he didn't,' says Michaela. Her face betrays no sympathy, but Harvey cannot work out if this is because her overweening commitment to her daughter's career has made her cold and unfeeling or because her face betrays nothing of anything any more. There is a short pause, during which his eyes flick across towards Lark. He thinks he picks up, in the move of Lark's eyebrows, some concern for him, but he cannot look at her for long, she is too beautiful: it is like staring at the sun.

'Well, so I haven't been able to spend as long as I would've liked working on this …'

As he says this, Josh picks up a mock-up of Lark's autobiography, which sits on the table between two teapots. The cover image – fitted around a hardback book – is Lark, looking up; her hair falls around the already decided title: *Lark: A Songbird's Story*. Josh holds it up with both hands, and stares directly over the book at Harvey.

'… but it would be a very interesting book to write, obviously, and I have had some thoughts.'

He launches into a rotation of all those words again: relevance blah style blah contemporary artist rhubarb rhubarb MySpace generation. He says this stuff on autopilot: his mouth is saying it, while in his mind he is still wondering what it is about Michaela's face that marks it out as not-young, despite every mark of ageing having been erased from it. It makes him pleased that he has never brought up the subject of plastic surgery to Stella – it has occurred to him, of course; he has sneaked a look at those Holocausty before-and-after photographs on surgeons' websites – as the trauma would clearly not have been worth the final result.

'Sounds great,' says Josh, when he has finished. Josh beams, his teeth so American white against the blackness of his hair they seem actually to be coming out of his mouth.

'I don't know,' says Michaela. 'It all sounds a bit like PR bull to me. What about getting to the heart of Lark?'

The heart of Lark?

'Well …' Harvey wonders whether to say this. It is the baby elephant in the room. '… The thing is, Lark … she is … very young.'

The three of them look at him. To avoid their gaze, Harvey stares down into his tea. It is English Breakfast. The surface of his cup is dappled with a white froth, the result of him pouring into it three pink packets of Sweet 'N Low. Sweeteners are Harvey's main dietary weapon against weight gain. Yes: he is one of those fat blokes who will slaver his way through innumerable cakes and fried breakfasts and curries thinking this is somehow offset by keeping all beverages sugar-free.

'And?' says Michaela.

'Well, that makes an autobiography quite a … challenge.'

Michaela frowns, which makes Harvey anxious, as he had not thought her forehead capable of it. It flashes through his mind that to register the truth of her reaction to his comment, he needs to think of it along the lines of an equation, something like: D (the actual level of Michaela's displeasure with his remark) = S (the strength of her frown) – B (the amount of botox in her brow).

'Well, firstly, Mr Gold, that is your job,' she says, her accent – Northern Irish – becoming more tart. 'Secondly, have you not read the PR biog? Lark was a child star. She's been on TV, in movies …'

Harvey looks across to Lark – he feels, if her mother is going to continue to talk about her daughter as if she is not here, or, more likely, as if she is such an icon already that she can only be referred to in the third person, that he has licence to look. Lark is unreactive – but not in a grand way, not in a way that implies that it is second nature to her being spoken about in this eulogizing manner. She just stays composed. In any case, it is hard for Harvey to make out from her features what might be going on inside her, because inside *him*, her features make him melt, into one big complacent eye.

Michaela finishes her tirade, her list of Lark's incredible-for-one-so-young accomplishments. Harvey has a sense, from the way she is fixing him in her glare, that things are not going so well.

'Maybe …' he says, one last throw of this shit dice, '… if I could listen to some of the songs?'

Lark looks up at this, and her head seems at least to nod. But her mother raises a barrier pair of hands.

'I'm sorry, Mr Gold, but as I told Alan, all of Lark's songs are embargoed until the release date. Obviously you understand, with piracy being what it is these days.'

'So – just let me be clear – I'm supposed to write her autobiography without hearing her sing?'

Michaela takes a deep breath in through her nose; a glance passes between her and Josh.

'Again, as you should know – I'm beginning to think you didn't read the brief we sent through at all – the first volume of the autobiography will cover the years up till the date of the publishing contract we signed last April. During which period Lark was not, of course, a recording artist. Volume Two will cover the next ten years, of success. Then, of course, *everyone* will have heard her songs.'

'But –'

'When the time comes – I mean, when you come to write the relevant chapters, you will be provided with some home video footage I took of Lark singing at various school functions, and some teenage demo tapes which I have transferred to MP3. But until the embargo is up, not the new songs. There's no need.'

Harvey, not knowing what to say, nods and sips his tea. The chemical Sweet'N Low backwash makes him wish he'd brought from home his favourite sweetener, Splenda, in its handy yellow dispenser. His hand even makes a small inward clicking motion as he thinks this, as if to force a tiny phantom pill fall from a phantom dispenser.

'Josh?' says Michaela, standing up. Josh, who is the person Harvey has been looking at least, but who it seems has been smiling the whole time, glances up. 'Perhaps we should just step out of the restaurant for a second ...'

'OK!' says Josh, in a very upbeat voice, and widens his smile at Harvey, despite the couldn't-be-clearer implication in Michaela's voice that the discussion they are about to have, re Harvey's suitability for the job, is only a formality. Harvey feels himself smiling back at Josh, as, faced with such a big mouth full of teeth, he has to. Inside, though, he despairs. Why did he agree to this? Why did he not just ignore Alan and his stupid urgency? Why, on finding out that Lark was the woman at JFK, did he get impelled by some idiot idea of synchronicity? Of – for fuck's sake – fate?

'Mum says you're staying here ...?'

He looks up. Lark is looking at him properly, it seems, for the first time. The absence of her mother seems to have thrown a switch in her. There is still something disconnected, though, about the look. It reminds him of something: what exactly he cannot place. 'Uh, yes.'

'So are we.'

'All of you?'

'No, Josh – he lives here. In New York.'

'Yes.' He notices she does not seem to have a trace of her mother's accent. She speaks in that part-estuary, part-American voice that all young people who live in London do, but overlaid with a blankness so deadpan it reminds Harvey of the female voice that he has set his satellite navigation system to speak in back home. He always sets his sat nav to this voice, as, still, many years after the 1980s, he feels more comfortable following the directions of women.

'But me and Mum have a suite on the top floor.'

'Oh, right.'

'It's *amazing*. It's got a piano, and a kitchen and a library full of old books ...'

'And a set of Lars Bolanger lacquered boxes and a sage velvet seating area?'

She blinks. Her eyes are as blue as robin's eggs.

'Yes. I think so. How did you know?'

Harvey shrugs. He feels himself unable to meet her eyes, or, rather, her face. Her beauty makes him dizzy: he imagines himself fainting, pissing his pants and gasping *I love you!* all at once. He looks away like a shy teenager, or like Jamie, who looks away when talking to everyone. To find something else to rest his eyes on he picks up the mock-up of her autobiography, although this still involves looking at her, because she is pictured on it. He feels assailed by many Larks, by an army of beauty.

'This looks great,' he says, just for something to say. She nods. He lifts the book up over his face, a shield between him and her, but the cover, which has not been fitted especially well on the hardback underneath, slips off, in a way that he can only think of as sexual.

'Oh!' he says, 'Sorry.' The book lands on the table. Harvey feels the lightness of the glossy print of Lark in his hands before looking down. On the cover of the book itself he sees a shape, an abstract imprint of a man's face, sort of a silhouette and sort of not, and a familiar 1950s font.

'Fuck.'

'What?'

'It's *Solomon's Testament.*'

'What's that?'

'It's by my dad. His first book.' He flicks open the front. 'It's a first edition, too. Where did you get this?'

'I said, there's a library in our room. It's full of old books. Josh just took that one off the shelf to put our cover on it.'

He opens the book. *I am Solomon Wolff, and this is my testament.*

'So, Mr Gold …' Harvey looks up. Michaela and Josh have returned from their conference, which was shorter than even Harvey expected. Michaela's hardly moving features have been arranged into a Sir Alan Sugar/Simon Cowell get-ready-for-something-cruel-but-honest mask. Josh is smiling.

'Look,' says Harvey, 'Let's save ourselves the bother …'

'I want him to do it.'

Michaela, Harvey and Josh turn. It is Lark who has spoken.

'Sorry, Samantha?' says Michaela.

'Samantha?' says Harvey.

'It's her real name,' says Michaela, with some irritation, as if only the surprise of the moment had let it slip out.

'I want Harvey – that's your name, isn't it?'

'Yes.'

'I want him to do my autobiography.'

Josh and Michaela look to each other. For a second, even Josh's smile seems to falter.

'Why?' says Michaela. Harvey feels like saying 'I am still here, you know.' Another part of him, however, feels like saying, 'Yeah … why?'

'His dad wrote this book. The one that was underneath. Underneath the cover.'

'He did?' says Michaela. Josh picks up the copy of *Solomon's Testament*, and flicks through the opening pages.

'Yes.'

'OK, Samantha … and?'

'Mum. That can't be a coincidence. It's got to be a sign.'

'Oh. I see.' Michaela scratches her chin. She is clearly doing some mental calculation, one she perhaps has to do a lot, as to whether it is worth challenging her daughter once she has made a mystical decision of this sort. Harvey notices that even the skin on the back of her hand matches that on her face. He had not expected this shift in the balance of power: it had seemed as if Michaela would brook no dissent over her daughter's career. But it seems she does, at least *from* her daughter. After a short, poised pause, she moves her hand down towards him. 'Welcome aboard, Mr Gold.'

Harvey looks to Lark. She looks back at him, neutrally. *I love you!* Piss, faint. 'Thanks very much,' he says, taking her mother's hand. Josh leans in, above their handshake, like someone coming into frame. He is still holding *Solomon's Testament*; Harvey notices that, for the first time, he is not smiling.

'Harv, you don't write like *this*, do you?'

* * *

209

So today this happened. When we came in this morning, Dr Ghundkhali took Mommy away to the window and was talking to her over there in a whisper and then she started to look really upset and she started saying, 'No. She's old enough. She has to hear it, too' so I knew straight away there was some bad news and that I was gonna have to hear it.

I didn't know how Dr G could see that Daddy was getting worse. He looked exactly the same. Maybe all the big machines that are around his bed were giving off signals saying it. When I realized that it was going to be bad news I looked at Daddy and tried to see it. I thought at first that Dr G was going to tell us that Daddy was gonna die, like, today or tomorrow, and so I looked really hard. I wanted to see if I could see that he was about to be a dead person. I couldn't. I guess he has been dying for quite a long time now so maybe you can't tell just by looking at him anyway. If someone is dying, I don't know when the bit where they're *really* dying starts. But I looked anyway.

So then Mommy came over and crouched down and she made her face go that way it goes just before she's gonna say something really important where her eyes go stary and sad at the same time. But before she could speak, I said:

'I know, Mommy.'

She didn't say anything then. Just nodded. She grabbed my head and put it on her chest. I could feel her boobies, and beneath them I could hear her heart beating.

I think Mommy wanted that to be that. I think she thought we didn't have to talk about it any more. Like we both just *knew*. But then Dr G came over and said, 'Mrs Gold, if you're sure you would like Colette to be present, then …' And then he trailed off without finishing his sentence, like he does a *lot*.

So then we ended up in this little room down the corridor with lots of charts and black and white photos on the wall, and Dr Ghundkhali said: 'Eli has an infection now. Of the lungs.'

'That's what you breathe through,' I said. 'Well, you breathe through your mouth and nose. But the way you pump air in through your mouth and nose is by the action of the lungs.'

Dr Ghundkhali looked at me strangely for like three seconds. Then he nodded and said, 'Yes. Anyway, we could, of course, give him antibiotics, and it would probably clear up. But in these circumstances …'

And then he didn't finish his sentence *again*! I looked at Mommy, but she just looked pale and furious and like her lips were shut really hard. We were sitting on these two grey plastic chairs and Dr G was sitting on the table. Well, not sitting on the table, not like with his legs crossed or anything. His bottom was on the table, but his feet were on the floor. He has really long legs.

'What?' I said.

'Sorry?' he said.

'In these circumstances … *what*?'

He looked a bit surprised. It might have been because he didn't expect me to know as a big a word as *circumstances*. Or it might have been because nobody had ever asked him before about what he was going to say in one of those sentences.

He made a face and shook his head and looked over to Mommy, like she was going to help, like she must know what he was about to say and maybe *she* could tell me. But she just said:

'Yes, Doctor. What exactly are you implying?'

Then he just looked really embarrassed. He went red. I could see that even though he is from India and has dark skin.

'Well, Mrs Gold. In these circumstances, when a patient is, as we know your husband to be, terminally ill – if they do get an infection or a virus, sometimes it's felt to be best …'

There was another long silence.

'Yes?' said Mommy.

'… not to treat him.'

Mommy nodded. She took my hand, and squeezed it tight.

'Not to treat him?' I said. 'What does that mean?'

'It means, darling …' said Mommy, looking at me; but then she moved her head round to face Dr Ghundkhali, and she changed her voice, making it really hard, '… that Dr Ghundkhali would like to let your father *die*.'

I looked round at him. I felt my eyes go hard at him, as hard as Mommy's voice. But also I felt them start to feel a bit wet, like I was going to cry. And then I didn't know what to do.

'Mrs Gold,' he said. 'I would not *like* anything of the sort. I'm just telling you what the medical situation is. And, yes, in this situation, some family members sometimes feel that it is more humane to let the patient … go.'

Mommy squeezed my hand harder. I could feel the bad feeling that I sometimes get inside me when grown-ups talk like this. It's like a cloud in my tummy. And I really want it to burst and get rid of its rain but it just stays full in my tummy. Sometimes it moves around, like my tummy is a whole black sky.

'Dr Ghundkhali,' said Mommy. 'Are you aware of who my husband is?'

Dr Ghundkhali suddenly looked very tired. He looked like he was ill, like he should be the one in hospital.

'Yes, of course, Mrs Gold.'

'I'm not sure you do. Not really. I mean, you know who he is and that he is an important man. But tell me: have you read *Solomon's Testament*?'

He didn't say anything.

'*The Compliance of Women*? *The Teriblo Conspiracy*? *Criminality*?'

'*Mirror, Mirror*?' I said. 'When it came out it got bad reviews, but now it's considered a classic.'

He rubbed his face with his hand. 'I'm not really much of a reader of fiction, I'm afraid. I prefer history.'

'Oh … I see. Biography? The lives of great men, by any chance?'

'No, not really. I like microhistory. Footnote history.'

I turned to Mommy to say 'what's that?' but then she said: 'What's that?'

'It's books about the small stuff. The things we all take for granted. Books about – I don't know – salt. Mercury. Paper. Plastic. I'm reading one at the moment, would you believe, about dust. Did you know …'

'Yes, well,' said Mommy, 'if you had read some of my husband's books, perhaps you would have a sense of exactly what life you're

212

talking about …' and here Mommy did that thing she sometimes does of putting her fingers up around a word, and moving them up and down as she speaks, '… letting go.'

Dr Ghundkhali nodded. He rubbed his face some more. He opened his mouth. Then he shut it again. Then he looked back at Mommy. 'Right. So we'll treat Mr Gold's infection. No problem.'

'Good,' said Mommy.

She got up. I got up, too. Dr Ghundkhali got off the table. He opened the door. He held it open. He smiled at me as I went through, but I just gave him a look. I can raise my left eyebrow without raising my right. Mommy says it's a thing I can do because Daddy can do it, too, and I have seen him do it. He used to do it a lot when I was little. He used to do it when I did something funny or silly and he would do it and laugh at the same time. I used to love that.

But that wasn't the way I was doing it now. I did it without a smile.

The woman's breast is so rock-hard it squashes Harvey's nose deep into his face, making it difficult for him to breathe. Who, he thinks, wants breasts to be like *this*? The point about breasts, surely, is their softness? That's the great thing about breasts, isn't it? There's their movement, yes, their slow hypnotic swing, but that movement itself is soft, or at least redolent of softness; and breasts filled with silicon or shrapnel or whatever they put in them to make them like these ridiculous American ones now suffocating him don't move or swing at all. The two breasts are seemingly no longer two at all. They move in a block, comically, like feet in a single big slipper; there is no movement independent of the rest of the body, which is what gives the breast its iconic, thing-apart status. And, besides, soft: that's what makes breasts nice to hold, and to bury one's face into.

What *do* they put in them, Harvey thinks, as she moves them back and forth across his face, semi-proving, with a shift of weight across her shoulders, Harvey's semi-point about false breasts and their lack of independent body movement. It feels like small, flat punches, like soft jabs from a practising boxer. Perhaps I should wear one of those head protectors. How hard would it be to find something soft? Feathers? Sponge? Kapok? Although Harvey has never been entirely sure what kapok is.

'I sense you're not focused, Gold,' says Bunce. Harvey, aware that his mouth is still open, and thus that he looks like a mouth-breather, looks over, to where another lap-dancer is sitting astride his American

214

friend, facing away, rubbing what Harvey knows Bunce would call her *butt-cheeks* across his groin. He is leaning back, his big square head a counterweight to her entire body.

'How do you know that?'

'I feel no electric current of desire coming off you.'

'Really.'

'Yes. None. And you should. She's good. She's very good.' A flicker of a bored, practised smile shimmers across the dancer's face as she moves. 'And I'll tell you what I really like. She looks like that girl-child opera singer from your country. The one who's grown up now.'

Harvey looks at her. He is uncomfortable about many things in this situation, not least the clearly assumed licence to talk about the woman naked in front of you as if she is not there. This seems odd to him, as he has never experienced someone so clearly *there*. The phantom feminist in his mind deconstructs it as yet another type of objectification, as if there weren't enough going on in this room: a way of rendering her a body without consciousness.

'Charlotte Church?' he says.

'Yes. God. I love her. I'd fuck her until my dick became Welsh.'

'Do you feel an electric current of desire coming from …' Harvey twists his neck, with a stab of pain, around the side of his dancer's left breast, in an attempt to nod towards Bunce's one.

'Susan?'

She turns round, on the hearing of her name. She is blonde, and her eyes are not *especially* dead.

Harvey frowns. Susan? *Not Jenna? Chelsea? Angel? Shyla?*

'Most definitely a girl named Sue,' says Bunce. She laughs, but Harvey thinks she may – just – have heard this joke before; and then goes back to the groin-grinding.

'But no …' continues Bunce, leaning over so that his mouth is close to Harvey's ear, and his big head close to Harvey's dancer's – whose name he does not know – still slowly moving breast. He worries about the matter/anti-matter, Higgs Boson-creating style explosion that might happen if these two heavily gravitational objects collide, but they do not, '… I don't feel much in the way of desire coming off Susan. Which is not to say, as the myth would want us to believe, that strippers stroke hookers never get any pleasure from their work. Obviously, some do and some don't. But, no. Susan, my guess is …' and here he looks directly at Susan's buttocks, moving at exactly the same speed as Harvey's dancer's breasts, in time with the terrible R 'n' B song banging out of the enormous speakers hovering like UFOs from the ceiling of Exotique Manhattan Table Dancing, 'my impression is, for her, it's just a job. Neither pleasurable nor unpleasurable.'

'Right …'

'Which is fine with me. One thing I've never understood is the idea that, sex-wise, men need women to feel pleasure. I mean, sure: it's a bonus. It's good. I'm happy if they've had a good time. But it's not crucial. The key area, for me, is me. To be specific, my balls. Are they empty? As can be? Check. Job done.'

Bunce smiles as he says this. It is part of his trick. Bunce wraps all his attitudes in just enough self-awareness and irony to pre-empt disapproval, or, at least, to render it po-faced. Smiling, however, does not really suit him; it makes his face look suddenly boyish and over-pleased, in direct contradiction to his given mode of being, the thinking man's jock.

'Such an attitude would, I assume, allow for sex with a *lot* of hookers,' says Harvey.

'Well …' says Bunce, 'It would. But no, I'm waaaaaay to cheap for that. I hate spending money on a date, let alone a hooker. And besides: with hookers, you lose the thrill of the yes, the gaining of the Golden Ticket, when you've persuaded and charmed and conned until she's reached escape velocity; and the next magic step where she puts her knees behind her ears and lets you sweat and grunt and punish like a bull mastiff on a toy poodle, and your inner voice is throwing both fists in the air and exploding between two thundery reactions: a) I fucking *won!*; and b) I cannot *believe* I'm getting away with this shit *again*.'

Harvey nods, remembering that an evening with Bunce involves listening to a lot of this stuff: this is how he talks, all the time.

'Yeah,' he says. 'You know this … what Susan's doing there, to your groin – that costs money? We're on a tab here?' Harvey hears himself speaking like an American, going up at the end of the sentence like the Bengali in the taxi, but without the excuse of having heard American speech rhythms burbling on behind him every day for the last however many years. The idea embarrasses him, makes his face go red – he can feel it, although knows it cannot be seen in the flashing dark – because there is something about accent-chasing, especially American accent-chasing, which speaks of desperation, of wanting so much to fit in. It makes him feel like an English fifteen-year-old obsessed by The Fonz.

But Bunce seems not to notice; he just shrugs, and says:

'Hey. I am large. I contain multitudes.'

The music stops, followed a split-second later by a calming of the lights. Both dancers get off both laps. There is an awkward moment, like a potted version of waking up the morning after a one-night stand, as they stand there putting their underwear back on. Harvey's dancer, demurely, turns away to do this. Susan is less bothered: she fiddles with her bra straps face-on, while fixing Harvey with a gaze that feels to him like a rebuke. He looks away, catching sight of his reflection in one of Exotique Manhattan Table Dancing's many mirrors. He looks, as well he might – right-on man gone wrong, new man grown old – ashamed.

'So, honey,' she says, 'wanna go upstairs to the private room?'

He glances over to Bunce, who, Harvey thinks, raises an eyebrow, although because he is absurdly blond, with eyebrows that verge on the invisible in daylight, it's hard to tell: it could just be some random crinkling above the contact-lens-blue pupil. Harvey used to be able to do a killer raised eyebrow – an inheritance from his father – but lately, the muscle seems to have atrophied.

'No thanks,' says Harvey. 'I've just found out I'm the Federal Reserve for the evening.'

She nods, and looks away, not bothering with a polite smile. *Why*, thinks Harvey, *am I trying to sound so fucking American?* He is trying, in fact, to sound at home here, to sound like the sort of person who comes to these kind of places often and is not in any way daunted by them, and thus has fallen into what he imagines might be the lingua franca of, say, a hedge-fund manager on a bawdy night out.

He wonders, too, as Susan and her beautiful buttocks – but why? What is so beautiful about the bisected pound of flesh? How can something so banal, something not actually that different, graphically, from the inflated Ws he would draw over and over again on rough-book paper as a child, drag his eye towards it so? – walk away, why he failed to take up her offer. It was not the cash, even though one of the reasons Harvey is trying to affect a breezy confidence is that he has no real idea how much the bill for the evening at Exotique will be. It had been Bunce's idea to meet here. He said he would rather get it out of the way at the start of the evening, so that they could talk properly for the rest of the night without having to think *When for fuck's sake are we gonna go to a strip club?*

So meanwhile: why not the private dance? Harvey had been more attracted to Susan than to his own dancer – not least because her breasts looked considerably more real – but had felt intimated by the forthrightness with which she had offered her services. Also, he had felt sorry for the other one, having made the assumption that her quietude was indicative of some secret sadness, which is the kind of assumption that soft-hearted men have always preferred to make about women who work in the sex industry, from Sir John Everett Millais onwards. Not that that makes any sense: because she looked maybe a little sad, he chose her, rather than her friend, for a lap dance; he did not whisk her away to a safe house and provide her for the rest of her days with a steady income.

The reasons why he doesn't follow Susan up to the smaller rooms on the first floor are manifold. There is the money issue. And then, Harvey is – this is key: this is his shield and sword against chaos – faithful to his wife. Within the confines of this faithfulness, pornography, street sexual anguish, feeling like he is going to faint in front of Lark and, once in a very blue moon, a lap dance, are containable. Beyond lie the great plains of infidelity; and Harvey feels that, right on the border to those plains, fringing it, like a fence that may be in one land or another or both, stands the private lap dance. Also:

218

Harvey is so aware of his own tendencies that he is frightened that the more intense, one-on-one intimacy of the private dance may lead him, instantaneously, to fall in love. Which would be both disastrous and embarrassing.

The music cranks up again. The thudding bass starts to give Harvey a headache, not helped by his having had two Budweisers, the second of which is sitting in front of him now, its last quarter, like all beers he has ever had, undrunk and turning sour. Away from the trance state that the gyrating female body inspires, a kind of alienation effect sets in, making him suddenly see no connection at all between the trimmings of this place – the bass lines, the lights, the mirrors, the velvet furnishings – and sexiness. As if to counteract this, two other dancers, who have been idling by the bar, move, with self-conscious slinkiness, towards him and Bunce. Harvey looks towards them, uncertain, but his fellow lap-dancee, sitting up and ready, has an air of knowing exactly what to do: he doesn't go so far as to wink at Harvey, but everything about his body language implies it. As the women get there, and settle, in front of the two men, hands on hips and eyebrows expectantly raised, Bunce yawns, theatrically, and says:

'Shall we make a move?'

'No. No. You're so wrong, Gold. The bigger and faker the better, and I think I like them even better when fully clothed. I like the cartoony element. I like them stretching out of a shirt or a suit or pulling some sort of fabric that doesn't want to be pulled any more. I want them larger than life, ridiculous, preposterous, because they appeal to my sense of the absurd, and my id's sense of the absurd; and I draw encouragement from the truth that the woman has spent a fortune and put herself into the hands of a mad scientist, has become Hanna Barbera's conception of a female, solely to draw men's sexual attention.'

Bunce slams his empty beer glass down on the bar as he says this. He is not angry, but Harvey confiding in him his uncertainty about false breasts has led to an outbreak of definitiveness on the subject. Bunce has no half-positions: he thinks in rant.

They are sitting in Why Not?, a bar on the corner of West 40th and 9th, overshadowed by the hulking concrete of the Lincoln Tunnel Overpass. Bunce, on leaving Exotique, perhaps to disperse pent-up sexual tension, had wanted to walk. It had felt directionless to Harvey, and when they ended up here, in the unhip section of Hell's Kitchen, he had started to feel anxious, a little because of an old 1970s sense that New York was dangerous at night, but more because the street-scape had started to resemble the badlands of his dreams. In his dreams, Harvey often finds himself lost in some tangled urban land-lock of shopless streets and dead ends and fenced-off areas and gravel-scrubbed waste grounds and closed industrial parks and half-finished bridges, black wires rising out of their broken struts and joists like the legs of insects trapped inside the masonry. This part of New York looks so like his dreams that he had started to wonder whether he had been here before, like something was jogging his unconscious. It gave him the creeps. The appearance of Why Not? felt oasis-like.

It is not, though, the sort of bar Harvey expects to find in Manhattan. This seems to be another trick, similar to his failure to find in the city a hotel room with the Promised View. What Harvey had assumed it would be was a long, narrow room, plush and hardly lit, with a bar flanking a series of narrow booths for the conducting of sexual and economic deals. Why Not? is not that. The fittings are pine; there is a jukebox, and a pool table, over which denim-clad men are bent; no women are present, apart from those serving drinks; and although there is not actually a confederate flag above the bar, when they walked in 'Tuesday's Gone' by Lynyrd Skynyrd had been playing. It feels to Harvey like reality is for once conforming to film and TV, except the wrong films, the wrong TV; expecting a bar out of *Sex and the City*, they have walked into one from *The Accused*.

Bunce orders two more beers from the woman behind the bar, who breaks the mood further by looking very like Angela Merkel.

'Bunce,' says Harvey.

'What?'

'Don't make me drink any more.'

'I'm not *making* you drink anything, Harv.'

'No. But you've ordered me another drink. And I'll feel the need to finish it, once it's here. And then I'll feel sick, and later – because I'm forty-four, and masturbation has, over many years, inflamed and swelled my prostate into a prostate wearing a fat suit – I'll spend all night going back and forth to the toilet.'

Bunce laughs, and Harvey smiles, although misgives a little inside, knowing that he has now started copying not just the accent but the speech rhythms of his alpha male friend. The fall in his stomach comes from a slippage of self, a knowledge that he is no longer quite his own man. The Harvey Goldness of him is vulnerable, easily contaminated.

The drinks arrive: Angela puts them down in front of the two men, and turns away swiftly in full, confident assurance of her invisibility to them. Harvey looks at it, finding as always the white froth more attractive than the urine-coloured liquid underneath. He wishes he had brought his last bottle of Extra Tart Sour Blast Spray with him. Perhaps he could have secretly gone into the toilet with it.

'So what the fuck are you doing these days?' says Bunce. 'Apart from waiting for your dad to die. Are you writing?'

'Yes. I wasn't for a long time. But, yeah. I just got a job here.'

'Here?'

'In New York. I'm writing an autobiography for a pop star. Well, I will be writing it. Once I get round to it.'

Bunce drinks, a big male glug: he drinks as if he is going to wipe his mouth across his face afterwards.

'Bono? Elvis Costello? *Beyoncé*?' He says it in an exaggerated black voice, with a snap on the last syllable. Harvey registers that Bunce is being cruel – ironically, obviously; it's all irony, everything is irony, the world is awash with irony – knowing that Harvey would never be in the frame to ghostwrite such people's autobiographies.

'No. Someone you've never heard of.'

'Some indie faggot?'

'No, but – you won't have heard of – of her.'

Bunce drinks more beer. Harvey can feel that the word *her* has made him want to interrogate further. It was partly the way he said it, stumbling slightly: like it was a secret. Harvey doesn't want to talk to Bunce about writing Lark's autobiography. He is embarrassed about it, because she is nineteen and hasn't done anything. But he also doesn't want to talk about it because he has been thinking a lot about Lark recently: a lot more than he really wants to. She is slipping out of her container.

'So anyway,' Harvey says, before Bunce has a chance to follow up on this line of questioning, 'how's sex crime?'

Bunce nods thoughtfully, before saying: 'I've really got to give it up.'

'Well, you haven't been caught yet.'

'No, but it's just a matter of time.'

Harvey smiles: this is the conversation he knew they would have. Bunce now works for the CSC, the Criminal Sexual Conduct unit of the Toledo County Detroit Prosecutor's Office. Bunce is an assistant prosecutor in the unit. He really is.

'No, but honestly – how the fuck did you end up in that department?'

'I dunno. The job came up.'

'What do you do all day?'

'I fuck up paedos. I take paedos down.'

'Great job description. Paedos? Not rapists? Flashers? Necrophiliacs? Horse-fuckers?'

'Not often any of those guys. We see all the colours of the male sexual rainbow in my work, yes, but generally we're dealing with the deepest, darkest black.' Harvey sees a gear change in Bunce's face, a shift away, amazingly, from irony, but not towards gravitas exactly; towards *OK, we're talking business now*. 'Say: rape. Sexual touching of children outnumbers it by at least fifteen to one. It is a fucking pandemic. Committed ten to one by men – overwhelmingly, white men. Also: ratio of touching by stepfather, as opposed to father, I'd put at about seven to one. There seems to be a taboo about one's own children, though it's often overcome. Stepchildren? Open season. Our office has five lawyers devoted full-time to prosecuting child molesters. And they are overworked.'

'Wow,' says Harvey, and then thinks how stupid a word that is in response to what Bunce has said. But Bunce has not noticed, has hardly paused for breath.

'And here's a weird thing. It is really common – heartbreakingly common – for the natural mother of the abused stepchildren to battle the prosecution at every step. Typical scenario: sexual abuse is detected; the stepfather stands accused; the mother of the children defends the rapist and focuses all her fury on the police, prosecution and children. Even when faced with conclusive evidence of guilt. Given the choice between her children and her man, too often there is no choice. The children are sacrificed to the lover. To the man.'

'But ...'

'What?'

Harvey doesn't know what to say. He wants to say: *But they are mothers.* Bunce takes his silence as shock, which it is. Harvey shakes his head, and takes a sip of the beer: sour, of course.

'I tell you, Harv, it must be the best sex ever, because I don't think you can ever rehab a real chicken hawk ...'

'A what?'

'Paedo. Child molester. That's what we call them in the biz. Let's say you lock one up for ten years, take everything away, stick him in a jail where he will be tortured every day as the lowest on the totem; beaten, spat at, pissed on, anally raped with iron bars, and that's just the guards – it's a fucking Hieronymus Bosch painting for them in there – and still: the moment he is released, he will not pause for food or rest or a hot shower, but will go right about the business of finding more young ass to penetrate. It is a drive unlike anything you or I will ever experience. My take? Easier to kick a fifteen-year crack habit than to curb your desire for young boys or girls. Harsh truth: the only thing we can do is lock them away. They haven't the strength to stop.'

Harvey nods, but doesn't feel entirely comfortable talking about this stuff. He knows what it is like to be driven and distorted by desire. He has no wish, however, to feel any kinship with these men. He shivers, repulsed by the thought.

'But how do you deal with it? Having to look at – whatever it is that you have to look at?'

'I deal with it by ... I don't know.' For the first time, Bunce's rhetoric falters. He shakes his head. 'It is hard. Some of the things I've seen

… I've been in rooms with people who like to think of themselves as the hardest of men – seen-it-all men, men who present themselves as having souls thick as lead – and evidence – films, fucking films, seized by the cops, that these scumbags have made of themselves with kids – has gone on the DVD player: and by the end, everyone – *everyone* – is crying.'

There is a silence. The image Bunce has conjured up has dried out Harvey's mouth: he has to drink some beer to rehydrate. Its effect is dizzying, as if the alcohol has been injected directly into his brain. Bunce breathes in. Harvey can feel him returning to earth, or at least Planet Bunce.

'And also,' he says, 'it doesn't make for easy chitchat. "Oh, hi, honey, what did you do today?" "Oh, watched another video of a four-year-old getting fucked. What's for dinner?"'

Harvey laughs, as he knows he has to. Laughter is the way of normalization; it's how modern man says whatever it is, I *can* deal with it.

'And what about sex – doesn't it weird up sex? Looking at that awful shit all day? Although you were always a bit weird about it …'

Bunce does a face of mock outrage. 'How so?'

'Oh, y'know. The way you always …' Harvey pauses, not sure whether he is straying into difficult waters.

'What?'

'Found fault. With women. You were always the guy who managed to find the fault. Even the most perfect looking women, you would scope it out somehow. Maybe that's why you went into sex crime.'

Bunce puts his glass down and considers. He is silent for so long Harvey starts to wonder if he had been wrong in thinking of Bunce as one of those people who it's impossible to offend.

'You're right,' he says, eventually. 'And you don't know the half of it. Not the quarter of it. Let me see. Reasons that I've broken off with women in my time include …' he spreads the fingers of his right hand and marks off the numbers with the index finger of the left, '… stretchmarks; too fat; too thin; facial hair; too much vaginal hair; too much anal hair; bad breath; too many moles; pores …'

'What about them?'

'Too big and open. Which suggested to me a weird kind of alien sweat; which I then started to smell on her. It may have been psycho-somatic. Irregular-shaped breasts. Irregular-shaped vaginal lips. Big hands. Veiny thighs. Protruding hips. Thin lips. I liked her.'

'What?'

'The thin-lipped one. She was great. Met her in a bar in downtown Detroit. I liked her a lot. But after about four dates, I was just thinking, so much: *if only she had just slightly thicker lips.* And I couldn't be doing with that thought in my head all the fucking time for the rest of my fucking life.' He sticks his left hand out now, and puts the right index finger on the left pinky. 'Shortness of neck.'

'Shortness of what? Are you mental?'

'A long neck, fellow. That's a great thing. Swan-like. You're a great writer's son, you should know. "Her neck was long, and finely tuned" – Henry Fielding, describing the beauty Sophia, in *Tom Jones.*'

'Yeah. Obviously, I knew that.'

'Cankles.'

'Fair enough.'

'Camel toe.'

Harvey frowns. 'But surely she could just have bought a less tight pair of trousers?'

Bunce shakes his head. 'No: it showed itself with every pair: I think maybe she had cloth-attracting labia. Spotty ass.'

'This is a different woman, now?'

'Yes. Unless I make it clear, each defect represents a separate reason for dumping a separate woman, OK?'

'You never operated a two – or even – three strikes and you're out system?' Why am I asking all these questions, Harvey thinks. Is it because whenever I meet men who can do this – go through women quickly, apparently unscarred; as if all the scarring has been inflicted only on the women – no, that's not quite it – *as if all the scarring of women has not scarred them* – I want to know how. I hate these men, and yet I admire them, Harvey thinks. I think of them, at some level, as courageous; as honest; as living a life close to the bone, the bad bone of what it is to be a man.

Bunce shakes his head again. 'One'll do it for me. BO.'

'BO?'

'Body odour. Smelliness.'

'I know what BO stands for, I just can't believe anyone's saying it when it isn't actually 1974.'

'Fuck me, man, she smelt like she last washed in 1974. Weird toenails.'

'Weird in what way?'

'Dinosaur weird. In my head I would imagine her cutting them with secateurs.'

'How many women have you been through?'

'A lot.'

'Is the dumping reason only ever physical?'

Bunce takes a sip of his beer; he chucks the liquid around his mouth before swallowing, to indicate consideration of this question.

'Generally. Although the finding of a personality flaw is, in truth, often concomitant with the finding of a physical one. One woman I thought was great. Dated her no problem for a month. Then it turned out that her hero, her fucking intellectual mentor-giant-guru-person-she'd-most-like-to-meet was Hillary Clinton. Five minutes after she told me that I noticed her nostrils were slightly different sizes.'

'Hmm.'

'And when I first starting working in Toledo County, I split up with an intern I was fucking – and she was gorgeous, astonishing, and properly fucking dirty, the imagination of an Arab dictator's harem-favourite combined with *circus*-level flexibility – because she told me there was a history of cancer in her family.'

'Oh, Bunce … that's terrible.'

Bunce does a *Hey, I don't make the rules* face. '*Breast* cancer. You can't be too careful.'

Harvey laughs, in spite of himself. He wonders, though, about a flaw that Bunce has not mentioned. He has not said: *too old*. I split up

226

with her because she was too old. Harvey has been thinking he will say it in a minute, fearing the saying of it, in fact, knowing it will pierce him. But so far he has not. Harvey wonders if Bunce, too, is part of The Great Silence; and then realizes no, he has not been with any of these women long enough for them to get old.

'You're such a cunt,' he says. Bunce smiles, pleased. 'And so *proud* of your cuntiness. It's incredible. What did you tell her?'

'I said *it's not you, it's me*. Of course.'

'Of course.'

'I said it with real tears in my eyes.'

'Yeah, yeah. Fuck, you've fucked a lot of women.'

'I have.'

'It's making me feel envious.'

'What did you think was the *point* of this conversation?'

Harvey laughs. 'But these are all still basically physical things. Hillary Clinton, yes, but then there was the nostril thing. And the poor intern, you split up with her because a picture of her in your mind with a double mastectomy made your cock shrivel.' He deliberately says *cock*, even though the word that appeared in his mind was *dick*: he is fighting the idiom, summoning his mental mujahedeen to resist America. 'There must be one –'

'Oh! Here's one! Do you remember that woman Bryony, who I was fucking at college, the one with the blind dad?'

'Yes! Fuck! Bryony! What happened to her?'

'I split up with her because she refused to believe that the Romans were ever in Britain.'

Harvey gasps. 'What? How could she not have known that?'

'I don't know, but the point is not that she didn't know it – although, yes, obviously, that's a sacking offence right there – but that having found it out – having had this piece of fundamental ignorance corrected, finally, at what, nineteen, twenty – she set her face against it. I tell you, I was still rowing with her and calling her a stupid bitch and telling her just to read fucking Gibbon long after I'd decided to split up with her. A voice in my head was saying, you don't have to do this – just walk out the door – but I just couldn't believe anyone I had ever been associated with could be so dumb.'

'Anything more to drink, gentlemen?'

Harvey looks up: it is the woman behind the bar. How long has she been there? As Bunce has warmed to his subject, and Harvey, drunk, has been drawn in by the tangy thrill of this unfettered man-to-man banter, he has lost track of the outside world, the two of them on their own in their unwatched-by-women bubble. But now he worries that she has heard much of it; that she may have been counting how many of Bunce's microfiche of female flaws she, a weighty woman in her mid-fifties, displays; and that therefore, any minute now, she will take a pair of bottles from the row behind her, smash their tops off and screw the zigzagged glass into each wrist, or, alternatively, his and Bunce's faces. Her expression, however, is unreadable.

'No, I'm OK, thank you,' says Harvey.

'Bring him one, would you?' says Bunce.

'*Bunce ...*' Harvey turns back to the woman: 'No, thank you.'

'You've got to drink. You have to toast me.'

'Toast?'

'I got married.'

Harvey opens his mouth in astonishment. His mouth is even more open than when, earlier, his nose had been crushed by silicon-impacted skin.

'You're joking.'

'No.' Bunce's expression is flat, but his eyes sparkle with the knowledge that he is upending Harvey's preconceptions. 'To my ongoing astonishment, I am a married man.'

'Who is she?'

'Her name is Kelly. Here.'

Bunce flicks open his phone, a BlackBerry. On its main screen is displayed a fair-skinned woman, with short, sandy hair, and an expression that says to the person with the camera: *I've got your number.*

'She's also a lawyer; a very unlesbianic tomboy, total extrovert, popular with women and men, unpretentious, non-neurotic, with good common sense that lapses far less often than with most women. I never wanted to be married – still don't. I'm radically unsuited to it, but I liked her so much as a friend that it turned into love. So here we are.'

'Fuck. For how long?'

'Getting on for two years.'

'What else are you going to surprise me with? Have you got kids?'

Bunce snorts. 'Fuck no. Being with a child? It's like hanging out with a drunk – the falling over, the incomprehensible crying, the even more incomprehensible laughing, the hitting, the shouting. But one you're not allowed to walk away from. Childlessness – and for that matter, petlessness – is a non-negotiable contract term.'

'What about her flaw?'

Bunce smiles. 'I'll find it eventually.'

Harvey glances back down to the phone, and thinks – based on an estimation that Kelly is about twenty-nine – *in about ten years time, Bunce, you and your fascist eye will be spoiled for fucking choice.*

'The fact of my being married is, of course, why I've packed, for this trip, a number of identical shirts.'

'Huh?'

Bunce is wearing what looks to Harvey like a 100 per cent cotton, white, button-down-collar, Brooks Brothers shirt. He raises his arm; The Material is streaked with brown.

'Something you need to know. American Caucasian strippers cover themselves in spray tan. It's happened to my buddies more than once: returning home to an accusing wife, standing in the foyer in hot denial, only to look in a mirror and see themselves covered in this brown chalky stuff nipple to knee, like they've just slid head-first into third base.'

Harvey immediately looks to his own clothes: the one pair of jeans he wears all the time, a dark blue Diesel pair he thinks don't make his hips look too bulgy and womanly, and a nondescript grey Gap top.

'You can't really see it on your trampy wear in this light, but I promise you it'll be there.'

Harvey brushes himself with his hand; sure enough, he feels the sticky dust clinging to his clothes. It sticks to his hand.

'I would recommend a very heavy laundering with starch at a Chinese laundry,' continues Bunce. 'Although that advice is based on my experience of wearing, y'know, proper clothes.'

Harvey looks down at the phone again. The image of Kelly clicks back to Bunce's home screen, a picture of himself that Harvey has seen before, on the Toledo County Prosecuting Attorney's website – Bunce, smiling, teeth forward, a kind of publicity shot, wearing a suit and tie, and underneath it, a white, 100 per cent cotton, Brooks Brothers, button-down-collar shirt. He lifts his glass, full of American beer.

'Congratulations, Bunce.'

And Bunce raises his, and they clink, and Harvey feels small drops of the beer fall onto his sticky hands.

*   *   *

Violet Gold sits in her room at Redcliffe House, holding her copy of *Solomon's Testament*. It has always sat on her little mantelpiece, next to a framed photograph of her nephews, a biography of Bruce Forsyth and two crime novels – one by Patricia Cornwell and one by Barbara Vine. She has never read the whole book, despite its dedication to her, printed after the title page. *To V.*

She wonders if now would be too late to read it. She has started it before, a few times. This copy, a first edition, was given to her by Eli on April Fools' Day 1953, three days before he left her. It is inscribed, below the dedication, '... *light of my life, love you still*'. And then he'd signed it: *Eli Gold*. She had thought at the time that that was a little strange – that he hadn't written Eli, or E, with maybe a few xxxxs. It speaks to her now of a number of things – Eli's apartness from her; his not wanting to put down in writing (especially not in writing) their intimacy; his grandiose sense of self, even in this, his first book, as if his name said in full had a power that diminutives would lack; his need to give her a clue that he would soon leave and therefore to familiarize her with a more formal type of address, a world in which pet names would be dead and awkward – but mainly she thinks *maybe he thought it would be worth more*. Maybe he thought, after I'm gone, she's going to need the money, and when I'm the most famous writer in the world, with my full signature that'll be worth something.

She tried to read it first on the night he gave it to her. Eli was out, again, as he was most nights towards the end of their marriage, and she went to bed early. She put her bedside lamp on, and read, like Eli did every night, although without all the sighing and blowing in frustration at the rival author. With the blankets around her, Violet felt a small thrill at the possession of her own territory, alone in their bed, reading. She didn't wear glasses, but considered looking for Eli's spare pair, not because the words were blurred on the page but because it would complete the picture of herself reading that she had in her mind.

But the book was difficult. She had read books before, schoolgirl stories, Angela Brazil, Dora Chapman, Elsie J. Oxenham, with titles like *Rosaly's New School* and *The Fortunes of Philippa*. These were about girls her age, and though their life and education bore no resemblance to her own – except on the odd occasion when Rosaly or Philippa would pass by some poor children and feel sorry for them – reading these books felt comforting to Violet, projecting her into a safer world, with rooms and fires and tea and turrets and rules that everyone knew without having to learn them. *Solomon's Testament* did not do that. It did not project her into any world. There were so many words in every sentence, and everything was *described* so much, that the only world conjured up by the book was a world of language – or, rather, a closed door of language, behind which lay the world of *Solomon's Testament*.

That was her first attempt. A few months later, after all Eli's things had gone from their bedsit, she picked it up again. But not to read it. It had crossed her mind to use the book to make some grandiloquent gesture, like women were supposed to in these circumstances – maybe burn the book, or tear out the pages one at a time, or write some obscenity across the cover and send it back to him in the post. None of which she did: when she thought about herself doing such things, it felt contrived, like behaviour copied from the movies. She knew that she wasn't coming up to the mark in terms of vengefulness, that the expected feminine response to being left by one's husband was rage, parleyed eventually into an air of good riddance to bad rubbish, but she didn't really feel it, however much she pretended it was the case to an encouraging Gwendoline. What she felt, in her heart of hearts, was that now at last she could get on with her life: the quiet, simple one she was supposed to have had.

Some years later, when Eli was long gone and had left his second wife, the French film actress Isabelle Michelet, she tried again, reading it not in bed but on the tube. The journey from Kilburn to Monument took over forty-five minutes in those days, and she noticed that a fair few people passed the time with books. She found that having a book with her made quite a difference to the way in which she travelled. Most importantly, it made her keener than ever to get a seat. She was, by then, over thirty: not old enough to have a seat given up for her in deference, nor young and beautiful enough any more for a man hoping to start a conversation to do it either. Or, at least, not considered so at the time; now she sees on television and in the magazines that women are allowed to hold onto youth and beauty for much longer, into their fifties even. So if she wanted to read she needed to find a seat: it was too uncomfortable to hold the book standing up all that way. She tried it once, but her hand began to hurt by Oxford Circus.

Mostly, though, she did find a seat, even in the rush hour. This was when she discovered her penchant for crime fiction. A good Agatha Christie, or latterly Patricia Highsmith, could wrap her in a bubble of narrative mystery, which protected her from noticing the packed groins in front of her face, or the rancid recirculated air of the tube. They also made her feel like she could read books for grown-ups, books about death and the dark side, and so felt minded to give *Solomon's Testament* another go.

It didn't work, though. Apart from anything, she was worried about the book's physical safety. The crime novels protected her; her copy of Eli's signed first edition felt like it was something *she* had to protect. Reading it on the tube, she was concerned that men might brush their grimy flies against its spine, or that if she put it down on the seat next to her it might pick up an imprint of the rough check, or that she might just leave it behind when she got off. The book itself made her feel more keenly than ever a sense that she was holding a rare jewel out on her palm for anyone on public transport to scratch, because the words within it so failed to create a bubble around her. They seemed designed, in fact, entirely to burst that bubble. *Solomon's Testament* made you aware all the time of the fact of reading – which made it very hard to go into the trance. And when you did, when for a couple of paragraphs she could follow it for long enough to feel that, yes, here was a story, then the character who she had hung her hopes on, who she would be using as a rope into it, would vanish, and a new one would appear, only for them to go a few pages later. Plus there would be characters who would recur, or at least Eli would be writing as if they were recurring, but she couldn't remember who they were, so she would have to flick back through the pages to try and find their first appearance, in order to identify and situate them in the crazed geography of the novel.

Sometimes, when she didn't have a book, she would buy a copy of the *Daily Express*, in order to do the quick crossword. She liked the replacement of one word with another, the filling in of blank space, the satisfying way the letters fitted together. But sometimes she saw, over the male commuters' shoulders, or on the backs of their copies of *The Times* or the *Telegraph*, the cryptic crosswords. She would stare at the clues and all they would do was stare back at her. 'A ring, found, makes the Hoover cleaner, perhaps'; 'The bell, not heard in this congregation'; 'Man, puts head in lion, tame?'; 'From Bletchley, a river next, sailed on by a sheikh'. They would not yield. Even when she saw an answer being pencilled in by one of the men, still nothing was clear – she still could not tie the answer to the clue, the meaning to the words.

This was what it seemed like reading *Solomon's Testament*. Like Eli had written a whole book of cryptic crossword clues. And what would be the point of that? Especially when he hadn't put in the answers at the back.

So she gave up again. And periodically, throughout her post-Eli life, she tried again. But it never took hold for her. And as her life went on, and her history with Eli became more and more unreal, there seemed less and less reason to read it. It was not her type of book. The only reason for her to read it would be her connection to the author, and as that connection frayed in her mind with time, the book sat on her mantelpiece: an ornament, a relic.

Valerie was always on at her to sell it. In the mid-1970s, she brought an antiquarian bookseller called Neville round, uninvited, to Violet's Cricklewood flat, in order to make an estimate. Neville was swarthy, and had a moustache whose tips ran all the way to his chin. He picked up the book and held it close to his face, as if sniffing it.

'I mean, who knows?' Valerie had said, flipping her arms up while keeping her elbows at her side. 'Some people *may* pay good money for it!'

She shook her head as she said it. Violet felt a little sorry for Valerie: she so clearly wanted this symbol of her sister's moment in the sun no longer to be around, but she also patently wanted to impress Neville, who Violet thought she may be having an affair with. She wanted him to make money from it; at the same time, she was desperate to suggest that the book was essentially worthless. Confusion rang out from her features, even as she pouted towards Neville.

'It's signed to you, I presume?' he said, looking at the frontispiece.

'Yes.'

'Did you know him well?'

'We were married. I am V.'

He opened his mouth, making his moustache curve down through the middle, like two arms describing the shape of a cartoon sexy woman.

'You were married?! To Eli Gold? Valerie, why didn't you tell me?'

Valerie raised both eyebrows and made a downward move at the corners of her mouth, as if to say: *Didn't think it was important.* They were having tea. The radio was playing tinnily in the background.

Violet had recently started to leave it on all day, perhaps as a counter-balance to living alone. She vaguely recognized the music as something by The Osmonds, that song with the sirens in it at the start. She didn't know anything about pop music, but she had seen them on the TV and found that the looks of the main one, the one with the teeth as white as a newly painted wall, moved something in her and made her want to blush.

'That's amazing. What's he like?' From the inner pocket of his tweed jacket Neville took out a packet of Menthol cigarettes and offered Violet one. She shook her head.

'Well, I don't know if I can say any more. We were divorced …'

'He left her,' said Valerie, taking a cigarette. She was supposed to have given up, but Neville being a smoker would have wiped out her resolution.

'… in the fifties. We were married ten years.'

'But still. *Eli Gold.*'

'I suppose he was –'

'Never mind about him,' interjected Valerie, waving a match out, as if its tiny flame were Eli's personality. 'What about the book? Come on, Neville – valuation's your strong point.'

Neville picked up the book again, and flicked through it with a certain self-consciousness, a sense that he was now performing the ritual which would demonstrate the truth that valuation was indeed his strong point. He drew deeply on his cigarette; a second later, smoke billowed from his nostrils. Violet imagined its tendrils snaking through the packed black nostril hair.

'Hmm … small amount of yellowing at the edges … in the original dustjacket … one tiny bump to the rear board … but overall a fine copy. And, obviously, the inscription adds a personal dimension, which a lot of book buyers love – Nabokov sometimes gives close friends copies of his books with a drawing of a butterfly on the flap: that'll add a small fortune to a copy of, say, *Lolita* …'

Valerie was nodding, as if this was all information that she, of course, knew already. She combined the nod with a smirk at the mention of *Lolita*, to suggest that such a reference must be flirtatious.

There was a pause. It was the kind of pause that in a few years, on *The Antiques Roadshow*, would be viewed often by Violet – though always with a certain level of discomfort, concerned that these people, normally aged and vulnerable, were about to be let down; or that, during the pause, they might not be able to keep the greed and hope out of their straining faces.

'Violet,' said Valerie crossly. Violet looked at her blankly. 'You're doing it *again*.'

'What … oh. Humming. Was I?'

'Yes.'

'I hardly know I'm doing it.'

'You always do it. The minute there's any silence. You've always done it. I wouldn't mind if you actually hummed a tune, a nice tune, but it never actually –'

'OK,' said Neville, breaking through the sisterly spat, which had rather destroyed the dramatic tension of his pause, 'I'd say, to a collector … if you were lucky … for this copy of *Solomon's Testament* …' He held it up, like a flaming torch, '… you'd be asking two hundred pounds.'

Valerie immediately let out a long, slow whistle, which, because it had so obviously been coming whatever figure Neville was going to quote, induced in Violet a shudder of repulsion.

'Oh,' she said.

'How *marvellous*!' said Valerie. 'Do you have a collector in mind?'

'I do, actually. Big modern classics lover. Jewish, so, you know – not short of a bob or two.'

'Although they don't part with it easily …'

'Don't I know it. But I think for *this* …'

'That's very interesting, Neville,' said Violet, getting up and brushing some biscuit crumbs off her skirt, feeling as she did so how wide-hipped she seemed to be becoming – *broad in the beam* her father used to call it, 'but I don't think I actually want to sell it.'

Neville coughed, and stubbed out his cigarette. Valerie narrowed her eyes at her sister, menacingly.

'Is the issue … commission?' said Neville. 'I normally charge fifteen per cent but in this case I was thinking – no more than ten …'

'No. No, I – I just think I want to keep it.'

'Right.' He scratched his nose. 'It's just that Valerie – I assumed … had you not spoken?'

'Yes! Of course!' said Valerie.

'*Val* …' said Violet.

'What? I remember quite clearly a conversation we had about what it might be worth.'

'Yes. Not about whether or not I wanted to *sell* it.'

'Well, what on earth else is one supposed to conclude from such a conversation?' said Valerie, raising her voice a notch not only in volume, but also in class. Violet had noticed long ago that her sister disavowed their background in the way she talked; when challenged, and angry, her vocabulary would not revert to type, like some, but instead become even more artificially refined.

'I …'

'Violet. Can I ask?' said Neville. 'If you don't mind, *why* don't you want to sell it? I mean, seeing as, as you said, it was all a long time ago …'

Valerie turned from him towards her, and nodded, slowly. 'Yes,' she said. 'Good question, Neville. *Very* good question.'

Violet was still standing. She felt awkward, as neither her sister, nor her sister's friend, had risen, which had the obscure effect, though she was physically above them, of making her feel the more bullied: as if both of them were simply ignoring her body language and its patent implication that this meeting was over. An answer came quickly to her mind: *That's none of your business.* It was followed almost as quickly, however, by a flash of uncertainty, an intimation that the phrase *that's none of your business* normally implied a clear, if private, motivation. But she did not know what her motivation was for not selling the book. Valerie was right, however sneeringly she said it: Neville's question *was* a good one. In the silence, surreally punctured by the fading of the synthesized sirens from the radio, various explanations did come to her:

I haven't even read it yet.

The smell of it reminds me of when I was young.

It's mine. It's signed to me. There's an inscription.

It's the only proof I've got that, once, I was married to Eli Gold.

The thought of saying these things out loud triggered in her a rush of self-pity. They made her sound so like a child; but she also knew, even as they appeared as discrete phrases on the wall of her mind, that she would never say any of them to these people, and felt sorry for herself again, trapped forever under the boot of inhibition. She felt a tear begin to appear and, for the first but not the last time, had an impulse not just to cry but to flood: to let all excreta come from all orifices at once; to respond to this question by melting in a heap of tears and snot and blood and shit and piss.

'Oh,' said Neville, flushing, 'I'm so sorry … of course. I'm sure it must mean a lot to you; please don't worry about it any more.'

'No, wait a minute, Neville …'

'*Valerie* …' This in a whisper. 'She's *crying*.'

Valerie frowned at her sister. For a split second her face softened, and there showed in it some sign of sibling concern, some trace memory of when she was five and Violet was seven and their father carried her in from outside because she had hurt her wrist on one of the cobbles, and Valerie's sky had fallen in. At this first intimation of life's capacity for damage she had begun to cry, much, much more intensely than Violet, and did not stop crying until Violet returned from hospital with her arm encased in a frayed, white plaster, and told her sister, many times, that she was all right. And then Valerie let this memory fall back into the velvet pouch of her soul, buried so deep now in the earth of her she had no idea it was still there: the softness vanished, no more than the faintest flit, to be replaced by the hard set of an eternal tut.

So now Violet opens *Solomon's Testament* again, which she has not done since that day in Cricklewood. She opens it at random. She knows that the opening chapter has defeated her, time and time again: the thought of starting again with *I am Solomon Wolff, and this is my testament* exhausts her, and, besides, she does not have the time. Eli will be dead soon, and so will she. That chronology – beginning, middle, end – does not apply any more. Near death, life shrinks to the quantum level.

She begins at a random page: 147. Dust motes rise from the page. She reads and reads: the one thing she has, even though she does not have it, is time. She has no time, and yet time stretches endlessly for her, here in the black hole of Redcliffe House, every minute an hour and every hour a lifetime. As she reads, something dawns on her: something so obvious, something which anyone who knew anything about books, and first novels especially, could have told her long, long ago, and which would have thrown the book into a new light, a light which perhaps might have allowed her to read it much sooner. But no one did tell her. No one told her that *Solomon's Testament* is about many things – America, Jewishness, language, class, comedy, food, sex, all that brave new 1950s stuff – but it is also, quite clearly, about her.

Harvey sits in his room, terrified. Like all people with anxiety disorders, he has read about the flight or fight response; about the amygdala and the hippocampus; about how the primeval evolutionary function implanted in us, designed to adrenalize the body when faced with a lion or a woolly mammoth, still squats in the brain like a blind, nervous toad, unable to see any difference between a woolly mammoth and a traffic jam, or a recalcitrant boss, or a computer malfunction: or, in this particular case, the possibility of illicit sex with a nineteen-year-old.

It's so useless, he thinks, the fucking flight or fight thing. If he listened to his body, now, it would mean either getting up and running away from the hotel screaming 'Help me! Help me! I might be able to have sex with a beautiful young woman! Aaaarggh!' or, alternatively, going up to the top floor, where Lark is waiting for him, and beating the shit out of her. Neither is a truly useful strategy for coping with the situation.

It was decided, after the initial meeting with Lark and her people, that the way forward with the autobiography was that there should be a series of conversations between the singer and her ghostwriter, which Harvey would record and make notes from, and then flesh out into Story of a Songbird. The first one was earlier this evening. It took place in a sushi restaurant on Madison and 97th. Harvey took his Dictaphone and his gold leather notebook. He also wore the black jacket from his one suit. He angsted about this for a while – should he really wear the jacket from his funereal robes? And why is he wearing it anyway? It's not a date, after all: not a fucking *date* – but after a while he just put it on. Stella called just before he went out the door; he didn't pick up.

At the restaurant, Lark, who had not dressed up – she was wearing jeans and a loose tartan shirt – told her story. She had been born in Belfast, but had been brought to London as a child. She had been a late birth for Michaela – an attempt, Harvey inferred, to save a fading marriage to Lark's father, who had already left the family house by the time she was born. Her father, who she'd seen irregularly after he left, died when she was twelve. As well as an actor, he had been a good amateur classical pianist and maybe this is where she got her interest in music. It was fortunate that Harvey had brought his Dictaphone to pick up these and other titbits from her life as concentration was difficult. The sushi, in particular, was an issue. Every time she brought a new piece up to her face, he became distracted by the idea that the raw pink fish flesh could seem, to a mind that might be led that way, like a little tongue fluttering across her mouth. Plus, knowledge of the behaviour of Japanese salarymen kept on urging Harvey's Tourette's head to shout, 'Hey! What don't you get on the table naked and let me chopstick this stuff off you!?'

He managed to control this urge. He did not control, however, his gaze. At first he would hardly look at her at all. He was too convinced his eyes would be see-through: too convinced, as well, that her beauty would rush in through them, like rapids flooding his heart. He had to protect it, this fragile place where his love – his exhausted, infiltrated, love – for Stella lived. But over the course of the meal he forgot about this need; and a cocktail of the natural body language of interview, three bottles of sake and Lark's blankness – it was as if he could stare at her all day and she might not pick up any agenda from it – brought his vision forward. As she talked, itemizing her life like a shopping list, he luxuriated in his licence to look. It was a liberation, for Harvey, not to look scurrilously, not to snatch secret glances. And as he looked, he let himself go. He let her beauty do its work. He let her beauty off the leash and allowed it to engender in him a deep, misplaced sense of peace.

On the way back to the hotel, Harvey felt that this was OK: that he had been granted an amnesty of sorts. Some climate confusion meant that the late August Manhattan air was colder than it should be, and he felt it as a slap, bringing him out of a trance. It allowed him to rebuild his defences, which he took to be unbreached. He could walk side by side with Lark, and look at her profile, and talk to her, and even play with the idea that this tableau, a man and a woman walking on a summer's night with Central Park on their right and Fifth Avenue on their left, might cause some onlookers to think – the ones who were not thinking 'nice to see a dad out with his daughter' – that they were lovers. He allowed himself to think, from behind a wall of what he considered to be ten-inch-thick self-awareness, 'Ah, in another life …' This is what the monogamous are often agonizing about: not the sex they did not have, but the lives. Harvey absorbed this thought, though, with equanimity. As they approached the Sangster, a senti-mental smile sat on his face like a meniscus of untroubled mercury.

And then she said: 'What floor did you say you were on?'

'The eighth. It's nice, but there's no view. And – well, I never seem to get a view when I'm in this city …'

'Come up to mine.'

She said it straight, with no hint of anything. They were standing just outside the lobby. Harvey felt his smile fade, and his anxiety levels shoot up. They don't build, his anxiety levels, they are faster than a supercar: they go from 0 to 100 in under half a second.

'Sorry?'

'Come up to my room. It's on the twenty-second floor. 2214. It's got an amazing view …'

'Yeah. You said that actually, when we first talked …'

'I know. I remember.'

Harvey nodded. He looked away.

'Well, OK, I will – at some point.'

'Come now. Mum's out with Josh. She won't be back for at least another hour; probably two. They're having an affair.'

Which is why he sits now, in his room, his skin tingling with sweat and his stomach churning like it's trying to make bile butter. He had made some ambiguous excuse about needing to go back to his room first – implying that, *second*, he would indeed be coming up to her room. She had said fine. They had shared a silent lift together, and he had got out at the eighth floor. He had looked back at her and she had looked straight at him, but he could not read it. He had no sense of what was going on inside Lark. He could see her but could not feel anything coming off her. It was as if she was looking out at the world from behind reinforced glass.

He does not, of course, think that Lark is interested in him physically, but he knows there are thousands of reasons why women sleep with men that have nothing to do with the male version of attraction. Women, sexually, have much more subtext. Perhaps she is doing it to get back at her mother for having this affair; perhaps she is impressed by the Eli Gold connection, although she has not mentioned it since their first meeting; perhaps she liked how he appeared to be listening raptly to her in the restaurant; perhaps she is just bored, and wishes to flex her beauty. It might be none of these reasons. She may indeed not even want to sleep with him at all.

Not that it would make things any easier for Harvey if Lark had said, in the same neutral way that she said everything else, 'I want you to come up to my room because I want you to fuck me.' Well: it would be easier in one way; insofar as Harvey would then not be facing the twin possibilities of rejection and humiliation – and, no doubt, removal from his first proper job for ages – along with the more direct ones of guilt, shame and destruction of his family life.

Harvey wonders how the other men – the ones for whom ending relationships is weightless; the ones who live close to the man-bone – would be in this situation. Is adultery also weightless for them? These sexual chances that tot up so apprehensively in the libido's memory – how unmanly is it not to seize them with both hands? To try and calm himself down, he starts a game of chess on his iPhone, but his thought process is so frazzled that even by his standards the game is short. Within seconds *Ting! Tiny wins*. He tries a mantra. *I would really like to have sex with Lark, but if I don't have sex with Lark, it's not the end of the world.* It does not engender even a flash of peace.

He tries it the other way. *I would really like to stay faithful to Stella, but if I don't stay faithful to Stella, it's not the end of the world.* He is considering that this second way does not quite work – the mantras are impulse controllers: they are meant to deflect desire, not duty – when he realizes how deeply, even though he has never said it before, he has internalized this idea, that he has always taken it for granted that infidelity to Stella would indeed be the end of the world. For the first time, his mind rises up against it. I am ill, he thinks, ill with attachment, ill with what time does, ill with love. Lark will give me a respite, won't she? A holiday from it all; a moment's health.

It comes to him that he knows who will provide the answer, at least as regards what a *real man* would do. It is too late to call, but he opens the Sony Vaio, and calls up Bunce's Facebook page. He types into the Instant Message box:

Bunce. Are you up?

A second later it comes back:

I was just thinking about you. Thinking about sending you something. I probably shouldn't but fuck it.

Whatever, yes. Do. Bunce: listen.

What?

He takes a deep breath and puts his fingers to the keyboard:

A woman – a young, very attractive woman – has just invited me up to her room. What should I do? And I know what you would normally say, but think about it for a second. You're married. I think that through all your big male bullshit you love your wife. I think even you would think twice. So. I love my wife. I really love my wife. But I'm fucked up. I'm fucked up about it all. What should I do?

244

He presses return. The reply does not come instantly. Bunce is doing what he asked: thinking about it. Harvey reads what he's written. It is a mess. It does not express how he feels at this moment, except in regards to being a mess. Then, these words appear in his inbox:

Yeah. It's a tough one. But here's the thing, Harv. Who do you want to be on your deathbed? John fucking Betjeman? Or Eli fucking Gold?

*   *   *

Last Saturday, Mommy arranged for Elaine to take me to the zoo. This was weird, because me and Elaine haven't done anything like that for ages, not since Daddy got ill. Because we spend all the time at the hospital. But also maybe because Daddy is gonna die soon, but nobody knows when it is and Mommy really wants me to be there when it happens, so, suddenly, it's like no daytrips, no play dates, and *definitely* no sleepovers at Jada's. Also the *zoo*; the *zoo!* Not like a museum, or a monument, or a music recital, or anything. I love those things, of course, but still, I really really really love animals.

And here's the *really* amazing thing: she called Jada's mom, and arranged for her to come, too! And Mommy never does anything like that. She never calls any of the other moms at the school herself, she always gets Elaine to do it. And she doesn't really like Jada. I know that's the truth. She would never say so, but every time I tell her about something Jada said or a TV show or a movie she's told me about, Mommy does that face that looks a bit like someone's pinched her.

And it is true that Jada never talks about books. I sometimes try and tell her about them but she always goes *bor-ing!* And does a big fake yawn. So I can see why Mommy doesn't like her. But the other thing is that Jada's mom doesn't like *her* going out with *me* when Elaine's so old! That's what she said, that she thought it was a bit weird that my nanny was so old and she had her own ideas about why my mom had hired someone over sixty. I don't know what that was about, and neither did Jada. But the point is, she thinks that Elaine might, I dunno, forget where we are, or fall over and break a bone in her skeleton or something while she's looking after us. It's crazy, she's not *that* old.

So that's why it's so AMAZING that Mommy sorted out a play date with her. And we had *such* a great time. We saw the lions and the zebras and the elephants; we saw the penguins being fed fish from buckets; and there was a monkey who was touching his winky-wonk over and over again! It was so funny! Although it looked a bit sore. And Elaine let us have an popsicle each – I had a Tangle Twister – *and* a bag of Toxic Waste to share. The sun was shining and Jada wasn't too *yeah, yeah* about it – she wasn't *yeah, yeah* about it at all – and even Elaine seemed to smile more than usual. I wish Jada's mom had seen her. She looked young: like, fifty.

After the zoo, we took Jada home. And then we went to the hospital. I thought we were just going in to spend a couple of hours in Daddy's room as usual before going home for dinner but then when we got there Mommy was waiting outside his door, standing next to John the security man. I got a weird feeling in my tummy when I saw her there, 'cos I thought: oh no, Daddy's died, and I wasn't there! But then she smiled, and opened her arms, and I ran into them, and she gave me the biggest hug.

I started to say 'What's going on …?' but she shushed me and held my hand and we started to walk along the corridor. We went past the little room that Dr Ghundkhali had taken us into that day, and then into another room. Mommy gave me a little smile, and then opened the door. It was quite a big room, although not as big as Daddy's. There was a window that looked out on all the skyscrapers. And there were two beds in there. One was bigger than the other. By the side of that one, there was a table, with a whole load of books on it, all by Daddy. And then there was a small bed. On that one, someone had put loads of my toys. I think it was meant to be all my favourite snuggle toys, but it wasn't. It did have my Baby Born and Dilip my kangaroo and Becky Boo who's a monkey that talks and I love all of them but then after them it just had loads of teddies and stuff that I don't even have names for any more, not since I was like six or something. Next to the bed was a little pink table, and on that was a frame with lots of little shiny jewels on it, and in that frame was a photo of Aristotle. Next to that was my Nintendo DS Lite, and Mommy's copy of *Mirror, Mirror* with all the crossed-out bits in it.

I turned to look at Mommy. She was smiling but it looked like she'd been smiling the whole time I'd been looking at the beds and the toys and stuff and now her smile was maybe hurting or something.

'Are we living here now?' I said.

'Well, darling. Yes. I suppose you could say that. Just for a bit.'

'How long?'

She stopped smiling when I said that.

'Darling … I don't know how long …'

I got it then. Whenever Mommy says she doesn't know how long we're going to have to do something, she means: until Daddy dies.

'Oh,' I said. I sat down on the bed.

'Don't you like it?' she said. 'We brought all your favourite toys.'

'You didn't.'

'We didn't? Elaine?' She was standing outside the room, but she came in when Mommy called her. 'I thought I asked you to make sure we brought all Colette's favourite toys?'

'Well, I …' said Elaine: she looked a bit upset, '… you know, Colette changes her mind quite a lot about which ones are her favourites.'

'I don't!' I said. 'And besides – I don't want to live here anyway!'

'You won't be living here, darling. You'll still be going back home some of the time. It just means that you can sleep here … now …'

'But I don't *want* to sleep here!'

She came over and sat down on my bed. She moved Becky Boo out of the way. She did a little nod, to Elaine, and Elaine went out of the room. She took my hand and put it in her hand. Her hand felt colder than I thought it would be because it's always quite hot in the hospital.

'Darling … you know we had that little chat with Dr Ghundkhali the other day?'

I nodded. I could feel that I wanted to cry. I was trying not to.

'Well, I've been speaking to him again … and: well, you remember he said that Daddy now … had something wrong with his lungs?'

'A lung infection. That's what he said. I remember.'

'Yes. Well, it hasn't got better.'

This made my tummy feel tight.

'But we spoke to him! We told him off! We said he mustn't let Daddy die!'

She squeezed my hand harder. 'I know darling. And he isn't doing … they have treated him. But it hasn't worked.'

'What do you mean it hasn't worked!'

'It hasn't worked! The lung infection hasn't gone away.' She shook her head and looked very sad. 'I don't know what else to tell you.'

I sat down on the bed next to her.

'Don't cry, Mommy,' I said.

'I'm sorry, darling,' she said. 'I …'

And then she did cry, really a lot. It felt really weird to see her cry.

She did cry before, when Daddy went into the hospital the first time, but this time it was much more. When she started she was just sniffling, but after a bit her mouth opened wide and even though no noise was coming out of it it was like she was screaming. Her mouth went all down at the sides of her face and she looked sort of younger, and much, much older at the same time. She put her hands up and covered her eyes, but she was crying so much that her tears came through the lines that your fingers make when you hold them together.

I held her hand and said, 'It's all right, Mommy. It's all right.' I said this even though it made me feel really strange inside that she was crying. Especially the way she was crying. I've seen grown-ups cry in the movies and they don't cry like that: they have a little tear and maybe they smile when they're doing it and they still look like grown-ups. Mommy was crying so much it was like she wasn't a grown-up any more.

I thought she might hug me or something when I said 'it's all right' but she just carried on crying. I didn't want to look at her after a while, so I looked away. Then Mommy said something, but I couldn't hear it at first.

'Pardon, Mommy?' I said, turning back. She did a big sniff. Her shoulders stopped shaking so much.

'I said …' She did a big gulp, '… does that mean you will stay here at nights now? Please? Until …?'

'Daddy dies?'

Her face went again then, all crumpled like a piece of paper you scrunch up.

'Yes! Yes! Christ, Colette, why do you always have to be so literal! Why do you always have to f-wording spell everything out!' Then she put her hand up to her mouth. She took a deep breath. 'I'm sorry, darling, I shouldn't have shouted. Or said that word.'

'It's all right,' I said. 'I've seen it before.'

'Seen it? What do you mean?'

'In here,' I said, picking up *Mirror, Mirror*. 'It's one of the words you crossed out.'

She took the book away from me. 'But when have you been reading it? When I'm not there?'

'Only once or twice. That time when you went to heat up Cuddles in the microwave, and once me and Jada found it in your bedroom.' She looked a bit shocked about it, so I said: 'I was only trying to show her what an important and clever book it is. Because she's always saying books are boring.'

'Right …' She had stopped crying now. She put the book back down by the side of the bed. Then she picked it up again, and put it in her lap. 'Well, it's a bad word.'

'Why does Daddy use it in his book then?'

She made a clicking noise with her tongue. 'OK, can we talk about this some other time? Just don't use it for now. And don't look it up on the internet.'

I nodded. Even though I already had.

'So: Colette. Please. Would you please agree to staying here, and sleeping in this bed, until – well, yes, perhaps, you're right: perhaps we just need to say it out loud – until Daddy dies.'

I looked at her. Her eyes were so red and wet. I felt really sorry for her.

'No,' I said.

*   *   *

RW: So your suicide note …
EG: Yes?
RW: Can I read it to you?
EG: Can I stop you?

[pause]

RW: Reading to Mr Gold case document R45/103. 'I have – of late, but whereof I know not, lost all my mirth.' Period. And it's signed, EG.

[pause]

RW: I said earlier on that Larry Barnett might think your note valuable as it's an original piece of writing from a Pulitzer Prize-winner. Of course, it's not …
EG: I guess not.
RW: It seems odd to me that you didn't want to write more.
EG: I have writer's block. I've had it for a few years.

[pause]

RW: Are you serious?
EG: Deadly. I have writer's block. That means I cannot write like I used to. Why would I want the last thing written by me to be substandard?
RW: So you chose instead to quote something that obviously is not substandard …?

[pause: sound of EG sighing]

EG: Not really, Commissioner. It's all more complicated than that. And at the same time, not. I did have a longer and more explanatory note planned. But when it came to it, that's what I felt like saying.

[pause]

RW: It does put the quote into an interesting new context, of course. I suppose it's art, in that sense. Conceptual. Like an installation. You've done a bit of that recently, haven't you?

EG: Yes.

RW: I saw the Butter Mountain thing. I liked it.

EG: Thanks.

RW: A way through writer's block? A way of still creating, without words?

EG: I really don't have time for this, Commissioner.

RW: Did you think of you and your wife's suicide as a kind of art?

EG: No, of course not.

RW: But you thought it would be beautiful. You wanted symmetry. Which is of course the basic component of beauty … conventional beauty …

[pause]

RW: Would you call yourself a perfectionist, Mr Gold?

EG: Not really.

RW: Well, I would. A writer – a great writer – who won't even put his own words on a suicide note in case it falls short of his standards? I'd call that a perfectionist.

EG: My suicide note is –

RW: A lot of great writers – great artists – great *men* – are perfectionists, aren't they? They have to have perfection around them. They have to have symmetry. Like … you know that bit in Bellow's last book where the Uncle guy says that even though his wife was fantastic and beautiful he had to leave her because he could never get over the fact that her breasts were slightly too far apart?

EG: Saul Bellow has written two books since *More Die of Heartbreak*.

RW: He has? Do excuse me.

EG: And – Jesus, I can't believe I'm having this conversation, here now – it's not Saul speaking. It's his character. Uncle Benn. That's what you people always get wrong, don't you? You always think that whatever's in the book is exactly what the author thinks.

251

RW: Yes, of course. Uncle Benn. I remember now. Who is – correct me if I'm wrong – a great man, though, no? In his field.

[pause]

RW: I'm not talking just about the fact that if you're a great man, you've gotta leave women. I mean, we all know that. That's part of the deal. I mean, you, you're a cast-iron Great Man. You own the patent. So you should know. But it's true, isn't it? I mean, just now, I read in the paper – can you believe this – Stephen Hawking – you know, the guy in the chair? The superbrain physics guy with the computerized voice-box thing? He's just left his wife. I mean, the guy can't even walk: but he's managed to get up somehow and leave his fucking wife. It's in your Great Man DNA.

[pause: more sighing]

EG: So what *are* you talking about, Commissioner? I'd love to know.
RW: I'm talking about how that connects to their work. Sometimes great artists – when they're with the wrong women – they get stymied, don't they? Their mojo goes. They need someone new to get the creative juices going. Like … I don't know … I'm sure you could come up with an example better than me. Picasso! He was all washed up, wasn't he, by the end of his first marriage – hadn't done anything good for years – then he starts fucking Marie-Thérèse Walter and bang – he's painting masterpieces like there's no tomorrow.

[pause]

EG: First, psychoanalysis. Then, high literature. Now, high art! My, my. How long did you spend mugging up for this interview, Commissioner?
RW: How long have you have had writer's block, Eli?
EG: Three years.

RW: And you and Pauline were married how long?

EG: Seven.

RW: And how long would you say it was before the marriage became … imperfect?

EG: Did I say it had?

RW: Well. They all do.

* * *

It is, indeed, a wonderful view of Manhattan from Suite 2214. It is an even better view than his father, if he could, would see from his hospital room. The view from Mount Sinai is beautiful, but it is across Central Park, which means it only really works during the day, and, looking through Lark's window, he realizes that the truly archetypal vista of Manhattan is at night. For all the force of the other images – the steam rising from the manholes one; the crisp, bright, walking-through-a-flea-market-in-Greenwich-Village one; even the City of Man from the Brooklyn Bridge one – it is this one – the skyscrapers attempting to outglitter the stars – that most chimes with the Platonic Idea of New York City.

It may be the case, though, that it just happens to chime most with Harvey at this moment, a moment he is desperately trying to lose himself within. If, as Dr Xu and many others believe, the secret of happiness is to live in the moment, then Harvey is certainly doing his best. He is trying to use the view, and the romantic whoosh it might generate, to shut out the future: to shut out any sense of consequence.

He turns to see Lark looking at the view, too, her profile unnecessarily well lit by the refracted city lights. Sometimes, in Harvey's tortured sexual aesthetic, young women are too young – some young women just look like young girls, and absurdly subject though he is to the tyranny of soft skin and unlined eyes, he is not attracted to youth per se. His obsession with ageing is mechanical – it is to do with skin, with the sliding of the soft machine, not some Nabokovian need for innocence, or childlikeness. But Lark, although clearly not old, has something unyoung about her; there is something in her impassivity

253

which translates as maturity, even wisdom. She turns to him with her blue-blank eyes and he feels this to be true.

'Amazing, isn't it?' she says. 'Some people think that only natural things can be beautiful. But man-made things can be, too.'

'Yes,' says Harvey. He glances away from her, because he cannot take her gaze and what it might imply. The clock on the bedside table, glowing red, says 11.15. He wonders what time Michaela might be coming back.

'Harvey …'

He hears, through the deadpan intonation, some hint of a cue. Like a whip crack, he switches his attention back to Lark.

'Yes.'

'There's a reason I wanted you to come up.'

He feels his anxiety rise past an unprecedented level at this confirmation. Why should desire, he thinks, induce such fear? Why should getting what I want scare me so much? She looks down, reaching up a hand to the buttons of her tartan shirt. Behind her, at the corner of the far wall, Harvey sees the black edge of a grand piano, a wall-mounted Bang & Olufsen, a set of lacquered boxes, a fireplace with faux-quartz logs, and an oak cabinet containing row upon row of old books: *Of Human Bondage*, *The Scarlet Letter*, *Jude The Obscure*, *What Maisie Knew*. He even sees, on the sage velvet seating area, the first edition of *Solomon's Testament*, next to the mock-up cover of *Lark: Story of a Songbird*. Lark shifts towards him, an angel in this hotel heaven.

He moves his face closer to hers. When she looks up his lips are open and ready and his need to kiss her is so strong that only a very tiny part of him is worried about his breath. A blur of silver juts in front of his eyes. He backs away.

'What's that?' he says.

'It's a dongle,' she says. 'For a computer.'

'Right …'

'It's got some of my songs on it. Five of them.'

'OK …'

She proffers the dongle again, like she might offer a suspicious cat a piece of fish. Harvey stares at her. He realizes that that is why she has just reached up a hand to her shirt: to take the dongle from her breast pocket.

'It's so stupid,' she continues. 'You were right. *Of course* you can't write my autobiography without hearing my songs. You can't know who I am without my songs. My songs *are* me.'

It is the most animated Harvey has seen her. She continues to hold out the dongle. In its tremulous gravitas, her attitude is reminiscent of a mother handing over her child for safekeeping. He looks out of the window. New York seems suddenly drained of glamour, just a bundle of corporate towers that leave their lights on all night.

He looks at Lark. Her face is blithe, blank and clear as a white wall; but then her eyes, betraying some fear, move away from his face to check the door behind. Harvey realizes that she is worried her mother may come in and catch her doing this: *breaking the embargo*. He breathes a deep sigh, of sadness but also of relief. God has passed from him his cup of delicious poison. He nods, and from her hands he takes the dongle, registering that this flash of her fingers across his will be the only time he will touch her flesh tonight, or any other night.

Later, much later, Harvey Gold is sitting in his own room, naked, staring at his laptop computer. He has masturbated many times for a man of his age. Next to him are five empty miniatures of various spirits. It is, as we know, part of Harvey's unmanliness that he does not like alcohol, but he can swallow it like medicine when he needs it to act on him like medicine. He has taken it now in order to make him sleep, but that has not worked as yet – first he has to sit through the drink making him drunk.

When he had initially got back to the room, the relief was still with him. The lack of anything happening between him and Lark allowed him to call Stella back, and to tell her he loved her without compunction. In truth, he could have come back from Room 2214 having impregnated Lark and it would nevertheless be absolutely the case that he loved Stella, but *I love you* was still easier to say having not done so. Four hours later, however, he awoke with a heart-stopping start, and, sensing anxiety spread over him like some awful spiritual dandruff, headed for the minibar. Now all he feels is furious and old and mad and drunk and sick and excluded forever from paradise.

On the side of the computer, in a USB port, is the silver dongle. On the screen is a new Word file, titled *Lark: Story of a Songbird*. He has written the opening paragraph of the first draft of her autobiography:

> My name is Lark. Actually, Samantha Spigot. I'm a 19-year-old singer. At the time of writing, I've done nothing special or interesting in my life so far. By the time this book comes out, though, I'll be a star. My face will be all over magazines and TV and what cunts who aren't funny call the interweb. This is nothing to do with my songs. It's to do with my face, which is beautiful. People will want to see my face and so they ascribe talent to it. Other people will back the desire to see that face with money, which is why you will have seen it everywhere. It will in fact be the reason you will have bought this book. But shame on you. Shame on me. Shame on all of us.

He wrote this at the height of his drunkenness, a drunkenness which has now fallen – as it does quickly with Harvey: the window in which he is actually drunk, as in whirling and uninhibited, is very small – into a scratchy, dizzy nausea. Surprisingly, he has rewritten it a couple of times, making a few judicious edits. He has attached it to an email, cc'd to Alan, Michaela and Josh, entitled Lark: Autobiography Intro … and then, in the body of the text, written 'hi guys. this is kind of the way I'm thinking of going with this. all comments appreciated. H' His thumb dallies over the track pad, ready to click send.

He can't see any reason not to click, even though he is sober enough now to remember that he does, actually, need this job – he needs the money, and, more than that, he needs the work: he needs something to employ and distract his mind away from bad rumination. But he does not want to write Lark's autobiography. It is not just bitterness: even in the face of all this belittlement, some tiny shred of self-esteem clings to his ego like a determined embryo to the walls of a threatened womb. He is Eli Gold's son, and should not be writing the life story of someone who has not yet had a life.

His thumb hovers again. The child's cry, *it's not fair*, sounds again like a bell deep in his being. But because Harvey, despite everything, is a good man – or at least, trying to be good – or at least, someone who has picked up enough from people around him to know what goodness is and feel that he should aspire to it – because of this, he is alive to other unfairnesses, even ones which might not be targeted at him: even ones which might be *emanating* from him. So, before clicking on send, he thinks, 'OK. Just one. I'll listen to one …' and he opens the MP3 files on the dongle, which is entitled, simply, *Songs.*

He highlights the first file, called *Astray.mp3*, and double-clicks. Some acoustic guitars, and then some words: the usual string of pop words, love words – heart, hand, hope, sun, rain, you, me. They don't really matter, the words. Even through the travel speakers, it is clear: the song is beautiful. Lark's voice is beautiful. The flat nothing of her sat-nav tone is transformed, through the alchemy of music, into a glorious breath instrument. This music will be beautiful, he realizes, long after Lark is not. And then another revelation comes to him: Lark has Asperger's. Or something like it – she is, in the modern idiom, on the spectrum. That explains the voice, the blankness, the complete failure to understand how the invitation to her room may have been misinterpreted, and why something about her manner has always seemed familiar to him. She is like his son. She is like Jamie.

Except in one respect, made clear by this song. She has a talent. She has an extraordinary talent, which Harvey cannot but feel is provoked in some way by whatever her place is on the spectrum. His finger goes back to the track pad on his computer. He highlights the paragraph entitled *Lark: Story of a Songbird*, and clicks delete. It goes, revealing only the white of the unwritten-on page, and he bursts, suddenly, into tears: not small dignified sobs, nor the pleasurable trickle-down-the-cheek inspired by sad films or sad songs – so much liquid pours from his eyes and nose he thinks he might dehydrate. It runs in rivulets along the corrugated lines his face makes as it contorts in a series of huge silent howls. He does not know what is making him cry, whether it is the music, or the blank white page, or his exile from the young

PART TWO

It is a mountain of butter. It really is, with peaks and ridges and outcrops. Roughly his height, it reminds him of the snow-capped ones that surround Utah Lake. He finds it confusing. He has come here expecting to find another reason to hate The Great Satan. Instead, there is something he likes about it. He gets it. He gets that it is interesting to see something so soft represent something so hard. He gets that it is like an old-style work of art, like an old-style landscape painting, but done in a newfangled way. He gets that it refers to a long American tradition of butter sculpting, because he has seen ones of cows and suchlike at farm fairs around American Fork: in Provo, a few years back, he even saw one that the local people had made of the Last Supper. And he likes the creamy, curdy, breakfast smell, rising into his nostrils in the cold, processed air of this semi-refrigerated room.

He is on his own in the room, just him and the Butter Mountain and the words '*Butter Mountain*: Eli Gold, butter, 1991'. He feels fury rising within him at liking it – more fury then if he hadn't, more fury then if he had just seen it and thought what a fucking waste of space. He is tired of confusion: tired of complexity, of feeling – what did they call it? – *conflicted*. He has not expected to feel like this. Confliction – he does not know if that is a word – has no place in his destiny.

On the side of the wall is a glass case, which contains a thermostat. He hits the case hard with his bare fist – it shatters easily and noiselessly – and turns up the temperature as high as it will go. He expects alarms to go off but they do not. He walks out of the Kneibler Project Space Gallery in SoHo, sucking the blood from his knuckles.

✳ ✳ ✳

Checking out of the Sangster Hotel, Harvey Gold feels bad. The man on reception, the same autumnal-suited one who checked him in, hasn't helped. He's making him sweat, something Harvey does a lot anyway these days. Sweat used to build up in him over time, and was a response to being too hot, or, less often, because he did it less often, exertion. Now it comes on in a clammy rush, with a prickle in the armpits, on a variety of dread triggers, some of which he knows – a call from Freda, Jamie starting a tantrum, Stella walking under strip lighting – but others of which are more obscure. This one is clear enough. The man is taking a long time over the checkout, scrutinizing the bill, frowning over the AmEx number, and, now, telephoning the bank. The grey plastic receiver is wedged between his chin and his ear, and he is fixing Harvey with eyes that somehow manage to be both dead and searching. Harvey stands by, his suitcase lying uncomfortably against his leg, feeling his pores ooze.

The problem is that Harvey has gone for it. He's put his bill on Eli's card, while remaining entirely uncertain if he's allowed to. When, yesterday at the hospital, Freda suggested he move from the hotel, he had wanted to ask about who would be picking up his bill – the thought of which brought on an armpit prickle all by itself – but the conversation moved so quickly into such complicated waters that he never got a clear run at the question.

When he arrived, Freda had been in the corridor, deep in conversation with an older woman. Harvey had noticed this woman last time he came to Eli's room at Mount Sinai: she had the big glasses and the woolly-hat hair of the eternal hospital receptionist, so that was what he had assumed she was. Freda, unaware of Harvey's approach, was saying:

'... you really can't? Not even if we up your wages to cover the sleepover time?'

The older woman shook her head. Harvey stood a few feet away, unsure of whether to interrupt. John looked at him, impassive as ever.

Harvey made a stab at a friendly, 'Hi' face, which gained, from John, continued impassivity.

'I'm so sorry, Mrs Gold. But my mother is …'

'Your mother, of course …'

Harvey was startled by this information, that the older woman had a mother who was still alive. So, he sensed, was Freda, even though she must have known it. He sensed that Freda was perpetually startled by it.

'… not well herself, and I really don't think I can just spend so much time away from her, at the moment.' She stopped, and took her big glasses off, and cleaned them thoughtfully with the satin material of her blouse.

'Oh God. You do realize the stress I'm under at the moment, Elaine?'

'Of course I do.'

'Not just Eli, but trying to keep on top it all – Colette, the media, the publishers, and now I hear that the Butter Mountain has started to melt …'

'Melt?'

'Yes! Kneibler just called me.'

'How?'

'Some problem with the temperature control.'

'Can they put it back together?'

'Elaine. It's a *mountain*. Made of *butter*.'

Elaine made a sympathetic face, and put her hand on Freda's arm.

'Look. Maybe you just need to talk to Colette about the idea of staying here again. I'm sure she can be talked round.'

Freda's head moved from side to side. 'I don't know. I think she's changed.'

'Well …'

'I'm sorry, Elaine, I do. Ever since Eli got ill. And especially since he went into the hospital.'

'Changed in what way?'

'She seems more aggressive to me.'

'She does?'

'Does she not to you?'

The older woman – who Harvey now understood as Elaine – shook her head.

'Is she just being more aggressive to *me*? Is that what you're saying?'

'I think,' said Elaine, 'that Colette is a very young girl, who, because of …' she waved her hand towards Eli's room, '… the circumstances is having to grow up very quickly. And that's going to have an effect on any eight-year-old-child.'

On the back of Freda's head, Harvey saw a tiny tightening at the crown, from which her black-grey curls spiralled.

'She is not *any* eight-year-old child, Elaine.'

For some reason, John the security guy chose this point to cough. Freda's face turned, into a sharp profile. John moved his eyebrows up, and nodded in Harvey's direction.

'Harvey!' said Freda. 'Wow! You are happy to turn up *whenever* these days, aren't you?'

'Sorry, I …'

'Hi,' said Elaine. 'You're Colette's half-brother, aren't you?'

'Yes. Hi. Nice to meet you.'

She put out the same hand, with its landscape of veins, bones and freckles, that had waved towards Eli's room a moment earlier. Harvey took it in his.

'I'm Elaine. I'm Colette's nanny.'

'Oh! Of course. Sorry, I couldn't help overhearing … what – what's the problem?'

Elaine looked to Freda for some sort of permission. Freda shrugged, sullenly. Elaine returned her gaze to Harvey.

'Mrs Gold has decided to stay here at the hospital at night from now on. She was trying to convince Colette to stay here overnight too, but … she doesn't want to. So she was asking me if I would move in to their place but …'

Harvey looked at Freda. 'You're staying here? Sleeping here?'

'Yes.' said Freda.

'Since when? I mean, from when? When's that gonna start?'

'As soon as we sort out the situation with Colette.'

Harvey found that he was rubbing his face with his hands. *Why? Why am I doing that?*

'So that means …?'

'It doesn't mean anything, Harvey. Eli has a lung infection. The doctors are working on it. I just – I wanted to take the precaution. Of being around, twenty-four seven.'

Harvey looked at the floor. It was weirdly black, he noticed for the first time. *What is that? Lino? Do they have lino any more? Did they ever have it America? What is lino?* He felt, inside him, a speech germinating. A speech that began: 'I'm his son. OK? I'm his *son*. I would like to be told, if he's about to actually …' but he never got to finish it, not even in his head, because Elaine said:

'Hey! Excuse me if I'm speaking out of turn, but … maybe … Harvey – would you be able to move into the apartment?'

'Sorry?'

'Eli and Freda's? Because you're staying at the Sangster, right?'

She pronounced her s's with a hint of a following h, like older people sometimes do: *shtaying. Shangster.* Something to do with the teeth, the way that after a while they begin to sit haphazardly in the mouth.

'Yes.'

'Well, that'll be costing a fortune. And you are family. It's …' She stopped here, realizing she might be about to cross a boundary. The sentence continued in the air: … *crazy that you're not shtaying at your father's apartment.*

Freda was frowning hard at Elaine. Harvey looked at her, expecting her to be so angry that she might catch fire. But then his stepmother's face cleared; she smiled, and turned to Harvey.

'You know, Elaine, that's a good idea. A very good idea. Can we sort that? How quickly could you move in?'

'Really? You want me to stay at yours?'

'Yes! Why not? I don't know why we didn't think of it earlier! I've been worried anyway about leaving the place empty for such long periods of time.'

'But Colette … will she be all right with …?' Harvey didn't quite know how to frame what the issue was here, so he just said: '… me?'

He remembers how her eyes had been so full of fury when she screamed that thing about Eli hearing everything still despite his coma, that time he was trying to tell Roth how much of a fan he was. It was almost like she was screaming it at him. But maybe it had just been a weird kid's tantrum, and he just happened to have been in the firing line.

'Oh, she'll be fine. She'll still be here most of the time. It's just at night. She doesn't want to sleep here at night.' On the word *here*, Freda waved her hand in the air, to indicate, simultaneously, *the hospital* and *it's just a child's silly nightmares*.

'And when Colette has decided something, she has decided something,' said Elaine.

'Yes,' said Freda. '*Exactly* like her father.'

She beamed at him. Freda had managed, in this small time, to convert Colette's resistance to her wishes into something positive, by rewriting it as a dramatization of her daughter's genetic inheritance; as a realization of her inherent, inescapable Eli-ness. Harvey wondered if she could ever recognize such Eli-ness in him; whether she even remembered, when telling him what Eli was like and how alive such traits were in Colette, that he was her husband's progeny, too.

Elaine excused herself, tactfully – having put this particular cat amongst these particular pigeons, Harvey sensed in her the grace to let him and Freda discuss it in private. He didn't, however, immediately know what to say to this request – which, he noted, had not been phrased as such. He knew – or certainly had come to understand since being in New York – that the reason he had never been invited to Freda and Eli's apartment was because to set foot in it would have been to encroach onto a sacred space, a space from which he was *more* barred as a result of his family closeness, disturbing as it did Freda's preference to airbrush Eli's previous families out of history – but that now, the site of that sacristy had shifted to the hospital. Thus her sudden acceptance – positive endorsement, in fact – of Elaine's idea, because it allowed her to do the thing that Harvey has realized she always needs to do, which is to consolidate her position at the top of the nearness-to-Eli hierarchy. Harvey moving into the apartment does that, relegating him to a Colette consort, an on-call driver for Eli's daughter should his father start to breathe his last. It occurred to him, therefore, that the best way to challenge this hierarchy – he heard Stella's voice in his head encouraging him to do exactly this – would be politely to refuse the move, and ask for a room at the hospital himself. But he didn't. He couldn't be fucked. Freda has so much more energy for all this than he does. Plus he won't have to tip some flunky every time he fucking moves. Plus he won't have to fear bumping into Lark or her mother in the lift. Plus it'll be more comfortable.

'Um … OK.'

Freda smiled, a really big one, her top lip going up above her teeth to reveal a layer of gum as pink as bubblegum. She looked genuinely grateful, and Harvey felt suddenly sorry for his stepmother; he felt how hard all this was for her, how long it had been since something good had happened to her. She put one of her hands on Harvey's chest, fingers outspread, and raised the index finger of her other one. 'You have to promise me one thing though.'

'Yes?'

'You have to keep your cellphone on at all times. Because …' She looked through the porthole to her right; Eli's oxygen-propelled chest was just visible, rising and falling above his bed sheets, '… I may need you to bring Colette down here. At any time, day or night.'

Her eyes came back to Harvey. They were fierce with gravitas. Her finger was still in front of his face, an antenna twitching with seriousness.

'And Elaine – I mean, she's amazing, Elaine, a fabulous child-minder, but she's, you know – old. She doesn't always hear her cell. She doesn't always remember to charge it up. She basically doesn't quite *get* cellphones.'

Harvey nodded. His mother had been the same: *Why would I want people to be able to contact me wherever I am all hours of the day*, Joan had said when he, concerned about how regularly she was getting lost out on her daily walk, had bought her a mobile. 'Because if Eli – well, you know what I mean.'

'Yes.'

'You need to be ready for that call, Harvey. OK?'

Harvey, feeling a need to respond with more than just a nod, wanting to move past whatever block he always felt with his father's wife, reached out for her with his hand. Her hand, however, was still raised in front of his face, index finger-first; which caused him to grasp her finger, and tighten his fist round it: which both looked and felt weird, and not a little inappropriate. She looked at the hot-dog shape their hands made together, then at Harvey. He relaxed his grip. She pulled her finger out.

So that is why, sweatily, Harvey is leaving the Sangster Hotel. Beautiful women pass by in the lobby, as they do everywhere expensive. His eye is drawn to them, but also to a black – African-American? Is that right? Harvey knows it is but finds it an uncomfortable phrase, because of the implication that black Americans are not totally American – woman behind reception who he has not seen before. His guy is still on the phone, so he turns to her.

'Hi.'

'Hi!' she says, startling him with her upbeatness, although he should be used to it now. He's been in America for a while.

'I'm just checking out …'

'OK, sir. I do hope you enjoyed your stay.'

He feels his honesty imperative tingle: *Well, just a couple of nights ago I was up at four o'clock in the morning drunk and weeping and hitting myself in the genitals …* but he swallows it.

'Yes, thank you very much.'

'Great.'

'I was wondering: could you make sure this gets to the woman in room 2214?'

He hands over an envelope, on which he has written Lark. Inside is the silver dongle, and a note which says, 'Lark: Your songs are beautiful. But I'm not going to be writing your autobiography. Sorry. Best of luck, Harvey.' He had wondered about saying, after 'your songs are beautiful', 'as are you'. He had wondered about one or two kisses after his name.

'OK, sir. I know the ladies in room 2214, so that'll be fine.'

He feels a small ball of anxiety burst in him, like a bath bomb. 'Yeah. The *younger* woman …'

'I'm sorry, sir?'

'Well, as you say, there are two women in that suite. That package is for the younger woman not the …' He hesitates: the phrase *older one* weighs heavy in his mouth: is it unacceptable? What's the equivalent of *African-American* here? '… It's a mother and a daughter. Can you make sure the daughter gets it?'

'We'll do our best, sir,' she says, '… although sometimes I see those two about the hotel and they look just like sisters to me!'

She laughs, and he does his best to laugh along with her.

'No. Yeah. OK. Thanks. Bye …' says the man on the phone to the bank. He puts the receiver down.

'No, that's fine, Mr Gold,' says the man. 'We can charge everything to that AmEx card.'

'We can?'

'Yes, sir. That's what the bank is telling me.'

'Extras, too?'

The man looks up and smiles. Harvey cannot read his face but thinks it might be in reaction to his silly, instant hopefulness. He hopes it's nothing to do with any particular item on his Extras bill.

'Yes, sir. I suspect you could have upgraded yourself to a much superior room if you'd wanted to. Perhaps on the twenty-second floor … the view from there is *remarkable*. Still: next time perhaps?'

*   *   *

– What are you doing?

He looks round. At first, he does not recognize the woman who is speaking, but then realizes that it is the one with the woollen tri-coloured hat, only she is not wearing it. It must be a defining item for her, because she looks like a different person without it. Her hair, the colour of straw, is in pigtails, which does not have the effect of making her look young.

– I'm taking photographs.

– Of the hospital?

269

– Yes.

He continues with what he thinks of as his work. He points the camera up, towards the top of the building. She frowns: he is aware of it in the corner of his eye. It distracts his concentration.

– You're trying to get … shots of Eli?

He doesn't answer. The sun, breaking free of weak clouds, moves around a triangulated section of the roof. Its light burns into his lens. He shuts his good eye, leaving the stuck one to perceive the brightness.

– But he's in a coma. He won't come to the window.

She has corralled his work into her world. His actions must be an act of fandom, and thus a challenge, to her own. Her words mean: I have of course already considered trying to photograph Eli from here, but because of my greater knowledge of his condition I knew that it would be pointless.

– I know he's in a coma.

– So why are you doing it?

He looks at her. A flash of anger goes through him. He imagines taking out his Armscor 206 .38, and shooting her there and then in her expectant, unknowing, irrelevant face.

– Because …

He hesitates, not because he has to search for a lie, but because the real answer to that question is not clear. When he got up this morning, after he had prayed, and after going through The Material again, he had felt at a loss. In moments, he feels a great pressure inside, a voice telling him just to get on with it, to do it now, what was the point of waiting? That was what he had felt in front of the Butter Mountain. But the pressure does not build up, it comes and goes, dispersing like steam. He needs something else. *Give me a sign*, he had said, to the Jesus on his wall. Not that my mission is just, he had thought, I know that: but when to begin it. Show me the day of my destiny.

No sign emerging, he had come here, and, on the way, because it was in a sale, he had bought a digital camera. The shop was called B & H, an enormous camera store on 34th and 9th, and he had been drawn in because everyone serving there was a religious Jew. It was astonishing, he thought: a temple of modernity, all the most state-of-the-art devices lined up like icons on the shelves, and yet the men tending to them were all dressed like Talmudic scholars from the seventeenth century. They were dressed, in fact, like he would be dressed, if he were not here but back in Utah. One of them – Hyam Lederhandler it said on his name badge – showed him this camera, a Casio, and offered to do a deal on it.

He doesn't have very much money – before leaving home he had withdrawn all his savings, and had only this morning been worried about the possibility of them running out before the day of his destiny – but Hyam kept on pushing him, and offering different ways in which he could organize the payments, and eventually he had said yes. He had felt in himself a desire to please Hyam. He knew from Father McIntyre's sermons that Mormonism and Judaism had much in common: that the reason that Salt Lake Assembly Hall was adorned with a Star of David was because the two religions were brother and sister, and that, as a Latter-day Saint, he was a direct descendant of the House of Israel, a member himself of the tribe of Ephraim.

It was easy to operate. Hyam had put a battery in free of charge, so he could use it immediately. It would do moving pictures as well. He was pleased with his purchase. It was only now, now that the woman had asked him, that he realized he didn't really know why he was taking photographs of Mount Sinai Hospital.

– I want to have a record of these – of his last days.

She thinks about this for a moment, and then, with a blink and a nod, accepts it, as within the canon of what a fan might do.

– A record is important.

– Yes.

– Are you OK, she says?

– What?

– Your hand. It has cuts on it.

– I'm fine.

She starts looking through her bag. His eye on her feels benign. He does not know why this should be, but then recognizes that the

271

dress she has on, of red and white plaid, is very similar to one his sister used to wear. A sign? His thought is broken as she fishes a black file out of her bag, on the front of which she has stuck the photograph of The Great Satan when he was young that has been in a lot of the newspapers since he went into the hospital. He wears a suit: natty, his mother would have described it. It is a big file, but not big enough to contain all the stuff within it. Two bits of paper immediately fall out.

– Oh! she says. He picks them up, because they have fallen closer to his feet, and it would have been rude and weird to let her do it. He looks at them. One is a review of one of Eli's books, cut out from a newspaper; and another is just a piece of paper with some handwriting on it. He hands them back to her.

– That's the *New York Times* review of Tolon's biography.

He nods, not knowing what she is talking about.

– If you look, you can see all the places where I've agreed I've underlined in green, and where I disagreed in red.

She is holding up the cutting as she speaks. It is a mess of lines, more red than green. He scans it quickly, though, for the information it contains.

– And …? He gestures towards the handwritten paper.

– Well, after I did that I wrote my own review and then stuck it with a paperclip to the *New York Times* cutting, like an addendum.

– Right.

She opens the file. It is full of other cuttings, papers, photocopies, photographs and cards: also many more handwritten notes.

– This is *my* record. Of his whole life. And also mine, I guess. My life as it has been defined by the work of Eli Gold.

– Right.

She is staring at him very intently. He finds it difficult to handle, so he turns and starts taking photographs again, this time of the canopied entrance area, just to put his eye out of her line of vision.

– It's so great to meet another properly committed fan, he hears her say.

– Yeah.

272

– I've met so many people who say they love his work, and then they just don't. Not like I do. Not like … And now he hears the shy insinuation in her voice … *we* do.

He moves the camera up to the top of the hospital again. Seen through the lens of the Casio, his hand making the image move and shake, what he is seeing takes on the quality of a film. If it was a film, he, as the director, would make Eli – ah: he has let the name into his head: that is her fault, for saying it over and over again in that breathy, hushed tone – The Great Satan, rise from his bed, and appear at the window. Then he would know exactly what room he is in. He thinks, when the time comes, he will be able to find it anyway. He will be led there by God. But he would like to know now, to be sure. He would like The Great Satan to appear in his sights, and then click. Click.

– Tolon's biography, he says, still looking into the camera.

– Yes …?

– It was published in 2003. He has gleaned this from looking at her cutting.

– Yes.

– Just remind me … did it say anything about … his marriage to Pauline Gray?

She does not respond. He takes his face out of the camera. When he looks at her, her face looks childish, confused.

– Of course, it has a section about it. Why do you ask?

He can hear an urgency in her voice, like someone whose button has been pushed, ready to defend, ready to fight their corner.

– No reason.

She sniffs. He can tell he has made her suspicious, but her urge to demonstrate knowledge of her subject is too great.

– Yes, well, he's more fair-minded about it then some, at least. Kerensky is the worst. Worse even than some of the things you can find on the internet. Kerensky should be put in prison, I think, for some of the things he says. You read that biography without knowing all the facts and you would think …

She halts. He finds he can't resist it.

– That he murdered her?

273

She is looking very upset now: he thinks she might cry. The thing that drives him, that informs his being, cannot, for her, be voiced. He has said it as blankly as he can, but he knows that in his tone there was an edge. He needs to control himself.

– Terrible, he says. I hate Kerensky.

For a second, he thinks she is going to throw her long arms around him.

He had thought there might be one. Maybe when he was a kid. A baby. Or maybe of his and Stella's wedding: he had sent him one (he had *invited* him, but received no reply). There could be *one* photograph of him, somewhere in his father's apartment.

Perhaps in Eli's study, a space could have been found in between the photographs of Eli. Eli with Arthur Miller. Eli with James Coburn. Eli with W. G. Sebald. Eli with Gloria Steinem. Eli in a group with Joe Namath, Walter Kronkite, Warren Beatty and Bill Clinton. Eli on a beach with Eric Idle. Eli with Jack Kerouac. Eli with Bob Dylan. Eli with – fuck me – with Picasso. When did Picasso even come to America? Or is that Paris? Eli with Dick Cavett. Eli sharing a laugh with John Updike. Eli dancing with Madonna. Eli, smoking, with Kingsley Amis. Eli with ELVIS! Shaking hands! Eli with some people who Harvey doesn't know but they look very important and clever: academics? Eli with Jackie Onassis. And Eli on his own, over and over again, young, moodily backlit in black and white, or smiling, throwing his head back, in colour so rich it looks like a still from a Super 8 film, or white-haired and kindly faced, in a sepia-treated circle of light, or wackily positioning his glasses in a 1970s shot which Harvey remembers having seen before in an old copy of *Vanity Fair*, subtitled 'The Seer'.

Or perhaps in the lounge. And if not of Harvey, surely: one of Jamie. For fuck's sake. His grandchild. On this ornate Edwardian mantelpiece, there might be room for one, *one* photograph of Jamie – doing that heartbreaking thing he does of smiling but not at the camera – amongst the endless frames of Freda and Colette and Eli, and Freda and Colette and Eli together, and Eli with what looked to him like Freda's mum and dad; or on this minimalist coffee table, cheekily mismatched against the generally antique aesthetic, with the picture on it of Colette and Eli and Freda with Nelson Mandela; or maybe on this beautiful fucking nineteenth-century fucking – I don't know – *armoire* or something, next to this one in the fucking frame of the fucking fucking cat.

'Are you looking for something?' says Elaine, standing in the door-way to the lounge.

'No,' he says. 'Not really.'

'Just admiring the furniture?'

He nods and smiles awkwardly, like people do when other people say things like that.

'It is beautiful. They have a lot of very lovely pieces.'

'Pieces. Yes.'

'That's Freda, mainly. Mrs Gold. Before they met, Eli – well – as long as he had a chair and a desk, he didn't care.'

Harvey nodded, repositioning his awkward smile around his face. The number of people, he thought, happy to tell me what my father is like.

'And his books, of course,' she says, gesturing towards the shelves, which are packed. Elaine walks over to them. 'This is just a fraction of them.'

'At least they're not arranged alphabetically.'

'No, Freda wanted to do that, but Eli wouldn't let her.'

She makes a knowing face – knowing, that is, about the dynamics of her employers' marriage – and Harvey does his best to smile in appreciation. Some of the books sit in towers on the front of the shelves. These seem to be mainly Eli's works, suggesting, perhaps, that those were the ones he most frequently took off the shelves. From the top of one of these, Harvey picks out *Chess*, Eli's slim essay on the game, and idly flicks through it, wondering if there might be some tips here on how to beat Deep Green.

'So,' Elaine continued, 'are you OK with everything? Your room OK?'

276

'Yeah. Yes.'

A great chess player, like a great novelist, requires a very particular, almost contradictory, combination of ruthlessness and empathy. Because you need to be able to imagine what another might do in any given circumstance; and you also need, when the moment shows itself, to be able to kill off that other: quickly, decisively, guiltlessly.

'That room is a little small, but Mrs Gold thought … uh … that you would like it.'

He shuts the book. Did she think that? Or did she tell you not to put me in the bigger and more salubrious spare room, the one I saw in passing at the other end of the hallway, in case – I dunno – *Jesus Christ* shows up needing somewhere to doss for the night?

'It's fine, yes … although it's been a while since I slept in a single bed …'

Elaine looks at him sharply: whether because he is breaking some kind of etiquette by registering a complaint, however mildly, or because it's not been a while for her, he cannot tell.

'Well, if you're not comfortable …'

Harvey, who is never comfortable, says: 'It's fine.'

Elaine nods. She moves into the room, towards the deep cream sofa which stands in its centre, and, with some kind of robot-lady instinct, plumps the cushions scattered around it, of which there are too many, and which match the fine Persian rug underneath the sofa, and the velvet curtains behind it, too tastefully. Harvey takes out his iPhone, looking for a wi-fi signal. There isn't one. This is bad news. It means that when he wants to masturbate, which he will want to do to streaming internet pornography, he will have to do it in his father's study. He looks out of the wide window. A barge of some sort, loaded with timber, is chugging methodically down the Hudson, every few seconds belching out a small, indolent puff of smoke. Harvey wonders if Freda somehow hired these barges, to convince Eli that his vision of New York was still intact.

Elaine stands up again. Her hands are pinioned behind her back, elbows crooked, the shape that pregnant women sometimes make to balance the weight of their stomach. Harvey puts his iPhone back in his pocket. Into the room comes the cat, looking much fatter than it does in the photograph. Harvey makes some chucking noises and reaches to stroke it: it runs back out.

'Don't worry, he's like that with everyone except Colette. Would you like some tea? Coffee?'

'No, it's OK. I mean, yes, I would but I can do that. Y'know. Probably best for me to find my own way about the kitchen.'

'You sure? They have a Rayburn. Do you know how to work that?'

They have a Rayburn? In their Manhattan apartment? Really? 'Um … yeah. Maybe. I don't know how much cooking I'm gonna be doing anyway. Probably just get takeouts.'

'Oh. Yes. Of course.'

Harvey coughs: not his anxiety retch, just one of those self-conscious coughs that people do to fill the air. He sits down on the sofa. He tries to sit back on it, but there are too many cushions. The Filipino maid comes in to dust, taking great care over the pieces. Her face is as sombre as a Nigerian hawking DVDs on a Costa del Sol beach.

'If you can check on the mailbox from time to time,' says Elaine. 'I can do it when I visit but I seem to always be carrying things when I come to this house.'

'Right. Sure …'

'It's downstairs in the lobby. A box with twenty-three on it, same number as the apartment, of course. Just bring it up here and leave it on the kitchen table. If I see anything that looks important, one of us can take it down to Freda at the hospital.'

He nods, only half listening, as he does when people start going into domestic details. The Filipino maid goes out.

'So …' he says, 'where's Colette?'

'She's at the hospital.'

'Right.' He looks up at Elaine. This, he knows, is the worst angle to look at an older face: if worst is understood to mean the angle that will make the face look oldest. From below, the up-ness of the eyes accentuates the down-ness of the skin. He wonders, of course, how attractive Elaine might have been, twenty or thirty years ago: if you can see through the skin to the face, the ur-face. His calculations are that she might have been pretty. But what can you do with that? You can't even *say* it. At a party given by his publishers, once, he had met Joan Bakewell. He had seen clips, on YouTube, of Joan Bakewell on *Late Night Line-Up* in the 1960s. There were not enough clips of her on YouTube for him to track her life, so she had never joined Linda Ronstadt in the obsessive search for peak beauty, but there were enough for him to know that she was gorgeous. On meeting her, this was what he wanted to say: *Joan. You were so beautiful.* But the use of the past tense would mean that this, meant as a compliment, would be taken as insult. Grammar would make it into an insult. It was an insult, to say of beauty, that it was. But how, then, could you ever mark its passing? Was it something you were only allowed to say after death, as an epitaph? *She was so beautiful.*

'She'll be back later,' she said. 'I will bring her back, for bedtime. I'll put her to bed.'

'OK …'

'And then tomorrow, I'll come and pick her up about nine …'

'Nine? What time does she wake up?'

'About seven.'

'And breakfast … what about …'

'She's fine to get her own breakfast. She has a menu. You can see it in the kitchen, it's really cute. She writes it herself. Tomorrow is uh …' She screwed up her face. Harvey sees how, when she was young, this expression would have been cute. The lines under her eyes scrunch and fill. He thinks about the urge he gets, while looking at Stella, to pinch the skin under her eyes where the lines congregate, and cut it off with some scissors. In his fantasy this leads to neither blood nor pain. The two flaps of skin created just meld.

'… I think it's oatmeal. With cinnamon and brown sugar. She *loves* that.'

'Yes. Well. Good. My son has a kind of menu thing, too …' This is sort of true. He doesn't explain that the menu consists entirely of cereals from those mini cereal selection boxes, Coco Pops on Monday, then Corn Flakes on Tuesday, then Rice Krispies on Wednesday, then

Corn Flakes again on Thursday, then Weetabix on Friday, and that he has to have all the boxes lined up every day in the right order, otherwise he will refuse to eat at all.

'Oh! You have children?'

'Yes … just the one. Jamie. He's nine …'

'Oh. It must be really difficult, being away from him for so long.'

'Yes. It is.' It is. He really misses Jamie. He is struck with love for him, four or five times a day. Jamie remains the nearest thing Harvey has yet found to an antidote (to depression, to despair, to disgust, to whatever else it is that squats in his cells). It is love, of course, that is the cure, but love not weighed down and complicated by sex.

Elaine looks at him more softly now, almost as if she sees him with his son on his lap. She sits down next to him, smoothing her plaid skirt. Harvey imagines – or, rather, cannot stop himself from imagining – what her buttocks must look like under the skirt.

'You'll be OK with Colette. She's a very sweet girl, really. Very clever, of course. For her age. As you would expect. And sometimes that cleverness can seem a little … precocious. And, hey, as Mrs Gold says, she's a girl who knows her own mind. But, as I say, underneath she's a sweetie. It'll be nice for you to get to know her.'

She puts her hand on his knee as she says this. Harvey nods, adopting the role of the child, even as she is talking to him about another child.

'Thanks for the pep talk, Elaine,' he says. Elaine smiles. She is a nice woman. Harvey hates himself that he cannot end his thoughts about her there. What a great thing that must be, to be that person, the one who just looks about the throng and thinks: she's a nice woman; he's a nice man; she's not a nice woman; he's not a nice man. He imagines this person as living in the 1950s, in an English market town, resting his or her weight on a fence between backyards, watching the smoke curl up from the 1950s chimneys.

'It's what I do,' she says. 'Someone has to …' She gets up, smoothing the skirt again. 'Anyway. It was super to meet you properly.' Super: yes. 'I'll see you later, when I bring back Colette.'

'OK.' He stands. This is what people do, isn't it? They stand when someone else is leaving. And arriving. Harvey doesn't know why, nor why it might be rude to stay sitting down. She smiles once more at him, and moves away. He judges that it is OK to sit down again. At the door, though, she turns and says: 'Oh. And Harvey … I should have said this earlier, but I'm so sorry about your father.'

There it is again, that h after an s: *I'm so shorry about your father.* Harvey wants to say: he's not dead yet – but he admires Elaine for this, this saying of the same sentence she will say when he is. He likes, too, that at last – and in this house, as well – there has been an acknowledgement that he also is someone who sorrow needs to be conveyed towards: someone who people must apologize on behalf of death to.

'Thanks, Elaine.'

She makes a face expressive of sad wisdom, and leaves. Harvey hears the click of the door, and makes his way down the corridor to his father's study.

*   *   *

I just cannot believe that Mom has moved in The Larvae! I cannot! And she didn't even ask me!

This is what he does, OK? He sleeps till about ten thirty. Ten thirty! Like a teenager! Then he gets up and wanders about in his dressing gown. There are some things you *need to know* about this dressing gown. One: it's brown. With weird stains on it. And, secondly, he never ties it up properly. And, thirdly, *he wears it without pyjamas.* Which means that he sits in the kitchen eating eggs and sausages with it all flapping open! He doesn't seem to care! I haven't seen his winky-wonk, thank God, but the way he sits without ever sorting out the belt or anything, I probably will soon! Maybe then I can call the police or something and he'll have to move out.

What I DO have to look at all the time in the morning is his chest. It's all hairy but loads of the hairs are grey, like Daddy's. But then he's got these boobies. He's a man and he's got boobies! They hang off him like two hairy haddocks! It's sooooo disgusting. Thank God he DOES get up so late and I don't actually have to eat breakfast with him. I wouldn't be able to eat my granola.

And then he tries to talk to me. I can't stand it. I always know it's going to be one of those questions 'cos he always starts by saying, *So, Colette*. 'So, Colette … what kind of things are they teaching you at school?' 'So, Colette, do you like living here?' 'So, Colette, do you like Harry Potter?' And I don't say anything. Well, not nothing at all, like I'll just nod or say, 'Y'know … loads of stuff' or 'Whatever'. And then usually he looks a bit sad and shuts up.

I feel bad sometimes treating him like this. I mean, I know he's my half-brother. But it's so hard to think of him as any sort of brother! Jada has a brother – Emile – who's a bit of a pain, really, what Daddy used to call a pain in the ass when he thought Mommy wasn't listening (he didn't mind me listening – I think he quite liked me hearing rude words from him, sometimes he'd say them and wink at me). But he's only two years younger than her! At least when he's not being too much of a pain and not being too rough or crazy you can play with him. You can't play with The Larvae. What would we play?

Here's the problem. He treats me too much like a kid. He thinks I won't understand anything! He doesn't understand that I'm different from an ordinary eight-year-old! Like yesterday, OK, he showed me a photo of his son on his iPhone. Which was an OK thing to do, I guess. I mean, he looked nice, his son. He's called Jamie. He's got red hair, which is a bit weird, 'cos Harvey hasn't – he hasn't got much hair at all, and it's mainly grey, but I guess when he was younger it was black – and brown-green eyes. He was wearing some kind of red shiny shirt thing that The Larvae told me was a football shirt, and then he started going on about how it wasn't like an American football shirt, it was a soccer shirt, and he said soccer in a weird way like I would never of heard of it, so I said:

'I've played soccer. And my friend Jada is like the best player in the school.'

'Oh. Yes. Of course. I forgot that American girls play it.'

'How old is Jamie?'

'Nine.'

'A year older than me.'

'Yes.' Then he looked at me. 'Maybe if you come to England ever …'

And then he stopped. I don't know why. Maybe because he didn't really want me to come.

'Why is he looking away?'

He didn't say anything.

'Harvey,' I said. 'Why is Jamie looking away? Have you got one of him looking into the camera?'

'Well …'

'He is smiling though. I always smile in photos. Sometimes I say cheese. My friend Jada says smelly subway sausages!'

He looked back at the phone.

'Jamie has got an illness.'

Then he stopped again.

'What is it?'

He didn't say anything.

'Is it cancer?'

He didn't say anything.

'Diabetes? Parkinson's? Kidney stones? Arthritis? Heart trouble? Migraine?' I know about all these diseases. They're all ones that Daddy has had.

'No, it's none of those.'

I thought about it for a bit. 'Is it AIDS?'

I said it quite softly 'cos Jada has told me about it and she says it's a really bad one. He looked quite surprised. Then he laughed! He's such a weirdo. What's funny about such a terrible disease?

'No, Colette, my son doesn't have AIDS.'

'So what is it then?'

'Asperger's Syndrome.'

'What's that?'

'It's a … do you know what autism is?'

'Yes. It's that disease where you can do really clever sums. I saw something about a guy with it on PBS. Mommy lets me watch PBS.'

'Right.'

'But how is it a disease if it means you're really good at sums?'

He went quiet again.

'Harvey?'

'Yeah, it's complicated, Colette. People with autism aren't necessarily really good at sums.'

'They aren't?'

'No. And Asperger's is kind of different. It's really hard to explain.'

'To a kid, you mean.' This is what I mean. He thinks *I won't understand*.

'Well … no. It's hard to explain in general. Lots of people don't really understand it.'

He got up then and went into the kitchen. I looked back at the picture of Jamie. Even though he wasn't smiling, he had a nice face. It made me wonder. He didn't look much like Harvey, except maybe round the mouth. He doesn't smile much either.

I had seen how he flicked his finger across the screen to move to a different photo, so I did that. There was another photo of Jamie, not as good. Then there was another photo of Jamie with a woman. The woman was smiling. She was hot! That's something Jada says. I know I'm not supposed to say it. I once said it about one of the ladies on the cover of a magazine that we saw in the drugstore, and Mommy got really cross. She explained to me that ladies on the cover of those magazines are just there to sell the magazines, and, even though they might be beautiful, that's what their beauty is being used for, to sell the magazines, and that was bad. She said: I'm going to have to explain to you what sexism is. And I said, is that something to do with sex? And she didn't say anything, so I said, because you haven't explained what that is to me yet. This was a while ago, when I REALLY didn't know what it was. Like, seven or eight months ago. Anyway, she said the point is saying things like 'she's hot' is offensive to women. Not to mention vulgar. I was going to say what does vulgar mean but I didn't.

'Who's this?' I said to Harvey, when he came back into the living room. He did a funny scrunched-up face and came over. I held the phone up to him.

'It's my wife,' he said. 'Stella.'

'Wow,' I said, 'she's hot.' He looked at me weirdly when I said it, so I guess he must think all that stuff my Mom thinks, too.

*   *   *

It is hard, really, for Violet to focus on the bingo. She likes bingo. She used to like it a lot in the old days, when she played in the Galtymore on Cricklewood Broadway. That that is the old days – even though she first went there in 1971, when she was already approaching fifty – surprises her. She wonders how old the really old days must be.

Joe Hillier is the caller. It used to be a member of staff, but Joe decided he really wanted to do it, because of his names for numbers. He has thought up a lot of new ones. Violet did think some of them were funny when he first did it, but now everyone in Redcliffe House has heard them a hundred times on Bingo Nights.

'My age: forty-three!'

This is greeted with silence, although it is the silence of concentration, of the crowd staring at their cards, rather than simply the silence of non-laughter. About fifteen residents have turned up. The seat that Meg Antopolski normally sits in has been left empty, as if out of respect.

'Will you still love me now that I'm way past it ... sixty-four!'

She almost misses it: she has a sixty-four. It gives her a horizontal line. But there isn't that much point in shouting it out, as only a full house leads to a prize, which tonight is a book, a second-hand autobiography, sent in as a charitable offering: *Chris Noth: Bigger Than Big*. She doesn't know who Chris Noth is – and thinks that that must be a misprint: North, surely? – but he looks like a nice man, from the cover.

In a way she wouldn't mind winning it. It would be nice, she thinks, to read something nice, something easy, after *Solomon's Testament*. It might clear her head, in the same way that Valerie once told her, at that posh meal she once took her for, that a sorbet cleanses the palate. She still hasn't finished her ex-husband's entire masterpiece, or doesn't think so, because she has continued just to open it at random. She will read the pages for as long as they hold her, and then stop, and then open it again somewhere else. She knows that it is more likely to hold her attention if she divines herself in the text; part of her wishes Eli had written it with an index, so she could refer to that, like:

Queenie 5–12, 16–30, 34, 38, 42–7, 53, 55–69, 75, 80–82, 110, 111, 113–22, 127, 159, 170, 177, 183–99, 202, 204, 208, 222–34, 251, 258, 267–80, 287–97, 301, 323, 344–56, 390–411, 413–14, 420–22, 443
    Body of 6–7, 34, 45, 55, 60–64, 115–20, 177, 185, 231, 269, 293, 348–50, 414, 422
    Cooking 28
    Death of 420–22
    Face of 8, 23–5, 45, 81, 186–7, 228, 289, 351, 409
    Habit, biting bottom lip 81, 301
    Habit, blinking fast 345
    Habit, dressing uncaringly 188
    Habit, humming while eating 159, 185
    Habit, speaking in rhymes 60
    Habit, speaking ungrammatically 347
    Habit, twisting hair 18, 189, 399
    Habit, washing herself methodically 65, 396
    Non-Jewishness of 184
    Smell of 44, 392
    Solomon's disgust with (sense of imprisonment by; uncertainty about beauty of; projections of future with; feelings about when drunk; paranoia about sexual past) 17, 58–61, 114–15, 188, 189, 227–30, 269, 222–9, 273, 290–93, 348–50
    Solomon's love for 34, 36, 55–9, 82, 184, 233
    Stupidity of 114, 230, 288
    Stupidity of, reconfigured as innocence 441
    Virginity, uncertainty about 58

That would have made it all much easier.

'The man who lives here really wants to be at Number 10 … Number 11!' She does not think that she is upset by the book. Even though Queenie is hated by Solomon, she isn't *simply* hated: she is also loved, lusted after, feared, envied, made fun of. She is, primarily, explored: she is the object of fascination. What it calls up in Violet, even as it intrudes on her, is the comfort, the repletion, she used to feel when opening her body up to Eli's eyes, that here at last she had his full attention. It reminds her of something she lost such a long time ago that it feels no longer even a memory: the ability to hold a man's gaze.

'Mid-life crisis at ... fifty-two!'

Of course, there are the affairs that Solomon has (ideally, she'd have liked the pages that described those indexed, too). It does not, however, enrage her, or make her feel humiliated, or wish for revenge, or even sad, that Solomon Wolff has affairs. Any of these responses feel ridiculous, now. It does make her try to think of anything she can remember about her eight years with Eli that would prove he had affairs, but there is so much proof of that, and none. He would stay out a lot. Sometimes he would smell different. Odd nights there would be when he wasn't interested in her sexually. It is a strange exercise, trying to relate incidents in the book to her actual memory: there is something monastic about it, like transcribing from one ancient language to another.

She knows she never interrogated Eli on the subject back then. Perhaps she should have done. That's what wives did: do, for all she knows. Gwendoline would sometimes bully her about it, saying: 'Are you keeping a close eye on him?' (And often: 'He's half-Jewish, isn't he? They're always at it ...' and 'He's like Henry, I can tell: *a ladies' man*', this latter phrase solemnly intoned as if packed within its walls was everything that could be said about gender and its troubles), to which Violet would nod, and say yes she was, but internally think no: he is the one who looks; I am the looked-at.

She's found three infidelities in the book so far, but thinks there might be others, some of which may or may not be fantasies. This is the other problem with the book. It is, she understands, a work of literature; she understands, too, that it is a modern work of literature, and so it isn't just going to straightforwardly tell a story – there are bits that you're supposed to think, *Did this really happen*? Not did this really happen like she sometimes thinks when she reads the *Daily Mail*, but did this really happen in the book, which she knows is not real?

Except it is real for her. It is her life, refracted. But her life is already refracted, by time and space: and, more, by disbelief, a pushing away of her history from herself. Reading the book is like remembering a dream, only not halfway through the morning, but years and years after waking. It is discomfiting. At the same time, it gives her something back. This is something she has sometimes heard celebrities say on the telly, when they have done a good deed, or appeared on a funny event for charity: I'm trying to give something back. She was never sure what it meant, but she feels that *Solomon's Testament* has given her something concrete back, a version of her youth that she had begun to doubt ever existed.

'Better get her married before this number of months goes by … nine!'

Idly, Violet crosses off this number on her card. Then, with a small double-take, she realizes that she has a full house. She feels both excited at the prospect of winning, and frightened of drawing attention to herself. In *Solomon's Testament*, she recalls, there is a page-long rant by Solomon at Queenie, in which he says, 'You're so full of fear for what you want!' Maybe that was true. This was going to be a thing, she knew, her life, or what was left of it, back-referring to the book, trying to see how much she was living out those old words.

'House! Housey-housey!'

She looks over. It is Pat Cadogan, rising from her seat so fast Violet fears for her joints. She is waving her card about her head. Joe Hillier looks disappointed, firstly because he detests Pat, and secondly because that's the bingo over. They only have the one prize, and even though everyone usually carries on playing for a bit after this point, the heart goes out of the night.

'Can you check?' says Frank to Corrinda, the staff carer on duty. Corrinda, another large black woman, who breathes heavily at all times, even when seated, gets up slowly, and moves her neck backwards and forwards.

'Oh, *I* see …' says Pat.

'It's procedure. We always check.'

'Yes, that's right, Pat,' says Molly Bowen, one of the wheelchair-bound residents, 'you remember I won last week – the Marks & Spencer's Cheese Selection? – and Joe checked my card himself.'

'Well exactly, himself. He'll have just glanced at it. He didn't insist on an *independent adjudicator.*' She says this, looking at Corrinda – who has begun to amble over, still moving her neck from side to side – with menaces.

'Oh for crying out loud, Pat,' says Joe. 'It's only a book.' He pronounces it *buke.* He looks at it, raised on the table by some form of plastic stand. 'By Chris North.'

'Right, then …' says Corrinda, holding Pat's card out in front of her, 'You, Mrs Cadogan, are now the proud owner of …' she picks up the book and hands it Pat, 'this *buke.* I imagine you're a big *Sex and the City* fan, aren't you?'

And with that, she moves away. Pat looks down at her prize uncertainly. She sniffs. Eventually, she holds it up:

'Does anyone else want this?'

The residents shuffle in their seats. The man who Violet now knows to be Frank takes a handkerchief, embroidered with a blue F in one corner, out of his jacket top pocket, and sets about cleaning his glasses. Molly Bowen adjusts what Violet assumes to be the gears in her wheelchair.

Violet looks again at her card and at all the numbers crossed out. She thinks of all the pages, all the numbers, in *Solomon's Testament* that speak of her: of Queenie.

'I'll have it,' she says, putting her hand up.

Harvey is in the sauna. Eli's apartment has a sauna. It is in the back of his and Freda's en-suite bathroom. He is not entirely sure he is allowed in either the sauna or the whole bedroom area. It makes him feel – well, it makes him feel like a child going into his parents' bedroom when they are not there. This raises in him complicated issues. When he was young, his bedroom was next to his parents'. His nights in it are one of very few memories he has of the time when Eli and his mother were still together, because of the noises. It is possibly these noises – more than his mother's slander, more than the world's assessment – that shaped Harvey's early idea of his father.

Many children, of course, have to deal with the noise of their parents' lovemaking, but the sound of Eli and Joan making love was particularly disturbing. Joan emitted a high-pitched note, not unlike a yodel – which would not in itself have been unpleasant, were it not accompanied so discordantly by Eli, who wailed and roared like a wounded walrus. To a five-year-old boy this sound was terrifying. Once, he had got out of bed, having wet himself in fear, and knocked on his parents' door, screaming *Daddy, daddy, what's the matter?*, only to be ignored; not out of neglect, but simply because his sobbing whisper was inaudible beneath his father's outpourings.

The sound that orgasm forced out of his father's mouth was so seared into the young Harvey's brain that, if asked, he could still do a passable impersonation of it now, thirty-eight years or so since he last heard it. He has actually once publicly reproduced it, as a teenager, during a discussion amongst his friends about how disgusting it was

290

to imagine parental sex. This led to each of them in turn doing an impression of the illicit sounds they had variously heard through their bedroom walls, and much scornful giggling. When it came to Harvey, who took a deep breath in and gave it everything – he was, he remembers, rather pleased with the accuracy of his rendition, having never ventured it out loud before – there was no giggling. All his friends just stared at him. Some of them looked like they might cry.

One side effect of having this sound echoing round his head his whole life has been a nagging conviction that none of the sex he has ever had can possibly have matched up to his father's experience of it. No matter how much he enjoys sex, Harvey has never felt the need, at orgasm, to keen like a mourner at an ayatollah's funeral: thus he feels that he is missing out. This inferiority pleasure complex is not helped by Eli's own delight in his own sexual self-image. In the mid-eighties, the *New Yorker* had printed a cartoon of Eli as a satyr, dancing on a pile of books and wives. Eli had had it framed: it was still up in his study, in pride of place above his desk.

Harvey has taken his iPhone into the sauna, and is listening to a playlist in there, through his Bose headphones. He has also taken a book, a paperback copy of *Mirror, Mirror*. It is the same issue as running: although a sauna is supposed to be relaxing, it is, in the main, uncomfortable and boring, and the only way he can get through it is with distraction. Harvey has no willpower for discomfort and boredom: considering how much he has to have on board to get through a run, or a sauna, he often wonders how he would have managed in a labour camp, or the fourteenth century.

Initially, he took his laptop in as well, but while replying to an email – from Ron Bunce, asking for his present address – he found that he was dripping onto the keys, so has left that outside the door. He thinks, though, that the iPhone should be fine: they have mobile phones in hot countries. He is not sure about the book, but it is one of ten copies he found in a box underneath the stairs. Eli and Freda's apartment has two floors. On the wall as you step up the stairs, there is a series of sketches by Matisse; a gift, Elaine has told him, from Henri's son Pierre.

He has created a sauna playlist. It has no theme. He considered basing it on being in the sauna, but then realized that songs with the word 'hot' in the title would refer to the wrong sort of hot. 'Hot' by Avril Lavigne; 'Hot In Here', by Nelly; 'Don't You Wish Your Girlfriend Was Hot Like Me' by The Pussycat Dolls. Despite being someone for whom desire feels like it was always in the front of his brain, plastered there, a D where Hester Prynne has an A, pop music that was too upfront about sex made him feel uncomfortable. He did do a quick iTunes search, and discovered that there is an Elton John song called 'Sweat It Out', but the idea of Elton sweating – perhaps with the flu – made him feel a bit sick.

He sits naked on the second level of the sauna, a white towel protecting his buttocks from the heat of the pine boards. Most of the sand in the wall-mounted hourglass near the door has already emptied out of the top bulb. Harvey turned it round when he came in, but he does not know how long one inversion of it represents in time. He assumes not actually an hour. The sauna coals sizzle with water poured on them from a wooden bucket on the floor (he hadn't bothered with the ladle, preferring the excitement of the heat hit that comes from sploshing the entire contents straight on). He watches his stomach as the droplets form, forcing their way through the folds. He knows it is just water, but thinks it must be pushing some fat out too. The dry air burns in his nostrils. A small bottle of Volvic – of which there are about fifty in the apartment's enormous four-door fridge – sits by his side: it is already too warm to be pleasant to drink.

Mirror, Mirror sits unopened by his side, its pages tickling his right haunch, making him aware of the fact of his buttocks spreading. He thinks it would be good for him to read it, but he becomes more interested in his varicose vein. Harvey has a varicose vein on his left inner thigh. He doesn't know how long he has had it. There seems, in the case of the varicose vein, to have been no starter vein, no tiny lesion that he might have thought 'Hmm?' about before realizing what it was and becoming obsessed with its growth. No: one day it was just there, vivid and red and scratchy, like someone overnight had grafted a tiny leafless tree just under his skin. It revolts him, the varicose vein, but it entrances him: a combination he is familiar with. The heat seems to make it more livid, because he can see it clearly even in the dim light of the sauna; its flattened-insect irregularity contrasting with the clean lines of the pine beneath.

He takes a swig of the warm Volvic and attempts to switch his attention to *Mirror, Mirror*. As sometimes when the physical world – and, particularly, his physical world, his body in all its heavy presence – threatens to overwhelm him, he imagines that there is an escape that can be made to the life of the mind. Thus Harvey has at home books about, for example, chess; quantum physics; Kierkegaard; Stalingrad; the new economics; the history of Islam; modern British art; cosmology; Renaissance architecture; the psychology of apocalypse; Benjamin Britten; and many others of that ilk, all of them purchased not because of any innate interest in their subject matter, but because of this notion that people who think about such stuff – about Kierkegaard or quantum physics or Benjamin Britten – must therefore not spend all their time thinking about the unending itchiness inside their testicles, or how much they want another sour sweet even though their stomach already hurts from the acid, or the lines on their wives' faces. Harvey does not know whether these people do or do not think about such things; but he knows that he only ever reads five pages of these books before needing a shit, a wank or a cry.

He opens *Mirror, Mirror* at the first page, but only gets as far as *In this land of ours,* before a fat drop of sweat lands on the prose. Fuck. He looks around for a towel, pointlessly, knowing that you cannot dry paper with a towel, and then the music coming into his ears – Spandau Ballet's 'Through The Barricades' – halts, as a call comes in. Shit. You can forget that the iPhone is a *phone*. He feels caught out, for a host of reasons. He is naked, in the sauna, a sauna he's not absolutely sure he's allowed to use. He's just dripped onto one of Eli's lesser works. And he's listening to 'Through The Barricades' by Spandau Ballet. Although the call has cut off the MP3, he still thinks that maybe the caller will somehow know.

He holds up the phone to his eyes. It is hard to see. He has to blink sweat out of his eyes, plus the screen has misted up. He can't see the name. Perhaps this was a bad idea. He decides to chance it.

'Hello?'

'Harvey?'

Shit. Shit shit shit shit shit.

'Dizzy.'

'Hello, Harvey. How *are* you?'

Why the emphasis on the *are*? Harvey puts the phone down on the wood: he can speak via his headphones.

'I'm OK, thanks.'

'Good. Great.' There is a pause: Harvey imagines that Dizzy is looking at the mirror that sits above the mantelpiece in his room, straightening his bow tie.

'So … the session has come and gone.'

'Yes.'

'I didn't get a message that you had found anyone else to take up the time …?'

'No … I didn't … I kind of forgot about it.'

'Ah.'

'Sorry, Dizzy. I also – I couldn't think of anyone who I could ring up and suggest therapy to. Seems a bit … rude.'

'Ah …' says Dizzy. Dizzy is king of saying *Ah* in that leading way, the way where you can almost hear the ellipsis.

'Well, don't you think?'

'No, I don't, actually, Harvey. I think that shows a rather one-dimensional attitude to therapy. The implication that needing it is a failure, and that therefore to suggest to someone that they might need it – even just try it out for one session – would be to imply a failing on their part. Surely that isn't something you think?'

'Er …'

'And, besides, I think it rather depends on how you make the suggestion. And who to. Someone close to you would surely appreciate it. Stella, perhaps? Did you ask her?'

'Stella?'

'Yes.'

Harvey bristles at the mention of her name. He does not feel it is in Dizzy's gift to bring her up. And he worries about Dizzy's knowledge: is there in his tone an element of blackmail? Like, if Harvey doesn't pay up this £130, he will go to Stella with what he knows? With his knowledge of all Harvey's fears?

Aha! Harvey wants to say. *But she knows! I have told her!* The excitement of this triumph over Dizzy is, however, quickly deflated by the memory of the conversation in question. He had thought, that day at Tower Bridge, that he never could tell her, that he must swallow this pitiful pill and never even shit it out it was so shameful, but it was too big inside him: he felt the pressure of it at all times, pushing and kicking to get out like some devil baby from a Hammer Horror film. And, of course, Stella was his best friend: who else can you tell your terrible secrets to?

He told her, having built up to it for weeks, finding every excuse possible why he shouldn't say it today, knowing that the truth was that he shouldn't say it any day. But one night, chock-full of depression, allergic with anxiety, it spilled out of him, in a mess of apologies and qualifications and protestations of love despite this terrible thing that he was saying. What did she say? Just what a lady ought, of course. *Fuck off, you cunt*, is the thing he remembers especially clearly: said, not shouted, deliberately, straightforwardly, even-handedly; and followed the next morning by her packing two suitcases and leaving with Jamie, before Harvey, exhausted with the telling and the crying and the sleeping on the sofa, woke up.

During the two-month period she was gone, Harvey cried almost solidly. He found after a few weeks that many of the daily things that you would have thought you would have to stop should you burst into tears in the middle of them were in fact perfectly doable while crying. Making a sandwich, watching daytime TV, sitting on the tube, masturbating: all these things, once you got over the initial self-pity/humiliation hump, were more than manageable with salt water flooding down your cheeks. If, however, as it sometimes did, the crying became howling, with added face-crumpling and mouth-wobbling, most of these activities became untenable, with the exception of masturbation, which became, if anything, more piquant.

Crying was also a particularly prominent activity for Harvey during the many, many phone calls to Stella that he made at this time and also in the three meetings they had: once at the flat she was renting in east London, after Harvey had banged on the door in the middle of the night, and twice at a service station on the M2, a venue chosen by Stella, possibly because it was equidistant from each other's dwellings, but more likely, Harvey thought, because the light was incredibly harsh in there, designed to make everyone underneath it look like all they ever consumed was tobacco and scratch cards; and that therefore, in a very Stella-ish way, she was deliberately presenting him with the worst possible view of the thing he was frightened of: with her worst possible face.

But when he wasn't tied to her – when she wasn't his woman – this didn't work. When she wasn't his woman all he could see, even in the Medway Moto Canteen, was that she was beautiful, and that he missed her and Jamie more than he could express. There was much pleading and convincing and pledges of change, and eventually Stella and Jamie came back. Harvey was overjoyed; his heart brimmed with love and relief; things were better than before, because they had been pulled back from the brink; and so he felt, right up until the moment, two weeks after Stella's return, when the three of them went out for a blowy country walk under an especially harsh slate-grey sky and he turned to his love and all the bad feelings started again.

'Thanks for the thought, Dizzy, but I don't actually think Stella is in need of therapy.'

There is silence at the other end of the line. Is this costing me, thinks Harvey? It is, isn't it? It costs me when someone phones me abroad.

'OK,' says Dizzy, eventually. 'Well, I'll expect a cheque in the post, then.'

'Yes. A hundred and thirty pounds.'

'Two hundred and sixty now, I'm afraid.'

'Really?'

'You were due to have a session this morning.'

'Oh. Sorry, I forgot.'

'Obviously, you're still away. You didn't think about letting me know that?'

'Well. Would it have made any difference?'

'To what?'

'To the charge.' Fuckhead, Harvey is desperate to add.

Silence again. The break in the conversation makes Harvey realize he is sweating astonishingly. It is as if he has been out naked in the rain. In the auricles of his ears, underneath the padding of the Bose headphones, there are two small ponds. He feels that if he moves his head quickly, they will overflow.

'And what about *next* week's session?'

'I don't know, Dizzy. I very much doubt I'll make that either.'

'Perhaps we should think about stopping.'

This comes rather abruptly, without, as Harvey would have expected, a big dramatic pause, indicative of the immensity of such a step.

'Um ...'

'If you're going to be, as clearly you are, away indefinitely ...'

It *is* indefinite, thinks Harvey, isn't it? Death. Even as it is *fucking* definite, even as it is the definite thing. And then he thinks, yeah. Let's stop. Let's stop this shit, this talking and talking and talking about me. But as he thinks about it, he can feel, his heart rate, already far too high for a man of his weight because of the sauna, rise, and more sweat come through his skin. He shifts his buttocks to stop them sticking to the pine. Why this anxiety? Do I think that maybe Dizzy and his mantras and his whole shift-a-must-have-to-a-preference shtick is going to work? Or is it just that all break-ups terrify me, all goodbyes?

Harvey's uncertainty allows Dizzy an opening:

'Well, we needn't decide now. But obviously, the longer it goes on ...'

'The higher the bill,' says Harvey.

297

Dizzy sighs, the sigh of the higher man, the one who is tired of dealing with all these people who must bring him down all the time.

'… the longer it will take for the treatment to have any effect. But, meanwhile, if you are going to worry about the cost of keeping the sessions open, remember you could still take my advice about asking a friend to take them up.'

'Right.'

'And also …'

Harvey suddenly cannot hear what Dizzy is saying. He suddenly feels too hot. It occurs to him that he feels dizzy, and this doesn't help the situation, as the idea of feeling Dizzy, perhaps untying his bow tie and then unbuttoning his shirt and fondling him sexily up and down his concave chest, infects his imagination and makes him feel nauseous as well.

'Dizzy, I've got to go.'

'Right, well …'

He can hear that Dizzy is continuing, but his voice sounds more and more distant, the sonic equivalent of looking out from a rising plane and seeing the landscape miniaturize. It makes Harvey think that he may be slowly blacking out, fading out like a disco track. The phrase *Mine is the last voice you will ever hear* comes into his head, the thing that was said at the start of some CND movie he remembers from the 1980s, before all this started, when all his anxieties were simply political – and he desperately doesn't want that last voice to be Dizzy's, which now sounds not unlike that of the human-headed fly quietly screaming 'Help me!' as the spider approaches at the end of the 1950s version of *The Fly*. Or perhaps it is his voice; perhaps he is the fly and Dizzy the spider. Either way, he has to get out. He stumbles down from the second level of the sauna, narrowly missing knocking over the hot coals, and falls through the pine door with its little window, noticing as he does so that all the sand in the wall-mounted hourglass has seeped out of a hole in the bottom.

He blacks out, and then comes to, his cheek cold against the tiled floor of Eli and Freda's ensuite bathroom, a minute later, or it could possibly be three hours. He feels as if there is something on his head, but in a phantom way, like you sometimes feel two hours after you've taken off a hat. It is his headphones; they are still on his head, but not pressed close to his ears any more. Harvey takes them off, and realizes what has happened: the plastic on the headphones has melted in the sauna, and warped, moving the earcups away from his ears. Once shaped like a sideways C, they are now more like an upside-down V. It's as if, while in the sauna, each side of the earphones has developed a lazy lob.

He realizes now that this was what had been making Dizzy's voice fainter while in the sauna – and therefore what had induced his panic attack. He sits up, and crosses his legs, and tries to force the headphones back into shape so that they can fit onto his head. They snap in two. He has a moment of pure depression, so total and so instant it feels cartoonish, like his Buddha-like body has been covered, suddenly, in tar.

*   *   *

Today he does not go uptown. Today, instead of walking all the way up Park Avenue, or taking the subway from 23rd straight up the green line to 86th, he takes it downtown. He is searching for the final sign. He cannot quite find it, in the Condesa Inn, in The Material, outside Mount Sinai. There have been some half-signs – the picture of Jesus, the steps marking his stepchildren – but he is looking for the last one, the one that will jump-start his destiny. What he wants is certainty: moral, religious and temporal, something that will make him know that now is the time. So he is going to Ground Zero.

He feels, as he rides towards the World Trade Center station, like a spy, undercover, much like the way he does at the hospital, amongst people, like the blonde woman in pigtails, there to pay their respects. Because he is not going to Ground Zero to pay his respects either. He is going there because he wants to feel as certain about his destiny as Mohammed Atta did about his.

Plus: his opinion of the 9/11 attacks is not the same as most of his countrymen, or indeed most citizens of the West. In their church, members are encouraged – through claiming as many state benefits for their enormous families as possible – to Bleed the Beast. The Beast is America. That is how his Church thinks of his country. Sometimes this attitude fights with that part of him which remembers loving The Outlaws, or which can still feel the outline of the Confederate flag underneath his skin, but then he thinks about how the America that he used to love, the one that Hughie Thomasson sung his heart out for, is nothing like the wide godless swathe that he has travelled across to be here.

When the World Trade Center was blown up, it wasn't taken in the usual way in American Fork. It did not shock his community. Like all members of all the Churches of the Latter-day Saints and all their sects and offshoots and splinter groups, he knew what it was: a herald of The End of Days. There had been so many portents, and he had committed them all to memory: the pure gospel of Jesus Christ, restored, and taught in His Church – this happened, on 6 April 1830; Elijah returning and giving the priesthood keys – this happened, on 3 April 1836; the Jews returning to Jerusalem and Israel – this began in 1881. Some of the portents had yet to occur. The building of a Mormon temple in Israel; a meeting of the Leaders of the Church with angels and Jesus in Adam-Ondi-Ahman, the site – in Missouri – where Adam and Eve lived after their expulsion from the Garden of Eden; and a separate appearance of Christ at the Temple in Saline County, Illinois. These things had not happened. But the Book of Revelation was clear: wars will be poured out upon all nations; nations will gather to fight Israel; and the wicked will be consumed by fire. Who were the wicked, if they were not the men and the women feeding the Beast financially? The very same men and women consumed by the jihadis' fire on September 11, 2001? And was it not the case that *The Book of Mormon* teaches that we must welcome these signs, these symptoms of His Coming, for they portend only the final and eternal triumph of the Just? *If ye are prepared, then shall ye not fear*, says the Doctrine and Covenants of Joseph Smith. And he is prepared; he is prepared.

Coming upon the site, he is surprised at how destroyed everything still is, a carved-open dust bowl, as if the attack only happened last week. There is something magical about skyscrapers, which makes it seem as if they should be able to rise up again just like that. But no: nearly a decade later, and still they seem only to have laid the foundations of the Freedom Tower and the Memorial and whatever else they are building here. It is a wilderness of canvas and tents and POST NO BILLS fences. He wonders if it would have been better if they had just cleared the area and left it empty: if that would have been more conducive to standing here now and remembering the dead. It would certainly have been more conducive to his own needs. He feels, looking at the multitude of JCBs shifting mountains of mud from one place to another, and the crazy mess of scaffolding and brickwork, the prickle of frustration that he has felt often on this trip – this mission, as he thinks of it – that the world will not conform to his destiny. He has come here expecting epiphany, expecting revelation, but those things are hard to find on a building site.

He decides to take one of the many tours on offer. There are seven men and five women on the tour, all tourists: Germans, Japanese, one or two other Americans. They stand on one of the platforms looking over the site, huddled together, while Sylvia, a woman with oval glasses and close-cropped hair, wearing round her neck a laminate, which says TributeNYC: OFFICIAL TOUR GUIDE, begins to speak, loudly, above the noise of machinery:

– So, everyone happy? Can everyone see me? Does everyone speak English?

She has an upbeat, driving voice. There is some awkward shifting about, some nodding; a German says *Ja*.

– So, first, some history. The Twin Towers were dedicated in 1973. They were originally very controversial. Oh my Lord. Bigger than the Empire State Building! People weren't sure about that. People said they lacked character. That it was bad that they were bigger than the Empire State Building, trouncing on such a great symbol of the city. But very soon they became part of the New York skyline. And people began to love them more than the Empire State Building. When you went up the Empire State Building, you were *away* from the view. But

301

here, in the World Trade Center elevator, it was just glass, straight glass, and your stomach – well, it went a little crazy!

He drifted off. He felt tired. It was difficult to sleep in the Condesa Inn, even more difficult than at home, where sheer numbers in the one house mean that some bed is always creaking, because the man next door has continued to do that thing of dragging his nails down the wall in the middle of the night. He would wake to hear it every night, terrified, scrabbling for the light: the sound was too frightening to listen to in the dark. He has knocked on the wall. He has shouted: stop that! He has prayed, and wondered while he was praying if the sound was itself a sign, or Satan, who always lives in the room next door.

His attention refocuses on Sylvia as she begins to speak about it, the thing he wants to hear:

– Many people do not know that September 11, 2001 was not the first day that the World Trade Center was attacked by Islamic terrorists. On January the 26th, 1993, a truck filled with 1500 pounds of explosives, planted by a man called Ramzi Yousef, detonated in the underground garage of the North Tower. Six people were killed. Although their deaths have been overshadowed by more recent events, we do not forget them here today. No, sir. But it makes you wonder, don't it? They tried before. So. What is it about this particular building, these two towers, that so outraged the fundamentalists?

It's the height, he thinks, immediately, pleased at the quickness of his mind's answer, pleased to know instinctively what it is for them. It's the height. The arrogance: it's the saying that we, us, America – we've got the biggest cock in the world. That, plus the Babelness of it, the reaching into the sky to disturb God.

– Which brings us, neatly I guess, to those more recent events. She takes a deep, dramatic breath. And out. It was the first day of school. It was primary day. It was the day we New Yorkers were viciously, horrifically attacked.

Sylvia's expression has hardened; her voice has slowed, to a more emphatic rhythm. His fingers reach for the photograph in his pocket. He has not brought the one of his sister on her own, smiling and waving, looking so fine: he has brought another one, of him and her when they were toddlers, being held up by their mother. He slips it out of his pocket and stares at it, listening all the time to Sylvia's voice become more outraged.

It is a black-and-white photograph. Their mother is standing in front of Lake Utah, holding them both up to camera. She is smiling, but her eyes betray boredom, in tune with his memory of her, a woman whose commitment to herself had remained entirely undented by children. This was not a political position: even if feminism had ever made it to Utah – instead of falling, with all the other great irruptions of the 1960s, into the Grand Canyon – it would have been irrelevant to how his mother chose to live her life. She had no sense of the world beyond.

This is why he loves his sister so much. Their father being mainly drunk, and their mother mainly herself, he and his sister had brought each other up. He has not had therapy, or any of that faggy shit, and is not given to self-analysis, but he knows in his bones that this is why his sister matters so much. She made him his breakfast, taught him how to tie his shoelaces, rubbed his back when he had childhood bugs that made him throw up all night. He knows that when he thinks of his sister, after all the grief and the anger, and the burning, religious need for revenge, underneath all that there is gratitude, the gratitude that he assumes people who have been brought up properly feel in the pit of themselves for their parents.

They are – were – twins. Being boy and girl, they are – were – not identical. Except in this photograph. In this photograph he thinks they look identical. They could both be boys, or girls. He has often wished that, somehow, they could have been identical. More of her would seem to have survived. He could look in the mirror and see her. Dimly, he senses there is something else: a need to merge with her, to bring back childhood and safety and someone looking after him, because the five wives and the fifteen children do not look after him, they look to him to look after them. If he merged with her, he would hear her, and she would tell him, surely, that his destiny was right, needed, and at hand.

– Imagine, if you can, how it was for the people who worked in the towers that day. To be at work – a normal day – with your colleagues and friends. Maybe sharing a bit of gossip before you actually got down to it. We all do that at work, don't we?

A couple of the group laugh politely; the Japanese couple genuinely.

– Maybe, because you work in the World Trade Center – because you work in the *tallest building in the world* …

Sylvia says this with intensity, and pauses after it, as if it has some moment beyond the obvious: then takes a deep breath and continues,

– … perhaps you look out at a clear and cloudless blue sky, and think about how nice it might be to be outside, soaking up the sun.

He concentrates on the photograph. At the same time he takes Sylvia's advice; he imagines how it was for the people that day. But not the people that she is talking about, the ones who worked in the towers. He thinks about how it must have been for the hijackers, in their cramped, sweaty cockpits, fighting off uncertainty and panic and confusion and the sound of the passengers wailing and banging on the door, with the repeated hammer of *Allah Akhbar*: God is great, God is great, God is great, over and over and over again. Finding in those words their destiny. Building a wall with those words against the unfitting flailing world.

He looks at himself and his sister held up by their mother and thinks of the 9/11 hijackers. Grant me that certainty, oh Lord. Just a piece of it. Show me a sign. Sylvia says:

– And then perhaps you might imagine how it was for me, just setting off for work, just checking my hair in the hallway mirror, when I heard a voice on the radio say that an aeroplane had crashed into one of the towers at the World Trade Center. Which one? I thought. Which one? Kept on repeating in my head. And God forgive me, God please forgive me, I was praying that it was the North Tower. Because my brother, my darling dearest brother Dan – he worked on the ninety-fourth floor of the South Tower.

He looked up at Sylvia. She had looked away from their group, up, into the empty unbuilt-upon sky, to that phantom ninety-fourth floor. He had been expecting her to say her son or daughter. She looked old, at least as old as himself, but that did not of course mean that the person she was grieving for was her child. That was just what he had expected. Something to do with her being a woman: that's who women grieve for, their children.

She stays looking, up, up. The sky is not so blue today: it is greyer, sitting heavy on the air and making it muggy. But Sylvia still peers into it, narrowing her eyes as if indeed it was that other day's blue sky and within it her brother has come into focus, waving, or falling, or stringing a tightrope between buildings to escape. This is the sign, he is sure: this sister looking for her brother.

– He was my younger brother. He'd only just got the job. People think that it was just financiers and moneymen working in the towers, but there were many other firms who rented office space there. He just worked for Regus, an employment agency: manning the phones, helping people find work. He had brown hair, brown eyes, he was maybe fifteen to twenty pounds overweight, he liked prog rock, and he was the proudest father of his two kids, my nieces, Faye and Zoe. All he ever wanted was for life to be good for them. Better, maybe, than it was for us. And you know what? Until September 11, 2001, he was doing really well with that.

She keeps looking in the sky all the time she is talking. A sister looking for a brother; for vengeance; for destiny. He is so sure it is the sign he feels tears in his eyes. Tears of joy, tears of thanks, tears of finally found purpose. Not tears, he is absolutely certain – he knows this because he can see them welling in the eyes of others in his group, and he needs no mirror to know his are shinier, brighter, fatter with truth – not tears of sadness over the wasteful, useless death of Sylvia's darling dearest brother Dan.

* * *

I love Daddy so much – with all my heart – but he's really starting to smell. Today, when we arrived at the hospital, I went to kiss him and tell him I love him like I always do, and I noticed it even before I put my lips on his cheek. I like kissing Daddy, even though the look of his skin since he's been in hospital does make me feel weird. I used to like it a lot when I was little. I liked the feel of his beard, all rough on my skin. I didn't like it when he shaved, like he sometimes did before he went out at night to get a big award or something. Sometimes he would kiss me on the lips, but sometimes he would move his face so that his cheek was there for me to kiss. He would move his face in a funny way that made me laugh, like someone had snapped his head to one side.

The thing is, I've got a really AMAZING sense of smell. Jada says it's like a superpower; like I should have a secret identity, and be called Smellgirl or Supersmell (I wasn't so sure about that because the trouble with the word smell is that even though it can mean that you've got a great sense of smell it can also mean you smell, so Smellgirl or Supersmell might be superheroes who just smell a lot. I wouldn't want people to think I was like, the Human Skunk). I don't know what this superhero would do – I guess I could follow the trail of a baddie, if I knew what he was supposed to smell like.

So when I got close to Daddy today I suddenly caught this really gross whiff. Like gone-off broccoli. It made me feel sick, so that I didn't want to kiss him. So because Mommy was talking to Dr Ghundkhali, and no one else was looking, I didn't kiss him, I just moved my head away at the last minute.

I didn't say anything to anyone about the smell. I wanted to, but I knew it would just sound really childish, saying to one of the doctors, 'Why does my Daddy smell so bad?' And anyway, I *know* why he smells so bad. It's because he's dying.

(I did tell Jada about it when she phoned me – she has her own cell! – after we got back home. She said: 'Maybe they should make like special deodorants or something for people who are dying.' Which I thought was a really good idea. I mean, just because you're dying doesn't mean you don't care about that stuff. It's never too late to make a first impression, Elaine says. Although I guess this would be more like a *last* impression.)

The thing was, though, I felt really bad about not kissing Daddy. I started to think that maybe if I didn't kiss him like normal at the start and at the end of my visit then maybe he would die. I mean, like, straight away, maybe as soon I went home, or maybe even when I was there. And then as soon as I thought that all the machines started beeping like mad, and he started making that awful groaning noise he makes, and the nurses started rushing in and crowding round his bed, and I started to feel really bad because I thought it was all my fault, that because I didn't kiss him he was going to die. So I rushed over to his bed, too, but I couldn't get through to Daddy because all the doctors were all there, all five or six of them and some of the nurses and Mommy, too. I wanted to scream, 'Let me through! I have to *kiss* him!' but I knew they would all just think I was being a stupid little kid. So I told him in my thoughts. I thought maybe if he can hear me when I talk to him even though he's in a coma maybe he can hear my thoughts as well. I told Daddy in my thoughts that I was really sorry that I hadn't kissed him, and that I would definitely kiss him before I left, whatever he smelled like, double extra hard, and please don't die before I do that.

Anyway, after about five minutes, the machines stopped beeping and everything calmed down, and the doctors moved away, and then it all went back to normal. Then, when it was time to go, I went over to Daddy's bed again. His mask was on his face again. It looked like it was too tight, like when they take it off there would be red lines on his cheeks. His hair was lying over his forehead, which was all sweaty. It was like whatever had happened today, when he'd started to make all that noise and the doctors had all rushed round, had been really tiring for him. I brushed his hair back, and said: 'That's better, now.'

Then I reached up on tiptoe and put my lips against his cheek and gave him the double extra hard kiss I had promised. If my kisses do help him live then he should live twice as long as he was going to because of that one. I would have made it even longer but I was holding my breath because of the smell.

* * *

In one hand, Violet Gold holds *Bigger Than Big* by Chris Noth, and in the other, *Solomon's Testament* by Eli Gold. Eeny meeny miny mo, she thinks, catch a nig– but then she stops herself, even in her thoughts, remembering that that word was out of bounds now, and feeling the fear and confusion that she always feels around the shifting sands of linguistic acceptability, the dread that she is going to get it wrong.

She opens *Bigger Than Big*:

It is 12 May 2008. Tonight is the night of the premiere of the *Sex and the City* movie, in London. Hundreds of screaming fans line the red carpet outside the Odeon cinema in the city's famous Leicester Square, waiting for a glimpse of their heroes: of the women who play Carrie, Samantha, Miranda and Charlotte. And of me. I play Big. The male lead in the movie. The sex object, people say, for the millions of women who have religiously watched the TV series for years. And yet I am not there. I have chosen to be with my son, instead. He is four months old.

She puts it down. She feels that flatness behind the eyes she sometimes feels when reading Eli's book, that sense that these words are not meant for her, and that understanding them will be hard work, like reading in a language enough like English to pick up about a quarter of the meaning.

She holds up *Solomon's Testament* again, without opening it. When she does this – when she just feels the 530-page heft of it, and looks at the first edition cover, with its strange abstraction of a face, an image once so modern, now so dated – the book loses its new fluidity and reverts to what it has been for her for many years: something stolid and fixed, an ornament, a keepsake, gathering dust on her shelf harking back to an ever-receding point in her life.

Violet remembers when Eli first came home with a copy of the book. He was so happy, as happy as she had ever seen him. He kept on reading it, which seemed odd to her, as he had written it, and so must have read it many times already. But she could see he got so much joy out of seeing his words in print and between covers. It had taken him a long time, and involved overcoming many obstacles, to

308

force it into that form. Before embarking on the novel, Eli had written a number of short stories and submitted them to a magazine called *Horizon*: they had all been turned down. His pages would be returned generally with a cursory note, although once a man called Cyril Connolly had written a few paragraphs acknowledging that he had talent but explaining why his writing wasn't quite right for them. Violet remembers his name because she remembers reading the letter over Eli's shoulder, and saying that she thought it was nice that Mr Connolly had taken the trouble to write, considering that he wasn't going to use any of the stories. She shudders at the memory of it: both at her cloying naivety and at the image lodged in her mind of how Eli had looked round at her, his normally lazy eyes electric with rage.

'I'm so full of it,' he said.

'So full of what?'

'Of everything he says. And it's all so wrong. So fucking wrong. Now I have to live all day with all the reasons he's so wrong. It's like a letter in my head.'

'Are you going to write it?'

'What?'

'The letter. To Mr Connolly.'

He squinted at her, like he couldn't make her out.

'No, Birdy. I just meant that my mind is full with a letter I *could* write. But, I could, I guess … what do you think?'

Violet, not entirely used to offering her husband advice, nodded. 'If you think it might change his mind,' she said.

Eli laughed. 'It won't do that.'

'Won't it?'

'No. You can change people's minds about politics, and you can change their mind about whether or not they want a slice of cake. But you can't change their mind once they've made a statement of taste. You can argue with them all you like, but the best, the absolute best you can get to, once they've said they don't like something, is a shake of a head and the words: *I'm sorry, I'm simply don't like it.*'

'So …'

'So, you're right. I should write a letter to *Mr Connolly*.' The name came out super sour: Violet blushed, aware that he was sarcastically echoing her politeness. 'It won't achieve anything, but it will make me feel better, and it might stop me hearing all the arguments in my head all day.'

Violet felt guilty about this conversation, even though she never found out whether or not Eli actually posted the seven-page letter that he wrote in response to Cyril Connolly's rejection. The fear that he might have – and that it might have made things worse for him – hung heavy with her for weeks.

She eventually realized, however, that in some fundamental way Eli did not take these rejections to heart; or, at least, did not store them in that part of his heart which had any bearing on his stone-cold sense of his own genius. When, on occasion, Mr Harlow, the boss of International Shipbrokers Ltd, had called Violet into his office and reprimanded her for typing errors, her first instinct was always that he was right, that she was a poor worker, and that her typing should really be much better by now. But even though they made him first angry and then depressed, the rejection letters did not make Eli question whether there might be something wrong with his work. He did not even consider it: his self-confidence acted like a silver shield to criticism, against which it deflected and dispersed like light. Criticism existed only outside of himself, evidence of the world's stupidity, or, at best, of its unreadiness to accept his genius as yet.

It was typical of Eli, Violet thinks with hindsight, that he should have given up trying to get short stories into magazines like *Horizon*, and chosen instead to leapfrog that hinterland of a writer's career and get on with a novel. His *prove-them-wrong* engine just continued expanding. The fury that fuelled seven pages of pointless prose to Cyril Connolly combined with all of Eli's other furies to create the fire underneath *Solomon's Testament*. He received numerous rejection letters for that, too, but by then it was like he had built from them a paper ark, on which he was sailing confidently against the current of their idiot opinion towards the harbour of his success. And when, eventually, in 1954, Weidenfeld & Nicolson published the book in a small print run of only two thousand copies, he gathered up every rejection letter he had ever had – including Cyril Connolly's – and threw them down the toilet.

'Why didn't you put them in the fire?' she said, putting her coat on to go down to the box at the end of the street and telephone a plumber. It was mid-winter. 'At least then they might have helped to warm the room.'

He smiled at her and shrugged, and did not say *Because that would have been too glorious for them and because the act of throwing my rejection letters down the toilet makes a statement about what they are,* as the symbolism would have been marred by an admission of its meaning.

Sitting in her room at Redcliffe House, with the sky darkening outside her window and the smell of lunch still seeping through the floorboards, she remembers the first arrival of Eli's book. It did not come in a parcel – although other copies would, many of them, cluttering up the place; her husband brought it home from the publishers. He kept reading it and laughing, as if it contained jokes he had never seen before. He sat in the one comfy chair they had in their bedsit, letting the fire go out, and laughed and laughed. This confused Violet still further, as the few glances that she had stolen at the manuscript had not revealed anything that she, a fan of Tommy Trinder, could conceive of as funny.

The very first time he came home with the book, he was, for a moment, like a little boy. It turned out that he had walked all the way from Soho to Walthamstow – and had run the last two miles, holding the book aloft like an Olympic torch. When he came through the door, the first thing he said was 'Birdy!' He called her: and when she came, wiping her hands on her apron, he kept saying it. 'Birdy! Birdy, Birdy, Birdy …' And he held the book out for her; not to read, but just to see, like a prize he had won, and won, it sounded to her ears, for her.

In fact, as she would come to realize later, what Eli had brought home was a bomb, ticking and ready to smash through the windows of their life. The fuse was not yet lit, but it was when the first significant review came out – a rave in the *Daily Telegraph* by Donald Davie ending, '*Solomon's Testament* drags the novel, kicking and screaming, into the future.' Violet had not considered this. She had accepted for a long time that Eli was writing a book, and that that was something mysterious and not for her, but she had thought of it as a closed act – she had not imagined any life beyond it, except that perhaps, at some point, Eli might write another book. His writing, she assumed, would carry on in parallel to their lives – he would still work at the Post Office, and she at International Shipbrokers Ltd – and that he would no doubt carry on writing much as other men carried on flying pigeons or collecting stamps. She thought of it, in other words, as a hobby; and in so thinking, she felt she was not diminishing it – many of the men she had known before marriage who flew pigeons did so with the same passion and intensity that Eli wrote.

What she was not expecting was that with the book would come the world: the world, that is, of the newspaper and the radio and the television, the world as projected onto the imagination of the ordinary by the mechanisms of fame. This was the great surprise. Today, sometimes, she watches the TV or sees the garish colour photographs in the newspapers, and thinks that children growing up now must see through to that world as easily as she once saw through her family's kitchen window to their back garden, and that getting there must feel as simple as walking through the door. But when she was young, there was no passage there at all. She went to the movies, and she listened to the radio, and the life that was represented there – both the fictional life, and the life of the stars, which seemed, when she read about it in the newspapers, no less fictional – seemed to come from some other side, like the dead to the living, or perhaps the living to the dead. It would have been as easy for her to enter into that life as to enter into the cinema screen or the radio valves. Indeed, such a wish – even as she might dream of Stewart Grainger or Eric Portman – never even occurred to her. The idea of being famous herself, which so stalks today's young that it seems not even an aspiration but an entitlement, would have been for Violet so far away from possibility as to live beyond the realm of the imagination. Fame was another planet; another dimension.

With hindsight, however, she could see how it was not like that for Eli. After the *Daily Telegraph* review came out, a journalist came to see him – a hunched, little man with a bad cough, who just knocked on the door, without a by your leave – and Eli didn't blink. He led him straight through to their tiny room, and when, a couple of minutes later, she walked in with cups of tea for the both of them, her husband was talking freely of his destiny: of *always knowing he would be a writer*, of *being sure from the beginning of his muse*, of *realizing very early on that he wasn't meant to work in the Post Office for the rest of his life*. She knew it wasn't a lie, it wasn't put on for the journalist: he had always been like that. It just took it to happen for it to become clear. Eli slid into fame as though into a bespoke tailored suit.

For Violet, though, fame was like finding a secret room in a house that you had lived in for years, a room you never knew was there, and, through a combination of fear, and uncertainty about whether you were allowed to, never went into. The nearest she came to it was a reading Eli gave at Foyles two months after the publication of *Solomon's Testament*. She had never been into Foyles but had passed it on Charing Cross Road, not bothering to go in, most of the titles on display in the window being by writers that she had only heard of via Eli's furious bedside rants. When she arrived – it was a Wednesday night, and cold – she was taken aback by the sight of a series of posters which had been put up on the main window. These posters had an image of the book cover on them, and the words 'A READING FROM THE NEW LITERARY SENSATION' written below. Above was the date and time, and then Eli's name, and then a photograph of her husband which she had never seen before. Such was the economy of expectation at Weidenfeld & Nicolson regarding *Solomon's Testament* that the photograph of Eli on the back inner flap of the first printing was simply an old picture that he had provided: a photograph of the two of them, taken on Brighton beach the previous summer, from which Violet had been excised. In that picture, Eli had looked like he always did when having his photograph taken: smiling not entirely naturally, his arms folded, a little hunched against the sea wind, but with some real joy breaking through the self-consciousness. He was both at ease and ill at ease, as people are having heard someone shout the word cheese – in this case Gwendoline, the only one of her friends to own a camera, who Eli had rather surprisingly allowed on this daytrip. But in this other photograph, the one in the window at Foyles, he had acquired *that thing* which people who are regularly photographed have, that way of looking and being looked at that seems at once utterly natural and completely mythological. How did he know how to do that? she thought. And so quickly? Was it the cameraman telling him what to do, or had he just done it, instinctively?

When she came into the shop – it felt exciting, going into a shop after six o'clock, like Christmas, when they stayed open late – about two hundred chairs had been set up in front of a small wooden stage, to create a mini-theatre. It was not enough: the place was packed, and many people were standing around behind and by the side of the chairs. She was taken aback by the audience, who were all younger and better looking than she had expected. An assumption remained within Violet, that people interested in books must be either old, or old before their time: but this crowd seemed to be mainly in their twenties, and fashionable. A lot of the men had glasses, but not wiry old-man ones – thick black ones which they wore in a way that suggested a sort of arch thoughtfulness, rather than myopia. The women were pretty: most of them wore trousers and some denim jeans, which Violet had seen in the shops but did not own a pair of. She felt old in her pink striped silhouette dress, which she had picked out especially for tonight. She couldn't make out whether she was, in fact, older than most in this audience: when she looked closely, some of them, both men and women, seemed more lined than her, and one or two might even have dyed their hair, but everyone gave out some overall message of youth, some indefinable mix of confidence and fashionability that Violet had thought did not extend beyond one's early twenties.

A woman in a smart blue dress suit was taking what appeared to be tickets, which inspired in her the familiar stab of anxiety that she had got something wrong, having arrived without one (not realizing that tickets would be needed for a reading in a bookshop). She thought about turning round and leaving, to spare everyone the embarrassment, but then a bald man with glasses appeared and said:

'Mrs Gold?'

'Yes?'

'I'm the duty manager for tonight. Can I get you a seat?' He pointed her towards a chair in a middle row, over the back of which a small piece of paper had been folded, bearing the legend RESERVED.

'Thank you,' said Violet.

'My pleasure,' he said, turning to go. Partly to delay the embarrassment of forcing the people already seated in the row to stand up and partly because she really wanted to know, Violet touched his arm at the elbow, saying:

'Excuse me … sir.'

'Yes, Mrs Gold?' he answered, smiling, she assumed at her use of *sir*.

'How did you know it was me?'

He reached into his inner jacket pocket and produced a torn piece of paper. He handed it over. It was a picture of her, waving, and grinning, and holding her coat against her body for warmth. It was the other half of the photograph of Eli on Brighton beach that had served, originally, as his book jacket photograph. She knew that Eli had had the photograph returned from the publishers, although she hadn't seen it around their bedsit for a while.

'Mr Gold gave me this and told me to watch out for you. And make sure you got a good seat.'

She looked up at the duty manager. He, at least, looked as old as his years. She held out her hand, offering back the photograph.

'No, no. Please. I don't …' He trailed off, avoiding the phrase *need it any more*. 'Have a nice evening, Mrs Gold.'

She is moved enough by the memory to go and fetch the photograph from her shoebox, now perched on the bedside table – she had no wish to go through the palaver of fetching it from underneath the mattress again. It lies on top of all the bits and pieces of her life, just below her wedding photo. Barring some yellowing at the edges and a certain cloudiness about the image that she does not remember, it has

315

not aged much: certainly, she thinks, glancing up from it to the mirror on the wall above, not as much as her.

She holds it to the mirror, just above her face, a bit like the referees in football matches do their red and yellow cards. Because the photograph is blocking one eye she can see it better, the enforced wink helping to break through the minor cataracts that blur her peripheral vision. And she thinks how wrong it all is. Not time, or the loss of herself, the disjunction between this woman in the photograph and who she is now – despite those things creating in her a visceral sense of wrong, she knows that they are deeply right, or, at least, deeply true – but how none of it means quite what it should. If this was a film, she would still possess both halves of this photograph, and the camera would close in on both fragments now, with her sad face hovering above the tear, a clear symbol of her fractured marriage. Or perhaps the photograph she would own would be the glamorous publicity one of Eli that had been on the Foyles poster, and that would have been torn away from some image of her, to suggest how fame rent him from her. It makes no sense that this photograph of her, ripped away from the image of Eli, actually stands as a keepsake of a moment of kindness towards her; of a small break in his solipsism which surprised her by making her realize that he did sometimes care for her when she was not there.

It is this that Violet Gold remembers most from that night: this realization, forming a small protective armour around her during the reading, so that even as the evidence of Eli's inevitable excision from her life by celebrity came alive – in the tense wonder with which the audience hung onto each word, in the shared conviction that they were witnessing the birth of a star, but above all, in the rapt attention of the women, an attention that was also, she could sense, a waiting, for the moment in which Eli's eye would alight on one of them and *choose* – even as all this seethed around her, she felt protected; she felt contained.

She puts the photograph down, and picks up the book.

Since Harvey has been staying at the family apartment, some relaxation seems to have occurred in Freda's timetabling of his visits. It was Elaine's doing. Coming into the living room to pick up Colette the day after Harvey's unfortunate blackout in front of the sauna, she said, while waiting for her charge to put her coat on:

'Coming?'

Harvey looked up from the TV: *American Idol*, a rerun. 'Sorry?'

'To the hospital.'

He switched the sound down on the remote control, although he had been quite enjoying this particular rendition of Shania Twain's 'You're The One'.

'Er … am I …?' He didn't want to say *allowed*.

'Yes, Harvey, are you coming to the hospital?'

Colette appeared by her side: she was dressed in some weird polka-dotted dress, making her look like a miniature 1950s housewife. Harvey saw the girl's face fall at her nanny's question. *Why does she hate me so much?* He glanced back at the TV. The commercials had started abruptly, like they do on American channels. It was one of the very many adverts featuring handsome men of a certain age working hard and playing hard – in this case, canoeing, playing basketball, riding along a sunlit coastal road in a convertible, five of them in one car, laughing, their full grey hairstyles bobbing in the wind – which turn out to be for drugs which will reduce the size of the prostate. They were all so happy, these men: smiling and waving and looking so fine. The picture froze on their exultant faces, and the words

Improved Flow, Comfortable Release, Less Urgency, Fewer Visits, Relaxed Passing came up in a tower on the right-hand side of the screen. Then, with the sound dipped, an authoritative male voice quickly listed the side effects: drowsiness, headaches, nausea, dizziness, in rare cases the development of breast tissue.

'Obviously, if you're *busy* today ...'

Harvey looked at her: she was smirking a little, but it was not unfriendly – her sarcasm was not malign, insofar as it was provoked by an assumption that to be by his father's bedside was, after all, the reason he was here. He flicked at the remote control, but failed to switch off the TV: it changed channels instead, to a film, *Austin Powers*, the first one, the moment when the wife of one of Dr Evil's henchmen receives a phone call about the death of her husband.

'No, no. Just give me a minute.'

On their arrival at the hospital, Harvey felt, for the first time, unquestioned: John the security man may even have given him what he likes to think of as a friendly nod.

Since then, there have been more visits, and he is beginning to feel part of the Eli deathbed elite. He knows, of course, that the key is Colette, that she is operating for him like an Access-All-Areas laminate, and that if he did not have her by his side, then things would revert.

This access is, however, something of a double-edged sword. Fighting to get into the room, however damaging it may have been to Harvey's much-damaged self-esteem, did at least give his visits a focus. It also meant that he didn't have to spend all that much time there. Now, he realizes, actually spending hours and hours in a room waiting for the occupant of that room to die is – what is it? For some reason he thinks of it in terms of what footballers say about a difficult match ahead: *a big ask*. It is *a big ask*. Most of the time he simply does not know what to do. Freda is in near-constant consultation with the doctors: when she is not, she seems perfectly able – serenely happy, in fact – to minister to Eli, to do all the things Harvey would feel incredibly awkward doing, mopping his brow with a damp cloth, stroking

318

his hand, talking – fucking *talking*, she has no problem with, no self-consciousness about – to him. Colette spends much of the day playing with her various toys, or reading, or being taught by Elaine in the other room, the one that Freda now sleeps in, or doing some mopping and stroking and talking herself. Sometimes she writes her diary.

Harvey finds, as well, that he cannot look at his father for long. It is a bad word, but what he feels is disgust: and not a moral disgust, but straightforward disgust: disgust at the smell, and the bedsores, and the sight of bone through skin. Sometimes, it is in the mix of mechanical and organic that disgust will burrow – for example, in the nasogastric tube that goes into his father's nose. As a child, Harvey had been fascinated and horrified by the inside of his father's nostrils, how they could possibly be so hairy: it seemed to him that the hair in there was so thick and packed that surely he couldn't breathe, the ends of it sticking out like fronds, so strong and pointed he used to think that if you were to tweak them like a Jew's harp they might make some discordant music.

The sight of the white wire ploughing through this now wilted nasal forest adds a new layer of disgust to the old. Harvey has read somewhere about disgust – that it will turn, if the mind starts to feel trapped within the orbit of the object of disgust, to fear. He is used to wanting not to see the bad thing but knowing it is there so having to look regardless: all those fucking idiot mind games that his mind plays on itself. So he finds himself making more and more excuses to leave. He gets cups of coffee from the café, or loses chess games to Deep Green, or heads outside to get some air and see if he can spot any of the regular Eli-weirdos hanging around waiting for news – there is a blonde woman in pigtails who has caught his eye a couple of times – or just wanders round the hospital. He has become quite well versed now in all the departments: Cardiology, Haematology, Oncology, all the proper medical words for what can go wrong with the human body. They make him think of that BT advert on British TV in the 1980s with Maureen Lipman saying to her O-level-failing grandson, 'You've got an 'ology!' He wonders if the boy she was talking to has, now, got one of these other 'ologies.

He also finds himself going on the first inkling of pressure in bladder or sphincter, to the toilet. He has discovered that, compared to the atmosphere around Eli's bed, it is indeed something of a restful room. Returning from the toilet on his last visit, he bumped into Dr Ghundkhali in the corridor, who said:

'Are you OK?'

Harvey looked at the doctor's concerned face. He was so taken aback by the approach that the normal response – *No I'm morally and intellectually bankrupt, my body itches all the time, my therapist is charging me for all the time I'm away, my half-sister hates me, I've been here too long now to still be jet-lagged, but somehow I still am, and of course all the other stuff: wife, dad, blah blah blah* – did not even properly run through his mind before he said:

'Yes, I think. Why do you ask?'

'Well because – I hope you don't mind me saying this, but I've noticed you go to the toilet … a lot.'

'Um, do I?'

'Sorry, I – it may be, of course, that you're just under a lot of stress.'

'Yes, I guess.'

'That can have an effect on bowel function. But you also seem to spend an awful long time in there.'

Can't a man go the shitter without surveillance? formed in his mouth, although it wasn't really what he wanted to say. What he wanted to say was: it's nicer in there than – pointing to Eli's door – in there. Come in with me, doctor, and I'll show you. You can even have a go on my chess app.

'No, really I'm fine. Although …'

'Yes?' Dr Ghundkhali brought his hand to his radically clean-shaven face and pinched his thumb and forefinger together, dimpling his chin.

'I do worry about … the other thing.'

'The other …?'

'Urination. I do do that a lot. I wonder if I should have my prostate checked out.'

Can you make me like one of those men in the advert, doctor? Smiling and waving and looking so fine? Riding the coastal highway into the far distance unconcerned by any need on their long great journey for a toilet stop?

'OK. How old are you?'

'Forty-four.'

'Have you had a PSI ever?' Harvey shook his head: he had no idea what that was. 'When was your last rectal exam?'

'Um … I haven't had a rectal exam.'

'At all?'

'Well, maybe when I was much younger.'

Dr Ghundkhali nodded, a measured, slow nod, like a man getting to the meat of the matter.

'Well, first thing we need to do is one of those.'

Harvey felt his mouth go a little dry. 'Now?'

'No!' he said, laughing. 'I'll organize one with one of our nurses. You're in here most days at the moment, aren't you?'

'Yes,' said Harvey, for it seemed that now he was.

Today, Eli is being washed. It is unlucky, or at least, challenging, that Harvey and Colette's entry through the door – Elaine having dropped them off at the entrance of the hospital, in order to go and visit her mother downtown – coincides with the nurse, with something of an inappropriate flourish, lifting the sheet off the lower half of his body and removing the bed pan, before applying a disinfected sponge.

Harvey looks to Freda, who is standing by the bedside, giving off a sense that this is a job she could do better. She turns: he expects her to glance at Colette, perhaps to register a desire to protect her sensibilities, but in fact her eyes alight on him. 'Should I take Colette down to the café for a drink?' he says, trying to help.

'No, no,' says Freda, irritatedly. 'She's seen him washed before. Haven't you, darling?'

'Yes, of course,' says Colette, going over and holding her mother's hand facing the bed, as if to make the point. Freda turns to look, too.

'But …' Harvey says, not sure what he is going to say.

321

'He never shrank from the body, Harvey. He made of the body, in all its oozing and flowing – in all its blood and horror – something beautiful. It's worth remembering that when you feel the instinct to look away.'

She says this – in that intent voice that she uses when she is being super-serious, and about Eli she is only ever super-serious – without facing Harvey, in order to illustrate, through staring at her husband, now having his legs being pulled apart, that *she* would never look away. But Jesus, Freda, Harvey wants to say, that's in his work: this is life. This is an old man in a coma having his frightful body exposed to pitiful sight. *I don't think it's what he would want.* It is pointless, however. Harvey realizes that, for her, Eli is, as it were, undegradable; even having his testicles lifted to wipe clean the terrible detritus underneath cannot demean him. He feels, too, a contradiction in her attitude, that despite what she has said she would quite like him to turn away, to turn away and go off on one of his aimless wanders through the hospital, because this ritual, of watching Eli being cleaned, seems to him less, in truth, about abiding by the great man's literary worship of all bodily form and function, and more about licence: about how because she is his wife and Colette is their daughter they can see this. They are allowed. This – this deep and awful intimacy – it is their final prize.

He, however, is not sure he is allowed, even though she has just told him not to look away. So he stays, locked into this contradiction: trapped near the object of disgust. He begins to feel nauseous. He tries to focus on a single point on Eli's body, a bit like when Jamie gets car sick and Stella tells him to stare at a stationary point on the horizon. His eyes fix on some innocuous part – a rib, a knee – but they are drawn back to the thing he most wishes not to see, his father's penis, a sickening bundle of skin framed uselessly by sparse tufts of grey-white pubic hair. All that trouble, Harvey thinks. All that trouble – all those wives, all those children, all those friends betrayed – in the service of this pallid balding grub.

'I'm going to the toilet,' he says.

In the taxi, on the way back to the apartment, Colette says:

'Harvey?'

'Yes.'

'Do you know any of our brothers and sisters? The other ones.'

'Yes,' he says. 'Well, no. I don't know them. I've met Simone. And me and Jules exchanged a couple of Facebook messages once. But he didn't seem to really want to be friends. Do you know them?'

'No. I knew Daddy had other children but me and Mommy never really talk about them. Although we did a while ago, for the first time.'

This corresponds to what he knows about Freda, who would under normal circumstances not countenance acknowledging the other marriages, and certainly not the fruits of them. He wonders if this conversation Colette had with her represents something of a breakthrough, like Arab countries deciding to recognize, if not condone, Israel.

'Why won't they come and see Daddy?'

They are in a traffic jam along Fifth Avenue. On their right, people file in and out of the Guggenheim Museum. Harvey has never been there, but he wonders how many Great Men's wares are shown in there, and how many of these men – while painting and sculpting their passports to Greatness – turned over poor old Peggy.

'I don't know exactly. I think maybe they feel loyal to Isabelle. To their mother.'

'What does that mean?'

'It means … I guess it means that when Daddy left their mommy their mommy wasn't very pleased about it, and so the children feel like it might be a betrayal – might be something that seems like it's against her – if they came.'

Colette's brow pinched. Harvey has a momentary insight into where the lines on her face would be, in years to come.

'So what about your mommy? Wasn't she upset when Daddy left her?'

'Yes. She was really upset, and really angry.'

He has a vision of his mother, tearing up Eli's clothes with her bare hands. When was that? The first or second time he left her? Did she

323

even do it? Maybe he has just transplanted this idea of what angry women do when left onto her history. He suddenly sees himself as the world might see him, the pole-axed son of the arch-feminist and the arch-misogynist. I never stood a fucking chance, he thinks about himself.

The cab turns along East 59th, into Park, but the traffic there is no better. A woman, beautiful from behind, walks up the sidewalk. He wants the taxi to move. He wants to see if the front confirms the back: it makes him anxious not to know, even though he is aware that such a confirmation will only depress him. A transit train rumbles past on the track to their left, taking passengers into Harlem, and The Bronx, parts of New York Harvey has never been and will never go.

'So why have you come?'

'Because she's dead.' Although so, Harvey thinks, is Isabelle, long, long dead. Perhaps her children hold her in the memory more than he holds his mother. Or perhaps they just hold the memory of her anger more. They are, after all, half-French.

'So you wouldn't have come if she wasn't?'

The jam clears a little, and the car begins to move. The woman comes closer, close enough for Harvey to track the seesaw-swing of her buttocks.

'I don't know,' he says, tearing his eyes away from the window. 'She never liked it that I got back in contact with Dad in my twenties. She thought it *wasn't* loyal. But it was up to me. It was what I wanted to do.'

Colette thinks about this, her face placid. Harvey doesn't know how much she understands of it. He doesn't know how much he understands of it. They are nearly past the walking woman. He turns to see her face, knowing he will only get a few seconds to make the judgement, to see if the promise has been kept, but the taxi swerves away, down 100th Street, back towards the park.

'Traffic,' says the driver, in some unplaceable accent. Harvey feels furious, cheated. He longs for the engagement he had with Jasvant Kirtia Singh. Colette comes out of her brown study and says:

'Daddy's winky-wonk …'

This breaks Harvey out of his self-pitying funk.

'Yes?'

'It made Jules and Simone. And me and you. Didn't it?'

'Um … yes, I guess. Not on its own, of course.'

'No, I know.'

Harvey looks at her, not sure what she knows. Him and Stella have not had the full birds and bees conversation with Jamie, even though he is old enough to hear it now, because of his echolalia. Stella in particular had been concerned that telling him about *all that* might lead him into something that would seem to others like Tourette's, saying penis and vagina and womb and sperm and egg out loud in all sorts of public situations. Harvey had gone along with it, although he wasn't sure, because he didn't want his son to be the only one at school who didn't know, and also because of a secret admiration he has for people with Tourette's – a belief that they are not diseased, but, rather, possessed of some virulent manic honesty.

She probably knows it all, he thinks. Nothing seems to have been kept from her. Although she did say winky-wonk, at least, a child's word; be thankful for small mercies.

'A long time apart …' he says.

'What do you mean?'

'I mean it made me in 1966. Or 1965, whenever him and my mum … and then you. Much more recently.'

Colette frowns. Tiny lines appear again above her bushy-for-her-age eyebrows. Harvey feels a sudden burst of affection and pity for her. She is, he can see, doing the maths, but he feels how she is also calculating – as she clearly has to do often – something which she should perhaps not have to do yet, some new and troubling equation of the spirit, one of many rebalances of the adult-child books.

'That's kind of weird, isn't it?' she says.

Harvey looks out of the window. They are at the park, passing Strawberry Fields.

'Yes,' he says.

*   *   *

He looks at his body in the mirror. It is good for his age, he thinks. You can see by his face and his skin that he is not young. But his body is wiry, taut, like Iggy Pop's. He sees his body and thinks that he is fit, even though he smokes.

He turns to look, over his left shoulder, at his tattoo. It's still there, just visible, a faded red and blue rash, now more like a birthmark than a tattoo. He never quite understood Uncle Jimmy's insistence on having it removed. Should, on the day of judgement, the Gracious Lord choose to resurrect him, He will, at the same time, banish all his wrinkles and stoops and scars – well, then, why could the tattoo not be done away with then, too? Are skin grafts beyond the Lord? he thought, and then felt bad for thinking it.

He opens the wardrobe. Hanging inside is a white shirt, with a black tie around it. He puts on the shirt, which is crisply laundered. It feels clean but stiff on his chest and arms. He does the shirt up to the neck, where it catches his throat, causing a concern that, on the day, he will be carrying around a sense that he is being strangled. But he does up the tie, flipping up the collar, twisting it round his neck. Even though some men in his community always wear a tie, he never does. He has to remember how to tie it by rote, the fat flap long, the thin one short. He will, on the day, be smart up top. He thinks that is safest, and somehow appropriate. But he has watched the doctors come in and out of Mount Sinai, and, to his surprise, noticed that only a few wear suits or are that smartly dressed and so, beneath, he has stuck with jeans.

He bends back into the wardrobe and takes out the white coat. He got it at Partydomain, a fancy dress site. It came with a stethoscope and a name tag. On it he has had printed the words Hughie Thomasson, MD, Faculty Physician. He is assuming that no one at Mount Sinai will be a fan of The Outlaws. He has another doctor outfit inside the wardrobe, also from Partydomain, a green surgical one, but it has a mask and a cap, and feels to him too much like a disguise. Also, he is not sure whether someone dressed as if about to go into an operating theatre would be able to walk into The Great Satan's room unquestioned. So he will wear white and black: white sacred undergarments, white shirt, black tie and white coat.

He takes the stethoscope out of his pocket. As all non-medical people do, he puts the blocky ends in his ears, and undoes a shirt button in order to place the metal disc on his chest. It is cold but warms quickly. It is a toy, but the disc still communicates sound through the rubber, and after three or four lifts and replacements he finds his heartbeat, faint, but strong enough. He feels it thud; then again; then again. He considers how strange it is that it happens without him; that it just goes on. Wanting to feel that he has control over his body, he decides to quicken the beat, which he does by thinking about his destiny. He imagines, on the day, putting on this shirt and this tie and this coat, and taking the subway to 103rd Street, and walking the six blocks to Mount Sinai; going in through the canopied door to the Fifth Avenue entrance, into the Guggenheim Pavilion, underneath its steel and glass slopes, and into the elevator at the far end. That is as far as his imagination takes him. It is far enough too for the thuds to speed up and get louder. He stops thinking. He lets his mind go blank, which it can do for a few seconds, before the fact of his sister's death turns it over again. It is in the moment of blankness that he hopes to act.

Through the stethoscope he hears his heart beat once more. He hears and feels its thud. The thud gets louder and quicker, more like a knock now than a thud. His mind is still blank. He is not thinking. He does not know what is making his heart beat faster.

Out of the corner of his vision he senses someone watching him. The stethoscope is still on his chest. He feels his heart trip, going through into some new rhythmic zone, more like the whirring beat of an embryo, or a small bird. He turns and realizes that it is Jesus watching him, Jesus who has turned from profile to face him, Jesus from whose face and body light is again pouring. It is too much to look at – his good eye will burn – so he turns back to the mirror, but the light comes again, enveloping him. He absorbs it, he reflects it, he shines in it, like the moon, like headlights on a desert road. He raises his hand to cover his eyes, blinded by the white of the white coat.

I wonder what my Daddy sees in his coma. I know he can hear, but what does he see? Does he dream? I dream every night. Sometimes I dream about Daddy, that he wakes up at the hospital and he says, 'Hi, Col!' or 'Hi, girly!', which is what he sometimes used to call me before he went into his coma. Sometimes I don't see him wake up. He just *has* woken up, and he's back at our apartment or maybe we're all at the Lodge in New England, or once I dreamt I came in to school and he was our headmaster!

They're the good dreams, of course. Sometimes I dream that I'm at the hospital and he starts getting out of bed but it's like he hasn't woken up, so he's just getting up with his eyes closed, like a zombie. I've had this dream a few times. I hate it. He gets up and even though Mommy and Dr G and everyone else is there, it's like no one notices what's happening. And then he comes right over to where I am and bends down with his eyes closed and puts his face really close to mine. Then he starts to speak but I can't hear what he's saying, or maybe he isn't saying anything, just moving his mouth. It's *so* weird.

I spoke to Jada on the phone yesterday. Her older brother – he's thirteen – says that my daddy might be having a Near-Death Experience. He says this is when you're about to die, and your soul leaves the body but you're not actually dead yet – so you can be on the ceiling watching. And then other times you see this big white light and then at the end of it all the people you've loved but who've died are there, wearing togas or something and smiling and saying come on it's lovely like people do when they're swimming in the sea and trying to get you to dive in. Daddy would have quite a big crowd at the end of the light, because he knows loads of people who have died.

I wonder if that is what Daddy is seeing. He certainly is near death. But he's been near death, I guess, for quite a long time. Months. So I don't know if all that flying on the ceiling and seeing the people you've loved and stuff can go on for months. The people would get bored, wouldn't they? The ones waiting at the end of the light, telling you to come and join them because it's lovely. If you didn't come, after a while they would say oh all right then, whatever, and turn away.

When I was on the phone to Jada, talking about this, Harvey was in the living room tapping away at his laptop like he does all the time. That guy seems to check his email five hundred times a day! I thought, wow, he must get so many, but then I sneaked a peek at his screen one time when he went to the toilet (something else he does, like, a LOT) and there weren't that many – and no new ones (the new ones are written in blacker letters, that's how I know). So I guess he must just check it a lot.

When I put the phone down, he said:

'Maybe I can help …'

'What?' I said.

'Help you understand what's happening to … your dad.'

'He's your dad, too.'

'Yes. I know.'

'It's hard to believe, isn't it?'

He looked at me for a while, doing one of those faces that grown-ups do sometimes after I've spoken, all big-eyed and nodding, like I've said something which means more than it does.

'Yes, Colette. It kinda is.'

He does this, too, trying to sound American. He keeps his English voice but says stuff that sounds more American. I was a little pissed (that's not a word I'm supposed to say but Jada says it and Daddy used to all the time before he started having his Near-Death Experience so I can't see why not). He had been listening to my conversation while pretending to work at his computer but not really.

'What do you mean, help me understand?'

329

'Well …' He looked confused, like he didn't really know how he could. 'Oh! Let's see!'

And then he typed something on his laptop. He looked at the screen for a bit.

'Hmm. I don't get anything for see in a coma.'

'See in a coma?'

'I was searching for it. On the internet. I'll try it with inverted commas round it.'

He typed some more. Then he shook his head.

'Nope. No one seems to have any idea what you see while you're in a coma.'

'Maybe that means you see nothing.'

'Maybe. Or maybe it means that when you come out of it, you can't remember what you saw.'

I thought about this for a bit. 'Come out of it?'

'Yes?'

'Daddy isn't going to come out of it. Is he?'

He made a funny shape with his mouth. 'Ah. No. I don't think so. But some people do.'

'Do they? Which people?'

'People who have been hit hard on the head, or have a brain illness, but they get better. Sometimes someone plays them a bit of music that they used to really like and that does it. Makes them wake up, I mean.'

'Really?'

'It happens a lot in films and stuff, but I think it really does happen in real life. Sometimes they get a celebrity in – like the person in a coma's favourite footballer or pop star – and when they speak to the person in a coma, they wake up.'

'Wow. Hey. Maybe I should be in a coma! Then I'd get to meet, like, Miley Cyrus or Justin Bieber.' Then I thought that – although I would really, really like to meet Miley Cyrus or Justin Bieber – maybe I should think of someone better. 'Or President Obama.'

Harvey smiled. 'I don't think that's a very good idea, Colette. You have to be hurt or really ill to be in a coma. And no one wants you to be hurt or really ill.' He looked at me very seriously, like grown-ups do when they say stuff like that. But then he smiled again. 'Although you're right, it would be a good way to meet superstars.'

'Is there a bit of music we could play to Daddy? Or someone we could bring in to meet him?'

'I don't think so. I think everyone famous has already come in. And anyway … Dad … Daddy … he knew so many famous people anyway.'

'Knows.'

'Pardon?'

'Knows. You shouldn't speak about him like he's already dead.'

He looked told off. Then he nodded. 'Daddy knows so many famous people anyway, I don't know who it would be – who could come and see him who would …'

'Make him so excited that he would wake up?'

'Yes. I guess.'

I thought about it. 'Could we get President Obama?'

He laughed. 'I don't think so. Bush, maybe. Or Clinton. I imagine Clinton would be a fan …'

'Who's he?'

'The one before the one before. You weren't born when he was president.'

I nodded, and said the name to myself to remember it – *Clinton*. He typed something else into his computer. I looked over. He had typed the word coma by itself into Google. He clicked on one of the websites. I read some of the words on it.

'What does that mean?'

'What?'

'That word.'

'Vegetative?'

'Yes.'

He shut the lid. He sniffed.

'It's what Daddy's in. What doctors call a permanent vegetative state.'

'Vege-tative?'

'Like … a vegetable.' He looked away, then back again. 'Look, Colette, maybe this was a bad idea, talking about this.'

331

'Why?'

'Well, I don't know how much I'm meant to speak to you about it. I don't know what Freda – what your mum wants you to know about Daddy's condition.'

This made me cross again, just as I thought I was starting to like him.

'Harvey. She wants me to know *everything*. She doesn't believe in the innocence of children.'

He looked at me like I was crazy. 'I beg your pardon?'

'She doesn't believe in the innocence of children. That's what she told me.'

'Did she …'

I didn't like the way he said that. 'Yes. Or … at least she said that Daddy said once that it was overrated.'

'Colette, do you even know what all these words mean?'

'What words?'

'Innocence. Overrated.'

'*Of course.*'

I do. Innocence means not knowing about sex and death and money and other grown-up stuff. And overrated means thinking something is great when it isn't. God: it's not like any of that is really difficult.

He shook his head. 'All right, then. Being in a permanent vegetative state means that Daddy is like a vegetable. Permanently.'

I screwed up my face. 'A vegetable?'

'Yes.'

'Are you joking?'

'No, I'm not joking. That's what doctors use to describe being in this sort of coma. It's like a metaphor.'

'A what?'

'Oh, you know what *innocence* and *overrated* means but not metaphor. I see, clever clogs.'

I looked at him and felt cross again. But I could see from his face that he was teasing me. I wasn't sure whether I liked him teasing me. I wouldn't have liked it when I first met him. But now it felt all right.

'Which one?' I said.

'Huh?'

'Broccoli? Carrot? Potato?'

He looked at me. I looked at him. He started to laugh. I did, too.

'If he's a potato, will he grow little green bits like a potato does when you leave it for a long time?' I said.

'No. And he's not a potato. Don't for God's sake tell your mum that anyone said that Daddy was a potato.' He stopped and tried to look serious. Then he said: 'Someone as important as Daddy would be a much more sophisticated vegetable. A butternut squash, maybe. Or asparagus.'

I laughed. That was a funny idea. 'Yes. That's what Daddy would be. An asparagus. 'Cos he is quite thin.'

'Yes.'

'And I love asparagus.'

He nodded. 'Yes. Good.' He looked, for a minute, really nice and kind. 'So do I,' he said. Then he did something a bit weird. He leant over and kissed me on the cheek. I wasn't really sure about him doing that – I'm not even sure he was sure about doing it – but it was OK. His face was a bit rough and his breath smelt funny, but I didn't mind.

'Harvey,' I said. 'Why don't you talk to Daddy?'

'Sorry?'

'Why don't you talk to him? Because even if he can't see, he can hear. I always talk to him. But you don't.'

He scratched his neck, and said: 'I have to call home.'

*　*　*

There is someone coming to Redcliffe House. Pat Cadogan has begun a rumour that it is a social services investigation. She has hinted, darkly, at abuses that have happened, perhaps to her, perhaps to others close to her. She has suggested that this confirms that Meg Antopolski's fall 'was not all it seemed'. Both Joe Hillier and his friend Frank have nodded, knowingly, at the suggestion. Norma Miller has told everyone not to be, as she pronounces it, *ridikalus*. She has also said that, with a bit of luck, the investigator will be a handsome young man.

But it is not an investigation. It is an initiative, endorsed by the social services. Violet reads the pamphlet, handed out to all residents at breakfast, by an unsmiling, unexplaining Mandy. It is called *Life Story Work in Care Homes: An Occupational Tool*. It says:

> *Life Story Work* is a way of making people enjoy their own history. It uses memory and imagination to build a narrative that helps the individual to find themselves within the larger framework of the history of their family and their culture. It is an interactive collaboration, exploring the person through their story. It is not psychotherapy: it is not an attempt to fix the past, or indeed the present, but to allow the individual to share their experience by presenting it as a story.

And then on the next page it says:

> In telling us a story about your own life, you do not have to tell us everything that has ever happened to you. Focus on a few key events; a few key relationships; a few key themes. You should highlight material in your own life that you believe to be important in some fundamental way: information about yourself and your life which says something about you and how you have come to be who you are. You can write this material down, or you can talk about it to the *Life Story Work* interviewer, who will record it, either on camera or on audio.

Then there are some photographs of smiling old people in groups, talking. Some of them are being filmed, or talking into microphones, or using computers. Some of them are writing on notepads. There is a flow chart in which, out of a central box with the letters L.S.W on it, the words IDENTITY and PURPOSE and MEANING and SELF-KNOWLEDGE sprout. On the last page it says:

> *Life Story Work* is a method of ordering selfhood developed through work with foster children.

Violet sits in the room, looking at the pamphlet. Outside her window the sun looks like it has been painted over with clouds, three or four coats thick. The person coming, then, is not going to investigate Redcliffe House, but its residents. They have not been asked about this. No vote has been taken. They have been treated, indeed, like foster children. The children will have been abandoned by their parents, and put in new homes and then removed to other homes for care: yes, she can see the comparison. She can see why the people at the social services might think it would work for them.

But it makes her feel very anxious. In the photographs, the old people, however much they might be smiling, are sitting around in large groups. She will have to share her life with everybody. She will have to expose herself. She will have to come out with things which she fears will make the other residents hate her.

She could, she supposes, not mention Eli. But that would be like – like – she once, some years ago, before she was living in Redcliffe House, saw an interview on television with the actor Christopher Lee about his career. And Christopher Lee talked fulsomely about being in *The Lord of the Rings* and *The Man with the Golden Gun* and a 1973 production of *The Three Musketeers*; he dwelt for some time on his role in a television production of Sir Walter Scott's *Ivanhoe*; he talked, in fact, about every aspect of his acting career. Except he didn't mention *Dracula*. This is what it would be like, if, when the *Life Story Work* people came, and asked her about her life story, she didn't mention Eli. It would be like Christopher Lee not mentioning *Dracula*.

She resolves not to do it. She knows that that will be frowned upon by the staff – if it is an initiative supported by the council then they will be keen that as many residents take part as possible, as Redcliffe House is part-funded by public money. She will pretend to be ill if she has to – an action which has its own risks, as it may lead to her becoming thought by the others as a dead woman walking.

Thinking like this forces her up out of her chair, towards the television. She feels how long it takes her to get there, the distance of ten feet or so. She has often thought how small her room is, but she has never wished it larger. She pushes the Hitachi's large oblong plastic button in. It is one o'clock, and the BBC news is on. The newsreader is talking about the Middle East. She stands by the television, watching until the next item, which is about the trial of a paedophile.

She does not want to watch: this is the danger of sitting waiting for news about Eli – she will have to absorb so much other news, so much other awful and contaminating information. It's all so alien; it all so wouldn't have happened when she was young; it all so demonstrates that life no longer belongs to her. The news is like one of those young people in hoods that she sees standing around on Fulham Road, speaking in a language she does not understand, always ready, it seems, to shock and abuse her. Ready to mug her.

It feels suddenly as frightening inside as it is out. Violet decides it is time for her walk. Because of the constant rain this month – it didn't rain yesterday, but the pavement would still have been too slippery to risk – she hasn't ventured outside for over a week. She needs to breathe a different air, one that isn't warm with radiator heat and food aromas; one that isn't redolent of last or nearly last breaths.

In the newsagent, on the corner of Finborough Road and Wharfdale Street, Violet steadies herself against a shelf of magazines, shifting her balance away from her stick: the pressure induced by walking even the few hundred yards from Redcliffe House has made the tiny bones in her hand ache. Her breath starts to come back to her. She turns to the rack. All these ones with the one-word titles: *OK!*, *Now*, *Heat*, *Closer*. So many: there had to be so many of them now because there were so many celebrities. Looking at their covers, you would think, though, that this expansion in celebrity numbers was entirely female. Always women on the covers. One woman or several women, but more or less the same woman, young, beautiful, long-haired, often in a bikini on a beach, occasionally contrasted with a picture of herself looking exactly the same, but described as radically fatter, or thinner. Both the magazines for women and the magazines for men had women on the cover. Correction, Violet thinks to herself, a word she remembers her dad used to say when admitting to being in the wrong: *young* women.

She picks up one of the magazines, one of the ones specifically for women, *Elle* – French for *her*, or *she*, Violet remembers. It is heavy in her hand: there seem to be as many pages in it as there are in *Solomon's Testament*. The woman on the cover is the woman – more or less – who is on all the covers, but Violet has a faint sense that this one is famous, rather than just beautiful – her smiling face has some words under it, saying 'Jen: How I Got My Mojo Back!' There are many subheadings, all about celebrity, beauty and weight. She sees one: *How to Stay Visible After 45*. Visible? She flicks towards it, with difficulty: her fingers do not have much flexibility, and the pages, slippery with gloss, move in chunks out of her control. And they are not clearly numbered: it is disorientating, like trying to find a house in one of those older London streets where numerical order is disregarded. The magazine seems to be all adverts for perfume and cosmetics. Many images pass by, all of women, all beautiful, all looking out at her unsmilingly, with what feels to Violet like reproach, for being their future. Finally, she stumbles upon it. It is a piece which suggests that it is a given that women become invisible at forty-five – invisible to men, but to women also, whose eyes, it would seem, have no function other than to compare other women to themselves. The piece lists a number of methods to combat this phenomenon, mainly cosmetic but one is a 'Have a look-this-way attitude!'.

Eli's marriage to Isabelle Michelet, she remembers, was covered in a celebrity magazine: *Paris-Match*. Gwendoline, whose attitude to Eli in the aftermath of his leaving was one of complete contempt, still bought a copy, and still showed it to Violet. The pictures of the wedding, so different from her own, made her feel jealous, of course, but only for the split second before her eyes fixed onto Eli's bride, a woman possessed of such immediate beauty Violet felt confused, dizzied almost, unable to tell if it was just the flashbulbs or an ideal, pure luminosity – some deep, shocking contrast between hair that dark and skin that white – which made her face shine so.

Violet had always known that Eli was going to leave her. The ticking of the clock of their marriage was apparent to her from the moment of their vows, perhaps even from that first night in the Eagle.

With or without fame, Eli's leaving always seemed built into their story. The fame, when it came, just made the end more apparent, speeding up the movement towards it. It still tore at her, but when he told her he was going – when one breakfast morning, he said her name, landing on it heavily, not Birdy but *Violet*, his face full of a sadness the mix of constructed and genuine in which she would never be able to work out – her overwhelming feeling was one of relief, of being glad that the bad thing that she always knew was coming was here at last. Now, looking back from her present age, she thinks how similar this is to what it's like waiting for death.

But all stories, even ones where you know what's going to happen in advance, need an ending, and Isabelle's beauty was it. She had looked at the photograph and understood: why he had left, and why, in the moment of leaving, over breakfast, he had, after the first few awful minutes, luxuriated in the telling. Not out of sadism, Violet realized, but out of love; love for Isabelle, which spilt out of him, eradicating all restraint and all sense of empathy with her, his wife. It was so predictable, and yet it was required. Isabelle's beauty still had to be put in front of her for Violet to sign off on Eli; for her to internalize the truth, that, yes, of course, she is more beautiful than me, so yes, of course, my husband who is now famous must be with her rather than me. A time would come which would define such a way of thinking not as truth but ideology, but for Violet it was too congruous with her idea of herself, and of the way things were, to disavow.

Her mind returns to the present and to the magazine in her hands. The article is illustrated with an outline of a woman's figure, wearing heels and a dress suit and carrying a handbag. She wonders how invisible a woman can be, if you become invisible at forty-five, and now you're eighty-five, and you already felt invisible in your twenties. There must be degrees of invisibility. Perhaps women who were less old, or had a *look-this-way attitude*, were, rather than invisible, murky, or shimmering like a ghost, before fading, as they were meant to, gently into nothingness.

She hears a cough. She turns round. The shopkeeper – Algerian? Serbian? They weren't even Pakistani any more – is looking at her with menaces, like she is a teenager come in to thieve, or browse through the magazines as if it were a library. He should recognize her, she thinks – she has come into this shop enough times in the last two years – but, then, she doesn't recognize him. He continues to stare at her: she feels the outline of her ancient body against the wall of youth and beauty. 'Sorry, I …' she says, but trails off, trying, at the same time, to put the magazine back between blocks of *Cosmopolitan* and *Vogue*. It hits the edge of the rack awkwardly, and the top left-hand corner falls forward, as if made heavier by grease from her hands, although they are dry: Jen's face contorts grotesquely. The shopkeeper folds his arms, into an expectant payment-demanding attitude, and Violet, out of shame and terror, does so, handing over the incredibly startling price of £3.70, and leaves, hurriedly. It is only when she gets back to Redcliffe House, and Joe Hillier's friend Frank smirks in her direction, on seeing that she is carrying a copy of *Elle*, that she remembers that her intention had been to buy some proper newspapers in order to check if there was any new information about Eli, and his dying.

*   *   *

RW: What's your feeling about women, Eli?

[pause]

EG: This is a tactic, is it, Commissioner Webb? After a couple of hours, you become friendly … first-name terms …. it's two guys, chewing the cud over chicks, we could be at a bar except there's no beers …
RW: Really, I'd like to know.
EG: My *feeling*? About *women*?
RW: Yeah.

[pause]

EG: Read my books.
RW: I have.

[pause]

RW: Perhaps you'd like to know which ones.

EG: Not really.

RW: *Solomon's Testament*, obviously. *Mirror, Mirror. Reluctance. Cometh the Wolf*, that's probably my favourite. Beautiful, but dark. That bit where Jimmy Voller forces his way into the brothel … amazing. And, of course, *The Compliance of Women*.

EG: Why of course?

[pause]

RW: You know what, I lied. I haven't read that one. But I love the title. What's it about?

EG: What's it about?

RW: Yeah.

[pause]

EG: You want me to précis one of my novels? Now?

RW: Well. I'd prefer you to answer my first question. About how you feel about women. But I thought this might be easier.

[pause; laughter, EG]

EG: It's about a man, a professor, at Yale, in his fifties, whose marriage – his second – is falling apart, and he's having an affair with a student, which he's trying to end but he can't because she threatens him.

RW: How?

EG: With coming out about the affair, of course. Telling the academic body. And ruining Henry – the professor.

[pause]

RW: So it's not really about women?

EG: Where might you be going now, Commissioner? Shall I call the *New Yorker* to listen in on this discussion?

RW: I mean: it's about men. It's about the restrictions women place on the sexual freedom of men. Like much of your work.

EG: Like much of my work …

RW: So what happens in the end?

[pause]

RW: What happens in the end?

EG: Oh Christ, Commissioner Webb. I mean, really.

[pause]

EG: She does come out with it – the student. His wife leaves him.

RW: Does he lose his job?

EG: No. He gets reprimanded but keeps it.

RW: And the student?

[pause]

RW: Mr Gold?

EG: Fuck. This is ridiculous. You know this. Pretending you don't – it's pathetic.

RW: Really – I don't.

EG: *She commits suicide.* OK? She commits suicide. Hey, you know what – like *my wife just did*! Like I just tried to do! Well, I guess that's proof, then, of whatever it is you're trying to fucking prove!

[pause; sound of paper turning]

RW: Is that the compliance? Of the title? Because it seems as if that's what your heroes are always looking for … I mean, on the surface a kind of sexual compliance, women to bend to their will either in bed, or in coming to bed, but there's a deeper need, isn't there? Which is for the women to leave. There's this thing people say about prostitutes, isn't there – it's clear to me from investigating them, and the men who use them – 'men don't pay prostitutes for sex, they pay them to leave afterwards'. But for you, or, sorry, *your characters* – your male characters, who are, after all, your *heroes* … the issue is how to make women, the ones who aren't prostitutes, comply with that demand: to leave. And the real compliance is that they leave without trouble. That they accept that their duty is to leave. Leaving a marriage is one kind of compliance of that sort, but that's messy – there's alimony, and custody and residual guilt and a whole wasteland of arguments still to be had – so really, the better option, I guess, is death. Not murder – that's crazy. But suicide – death, sweetly taken, as an option – self-murder, understood as leaving the man be, really properly leaving him be, letting him once and for all off the fucking hook: that's compliance. That's the compliance you – or, sorry, your characters – are looking for. Ultimately. Isn't it?

[pause]

EG: OK. Very good, Webb. Really. You're a very clever – a very *literary* police commissioner. Can I go now? I've been very patient with you. I haven't insisted on calling my lawyer. But if you persist you will have a writ in your office on Monday morning. I shall pursue a case of police harassment.

RW: I quite understand. I just have two more questions. Then you're free to go.

* * *

I'm starting to think Uncle Harvey maybe isn't so bad, you know. Yesterday, I came into the living room and he was tickling Aristotle's tummy. I said to him:

'Do you like cats?'

And he said: 'I love cats. Nothing's more beautiful than a cat's face.'

Which is sort of what *I* think, too. And Aristotle looked like he was really enjoying the tickling. Harvey took his hand away from Aristotle, but then he did this really cute thing of touching Harvey's hand with his paw, like 'Do that again!' It was so cute.

And he meowed as well.

'I understand cat language, too,' he said.

'You do?' I said.

'Yes. I understand all animal language.'

I thought he was joking with me – like saying the sort of silly thing a grown-up might say to a four-year-old or something – but I said: 'What do you mean?'

'Well, when Aristotle goes meow, like that, what he means is: *I want.* That's what all cats mean when they meow. Also all dogs when they bark, all birds when they sing, and all frogs when they croak.'

That made me laugh, that funny group of animals. Then Aristotle poked his hand again, and meowed again.

'You see?' he said. 'I want.'

And he started tickling Aristotle again. Who started purring, really loudly.

* * *

Harvey Gold comes out of the sauna, in good time to avoid fainting. His face, he sees in the mirror, is a healthy shade of red. He showers, turning the dial gradually from red to blue, the heat from the sauna seeming to stay deep in his skin, making the cold bearable. He goes to his room and, still wet, puts on his dressing gown. Harvey always travels with a dressing gown. Made of soft brown towelling, and only lightly stained in two places, it is his most worn garment at home, and he sees no reason why that should not be the case abroad. There had been a fluffy white one at the Sangster, which had made him annoyed – with Freda – because if he'd known in advance that he was going to be staying in a dressing-gown-providing-hotel, he wouldn't have packed his own one, taking up half the room in his suitcase. However, now that Harvey has moved into their apartment, he is glad that he has his to hand. It's clearly a genetic thing, this love of dressing gowns:

a cursory search of his father's bedroom turns up four (not including the one hanging up by his hospital bed that he never wears) all, like Harvey's, the fabric equivalent of comfort food.

Harvey is feeling, in his terms, happy. He has slept well. He isn't, for the moment, hungry, having gone to a diner on Broadway for breakfast. He had bacon, eggs, sausages, hash browns and pancakes with maple syrup and coffee. He considered grits, but has never known what they are and wasn't prepared to take the risk. Harvey loves American breakfasts. He also loves English breakfasts, but gets particularly excited by the spoiled-kid excess of the American one, the mixing of savoury and sweet breaking down the barriers of what you can and can't have, unfettered desire on a plate.

It did, of course, make him feel sick, but he worked that off by going into the sauna, letting the fat and sweetness and salt ooze out of his pores. He thinks to himself not *I am happy*, but *You know what: I don't feel half bad*. He has these sometimes, these respite moments. They come more often when he is away from Stella. The image he has of her in his mind is static, beautiful, unageing – a Platonic idea of her – and while apart from her he does not have to manage the daily confrontation with the plastic reality. These moments trouble him, but he allows himself them, letting his body indulge in the anxiety amnesty.

Beyond that, he seems to have reached some level of equanimity with Freda, and even, perhaps, with Colette, who no longer looks at him with fear and loathing. His father is still dying, he is still a ghost, a writer of celebrity autobiographies, his depression is still entirely there – he knows it has just stepped away for a moment, he can feel the penumbra of its shadow – but he savours the flash of contentment. He is just untying the brown towelling knot around his stomach and starting to make his way towards the toilet, finally to make peace with that breakfast, when his attention is distracted by a small package on the kitchen table.

Harvey, while not exactly one to shirk responsibility, is not given to augmenting responsibility with any add-ons: and thus, although he has fulfilled the basic brief of the one responsibility he was given by

Elaine while staying here – to pick up the mail from the pigeonhole in the communal hallway – he has not ordered or sorted the mail in any further way, but, rather, just left it, an ever-growing mound of envelopes on the kitchen table. Every so often Elaine has sorted through this mound, picking up anything urgent for Freda's perusal and leaving the rest in a neat pile, but then Harvey has messed this pile up again in the process of creating a space on the table, every mealtime, for condiments (Harvey likes condiments: he sometimes thinks he prefers them to main foods).

He notices the package, which may have been there for some time – it is lying next to some bills which arrived last week – because it has his name on it: Harvey Gold. He must have failed to spot it before amongst all the other Gold-addressed letters arriving in each delivery. Picking it up – it is heavier than he expects – he sees that it is marked with an official stamp: Toledo County Law Enforcement Office, it says. Bunce. Bunce has sent him some mail. A small shiver goes through him: this can't be good. But curiosity overtakes him, and he opens it. The thought goes through his mind of the small, ornate dagger that his mother's mother used to open mail with. There is an orange-brown book inside, like a school rough book. He opens it, scans a page or two, confused, not getting it at first, and then, in terror, shutting it as quick as he can. It is so quick that he is not certain what he has seen exactly, but he is sure enough to know he must not open it again. He feels white-hot fear mixed with repulsion: the image comes back again of the spider on Luffa's face. He cannot understand what he is holding in his hands. He checks the envelope. There is a note inside, printed on Toledo County Prosecutor headed notepaper.

Harv,
You seemed to be very keen to know about my work. So here's a taste
of the kind of shit I have to deal with every day,
Bunce.

So it is real. He will not open it again, but the images that he had seen, before he understood what he was looking at, coalesce like monsters forming from the fog with this new information. It was some words, some psychotic scrawl, illustrated with grainy images of – he stops his mind from saying it, thankful at least for the grain.

Bunce: what the fuck. WHAT THE FUCK. *What if someone else – what if Elaine had taken this along with the batch of mail to the hospital … what if Freda had opened it … what if …* But there will be time for that. First he must get rid of this book, quickly. Its very presence is contaminating. But he does not know how to get rid of it. He does not want to throw it into the trash – *fuck off!* He shouts at himself in his mind, for thinking in American even at this time of crisis – into the rubbish bin, the rubbish bin, as he knows that journalists sometimes go through the garbage – rubbish – of famous people. In fact, it happened to Eli, just after Pauline committed suicide. He could put it in a bag, maybe? And go and find a bin on the street? But he feels that his fear would radiate, making him give off suspicious vibes: he has a premonition of being stopped and searched by policemen, and then trying to explain to them: 'No, Officer, you see – I have a friend who works in sex crime, especially this kind of thing, and I was talking to him a while ago about his work, and clearly he thought I required further elucidation …' *Jesus.* His heart beats faster at the thought. Elaine, he knows, is bringing Colette home for lunch today, they could be back at any moment, and he isn't dressed yet, and he has to destroy it.

Burn it. Burn it, he thinks. His father used to have matches and lighters everywhere, before he gave up smoking. He runs into Eli's study and begins overturning everything – books, papers, photographs. Nothing. He goes to the living room. Surely there must be some somewhere, he thinks, surely Freda is one of those women who consider candles more vital than food, but a frantic search of the drawers and cupboards yields nothing. *Fuck fuck fuck fuck* metronomes in his mind.

He runs back to the kitchen. If only they had a gas stove … he decides to give the Rayburn a shot, even though he is frightened of it, the enormous green tinderbox, having preferred to eat takeout or microwaveable food throughout his stay. He picks the book up from the table, holding it at a comical arm's length, and goes over to the cooker. He lifts up the right-hand plate cover: it is like opening the lid of an enormous, overheated teapot. Then he lifts up the left hand one: the plate underneath seems to be hotter. He puts the book onto it.

Breathing heavily, he stands and watches. Nothing happens for a second. Then smoke begins to rise from underneath the book. The edges begin to blacken. *Good. Good.* He is still thinking *good* when the smoke alarm in the kitchen goes off. The sound is painfully piercing. It fills his already full head with its noise. He looks up. The alarm is above his head, a small beige circle of hell. There is a large soup ladle, one of many expensive looking utensils hanging on the wall behind the Rayburn. He takes the ladle off its hook and jumps up, trying to hit the alarm. He succeeds once or twice. It makes no difference. *What's best?* he wants to shout, *What should I do?* While it is still refusing actually to burn, smoke has begun billowing out from under the book like a Victorian industrial chimney stack, great big clouds of black, indicative, it seems to Harvey, of the boundless evil contained within. What, he thinks, is *Satan himself* about to emerge from it?

He decides to try and forget the alarm and focus on the book. First he must get it off the Rayburn plate, but that turns out to be no simple task. The bottom has stuck to the metal, and it rips, blackened bits of paper showering his face and hands. He throws it into the sink and turns the tap on: it hisses. He has to get a spatula out of the drawer, and begin scraping at the stove, trying to remove the black-brown square from the centre of it. The smoke alarm, impossibly, seems to increase in both pitch and volume. The paper won't completely come off, so he gives up and shuts the plate cover. Then the doorbell goes.

He throws the spatula down in rage, and goes to open the apartment door. It is the next-door neighbour, a middle-aged woman he has seen once or twice in the lift.

'Hi ...' he says.

'Sorry to disturb you, but I heard the alarm. Is there a fire? Do we need to clear the building?'

'No,' he says. 'No. It's just the smoke alarm going off.'

'Without a fire?'

'Yes. It must be – must need new batteries, or something.'

She looks uncertain: the alarm's ring, which must be much louder to her ears now that he has opened the door, does not sound like it is lacking in electronic power.

'But …' she says.

'It's fine.' He turns and shuts the door.

Back in the kitchen, the smoke hangs all over the air: Harvey experiences that moment of shock when returning to a room in which a fire has not been properly ventilated, of how much more smoke there is than previously realized. He goes to the sink, not really wanting to look into it. The remains of the book are now in the right-hand sink. In the left-hand one there is a waste-disposal hole. Is that the answer? The book is still too intact to go in there. He cannot imagine anything worse than blocking the waste-disposal unit with this. They'll get a plumber out, he'll pick it out of the pipes bit by bit …

He looks down into the right-hand sink. The book sits there like some awful cockroach that cannot be killed, one of the ones that will still be alive after a nuclear winter. The manic song of the alarm continues. Perhaps I should just kill myself, he thinks. After all, people must be used to members of Eli's family committing suicide by now. It might just be the simplest thing. Although then people will find the book and think I killed myself because I was a secret paedo. But what should I care, if I'm dead.

He looks round the kitchen. He has an idea. He turns the tap back on. He watches the book, already soaked, become more so, as if he is trying to drown it. Flakes float in the water as it rises. Then he lifts it, sopping, towards the food blender, which sits on the marble-topped breakfast bar conveniently close to the Rayburn. He drops the book into the blender. Even half-burnt and soaked, it doesn't fit very easily, and he has to poke it down towards the blades with a wooden spoon. Then, for good measure, he fills a cup from the tap and adds more water. It crosses his mind to add other ingredients, to make it mulch easier: vegetable oil perhaps? *Just do it!* screams the voice in his head.

348

But he has to fit the top of the blender back on, and then match up some small indentations on the machine between the plastic and the glass for it to work. This takes him six or seven goes: it is not an operation designed to be done under this kind of pressure. Finally, it seems right. He looks for the buttons. It is a Krups blender, much more expensive than the one they have at home, its base a chunky silver ballast dotted with switches. The top options are smoothie, milkshake, puree, ice crush and soup: below that, pulse or blend. He has never known what the difference is. He presses smoothie, and pulse.

The machine whirrs, and shouts, and in a nanosecond the book vanishes, transformed into gloop. He lets it run for a minute just to make sure, and then turns it off, its noise dying like a siren, revealing the continued pinging scream of the smoke alarm underneath. Harvey prises open the lid and looks down at his handiwork. A small grey bog bubbles at the bottom of the blender: something that looks less now like Satan might emerge from it than Shrek. There is no sign, though, of the images it once contained. He begins to breathe more easily for the first time since he opened the package. He wrenches the glass jug off the base of the blender. When he turns round, ready to pour it into the waste-disposal unit, Elaine and Colette are there. He hadn't heard them come in because of the smoke alarm.

'Hello?' says Elaine. 'Is everything OK?'

'Yes,' he says.

'Why is the smoke alarm going off?'

'I don't know.'

'You don't know?'

He shakes his head.

'How long's it been going?'

'A little while.'

'Were you cooking something?'

'Yes. I was cooking something.'

Elaine stares at him. So does Colette.

'What?'

'Sausages.'

It is the first thing that comes into his head. Elaine shakes her head. She looks up at the alarm.

'I'll go and call the super and he can come and sort it out,' she says, going out of the kitchen.

'Were you going to have a smoothie with it?' says Colette.

Harvey now stares at her. 'What?'

She nods at the jug he is holding.

'With the sausages.'

'Yes,' he says. 'I was.'

'Can I have some?' she says.

'Er ...'

'What flavour is it?'

It's kiddie-porn flavour, all right? It's a fucking paedo-delight crush.

'No ...' he says. 'It was meant to be ... I dunno ... kind of a mixture – but I think it went wrong.'

And quickly, before she can stop him – risking, in so doing, their fragile new-found amiability – he pours the horrible evil mess down into the waste disposal, and switches it on, making another awful screaming noise to add to the still-going smoke alarm. He watches it swirl round and round, washed away into the underworld.

He has just turned the tap on, to wash and wash again the glass jug, when Elaine comes back into the kitchen, holding his iPhone.

'It's ringing. It was in the living room. I couldn't hear it, but I saw the light come on.'

She hands it to him. He feels the back of her hand as she does so, gently wrinkled like a peach. On the front of the phone is the name Freda. He reaches for the green slide-to-answer box, but it's too late, it's gone to answerphone. A box comes up on the screen, with his stepmother's number. Missed Calls: 8.

Her name is Lisa. His name, he has told her, is Hughie. He had been approaching Mount Sinai Hospital when she ran up to him. As her smiling face approached, fast enough for her pigtails to fly across it, he realized that today was not the day of his destiny. That no day could be the day of his destiny as long as she was likely to be standing outside the hospital, which she did every day. She was always liable to get in his way, to want to talk to him, to ask him what he was going to do today. He should not have spoken to her in the first place: if he had ignored her, then she would have forgotten about him, and he could at any point, when the time came, slip in unnoticed. Now he would have to deal with her.

She was wearing the plaid dress, again; like his sister, again. He had got a sense that she had picked up something from him about this outfit, because there was no sign any more of the woollen hat. She was waving in front of her face a piece of paper. It was a print-out of a discussion on a website devoted to The Great Satan, allthatglittersis-not.com, in which someone on a forum was saying that the writer had had a miraculous recovery and might not die after all. He surveyed the excited words. It did not feel like truth; but it made him feel the need to get on with his destiny. He looked up at her thin, make-up-less face, the eyes brimming with false hope, and said:

– So we should go and celebrate. I know a great place.

She had thought he meant a bar nearby, but he wanted to be near his hotel; so they have taken the subway downtown, to a bar he has passed a few times, and liked the look of. All the fittings are

351

pine. A Confederate flag hangs on the far wall. The jukebox plays 'Sweet Melissa', by The Allman Brothers. The bar is called Why Not?

They sit across from each other at a central table. Her face is still alight with the same excitement that first burst out of it when he suggested this drink. He could read in it a release of pain. It may have been years since she has been asked on a date. She may never have been. He thinks that, perhaps, the obsession with The Great Satan operates as a compensation for that lack, and feels a rounded self-satisfaction at the acuity of his psychological observation.

Their drinks arrive, two Budweisers. He does not drink at home, nor has done since arriving in New York. He does not remember, in fact, when he last had a beer. It is quite a moment, then, to wrap his hand around the cold bottle, to feel the drips of condensation melt into his palm, to smell the hops as the fizz tickles his moustache, and, at last, to suck it down. The beer does more than quench his thirst: some deep part of him feels watered. She, meanwhile, glad-handles the bottle like a Southern Senator shaking hands with a black voter, shivering and grimacing with every gulp.

– You don't like the beer? he says

– No, no. It's nice. She untwists one of her pigtails, letting her hair on that side fall around her shoulder.

– The bar …?

She looks around her. Three or four men, all balding, with facial hair, sit at the bar. Two more, one wearing a cowboy hat, are playing pool.

– Well … it's a tiny bit … hick …

– I like it, he says.

– Ironically, right?

He shakes his head.

– We can go somewhere else if you'd like?'

– No, no. It's interesting, I guess, to be somewhere so … male. Men are good at that, aren't they? Just being men. But I've always felt – you know that bit in *The Compliance* – when Joanne says 'It's a front, being a woman, a construct. The hair, the make-up, the

352

unattainability, the sense of mystery: none of us really knows how to do it. The only people who really know – who really know what being a woman is all about – are transvestites.' I love that. It's one of the things you feel about Eli, as a woman reader, how unbelievably he's able to put himself into the minds and bodies of his female characters …

He nods. She looks at him, expecting confirmation, communion. But he can't give it to her. He is not like the Holocaust deniers, the men who so hate the Jews and their enormous lie that they have to immerse themselves in every last gas-chamber detail, stepping every day into a bath of everything they disavow, in order to shore up their truth. He has not read any of The Great Satan's books – the idea of doing so, in fact, revolts him. All he has done, and all he will ever do, is go see the Butter Mountain.

He will have to deal with her, now, before his cover is blown. And then something happens which makes him know that he is in the last days of his destiny. 'Sweet Melissa' ends, and onto the jukebox comes Hughie Thomasson's cracked and yearning voice, singing of *some place your soul can fly*. The Outlaws. The Outlaws.

– Lisa, he says. Would you like to dance?

⋆　⋆　⋆

Mommy swore a lot today. She said the f-word about a hundred times, the s-word about fifty times, and some others I haven't heard before but I'm really sure are swear words. When me and Harvey got to the hospital she started off straight away, in the corridor outside Daddy's room.

'Harvey!' she said. 'What the f-word is going on? I asked you to do one f-wording thing when you moved into the apartment. Keep your f-wording cell on. Listen out for it. And you can't even f-wording do that, you little s-word.'

I guess she was really p-worded off. (That's a joke, by the way.) Even John looked a bit embarrassed.

'Look, Freda, I'm sorry …'

'Sorry isn't good enough, Harvey!'

This is something Mommy says a lot. She says it to me sometimes, when she's cross. I never understand it. If you've done something wrong, you can only say sorry. So how can it not be good enough?

Dr Ghundkhali poked his head out of Daddy's room, but when he saw it was just Mommy shouting, he went back inside.

'Maybe we should go somewhere – your room at the end or something …' Harvey said.

'What for?'

Harvey nodded his face at me. I think he meant that they shouldn't have a big row in front of me. He doesn't know that I've heard Mommy having rows with lots of people. With Elaine, with Miss Howner, with people on the phone, even, once, with Daddy.

'Oh f-word off, Harvey. Colette's heard all these words before, it turns out. And like you care, anyway. If you cared about her feelings, you'd have made sure to listen out for your cellphone. It's about time that Colette realized what a useless half-brother she really has!'

I felt a bit bad for Harvey when she was saying this. I specially didn't like the way Mommy said the word 'half', like she was really saying that we weren't properly related or something.

'Mommy,' I said. 'I don't think it was Harvey's fault. The smoke alarm was going off and …'

'The smoke alarm was going off? F-word! Were you burning the place down, too?'

'Freda. Calm down, please. Look: we're here now. Your message just said to come and bring Colette as soon as possible …'

'Yes, well, you're too late.'

'Too late?'

'Yes.'

Harvey blinked. He looked round at me. I didn't know what face to make. I think I shrugged.

'What you mean … Eli – Dad's …'

Mommy frowned at him. 'No, of course he's not, Harvey! What is the matter with you?'

'Well, I assumed – I thought …'

354

'Bill Clinton!'

'I'm sorry?!'

'He was coming to see Eli! An impromptu visit! Today!'

'He was?'

'One of his assistants phoned an hour ago!'

'Right. So. Is he coming or isn't he?'

'Well, no! Not now! I had to put him off!'

'You put him off?'

'I told him Eli was too ill today …'

Harvey looked at her. 'Eli is too ill every day, isn't he?'

'Look, Harvey, it doesn't matter what I said. I put him off.'

'But why?'

'Oh God. Because I wanted Colette to be here. I wanted Colette to meet him. And by the time I'd called you the sixth time I realized that wasn't going to happen! OK?'

'Mommy …?' I said. She knelt down and started doing up some of the buttons on the front of my dress that had come undone. Her fingers were moving really quickly, though, and the buttons kept slipping away from them.

'Why did you want Bill Clinton to meet me?'

'He used to be president, darling,' she said. 'Before you were born. He's also a good friend of mine and Daddy's.'

'Then why don't I know him?'

'Well, because we've mainly met him at dinners and festivals and conferences and so on – we've never had a chance to have him round for dinner so that *you* could meet him. Which is why I so wanted you to be here today …'

'Can't President Obama come?' I said. 'I love him. He's so handsome.' When I said this I looked at John. I gave him a special look to let him know I really meant it. Mommy did one of her annoying laughs.

'Well, I would love that too, darling. But he's very, very busy.'

'Look, I'm really sorry, Freda. I am,' said Harvey. Mommy looked up at him. She breathed heavily, through her nose, like she does when she's about to forgive someone.

355

'Well, luckily for you, I just got a call from his office saying he could reschedule. Bill will be coming tomorrow!'

'Oh Mommy,' I said, 'That's great!'

'Right,' said Harvey. Over Mommy's shoulder, he looked quite cross. 'So if – if you knew already that he could rearrange – if you knew when we arrived that everything was OK – why …?' He didn't finish that sentence but I knew he meant: *why did you shout at me so much?*

Mommy stood up, brushing herself down. 'It's the principle of the thing, Harvey. You made me a promise. I mean, what if it *had* been – what if Eli *had* been …?' She looked down at Harvey but up with her eyes. He looked very sad. He did that weird cough he does. He wiped his face with his hands, like he had soap in it or something.

'OK, Freda. It won't happen again. I'll take her home again later and make sure that –'

'Well, I don't know. He's coming early tomorrow, just after breakfast. It's the only time he could fit in. She could stay over with me tonight. Elaine could bring in a change of clothes … would you like that, darling? Would you like to have a sleepover with Mommy?'

I looked at my feet when she said this. I didn't want to. I was going to be at the hospital all day. I wanted to go home later with Harvey. I wanted to sit in the taxi with Harvey and see if I could make him laugh, like I did before.

'Freda,' said Harvey, before I could answer. 'If it's about what happened today, please: don't be concerned. I'll make sure she's here bright and early tomorrow.'

'Yes,' I said. 'I'll make sure, too. I'll get up and dress myself.'

Mommy looked like she wasn't sure, like she didn't understand why I didn't want to have a sleepover with her, but then there was some noise from inside Daddy's room, which made her turn around.

'All right then,' she said. 'I'll call Elaine and she'll come round later and put out some clothes for you. But straight to bed when you get back. I want you here bright and early for Mr President. I'm counting on you, Harvey.'

'OK, Freda,' he said. 'Understood.'

And then she went back in. Me and Harvey went into the room together. I held his hand.

∗   ∗   ∗

He is surprised at himself. He does not commit adultery. He has many wives, but he has never been unfaithful. It had occurred to him to try and instigate some kind of impromptu celestial marriage service, here in his room at the Condesa Inn, under the eyes of Jesus; but they would need at least an Elder of His Faith, and he had no idea where to find one. Even if he could have found one, it would have been awkward, following the sealing, waiting for the Elder to leave. Plus, of course, he does not actually want to marry the woman with the pigtails. He is not sure he even truly wanted to sleep with her.

But when they got back to his room, there was, it seemed to him, no choice. He had to deal with her. If he slept with her – if she was in his bed in the morning – she would not be hanging around outside the hospital, obstructing his destiny. So when she stood there, raising herself up on her tiptoes, he knew the way through was to kiss her. Her mouth was dry and clamped shut, like a child's, but her eyes were closed as if in great passion, allowing him to look at His Lord and know that he forgave him this small sin in the larger picture.

Her dress had come off awkwardly: he had tried unbuttoning it at the back, but his hands were big and unused to non-Mormon clothing. Eventually, she stepped away and did it herself, pushing the plaid over her head, allowing him a moment when he could see her body but she could not see him. She was thinner than he had realized. She wore a white bra and blue panties. Her movements to shake herself free of the dress reminded him of her dancing in the bar, jagged, short, arrhythmic.

She dropped her dress by the room's only real piece of furniture, a hulking Victorian wardrobe with an oval mirror in the middle of it. When she turned to him, her eyebrows were slanted upwards, like someone hoping not to be hurt. He reached, seemingly to touch her face, and she bent her skin into his hand, but he was reaching for her pigtail, the second of which she had forgotten to untie. Loosening the ribbon stopped her from having lopsided hair, handing her the womanliness she did not know how to affect.

He took off his clothes, methodically. She waited for him, not knowing where to look. When he got to his white undergarments, he heard her make a noise of surprise. Folding up his clothes, he said:

– I'm a Mormon.

– No.

– Yes.

She looked at him. Her face was holding back something: laughter or fear, or both. Something seemed to cross her mind.

– You never talk about him.

– Who?

– Who do you think? Eli, of course.

– Hey, he said. Are we going to have a discussion about literature? Now?

– No, but …

And then he hushed her mouth with a kiss, a proper one, forcing her mouth open as he went, drawing on his experience with many women, many wives.

Now it is just before dawn. He has slipped out of bed and packed his bag, putting the white coat in at the bottom. He has shaved completely, lost both his moustache and the beginnings of a beard that has sprouted since he has been in New York. It feels right: cleansing. Some of the 9/11 jihadis shaved off their beards, too, on the day of their destiny, so as not to look too much like Muslims. He has put his holy white undergarments back on. In the front side of the vest, near his heart, his third wife Lorinda, the best seamstress, has created a pocket, for his pocket edition of *The Book of Mormon*. Within this, reverently, he places his gun, his Armscor 206.

He checks his wallet: he will leave enough money for the bill at reception. He is about to pull on his jeans when he sees, by his bare feet, the plaid dress. He holds it up; holds it against himself, looking in the mirror, like he has sometimes seen women do in the shops in Salt Lake City. He looks over to the bed. She is sleeping soundly, the

358

satisfied sleep, he thinks, of a chick who has not been fucked for years. He surprises himself by the words, which feel like they come from a previous self.

Then, in an urge that comes from he knows not where, he slips the dress over his head. It falls around him more easily than it had come off her. He looks up. Yes. His hair, of course, is shorter, but not that much, having grown since he begun his journey to New York. In the dim light of the room, all differences melt away. This is why God made him shave. He sees her in the mirror, still alive, the age she would be now: his sister Pauline Gray. He blesses their near-identicality. His gaze grows soft. He leans in and kisses, gently, their joint reflection.

– For you, he says. For you.

* * *

Mandy is angry with her. The nurse is standing in the doorway of her room with her arms crossed. Violet can see the biceps squeezing against the fingers: she is heavy, Mandy, but she also lifts a lot of heavy things – a lot of heavy people. She does not want for either fat or muscle.

'Come on, Violet. Let's not be mucking about,' she says. Mandy has no trace of a Nigerian or West Indian accent, but through Violet's hearing aid she still thinks she picks up on some cadence which speaks of heat and dust.

'But I didn't sign up for it,' she says. 'I don't want to do it.' She is sitting on her big velvet chair, facing away from the window.

'Don't be stupid. Just come down and see what it's like. Don't you want to hear everybody's life story?'

A child, she thinks. She is speaking to me like a foster child. 'Not really,' says Violet.

Mandy puffs her cheeks out and shakes her head. It frustrates Violet that she cannot explain to this nurse how she is not simply being a curmudgeonly inmate, perversely saying no to everything. Violet appreciates Redcliffe House. She does not like living here, exactly, but she feels grateful.

'I don't know what we're going to do,' says Mandy. 'The man is here …'

'Yes,' says Violet. She hears a tapping. It will be the branch along the window.

'He is here, and we were told that we needed to get at least ten of you down there to make it worthwhile.'

Violet nods. The tapping continues. She knows it is the branch, but something makes her want to turn and confirm that. There is no need to see, just as there is no need to ask, 'How many people have come?'

Mandy's cheeks bulge, betraying a smile. Violet remembers how, when she used to sulk, her mother used to say 'Come on: let's see those apples!' to make her smile. When she did so, her mother would pretend to bite her rounded cheek. She wonders now, when she smiles, what fruit her cheeks look like.

'Nine.'

Violet sighs and uses the back edge of the chair to lever herself up. She turns away from Mandy to do so. As she thought: it is the branch.

In the lounge, the man from *Life Story Work* has organized the ten of them into a semi-circle. He is standing in front of a screen, with a diagram on it very like the one in the pamphlet, with the words IDENTITY and MEANING and PURPOSE and SELF-KNOWLEDGE written across it. When she arrives they all turn to face her. Joe Hillier, who is sitting in a chair next to the screen, facing the others, taps his watch. Violet feels again the impulse to explain, to say that she is not late but was not going to come at all, and then had been forced into it by a mixture of Mandy's bullying and her own reflexive instinct not to ruin things. She feels this concurrently with the knowledge that she is going to remain silent. She wonders how much of her life has involved this swallowing of impulse.

A woman hands her a notebook, similar to ones she remembers from school, and guides her to the end of the row of chairs. Violet flicks through the book: it is a series of blank pages. She looks up. The woman, who is blonde – but dyed? – smiles and hands her a pen. Looking around, she sees that they all have similar books and pens.

'Hi!' says the man, who is holding a clipboard. He has what Gwendoline used to call an upside-down face: bald with a beard. Although it wasn't very thick; perhaps it was just that thing that men did now, of not shaving. 'I'm Daniel.' With an open palm, he gestures towards the blonde lady. His hands are small, like a woman's. 'This is Kirsty, who's helping me today. What's your name?'

Violet feels her throat constrict with anxiety, even at this question. 'Violet.'

He hovers his clipboard into view, poising a pen above it. 'Violet …?'

'Gold,' she says. 'Violet Gold.'

'Thank you, Violet,' he says, scribbling. *Mrs Gold. In the old days, he would have said Mrs Gold.* 'So … do we need to go over again what *Life Story Work* is?'

She feels a collective sigh of frustration go through the group.

'No,' she says. 'I think I understand.'

'Great! If there's anything you don't, at any stage, just let me or Kirsty know. Now, where were we? Ah, yes: Joe.'

Daniel moves aside, revealing Joe Hillier sitting with his legs crossed, looking at Violet impatiently. His right trouser leg has ridden up past his sock, revealing his shin bone tight against the skin.

'Well. I was born in nineteen thirty, in Sheffield. I …'

'Just hold on a minute, Joe,' says Daniel. He is bent over, fiddling with the controls of a video camera, which is behind the semi-circle of listeners. On the side of the camera, a small red light goes on.

'Sorry, carry on …'

Joe looks uncertainly towards the camera. His head moves around, as if trying to find some imagined centre of frame. He coughs, ostensibly to clear his throat, but brings up a gobbet of unwanted phlegm at the same time, which he has to spit into a handkerchief. He puts the soiled white rag back into his pocket, which seems to take an age.

'In Sheffield, as I say,' he says, finally. 'My father was a boilermaker. I was the eldest of seven. I was expected to become a boilermaker, too, but after a short time serving an apprenticeship I decided it wasn't for me. I worked as a postman, eventually rising to the rank of postmaster in our ...'

'Joe. Sorry ...' says Daniel. He touches a button on the camera. 'This is great. This is context. But – as I said, the point of *Life Story Work* is not to tell your whole history from top to bottom. I mean, you can if you want to, when you go off and write your story down, if you have the time and energy, you know, that would obviously be great. But, certainly, that's not the point *today*.' He says this with a little internal chuckle, to indicate that he is not telling Joe Hillier off. Joe nods, nervously. He is imperious, with other old people; not with the young.

'What we'd like today ...' this is from Kirsty, who has glided beside Daniel, '... is maybe just a retelling of some central life incident – what we call a Key Life Moment – which will give us some sense of who you are.'

'Well, I don't know that that works,' says Pat Cadogan, who has been seated with her arms crossed throughout, her face fixed forwards, but with an expression so avowedly negative it seems somehow to give off a sense of being shaken from side to side. 'Some of us have had very long and complicated lives, my dear. It's not so easy to draw out who we are from one incident.'

'Some of us find it a bit hard to remember, as well!' said Joe Hillier's friend, Frank. 'Bit hard to remember what happened yesterday, let alone forty year ago!'

'Oh, don't be such stick-in-the-muds!' This is Norma. 'I've got *bucket loads* of Key Life Moments! I just don't think I can say them in front of camera!!' She laughs, loudly, the kind of laugh that invites others to join in.

'Look,' says Daniel. 'It doesn't have to be such hard work.' His face has shifted to a frown, away from its former attitude of deep-set civic patience. 'Someone here must have some moment in their life that they think defines them.'

Violet looks round. She feels the blankness of all of them in response to Daniel's language. She wants Joe Hillier to carry on:

she is interested that he was a postman. She hadn't known that. He was a man, before, with a job and a uniform and promotion prospects. He walked from house to house delivering letters, which people in Sheffield waited for with hope and dread. We all did things, before, Violet thinks. Life is not moments – there is something patronizing about a life thought of in moments, rather than as an ongoing thing; it is a *young* person's way of imagining what it must be like to be old, projecting that identity will only exist then in fragments.

She wants to hear what Pat was – a dental receptionist, she once thinks she heard her say – and Norma was a dressmaker, Violet knows, before she gave up to have her four children. This is what *defines* people like us, Violet wants to say: jobs, children. What more do you want?

'Violet!' says Kirsty. 'What about you? Do you have a Key Life Moment you want to tell us about?'

She feels the stiff movement of bone as the room turns to look at her.

'No … I don't think so …' she says.

'What about that *man*?' a voice opines, loudly. She looks round. The speaker is Pat Cadogan. She is looking at Violet with her eyes narrowing as if holding the other woman in her sights.

'Man?'

'That one who was in the paper. Your … distant cousin. You must have some special memories of *him*.'

She says it with a heavy dusting of sarcasm. So it has already happened. Gossip has started; nodding, suspect conversations have been had, concerning the incident some weeks ago now when she asked Joe Hillier for his copy of the *Daily Telegraph*.

'Sorry,' says Daniel, 'I'm just trying to catch up here … you have a cousin who was in the paper?'

'That's great, Violet,' says Kirsty, before she has a chance to answer. 'Maybe you'd like to tell us about him … about your relationship with him … Joe, if you wouldn't mind?'

Joe, who has gone into a brown study, looks up at Kirsty. 'Hm?'

'If you wouldn't mind leaving the chair for the minute. Obviously, we'll come back to your story later.'

Joe rises. He stays there for a moment, his hands pushing the flaps of his tweed jacket into his body. There is a sense in the room that he has failed the *Life Story Work* test; that he has been bumped, like a chat-show guest, for someone more famous, or, in this case, for someone with more access to fame.

Violet looks at his vacant chair, then back at Kirsty and Daniel. Daniel has his finger ready to release the pause button on the video camera. She actually gets up – what am I doing? she thinks, why am I doing this? – and the words begin to form in her mind, bursting to get out. It has been so long.

'He is not my cousin. He is my husband. He *was* my husband. I am Violet Gold, the first wife of Eli Gold. The world's greatest living writer, although we did not know that then. We were married for ten years, between 1944 and 1954. Ten years, during which I was not happy, or at peace, nor even clear about what I was doing married to this person; but they remain the ten years that form the … that form the … the Key Stage Moment of My Life Story Work.'

'Eli Gold? You were married to Eli Gold?'

'Yes?'

'Sorry, Violet, but … are you making this up?'

'Why would I make it up?'

'I don't know. It just sounds … wouldn't we know this already, Kirsty?'

'No one told me, Daniel.'

'I'm not making it up. He made *me* up. I am Queenie. I am Queenie. I am Queenie.'

'Oh, my God, she's … please, Violet, pull your dress down … not on the lounge floor … nurse, quickly!'

All this goes through her mind as she makes her way gingerly round the semi-circle and towards the *Life Story Work* chair. She halts briefly when she gets there, her fingers resting on the top of it. The nine other inmates have become an audience. She sees the red light go on at the side of the video camera, a pinprick of red, like blood from the tip of a finger. She opens her mouth, at last, to speak.

'I know what *my* Key Stage Moment is, if it's any help …'

It is not her voice. She and all the others look over to the door. It is Meg Antopolski, in a wheelchair. She looks – well, she looks like Meg: white hair, brown eyes, Roman nose. She has not had that thing happen after a fall, where the fallen person no longer looks like themselves. There is a collective gasp from the room, not so much at the drama of her interruption of Violet, but at the fact that she is not dead. Pat Cadogan even looks a bit put out.

'Sorry, Violet,' says Meg, wheeling herself in, 'but I've been reading up about all this while I've been in hospital – you get a lot of time to read there … and when you stopped there, by the chair, I got the impression that maybe you weren't so keen on talking to everybody after all. Am I right?'

Violet, not knowing quite what to say, looks to Norma, who laughs and shrugs. Next to her is Pat Cadogan, who looks directly back with a face that says, *What did I tell you? Always barging in.*

'No, that's fine, Meg, please,' she says. 'You go. So pleased to see you back.'

'Sorry, who's this?' says Daniel, now making no attempt to hide the exasperation in his voice.

'Meg Antopolski, love. Write it down, even though I'm sure you'll spell it wrong. Help me with this stupid cartie, someone.'

Kirsty comes to Meg and wheels her chair forward. Violet moves back towards the chair she was in before, although she does not sit down.

'Ready for my close-up, Mr de Mille,' says Meg.

And then Meg Antopolski goes on to say that she has had many Key Stage Moments in her life, but she knows now that the Key Stage Moment of Key Stage Moments, the thing that defines her, is her fall. That in the instant of collapse on the white enamel floor of her shower, she was presented with the perfect choice: either to stay there curled up in a ball, ready to die of hypothermia, or somehow reach the panic button. And that this perfect choice – whether to give up or to carry on – continued throughout her time in hospital. That is the Key Stage Moment, she goes on to say: choosing between death or life. It's a choice

EG: Yes?

RW: The first question is: what age were all your wives? When you left them, I mean. You have left them all, haven't you? None of them have left you … why would they?

EG: Again, I really can't see the relevance of this …

RW: Humour me, Mr Gold. You'll be out of here in no time.

[pause]

EG: I have parted from all my wives by mutual consent. Except, of course, Pauline …

RW: Well. It was mutual consent.

EG: I beg your pardon?

RW: I'd call a suicide pact mutual consent. Wouldn't you?

EG: Very clever. Very good.

[pause]

RW: So?

EG: What?

RW: The age … of your wives. When you left them. By mutual consent.

EG: Oh, Christ, I don't know. Violet was thirty, I guess. Isabelle … yes, she was thirty-five. Joan, probably – thirty-seven.

RW: What's the cut-off point, do you think?

EG: I beg your pardon?

RW: For women.

EG: Cut-off point?

RW: Come on, Eli. It's just me and you here. I'll turn off the tape recorder if you like.

[pause]

RW: What's the cut-off point? When does the door shut? When do they turn into being on the turn? When do they become imperfect?

EG: What the fuck?

RW: What's the Fellini age? You know, like in that movie? The broads got to a certain age and they got kicked upstairs and that was that.

[pause]

RW: He was a great man, too, of course, Federico. So I guess that was why it was OK.

EG: I don't know, Webb. I don't know what the fucking Fellini age is.

RW: You do. You're the king of knowing that. I bet you could pinpoint it like a sniper.

[pause]

EG: Thirty-seven.

RW: Thirty-seven? Not forty?

EG: Forty's too obvious. Forty would be the answer of an unoriginal mind. Besides – as some people say who are in relationships with people much older or much younger than they are – it's just a number. One shouldn't isolate an age because it's round, because it has a zero.

RW: And thirty-seven is not just a number?

EG: I meant, as I'm sure a man of your delicate perception could have registered, a certain essence of thirty-seven. Or perhaps a certain essence of thirty-six, which is lost at thirty-seven.

RW: Right. I see.

[pause; the sound of laughter]

EG: Oh, my God, your face. Really thinking about it. A picture of earnestness and consideration. I'm fucking with you, Webb, can you not see that?

[pause]

RW: Of course you are. You were joking.

EG: Oh yes.

RW: You love a joke, don't you? Great men do. Great – what do they call it? – 'post-modern' men. They love the comic; they get such a hard-on, don't they, for *irony*. Irony is like a religion, isn't it, for men like you. Nothing a man like you puts down in words can ever be quite true. Every day, every page, every chapter, a new way to fuck with the world.

EG: Oh Christ … how much more of this …

RW: You know, I read this quote once. You'll know it. 'There is no better starting point for thought than laughter …' How does it go …?

EG: 'Spasms of the diaphragm generally offer better chances for thought than spasms of the soul.' Walter Benjamin.

RW: Walter Benjamin. Of course.

EG: He's right, though, isn't he, Commissioner? Where would we be without those spasms of the diaphragm?

RW: A very bad place, I'm sure. I mean, you should know, Eli. You're joking now: but three weeks ago, to be exact – you had, wherefore you knew not, lost all your mirth.

[pause]

RW: How old was Pauline, Mr Gold?

EG: She was thirty-seven. And you can go fuck yourself.

* * *

Waiting at the lights on 125th and Malcolm X Boulevard, Harvey Gold looks through the smeary taxi windows at the people outside. There are many of them on the sidewalk at this time of the morning, going to diners, going to work. One of them, although not a tramp – he is wearing a smart suit, from a designer who Harvey, if he was a different type of man, could probably name – is doing a tramp thing, standing there looking into the road, with his mouth open. He holds it wide open, although not quite wide enough to be a yawn. It looks to Harvey like he is screaming, although they are close enough to hear him, and he can't. It makes Harvey think about the human face, and its Emmenthal number of holes. Nose, mouth, ears, eye sockets: what's inside, so open to the elements.

'Was he a good president?'

He looks over. Elaine came this morning before breakfast, and dressed Colette. She is wearing a sky-blue dress and pink tights, and her frizzy hair has been combed almost straight. He had watched as Elaine had done this, methodically, tugging and pulling the strands free of knots like some dour ancient weaver, and had been amazed at how stoically Colette had accepted it. Elaine had left immediately afterwards. Harvey had thought she might want to come to the hospital, but she just laughed and said, 'Not for me: I voted for Ross Perot. Twice.'

'Yeah, I think. I don't really know. I was in Britain the whole time he was president.'

'How old is he?'

'Um … I dunno. Sixty-something, I guess.'

'Quite young, then.'

Harvey looks at her serious small face. He decides not to contradict her.

'Why did he stop being president?'

'Well, you have to, after eight years.'

'Oh, yeah. I remember that now.'

'And also, he got into all that shit with the fat intern chick …'

Harvey looks up. It is the driver. He is a squat man, completely bald: two rolls of fat protrude neatly from the back of his neck like

370

frankfurters. 'The cigar, the dress stains ... "I did not have sexual relations with that woman" – Oh, Jesus, it takes me back ...'

'Excuse me?' says Harvey.

'Yeah?'

'Do you mind? There is a child in the back here.'

His heart beats faster, like it always does with any confrontation, however small. He envisages the taxi driver immediately locking the doors and driving them to some street, some Bronx junction of Knife Crime Boulevard and Gang Violence Ave, and demanding that they get out right there. But the fat on the back of his neck just twitches a little, and his eyes in the rear-view mirror go blank.

Harvey doesn't turn to look at Colette immediately: it crosses his mind that she may not have liked this intervention – he has seen how little she likes being described as a child. Much of life – and death – seems to have been laid out for her already. I am a fool, he thinks, for shutting the stable door so long after that horse has been put out to stud.

He sits back, and to avoid her gaze buttons his jacket up. He is in a suit; or, at least, matching trousers and jacket. He was not sure what to wear for this visit. Just as on the non-date with Lark, he had felt superstitious about wearing the black suit prematurely. Instead, he put on the dark blue jacket that he wore for his first visit to Mount Sinai, and then, after some uncertainty – and another nervous trip into his sort-of parents' bedroom – found a pair of Eli's trousers of round about the same navy colour. They are too small for him – his father, despite his extreme appetite for food, has always managed to stay wiry, a physical trait consolidated, in the last few years, by cancer – but Harvey has managed to get them on by doing up the far catch and leaving the nearer one undone. Which means that his fly is open at the top. Which is why it is a good idea that he is buttoning up his jacket.

'Would you like some gum?' says Colette. He turns. She is chewing radically, like kids sometimes do, overdoing the facial movement.

'Er ...' he says. It's tempting: it's early in the morning and he is worried his breath might smell. He is worried about meeting Bill

Clinton with smelly breath. 'I would but when I chew gum I get terrible hunger pains.'

'Hunger pains?'

'Yeah. It's like if you chew gum, your brain thinks you're eating. And then your stomach acid gets all churned up, and if no actual food comes through … I dunno, it kind of attacks your own intestine or something.'

'There's *acid* in your stomach?'

'Yeah. That's what breaks the food down.'

'But how come it doesn't … like … burn through your skin. Like through your belly button or something?'

Harvey shakes his head. He feels as if he can make out the contours of his belly button against the waistband of his father's trousers. 'Yes, I really don't know the answer to that. You'd have to ask your biology teacher at school.'

Colette nods. 'I haven't been to school for ages. I did go, but when Daddy started to get ill Mommy took me out, so I did home schooling. Elaine does a lot of it.'

'OK. Well, maybe ask her.'

'Hunger … pains.' She seems to be committing the phrase to memory with each chew. She takes the sticky wet ball out of her mouth, and looks at it with concern.

'It's OK. I don't think everyone gets it from chewing gum, but I do, really badly. I get hunger pains really badly in general. Sometimes when I go out to a restaurant, and the food hasn't arrived 'cos they're busy or something, I have to go and lie down in the toilet.'

She laughs. 'In the toilet? Why?'

'Because I can't lie down in the middle of the restaurant.'

She laughs more, her mouth opening wide. Her teeth have that heartbreaking arranged littleness.

'You could under the table.'

'No. People would kick me.'

Her eyes sparkle with the idea. She has forgotten that she is going to meet an ex-president. She has forgotten that their father is dying.

'How do you lie down in the toilet?' she says. 'There's not enough room. Specially not for a grown-up.'

'Yes, it is a bit difficult. If you go with having your feet at the toilet end – because the cubicles normally have a bit of a gap between the edge of the door and ground, your head can poke out of that gap. But then, if you go the other way round, you have to put your head where all the poo goes.'

'Urrrrrrrrggggh!' she says. 'Shhhh.' She points at the taxi-driver, whose face is set fixedly forward. 'He might hear.'

'And sometimes, there's wee-wee on the floor, too.'

'Harvey! No!' She touches his arm with her hand, as if to stop him from ever lying down in a toilet again. He smiles: he feels the fondness, familiar to him from hearing one of Jamie's earnest concerns.

'It's all right. I don't do it much these days.'

She looks at him, eyes wide. 'Good,' she says, and puts the ball of gum back in her mouth. Harvey notices something, a flash of green, red and blue on her lap.

'Hold on a sec. What is that gum?'

She holds up the packet. 'Sour Razzles.'

'Sour Razzles?'

'It's not really gum. I don't know why I called it that. It's more like little chewy candy.' She rummages and gets out a small green square. 'This one's apple flavour. I *love* sour candy.'

He looks at her. He puts the index finger and third finger into a crook, and pinches her round apple-flavoured cheek. She smiles up at him.

'Don't mind if I do,' says Harvey, picking the green bliss-bomb out of her hand, the saliva already welling in his mouth.

When they get to the door outside Eli's room, for the first time for some while John the security guy blocks their way.

'Huh?' says Harvey.

He puts a finger to his lips, and raps a knuckle on the glass port-hole. Harvey can see the backs of many men's heads. A second later,

Freda opens the door: she is wearing a black dress suit, a sexy version of widow's weeds, making Harvey's heart miss a beat.

'Right. Good,' she says. Her attitude and voice are clipped, urgent.

'Is everything OK?' says Harvey.

'Yes, fine, fine. Bill arrived a bit earlier than his office said he would ...'

'He's already here? In there?' Harvey cranes his neck. Through the glass, he reviews the men's heads, looking for a back view of grey pompadour.

'Yes. Come in, Colette.'

Colette, her face in the set expression of a child called upon to behave appropriately during an important moment, passes through the gap in the door. Freda turns away.

'Hello?' says Harvey. 'Freda?'

She turns back. Her face is irritated, someone who does not have time to talk.

'Yes?'

'Am I ... I thought I ...?'

'What?'

'Aren't I coming in?'

She blinks at him, her eyelids fluttering with frustration. 'No, Harvey, sorry. We had to specify a certain number of people for Bill's visit, by name.' Harvey feels someone's eyes on him: it is John, standing to one side, indicating his clipboard, with a new raft of names on it for today, not including his. 'And, obviously, with the doctors and nurses around, and all the machinery – it would just be too crowded. I'm sorry. But many, many thanks for getting Colette here on time.'

She makes to go back in. In that split second, Harvey – who is a man who would normally not do something like this, who would normally let it go, and then just stew with it, going over and over in his head what he should have said, what he would like to have said, picking obsessively at the scab of his weakness – empowered by something, the moment of confrontation in the cab maybe, or perhaps just a deep, deep sense of the unfairness of things, grabs her sleeve.

'What if he died?'

She looks back, astonished.

'Who? Bill?'

'No, not Bill! Dad! Eli! What if he died, now? Would I be allowed in then? What if he *started* to go? What then? Would I – I'm his son, remember; his *son* – not get on the list? Would I still be just the taxi service for your daughter?'

'Harvey, I simply cannot discuss this now!'

'Who's got more right to be in there? Me or Bill Clinton? Who do you think, Freda?'

'Mrs Gold?' says John. They look to him. He glances from her to Harvey, just with his eyes, his wide forehead corrugating. The glance means *Shall I get rid of him?* Once again, for Harvey, that nightclub feeling: here I am, causing a disturbance, and the bouncer is going to kick me out.

'Harvey,' says Freda, her voice freighted with this-is-your-last-chance patience. 'Please. This is not the time.'

'It's not pass the parcel, Freda!'

'What? What is this, now?'

What is this, now? A memory passes through him of the same phrase, said to him five years ago by his wife, in the shadow of Tower Bridge.

'The one holding the prize at the end does not win! Eli would have left you, just like he left all the others! For fuck's sake, he's *about* to leave you! Only not for another woman, for death!'

He has said this much more loudly than he had intended. Her face meets Harvey's. A part of Harvey is calm, removed from his own fury and self-pity, and that part is already wondering what the point is of such an outburst. He is, he knows, doing that thing again; that Eli-inherited, *chess* thing of trying to win an argument through stepping back from anger and presenting his opponent with a cogent and detached deconstruction of their own unconscious motives. Only he has failed, completely, to present this strategy in a detached way: it is key, for example, not to shout the deconstruction. His stepmother's eyes, above their fine, fine lines, grow cold as stone.

'Goodbye, Harvey,' she says, and walks back inside. His fingers slip from her black sleeve as easily as they would have from Lark's cheek.

Between him and John, about what to do next, there is a moment of complete inertia, of the purest uncertainty, like God is saying Um. John shrugs, his shoulders moving like little mountains deciding, after all, to come to Mohammed. Then, from Eli's room, comes Dr Ghundkhali, his manner brisk, friendly.

'Hi. Harvey! I saw you here. I've been meaning to say: I've fixed up that prostate thing for you.'

'I'm sorry?'

'That prostate examination? We talked about it a while back? You were worried?'

Americans and their constant questioning. 'Oh … yeah … I was. I am …'

'OK. Well, no time like the present.' He takes a black pen, and a note pad, from the top pocket of his white coat, and scribbles something illegible down.

'Take this to Urology. Fourth floor. Diagnostics.'

'What, I can see someone now? Right, now? I don't have to make an appointment?'

He rips the note off the pad. 'Not with this you don't.' He slips it into the top pocket of Harvey's jacket. 'Enjoy.'

*   *   *

He had three or four other grown-ups around him, but I knew who he was straight away. My mom had shown me a picture, but she said that he was the sort of man who caught your eye as soon as he walked into a room. I didn't know what caught your eye meant but I worked out it means that you look at him before anyone else. I didn't know why that should be. He looked OK, I guess. His face was sort of red, and his hair was a bit funny, but I liked his eyes, even though they had big bags under them. They were blue, my favourite colour. Mommy introduced me, once she was done talking to Harvey at the door.

'Mr President,' she said. (I don't get that. He isn't the president, not any more.) 'This is mine and Eli's daughter, Colette.'

He crouched down and took my hand.

'Hi, Colette.'

'Hello Mr President.'

'Your daddy must be very proud to have such a beautiful daughter.'

That made me blush. He had a funny voice. It sounded like he had a sore throat. I hoped he didn't, because I know the doctors have said that no one is allowed to come and see Daddy if they are ill, in case he gets their illness and dies. I hoped they hadn't changed that rule just because he used to be the president.

'Thank you. I'm proud to be his daughter,' I said.

'Of course you are,' he said. 'Of course.'

And then he ruffled my hair and stood up. He moved away to talk to some of the other men. I think they were his friends. I looked at Mommy. She smiled at me: she seemed really pleased about how it had all gone. But I wasn't.

'Mr President?' I said.

'Yes, Colette?'

'When are you going to do it?'

He came back over, and crouched down again. Mommy stopped smiling.

'When am I going to do what, darlin'?' he said.

His eyes looked really kind. Really blue.

'Wake up Daddy.'

He blinked, a lot. His eyes got bigger.

'I beg your pardon?'

'When are you going to say something that makes Daddy wake up?'

He looked at Mommy.

'Colette, darling …' she said.

'Hey, Colette,' said Bill Clinton, holding up a hand to Mommy. 'I'd love to do that. I'd *so* love to be able to do that. But I can't. If the good doctors here can't do it, I don't see that I can.'

'But you're really famous!'

377

'Uh …'

'Colette. Please.'

'It's OK, Mrs Gold.'

'That's what wakes people up, when they're in a coma. If a famous person comes to see them! And because Daddy's so famous already, only a *really* famous person could do it! Like you!'

All the doctors were looking at me by now, and Bill Clinton and Mommy and all Bill Clinton's friends. I could feel that I was going to cry and I really didn't want to, because what I was saying was so important.

'I wish that was true, honey.'

'It is true. Harvey said so.'

'Oh, did he,' I heard Mommy say.

'Harvey?'

'He's my half-brother. He's outside.'

Bill Clinton turned to Mommy. 'Is that true? Eli's son?'

'Yes,' Mommy said. She'd gone a bit red. 'We were told – only a certain number allowed in today …' She didn't finish her sentence. He turned back to me.

'We can't have that, can we?' He nodded at one of his friends, a big man with sunglasses on top of his head. He nodded back and went outside.

'Now, Colette,' Bill Clinton said, taking my hand. 'Come with me.'

He took me over to Daddy's bed. We had to walk through some of the doctors to do that. They moved away really quickly. We stood by Daddy's bed for a little bit saying nothing. He still held my hand. Daddy looked bad. The oxygen mask looked really tight on his face. I wished I could loosen it a bit.

'Here's the thing, Colette,' said Bill Clinton. 'I really can't bring your Daddy out of his coma. If I could, I would. Honest to God, I would. But you know what? I think he's in a really, really deep sleep. He's at peace, like that. I think he's OK.'

I looked at Daddy. Even though Bill Clinton was saying he couldn't do anything, I thought maybe him saying that would wake him up. If you're that famous just hearing his voice would do. I didn't know if that was the kind of thing you were meant to say to wake people up from a coma. I wondered what Justin Bieber would've said if it was like a young girl in a coma or something. I guess he would've sung 'Baby', or 'Never Let You Go', which is the only song of his I like by the way.

I thought that maybe Daddy didn't realize it was Bill Clinton. He was the ex-President and he hadn't been on TV for ages. Maybe Daddy didn't recognize his voice.

'Daddy,' I said. 'It's Bill Clinton.'

He looked at me. I looked at him.

'Can you tell him? Just tell him you're here. Please.'

Bill Clinton looked sad then. He looked over to Mommy, who was looking really worried now. But then he nodded his head.

'Eli,' he said. 'It's Bill Clinton here.'

I closed my eyes. I could feel Bill Clinton's hand in mine. It was starting to feel a bit hot. *Wake up, Daddy*, I told him in my thoughts. *Wake up and say hi to Mr President. Please.* I kept them shut for a really long time. I could feel some tears start to come out of them but I kept them tight shut even so. I just knew that if I kept them shut for long enough Daddy would be awake and sitting up in bed when I opened them. And then I heard a voice.

'Colette,' it said, 'Colette.'

I opened my eyes. It was Bill Clinton's friend, the one who had gone out of the room to look for Harvey. He was standing on the other side of the bed. He bent his face down. I could see the reflection of me and Daddy and Bill Clinton in his sunglasses.

'Sorry, sweetheart, but there's no one outside,' he said.

*   *   *

The room is very white: Persil-white. Harvey, who is used to the off-white and off-greys of the NHS, is almost blinded by it. He sits behind a white screen, on a white couch, which is covered tight with a white sheet, and considers his own disorientation. He feels like he wants to double-take – he wants to have a moment of saying to himself: *Uh? How did I get here? A second ago I was getting on well with my extended family, I was about to meet Bill Clinton, I had access to my dad's death-bed, and now all that is gone, and I'm about to have a doctor stick their finger up my arse. That doesn't even make sense.* He wants to, but he has a feeling inside that it is not over; that this day may bring an even deeper double-take.

He waits for the doctor to appear. Dr Ghundkhali's note has worked the wonders that the flourish with which he handed it over suggested it would. His phone rings. Uncertain whether or not he is allowed to leave it on in this part of the hospital, he looks at the screen.

'Bunce?'

'Hey. What's happening?'

'What the fuck, Bunce! WHAT THE FUCK!'

'I'm sorry?'

'That fucking package you sent me! What are you fucking thinking about?'

'What's your fucking problem? No one else was going to open it. You do know it's a federal offence in this country, opening someone else's mail?'

'What's that got to do with anything? There's a little girl in that apartment! Did you think about that? At all?'

'But you said …'

'I expressed interest in your job! That was it! I was being polite!'

'Polite?'

'Well, OK, maybe I *was* interested. Yes. In your *job*, man.' He feels the by now familiar catch of embarrassment at the American vocabu-lary, but anger overrides it: and after all, this is the stuff the dialect was made for, 'In your *fucking* job. Not in the fucking evidence! Not in actual concrete examples of your awful dirty work! Can I make myself any clearer: I didn't want to be sent something from some fucking cache of child porn!!'

He hears a cough and looks up. The doctor is looking at him, hold-ing the screen aside. Where has he seen this one before? Oh, yes. Coming out of the toilet. He still doesn't know whether she is Korean, Chinese or Malaysian. He knows, however, from her intensely shocked expression that she has heard what he has just been saying.

380

'Well, fuck you, Gold. Fuck you and your fucking great writer dying dad. You can just …'

He clicks the phone off and tries to smile.

'Hi.'

'Um … hello.'

'Dr Ghundkhali sent me down here for a check-up. A prostate …'

'Yes, I know why you're here.' Just a trace of an accent, through the basic New York: doesn't help place her. 'Could you just hold on a moment?'

She disappears back behind the screen. A second later, he hears her voice, which she is quietening, but hardly. It's not even a whisper.

'Hi, Dr G? It's Dr Dahn. Mi-Yong Dahn, from Urulogy? This patient you've sent down here … yes, that's the one … I don't think I want to do the prostate check on him. I'm sorry.' Harvey strains to hear, but cannot make out Dr Ghundkhali's response. 'Yes, no I realize that. But I don't feel comfortable doing it. He was saying some very strange things when I came in on the telephone, his trousers are undone, and I saw him a month or so ago when I was coming out of the restroom on your floor, and I did not like the way he looked at me. I am not comfortable giving him the prostate check.' Harvey sighed and got off the couch: whether she was Korean, Chinese or Malaysian, she clearly had an Oriental straightforwardness about things.

'Yes, I can get someone else to look at him. To do the check. A man, I think, would be more appropriate …'

But it is too late. Harvey is walking out from behind the screen as she continues to talk, out of the room, out of the hospital, trying to do his trousers up more tightly as he goes.

* * *

He walks up Central Park, wheeling his suitcase behind him. It is still early. The sun is shining. He feels good about himself and about this day, come at last. He is walking because he wants to feel it; he wants to live, as Janey used to say we all must, in the moment, in this moment, his destiny. He can feel it better here, with the tall buildings framing the green, than in the subway, where the air is close and people sometimes stared at you like they needed to know your business. And also he has to find a trash can without people around it, and it's easier at this time in the morning in the park than on the street.

When he finds one he quickly takes Lisa's dress out of his suitcase and stuffs it in. He feels bad about it – it dents his sense of righteousness – but he is taking no chances. She was sleeping soundly when he left, but she might still have woken up and rushed after him. Without clothes, however, she cannot easily leave the hotel room, and this knowledge has freed him to have the time for this walk in the park.

Before he zips up the suitcase his eye flicks over the contents. He could not do a proper last check in his room because she was in his bed, and he did not want to turn the light on. But everything he needs is there.

Walking across the circle of concrete the trash can sits on the edge of, he notices some kind of memorial at the centre of it. He does not want to be distracted, but is curious enough to walk over. It is a smaller circle, a mosaic. Some flowers have been laid on its patterns. In the middle of it is a word: IMAGINE. He looks up, out of the park. The pointed roofs and high windows of an old apartment building is blocking the sun, throwing him into shadow. He grasps where he is, but, deliberately, does not grasp it fully; he holds off that knowledge, because he does not want it to muddy his purpose, already thrown off by his feelings about Lisa, waking naked and confused at the Condesa Inn. It's not even a coincidence, he thinks, as he walks out quickly onto West 72nd Street.

He stops at Hanratty's and orders steak and eggs for breakfast, as it is the thing that will keep you going whatever happens. This time it does not go cold. It arrives quickly, served rare by a waiter he has not seen before, a Mexican, and he eats every morsel, savouring the soft meat, the mixture in his mouth of blood and yolk. Afterwards, he goes downstairs to the toilets. It is empty in there. He takes his suitcase into a cubicle. Inside, he changes: the black jacket for the white coat. He hangs his jacket up on the hook inside the toilet. He has never known why there are these hooks, but he is glad of it.

From the suitcase, he takes what he needs. The photograph of his sister. The Amscor. And *The Book of Mormon*. But there is no room for *The Book of Mormon* inside any pocket. It is 531 pages long. He has a pocket edition, back in American Fork, but this is not it. He could carry it but he is worried that someone would notice and question him. But he does not feel able to leave it in a toilet. He has always planned to leave the suitcase here, but not The Book. He tries to make it OK by wrapping The Book inside a pair of trousers, and shutting the case, but as he begins to unlock the door, he falters. He sits down on the toilet. He does not know what to do. He opens the book. He reads.

In *The Book of Moroni*, the last Book of *The Book of Mormon*, it says:

> For behold, to one is given by the Spirit of God, that he may teach the word of wisdom; and to another that he may teach the word of knowledge by the same Spirit.

He sees straight away that God and Joseph Smith have given him the answer. He goes out of the toilet, and straight back up the stairs.

– Excuse me, he says to the waiter, who is standing by his table with the check, I'd like to pay that.

– OK, sir. It's $9.99.

He hands him a ten-dollar bill. It is the last money he has. He left the rest at the reception of the Condesa Inn. The woman who runs the hotel was not up when he went out. He would not like her to think he left without paying. The waiter looks up, expectantly.

– I can't give you any money for your service, he says. I'm sorry about that. But instead I'd like to give you this. It is the best tip I can give you.

He hands him *The Book of Mormon*. The waiter opens it at a random page, and reads. He feels good that today has also included this small piece of evangelism. He realizes now that his destiny is also, in a way, a Mission.

The waiter looks up.

– Can I ask you something?

He nods.

– When you came in here, you were like a regular guy. And then you went to the john, and now you're a doctor. And a Mormon. How come?

He does his best attempt at a beatific, mysterious smile, such as he has seen the priests and Elders of his church do when children ask questions the answers for which are too complex for them to understand, and walks out.

*   *   *

Then they all left. Bill Clinton, his friends, even the doctors. That normally never happens. There's usually at least two of them around, plus some nurses, but no nurses had been allowed in the room when Bill Clinton was there. Dr Ghundkhali said something to one of the other doctors about how it would be all right to leave for a little while because their bleepers would go off if one of Daddy's machines went wrong. I think they all wanted to spend more time with Bill Clinton.

I wasn't sure about leaving Daddy like that. As we were going through the door, I pulled Mommy's hand and said:

'Mommy. Will Daddy be OK?'

I knew this was kind of a stupid thing to say, because he is dying. But I think she knew what I meant. She bent down to whisper in my ear, but I could see she was still looking at Bill Clinton and the other people who were moving out of the room.

'Yes, darling. The doctors will come straight back if anything happens.'

'But he knows, doesn't he?'

'What?' She had started to pull me away. Bill Clinton and his friends and the doctors had gone through the door.

'Daddy. He knows. He can hear. He knows we're leaving him on his own.'

'Darling …' Even though she was saying darling, her voice had gone harder, like it does when she's cross, '… Daddy – of course, yes, he can hear everything – but remember, Daddy, you know, he's still a grown-up … he's been on his own before, many times. And we're really not going to be very long. So, Colette … could we hurry up, please.'

I let her pull me. As I went through the door I looked back at Daddy. I couldn't see him too clearly because of all the machines, but I said goodbye to him in my head. I tried not to make it too big a goodbye because I didn't want it to feel like I was saying *goodbye* goodbye. I didn't want him to think that.

*   *   *

Harvey strides under the glass of the Guggenheim Pavilion, looking out towards Madison Avenue, his eyes already searching for a taxi before he has left the building. He has decided: he will go and pick up his stuff at Eli and Freda's apartment and then go straight to JFK. He does not know when the next plane to London is – plus, it crosses his mind, doesn't it cost more to buy a ticket at the airport? – but *fuck it*, he thinks: I'm gone. I'm outtahere. In his head, he lets himself revel in the diction one last time.

People pass him, ill ones in, healthy ones out. He fishes his iPhone out of his pocket: the battery shows only a small sliver of red. He taps favourites star and calls Stella. It rings twice.

'Hello?' The sleep-slurred voice, again.

'Shit! Darling, sorry. Shit.'

'Harvey?'

'Yes, sorry. I forgot about the time difference. Again. Shit. It's the middle of the night with you …'

'Is everything all right? Are you OK?'

Before he can answer, he hears a voice in the background say: 'Dad?'

'I'm fine.' says Harvey. 'Well, I'm not fine. But I'm fine. I'm not ill. I'm coming home. Is Jamie with you?'

'Yes, he came into our bed. 'Bout two hours ago.'

Harvey's present energy, an arrow speeding away from the circus surrounding his father, is deflected by this callback to his domestic life, the thing his son does of coming up to sleep with his parents, even though, at nearly ten, he is too old for that. Stella, properly awake now, takes the silence as reproach.

'He's disrupted by you being away for so long.' Disrupt: it is their soft word, their euphemism, for their son's reaction to breaks in his routine. 'You're coming home?'

'Yes.'

'Right now?'

'Yes.'

She is quiet. Harvey knows what is coming.

'Is he …?'

'No. The old bastard seems to be hanging on for ever. But I've had enough. Look, I'm so sorry to ring you so late – and Jamie's already woken you up earlier.'

'Dad?'

Harvey stops. He is at the exit doors. He can see the taxis passing, stop-starting in the traffic – a faltering yellow stream, not unlike, he thinks, the one produced by his own knackered prostate.

'Jammy?'

Stella puts him on.

'Hi, Dad.'

'Hi, Jammy.' This is what he has called him since he was a baby. An old man in blue pyjamas being wheeled past him looks up sharply as he says it, as if he might be mocking him. It makes Harvey aware of how he should probably stop calling Jamie it, but that would disrupt him. It passes his mind that many parents fear their children growing older, losing their childlikeness. 'You couldn't sleep?'

'No.'

'I'm coming home soon. Now, in fact.'

'Is Grandpa dead?'

'No. No, he's not.'

'So why are you coming home?'

He could hear a familiar catch in his son's voice, an angry tremor.

'Because …'

'You said you had to go because Grandpa was dying. You said you would come back when he was dead.'

386

'Yes, I know but …'

'You've been away for fifty-one days. There's no point in coming back now. That would be a waste of those days.'

'Jamie. Jammy. Listen …'

'It would be a waste, Dad. It would be a waste of all the time you weren't here. You mustn't start something you don't finish. It's a bad investment.'

'Can you put Mummy back on, please?'

And bang, he does, even though Harvey knows his son is fixed and fervent in his position.

'Stell …'

'Harvey, I'm not sure this is a good idea. Whatever's happened, I don't want you – I don't want you regretting coming back too soon.'

Outside, Madison Avenue seems to beckon to him. There was a band called Madison Avenue once, wasn't there? They sung 'Don't Call Me Baby'. Perhaps he should check it out on Spotify. Or they were a girl band, weren't they? YouTube, then.

'Regret. That's OK,' says Harvey. 'You know what Eli said once, in one of his last interviews, when they asked him if he had any regrets? "I am besieged by regret, as is any thinking person …"'

'Yeah. Bollocks to that.'

Immediately, he hears a distant laugh, followed by the words 'Bollocks. Bollocks. Bollocks.'

'Now you've set him off.'

'I know. But honestly, darling, I don't care if your stupid Great Man dad embraced regret. Which he didn't anyway. That's just something he said: I can't think of anyone who lived his life less held back by the possibility of regret.'

'Stella …'

'Bollocks!'

'But either way, he's in a coma. If he ever did, he doesn't have any regrets any more. But you might. You will …'

Harvey takes a deep, self-conscious breath; he feels the air going into and out of his lungs. A family with three children, all apparently packed with health, bursts through the door: the mother shuffles them away from him, making him wonder if he looks mad.

'I miss you, Stella. I really deeply miss you. And Jamie. It's not just that I don't want to stay here. I want to come home.'

'Bollocks. Bollocks. Bollocks.'

Even though he knows his son is just echolalaing, he wants to say, No, it's not. He really wants to be there. He doesn't want to be in Manhattan any more. He wants to be in Kent, on one of those bright winter's days when the county's beauty is at its bleakest; when the air refuses to snow, and frost spreads across its raped-by-motorways countryside.

'I miss you too, darling. So much.'

'I should let you sleep. I'll be back by the morning. Your morning.'

'Bollocks.'

'Have you at least said goodbye?'

'To who?'

'To your dad.'

'Oh Christ, Stella ... not you too.'

'What?'

'That's what Colette's been trying to get me to do. Freda told her that in some mystical way he can hear everything, if you – I dunno – if you say it with enough love, or something. I've tried once or twice but I just feel like a twat.'

'Well ... OK ... I just think ...'

He never finds out what she thinks, because the phone goes down, the blue earth re-emerging complacently onto the screen. He looks at it. No great thoughts come to him about his tiny place in this vast universe. A man comes through the door and barges into him. He looks up: it is a doctor, clean-shaven, wall-eyed, who is staring at him in an oddly intense way, as if Harvey should have known not to get in his way. Something about the man's features touches his memory, but before Harvey's hyper-recall for faces can kick in, he moves on, without a word. Harvey says 'sorry' to his retreating back, even though he is blameless.

The sun comes out. The sky seems to pour through Peggy Guggenheim's glass. Turned around, facing back towards the hospital, still a little troubled by the sense that he has seen the doctor somewhere before, Harvey Gold thinks: OK. There *is* someone I need to say goodbye to.

*   *   *

He walks faster, convinced that the sudden break of sunlight bodes well for his destiny. He looks up and into it. He can look straight at the sun because of his bad eye, if he keeps his other one closed. If he does that, all he sees is light.

He does not know exactly where to go. But he has a plan. He needs a doctor. A small part of his mouth rises into a smirk at the thought, feeling the tiny smarts of the shaved upper lip: *he needs a doctor* – there will be some who think in a different way. From what Lisa has told him, he knows that he will need to go up, so he waits by the elevators; and here they are, two of them, one black and one white, coming through the doors talking to each other as they walk.

'Hi,' he says, standing in their way. They look at him, blank. 'Do either of you know Dr Ghundkhali?'

'Ghundkhali? He's head of Geriatrics, isn't he?' says the black one.

'Yes,' says the white one. 'He's the one who's been on TV lately. He's got that writer guy in his care.'

'Oh, right,' he says. 'Because I need to speak to him about some test results.' He has thought about this sentence for some time. *Because I need to see him* sounded not enough: they might ask why. So this is what he has chosen. I need to see him about some test results. Saying it now, though, it feels hokey, like something from a daytime soap opera. They will see through him. His heart beats hard, sounding in his head like it did through the stethoscope.

But they do not. Jesus and Joseph Smith are surely on his side.

'Uh, well, you wanna go to Geriatrics,' says the black one. 'Fourteenth floor. Although I don't know if he'll be there right now …'

389

A drop of fear forms in his stomach: have they moved him?

'Why?'

''Cos of Clinton,' says the white one.

'Clinton?'

'You don't know? Where have you been, man?'

'I …'

'Hey, Matt,' says the black one. 'Don't give him a hard time. He's just trying to do his job.' He smiles and does a head-throw towards his friend, indicating apology for him. 'Bill Clinton's in today. Visiting the writer guy …'

'Oh,' he says. He feels his heart fall. 'Does that mean … does it mean there'll be a big crowd of people up there? Maybe I should come back another time.'

'Uh … well, Clinton and his people came in like over an hour ago, so they're probably on the way out by now. They may not even be up there any more, probably. There's not much talking to the patient that can be done, from what I understand …'

'I think there's some kind of reception for Bill in the Annenberg Building. That's where they'll be now.'

'Yeah, but you don't want to go over there. If I were you, I'd just go up to Geriatrics and wait. Shouldn't be too long.'

'OK.'

'Just look for a huge black man.'

'Much more huge and black than me.'

'Yeah. He stands outside the writer guy's room, day and night. What is his name? Not the black guy, the writer guy?' The black one shrugs. 'Do you remember?' The white one says to him. He shakes his head. 'It was the one whose wife died in a suicide pact.'

'And *he* didn't, of course.'

'Yeah. Complicated.'

'Clever, some would say.'

He cannot bear this. But perhaps he needs to hear it; it will impel him on. The elevator tings. In a second, the doors will open. He moves off without a word. Behind him, he hears:

'Hey? You OK?'

He has no need to speak to them any more, but he does. He turns back, to the white man and the black man.

'Why is he here?'

'Who?'

'Bill Clinton. Why is someone so important visiting a man who did that? That ... suicide pact. Wasn't it a scandal? Don't ex-presidents normally avoid people involved in stuff like that?'

They glance at each other. He needs to move, really: this outburst may already have made them suspicious. But he stays to hear the answers.

'Well, I dunno,' says the white man. 'It was a long time ago.'

'Yeah, and he was never charged with anything, I don't think.'

'And hey, it's not like Bill was scandal-free, in his time.'

'Yeah. Although he never quite got around to *killing* Hillary.'

The black one laughs. He hears the elevator doors open behind him. People flood past his sides. The two doctors shuffle, wanting to move back to their jobs, their lives.

'And also,' says the black one, looking back, 'he's famous. And dying.'

'Yeah,' says the white one. 'That'll do it.'

He turns round and walks into the elevator. He watches them walk away amongst the crowd of people. On the panel of circles, he presses 14: its white circumference, encasing gold, turns red.

* * *

He had run as fast as he could – even thinking, at one stage, of getting out his iPhone and putting on the running playlist – but when Harvey arrived back outside the door to Eli's room, Colette had not been there; neither were Freda, or Bill Clinton, or even any of the doctors. Having ascertained from John that everyone had left on Clinton's coat-tails, Harvey had stood there for a while, bereft of purpose.

'You OK?' John had said.

'Er ... yeah. Fine.' And, finding that he had no one else to tell this information to, he told John. 'I was about to go, actually. Once I'd spoken to Colette.'

'Go? Back to the apartment?'

391

'No. Home. England.'

'Oh.' John blinked very slowly, an action that reminded Harvey of Eli. 'I thought you were gonna wait until …'

'He died.'

'I guess.'

'Yes, well I was, but …' He trailed off. John nodded.

'He's taking his time about it, that's for sure.'

'Yes,' said Harvey.

'He lived a long life. And from what I hear, quite a life. I reckon he's still not that keen to exit it.'

'Yeah. Well, anyway …'

'You not going in to say goodbye?'

Freda, Colette, Stella, now him: Harvey yields at last to overwhelming pressure. So he finds himself sat by his father's deathbed, at last alone, at last, surely, ready to speak to him.

But still the words don't come. He sits on the chair next to the bed, and feels only that he should not be there. He watches Eli's chest go up and then down again, blown by some electronic bellows he does not understand. He begins, once or twice, stumbling again on the first word: 'Dad … dy,' he says. 'Eli', he tries. 'Father', even, which he tries twice, but it sounds more ridiculous than all of them, the first time an Edwardian schoolboy writing home, the second seeming to require, afterwards, *forgive them for they know not what they do*. All he can think of is the idiocy, the pointlessness of words. It comes to him in an obvious wave: the irony – the stupid fucking useless irony – of this God of words, this High Priest of Language, being rendered dumb, and the stupid fucking useless pretence of all those around him that the coma which is causing such dumbness does not also render him deaf. He looks at his father's eyes, which seem even more shut than usual, screwed shut behind their matrix of unfine lines. Around the two of them Eli's electronic armour, the circle of machines preserving his priceless life, bleep and tick and whine.

Harvey wishes that a doctor – having to minister to one of the machines, one of the hanging bags, one of the charts and graphs – would come and save him from this. Then he remembers: he doesn't have to do this. He didn't even come here to say goodbye to the old man. He turns away from his father, and then, yes, a doctor is there. He has not heard him come in. Harvey looks up at him and smiles, although is careful to adjust the smile so that there is some sorrow in it, not just relief. Oh, he thinks, it's the one who I got in the way of earlier, at the exit door to the hospital. I hope he's not pissed about it.

Before Harvey even has a chance to reprimand himself for this latest piece of linguistic Americana, the doctor looks at him blankly, and draws a gun.

– Step away from the patient, he says.

He knows straight away that saying this is a mistake. He has been lucky so far: or, rather, he corrects himself, God has been on the side of his destiny. Bill Clinton drawing people away, the two doctors saying what he needed to know, the big black security man just nodding at him to let him into the room – it's like it's been laid out for him. It's like he planned it with God. But now he realizes this was too much: it has made him expect it to be too easy. He was expecting no one to be in the room apart from his target. And when he came in and this fat, balding guy was here – damn. He flipped.

Because he could have just carried on playing the doctor. Instead of drawing the gun and saying step away from the patient, he could have just said, Sorry, I need to examine the patient. Then the guy would have said Yes, of course, and moved away, and he could have got close to The Great Satan and put a fucking bullet in his skull.

A doubt crosses his mind. He had felt, coming into the room, exactly as he thought he was going to feel: nervous, excited, ready, elated. But he realizes now that he had felt something else, something he had not bargained for: a second elation, above and beyond that of being at last in the moment of his destiny, something that had only come about because of the unexpected chance that the room was not full of doctors and other people who he would have to shout down using his gun. He had felt that perhaps he was going to get away with it. And then he saw the guy sitting there.

– What the fuck, says the guy, standing up. He sees the terror on his face. Then he sees him look to the door, and open his mouth.

– I don't wanna kill you, he says, quietly. It's not part of what I need to do to kill anyone else. But if you shout for the security guy, I will. You'll have a bullet in you before he's through that door.

The guy holds his hands up when he says this. OK, he says. OK. Whatever you say. He notices something weird about his accent. Australian, or something.

– So keep your fucking voice down.

Holding the gun in front of him, he glances towards the door himself. He can see the wide back of the security guy's black neck and the edge of his Bluetooth phone in his ear. He moves backwards, to a point where even if the security guy turned round, he could not see him through the glass. All he would see is the Australian, standing there.

– Put your hands down, he says.

– OK, OK, says the Australian, doing so. It's OK. Everything's OK. What do you want?

– I want to kill him.

– But you're a doctor.

– No. I'm not.

The Australian blinks, shakes his head.

– No. Right. Course not.

– So, as I said. Get away from the patient.

He starts to move. Then he stops. The man's bulk is still in the way. He can only see the white of the bed sheet. He cannot see The Great Satan's face.

– Look, says the man. Can't we talk about this?

– No.

– People will be here in a minute. The security guy will come in. You'll be caught. You'll be executed.

– I don't care. Move.

The man breathes heavily.

– For fuck's sake. I can't believe this is happening.

– I don't want to have to tell you again.

– He's dying. He's fucking dying, man.

The 'man', he notices, sounds wrong coming from the Australian's mouth.

395

– He might be dead today. Tomorrow. In five minutes. Why would you need to kill someone who's about to die?

– I don't have to tell you that.

– I'm his son.

He frowns. This is not part of his destiny. He looks again at this man, newly revealed as The Great Satan's son. Although the man's face is weak and full of fear, he senses that he, too, is near the end of something, and is going to see it out until that end.

– And you know what? I've been hanging around in this fucking city, at this fucking hospital, waiting for him to die for two fucking months. I really really want to go home. So I should just say, go on. Please. Be my guest. You're doing me a favour. But I can't.

He remains silent, just pointing the gun. The man takes a deep breath.

– I don't live in the moment, you see. Something people are always saying I should. And because I don't live in the moment, I'm already thinking about the days, the months, the years ahead, where I will have to live with the terrible guilt of stepping aside and letting you kill him. So I can't.

– Fuck off, he says. I'm not interested in all that shit.

He thinks that he could just shoot him. But he does not want to. It will fuck up his idea of his destiny. And he knows, too, that the sound of the gunshot will bring the security guy into the room. He is not confident that he will have time for a second shot, especially if the fat Australian son isn't killed outright first time and continues to shield The Great Satan.

– Just tell me why.

– I told you I don't have to.

– Have some pity.

– What pity did *he* have? For my sister?

This is out of him before he can stop it. Plus: he finds that he *wants* to tell him. It is something to do with this man being a version, a proxy, of The Great Satan. In his dreams of this moment, the old man is always up and cogniscent and listening, allowing him to be told exactly why he has to die. He accepts the justice. Sometimes he even smiles a small smile of acceptance as the gun is raised.

– Your sister?

– Yes.

– Who are you?

– I am Pauline Gray's brother.

The Australian stares at him now.

– Fuck.

– Do you understand now? Will you move?

– But … hey. It was a suicide pact.

– I can't see much of your father. But I can hear that he's still breathing. Pauline's been gone over fifteen years.

– Yeah, OK, but …

– She was tricked.

– You don't know that.

– She would never have done it. *We are Mormons*, he wants to add, but does not.

– She was in love with him. He was clinically depressed at the time. He said he wanted to commit suicide, she said she couldn't live without him …

– No.

– Yeah, it's mad – I didn't even buy it myself at the time, but in Eli's world, for Eli's women, it's the sort of thing that –

– Go read The Material.

– I beg your pardon?

– On the internet.

He glances at his watch. Three minutes have passed since he entered the room. It feels longer.

– Are you talking about … do you mean that thing on unsolved. com?

He does not reply. The son's quick knowledge of it makes him uneasy.

– The whole RW/EG dialogue? Commissioner Webb? All that?

– Yes.

The son laughs, sort of. Or an action and a sound a little like a laugh, but so filtered through fear and self-consciousness as to be more like a very short fit.

– Eli wrote that.

397

– What?

– My dad wrote that. My dad wrote that and posted it on the internet himself. Or got someone to do it for him.

He feels anxiety suffuse across his stomach, like salt in water.

– You're lying.

– I'm not. Commissioner Webb … Did you honestly think there's a cop in the New York City Police Department who talks like that? With such knowledge of Bellow, and Walter Benjamin, and Federico Fellini? Above all, with such knowledge of Eli fucking Gold? No. He wrote it himself.

His arms feel heavy. He has been holding the gun up for a long time.

– Why the fuck would he do that?

* * *

Harvey looks back towards his father and thinks: it's a good question. It's hard enough to explain post-modern irony at the best of times, but when you're shitting yourself? And to a sister-avenging *Deliverance* nutter?

Although in fact he is not shitting himself. His head is clear. When the gun first came out, his mind emptied. He lived in the moment, and the moment was white fear. And then his depression began to serve him. He felt a stasis. He has read, somewhere, that depressives flourished in concentration camps, because at last their inner and their outer worlds matched. Maybe it is that. Maybe feeling so often like death has made facing it a doddle.

He hears the word doddle in his head, and shakes it out. It is not right. He is still frightened. But it is true that he is used to dread. He has lived so long with phantom anxiety that there is almost a detachment, a fascination in experiencing what it is like to confront real danger. His mind throws up questions: if Stella walked in here now, under these neon hospital lights, would he still be frightened by the lines on her face? More, or less, frightened than by the barrel of the gun? Does the calmness come from that part of him which yearns to give up to it, to end the bad feelings for good, by making his own suicide pact with this madman?

Enough: enough deconstruction. Something, perhaps even just adrenaline, has returned his mind to him, and maybe he is Eli Gould's son after all, because so far the one thing that has not failed him is words. If he can keep talking for long enough, John will turn round; the doctors will come back; everything will be OK.

'It's kind of a joke.'

Harvey sees straight away that this is the wrong thing to say. The man's face contorts; he raises the gun closer.

'Sorry. I don't mean a joke joke. I think … when the suicide pact thing happened … there were a lot of rumours flying about in the papers. And then it died down, but then when the internet took off it started again. And Eli: I guess … I guess he thought, if you can't beat 'em, join 'em.'

'What the fuck are you talking about?'

'I think he thought – I think he thought it was a good subject to *write about*.'

The man takes one hand off the gun and smoothes it down over his upper lip, repeatedly.

'Why would he put it on the internet?' he says. 'Why not in a novel? Or a play?'

'Well, because the … I'm sorry to use this word, really sorry, I can't think of another one … the *joy* of it is that people will think it's real.' He looks at Eli: the plastic mask is tight on his face, a penumbra of reddened skin around its white edge. 'My dad is – was – very committed to the idea of misrule.'

He returns the hand to the gun.

'What the fuck is misrule?'

'Messing about with people. With truth. With what's real and what's not.'

There is a pause, during which Harvey remembers where he has seen this man. He has seen him, two or three times, hanging out with the Eli-worshippers who congregate at the entrance to Mount Sinai. This gives him some small hope. It means that, for whatever reason, he's been waiting for some time to do this; which means he might be persuaded to wait just a little longer.

'How do you know all this?'

'I'm his son.'

'He told you?'

'Yes.'

'You're lying.'

He is. It is one of Harvey's problems. He is very readable. It is easy to see when he is lying. This is because he does not like lying. Even the smallest untruth will make him feel like he is riding a curve of uncertainty.

Up to this point he has not, in fact, been lying. All he has said is exactly what he thinks; what he assumes – and has always assumed, ever since one of his endless Google self-and-father-searches threw it up – to be the source of the interview of unsolved.com. But he has never actually had this assumption confirmed by his father.

'And, anyway, even if he did write it – maybe he wrote it out of guilt. Guilt for my sister.'

Harvey blinks. He has not thought of this – this interpretation. Before he has a chance to consider it further, the gunman continues, his voice now edged with genuine menace:

'Not that it matters. He deserves to die anyway, if he thinks that the death of my sister, from pills they took together, is a fit subject for some *genius* prank.'

Harvey starts: it seems strangely sacrilegious, and yet somehow refreshing, to hear the G-word said sarcastically in this room.

'So, listen. I don't want to kill you. But. You've done your thing, your bit trying to protect your father. OK? Your guilt – it's fixed. You tried to talk me out of it. It didn't work. You can remember that in years to come. You did your best. So now: I will kill you unless you move out of the way.'

Harvey's eyes swivel round. Behind the porthole, John the security guy has turned round. He is not talking on his Bluetooth phone. He is looking impassively at Harvey. Harvey, not wanting to chance any greater 'Help me' gesture, flicks his eyes away from his gaze, towards the gunman, whom he knows John cannot see, and back again. John frowns, shrugs, and turns away. Harvey sighs internally. He has only one card left to play. He picks his father's limp right hand up from the side of bed. His writing hand. It feels light in his own, like a dried leaf.

'Can I say goodbye?'

'What?'

'Can I say goodbye? To my dad?'

The gunman looks at him. The wall eye makes it difficult for Harvey to judge where he is looking – where he is *aiming*: at him or his father. He exhales, heavily.

'Make it quick,' he says.

*   *   *

Running back along the hospital corridors, Colette Gold is thinking only that she has to get back to her Daddy. She has been feeling more and more unhappy in the room in the other building, where the grown-ups have all been standing for far too long in a big circle around Bill Clinton. She can't believe that her mommy and all the doctors would leave Daddy alone for so long. She has said this to her mommy, but her mommy has told her to hush, they will only be half an hour, and then they will go back to Daddy's room.

Some of the grown-ups have talked to her for a little bit, but she knew they were only doing so in the gaps before they could go back and speak to Bill Clinton again. So she ended up on her own, looking out the window at the park. She could see a man down there with some kids, a boy her age and a girl slightly younger, trying to fly a red and white kite. They weren't doing it very well – it kept on flapping in the sky and falling – but they were all laughing and having a good time. She wished she were one of them.

The man and his kids had packed up the kite and started to go home. Standing alone by the window in that big room, her thoughts had crowded in on her. She didn't like the way that she had said goodbye when she had left her daddy's bedside just now: she thought he could have misunderstood it, that he might have thought she was not coming back. Plus she thought that maybe he might feel jealous, because she had been spending such a lot of time with Harvey recently,

401

and he had ended up seeming sort of like he was her dad. Which, even though she liked him a lot more than she used to, he wasn't, and never would be.

So when her mommy wasn't looking – when her mommy was laughing and throwing her head back at something Bill Clinton had said – she had slipped out of the room, and now here she is, running down the corridor of the fourteenth floor. Some grown-ups in the elevators and in the lobby have stared at her curiously, but she knows the hospital so well by now and is moving so confidently that no one has stopped to ask if she is lost. Her legs hurt and her chest hurts, but she feels happy in the sure and certain hope of making things better again. She runs so fast that she has to stop and walk the last bit up to outside her daddy's door. John is there, of course.

'Hi, Miss Gold,' he says. He always calls her this. Sometimes she wishes that John would have a nickname for her, or maybe just call her Colette. 'Are you OK?'

'I've been running.'

'Oh. OK.'

'Is there someone in there?'

'Huh?'

'I can hear someone in the room.'

John takes out the phone thing he always has in his ear.

'Oh, yeah. Mr Harvey went in a bit earlier, and a doctor.'

'Is that who Harvey is talking to?'

John looks round, through the glass.

'Uh … no, I don't think so. He's sitting by the bed. I guess … I guess he's talking to your daddy.'

'Oh!' she says. 'Would you mind … could you lift me up so I can see?'

'Well, you can just go in if you want.'

'No. I don't want to disturb him. I'll wait till he's finished. I just want to look.'

John smiles – she thinks how big his mouth is – and picks her up.

She watches through the porthole. Yes, Harvey is indeed sitting by the bed. She can only see his back, but – oh – he is holding Daddy's hand. Colette feels tears in her eyes. But not bad tears; happy ones. She is glad that Harvey has at last taken her advice. She feels proud of herself, thinking that it is her doing, her that has brought her half-brother to this better place. She watches them, and in her mind's eye the two men, neither of whom on their own are quite the father figure she in her deepest core feels she should have, seem to meld, each one making up the deficiencies of the other. She presses her ear to the glass of the porthole, in order to hear what Harvey is saying; she shuts her eyes tight, so as to help her remember his words, because she knows how important this moment is, and she wants to write them down later on for inclusion in her diary.

'... so Dad ... Daddy ...' Harvey is saying, '... I'm glad you're dying, really, Dad. I think it's best for you. Because you're a Great Man, Dad. Yeah. Everyone says you are. I fucking know you are. But no one is Great, any more, Dad. Greatness: it's gone. It's over. In the old days, if you got called Great, in the right quarters, that was that. You were there for life. Now there are too many people who can speak, who can have their say, who can say No, he's not great, he's shit. He's a fucking useless cunt. And they say that stuff all the time, because they all hate the idea that anyone is Great, because it means that they aren't. And that's just the half of it, the Great thing. The other half, the Man thing, that's gone too. Men can't be men, any more, not like you were a man. Destroying everything that came into the path of your cock. Flying through life holding onto that big blue vein, knowing that it would all be OK in the end because you were Great. All forgiven, because you were Great. It stops here. I should know. I'm the son of a Great Man. But I haven't inherited any of the Greatness. I'm not Martin Amis, or Kiefer Sutherland, or Sofia Coppola, or Rebecca Miller, or George W. Bush, or Jordi Cruyff. I'm not even Julian Lennon. So no Great genes. And you know what? I may not even have inherited the Man gene. Not properly.'

Some of this sounds strange to Colette. It is not quite the goodbye she was expecting Harvey to make. But she puts it down to words she does not understand. It is still good, in her mind. Then Colette hears another voice from somewhere.

'OK, that's enough.'

She cannot see this voice and, because she is, after all, a child, she thinks it must be her daddy, who she has been told can understand, somehow answering. It does not sound like him but that must be just because he is in a coma. Her heart beats like a butterfly at the thought.

Harvey says: 'Fine. Fine. Sorry, Dad. I did my best.'

She asks John to put her down. She bursts into the room. She says Harvey! Daddy! And Harvey looks up and he shouts her name and jumps towards her as if he is going to embrace her but he looks really weird and mad and then there is a loud bang and then everything goes black.

✶ ✶ ✶

[unidentifiable noise … EG getting up and going?]

RW: Just one more question … Mr Gold?

[unidentifiable noise … door opening?]

RW: When you get back home … will you be keeping to your half of the pact? Will you be trying again to commit …

[door slam]

Harvey is still not entirely sure he can use his phone in the terminal building at JFK. Speaking on it now, in the Virgin check-in line for Economy, he checks furtively every so often in case that terrifying flight marshal should be patrolling the area. All he sees, though, is an electronic poster advertising first L'Oréal, then some new Cameron Diaz movie.

'Oh, my God. My God. But you're all right. Are you? Are you hurt? What about Colette?'

It is his wife's voice. In the background he can hear the sound of a kettle boiling and cereal packets rustling. Jamie will be having his breakfast. Tuesday: Corn Flakes. The sound recedes as she moves through to their hallway to avoid disturbing their son with this story.

'No, I'm fine. She's fine, too. She didn't get hit by the bullet, just by the butt of the gun. She was concussed, but fine.'

He notices that a man from the group in front, who is very fat but carries only a tiny suitcase, has looked round at him. His eyes, tiny in the flesh of his face, demonstrate a clearly piqued interest. How long has he been listening? All the way from *Stella: my dad was shot this morning*? Harvey gives him a hard stare. The man turns round, with no sense of abashment.

'And Eli?'

'Well, obviously, he's dead.'

'Killed … Jesus …'

'No, I'm not sure.'

'What do you mean?'

405

'There was no blood. The bullet hit him in the side of the head, but no blood came out.'

'Is he a vampire? Sorry, darling, wrong time ...'

'No, that's OK. He might have been. But, no, his doctor said in all likelihood he died some time before the bullet hit. Some time during the scuffle. Or maybe even while I was saying goodbye. Which means, I suppose, that he – Pauline's brother – won't get charged with murder.'

The first group at the check-in desk move off, with their boarding passes. The line shifts forward. Harvey, who has no trolley, has to kick his luggage in the direction of the very fat man. How hard would I have to kick my suitcase for it to fly into his enormous arse?

'Saying goodbye, though. That was weird. I was just doing it to stall, really. And also, you know this thing they say in crime films – it happens in *Silence of the Lambs* – how you have to humanize the victim? Try and make the killer see him or her not as an object, but as a real person?'

'Yes.'

'I think that's what I was doing, sort of. Without quite realizing it. In the process of saying goodbye to him, I was trying to make Pauline's brother see him as a real person. Except ...'

'What?'

'When it came to it, the person that I made him see that Dad was – I don't know if that helped. I don't know if I made him seem like a person who shouldn't ... die. I guess.'

There is a silence at the other end of the line. He feels Stella's empathy cogs whirring.

'So, you never really said goodbye? It was all just a tactic?'

He considers this. In his pocket, his fingers play with the wrapper of a Sour Apple Bomb Colette had given him much earlier today.

'It was. But, no. I said goodbye. More than I ever thought I was going to.'

'OK, Jamie. Just hold on. I'm coming.' Her voice shifts down to a semi-whisper: their son's Asperger's radar is up. 'Fuck. What about the police?'

'I've given them a statement already.' He doesn't say that the name of the policeman who took his statement, in the privacy of Freda's little room down the corridor, was Webb, and that when he had asked him if he had a relative who had worked in the NYPD, the answer had been yes: his father.

'They said you can go?'

'Well, no one stopped me. It was chaos at the hospital. And John – the security guy who's been standing outside Eli's room this whole time? He was great, just led me through the madness.' To Harvey's surprise, John had also, as they had got to the hospital entrance, said, 'I owe you, man' and hugged him – Harvey, completely smothered by his puffa jacket, found it strangely blissful, security guy become security blanket. Once released, Harvey had wanted to say, 'No, I owe *you*, man' – after all it had been John who had actually fought the assassin, John who had brought him down – but he hesitated, not wishing to come over like a white man trying to sound black, and, in the moment of uncertainty, John had just turned and gone back to his job.

'I still can't get my head around this. Especially that you took him on.'

'I didn't take him on. I just talked.'

'But when the little girl came in …?'

'I just jumped up to grab Colette. Get her out of his way. Protect her.' *She is so unprotected.*

'Yeah, but you might have – darling, you could have been killed.'

The group in front shift to load their luggage onto the weight machine. The check-in woman, revealed by their parting heads, is smiling at them all. She wears a bright red blazer, with lipstick to match. Harvey's tired eyes begin their search of her face and body: and then, quite suddenly, he can't be bothered.

'You're a hero,' says Stella. She says the phrase without irony: something of an achievement, in this day and age.

'No.'

'Harvey. You are.'

He thinks: I suppose I am, of sorts.

'What about the funeral? You aren't staying for that?'

'No. That'll be Freda's gig. As will the enormous memorial service in a month's time. I don't think I can handle it. Plus I really want to come home.'

'How was Freda?'

'Distraught. But also … I don't know. I think the drama of it suits her. I think she wouldn't have been able to cope with him just quietly slipping away.'

'Was she thankful to you?'

'For what?'

'For taking on the mental man! For saving her daughter's life!!'

'Oh. Yeah, sort of.' In fact, Freda had been mainly concerned, reasonably enough, with Colette's welfare, and then simply with the fact of Eli's death. She had cried manful, stoic tears. In his mind's eye Harvey had seen her transform – in the bustle of the room, with bodies being moved out, and policemen asking questions – into a classical widow, assuming the mantle of dignified grief as easily as a great actress dons Jocasta's black. This is what she will be for the rest of her life, forever wreathed in the sad smile of memory: she will be her Yoko Ono. As he had left, though, Freda had grasped his hand and looked him in the eye for far too long, until he had to look away, embarrassed, which Harvey had taken to be the dignified grieving widow version of her trademark hug: and therefore forgiveness and thanks, of a type.

'I think,' he continues, 'she was already working on her speech to the reporters.'

'The news is out, then? Already?'

'No. But it will be soon. They know something's up. There were more than usual gathered outside Mount Sinai.' Loads of them: the weirdo fans were all there, too, one of them, the blonde in pigtails, barefoot, wearing a man's overcoat, much too big for her, and crying, as if she already knew.

'Has everyone who should know been told?'

'How do you mean?'

'Before it's in the news …'

'Oh. Yeah. The police or the hospital will tell Simone and Jules. They won't release the information to the press until after they've been informed.'

'God. I still can't get my head round it. I know this is a clichéd thing to say but – stuff like this doesn't happen to people like us, does it?'

'No,' says Harvey. 'But it does happen to people like Eli. He'd have loved it as a way to die. Now he'll be more famous than ever.'

He is at the check-in desk.

'Hello, sir,' says the Virgin Lady. 'Travelling to London today?'

'Yes,' he says.

'Listen, darling, I've got to go.'

'OK. Be safe. For God's sake.'

'Just one thing. Sorry, I'll be with you in a minute.' The Virgin Lady nods, and looks away discreetly. He bends his face more into the phone and lowers his voice. 'I think maybe – well, I hope – that now Dad's dead – well not just that, a whole load of stuff that's happened here – anyway, the point is, I think I might be: better. A bit. With everything.'

She knows, of course, what he is talking about. There is a silence at the other end of the line. He can hear Jamie humming in the background, a tuneless song.

'Really?' she says.

'Yes,' he says. He says it with emphasis, because he so wants it to be true. He has no idea whether it is.

'OK, good. Let's hope so.'

The Virgin Lady looks back towards him. Though she smiles radiantly, her eyes are saying that he and a number of other passengers behind him, some of whom are looking annoyed, have a plane to catch.

'Stell, I've got to go. I love you.'

It comes back unhesitatingly. 'I love you, too. And, Harvey, I'm sorry. About your dad.'

'Don't be,' he says. 'Really. It was time for him to go.'

He puts the phone back in his pocket, clumsily failing, under the social pressure of the check-in queue, to click END CALL properly. To his right, the electronic poster rotates once more, flicking from Cameron Diaz to a new beautiful female face: it is Lark, looking direct to camera, holding a guitar, and subtitled simply with her name and the word *Astray*. He does not see it; just as he does not hear a small voice, his wife's, continue from another part of the world:

'Harvey? Hold on. Isn't there someone else who should be told?'

*　*　*

Violet Gold is straining to put on a sock. It is a blue woollen one, one of a pair which are now slightly too big for her feet. Her feet – unlike other parts – are not a section of her body that she would have thought capable of shrinkage, but she is sure these socks used to fit her perfectly. Because they are too big, the wool always concertinas around her ankle when she stands up, and she knows how socks worn in that way can present a version of a person who has given up. Not so much, though, as not being able to get one on at all.

Some of the residents at Redcliffe House dress themselves and others don't. It is the Rubicon between the living and the living dead, and Violet does not wish to cross it, at least not today. She has managed to get the right one on, presumably, she thinks, because her right hip is in better shape than her left. She sits on her bed, holding the limp woollen tube uselessly in her hand. It is navy blue, to match her skirt.

She tries again. But she cannot bend far enough on that side; her body locks, with her fingertips flailing the sock halfway down her haunch. It is as if someone is holding her down there, forcing her to come to terms with the realization that the skin on her shin is so thin the bone is visible. She rocks backwards on the bed and tries to put the sock on from below, but her legs do not come up above her as they would have done when she was younger. Instead, her torso ends up flat on the bed, with her lower half hanging off the end. She is not sure she can move. Off to one side of the bed, within reach, is the red panic button. But pressing it – since she will be found with one sock on and one sock off, and therefore the evidence that she can no longer dress herself will be incontrovertible – means crossing the Rubicon.

She remains there for some time, the smell of the kitchen's numerous breakfasts fading in her nostrils. There is something pleasurable about it. With one sock on and one sock off, she can imagine that she has stopped time: nothing can progress until such an in-between condition is resolved. Life will not move on, surely, until her other sock is on, so perhaps it is best to just lie still and assume that she has found in this tiny domestic interstice the means to cheat death.

There is a knock on the door. Her heart beats fast: or, at least, fast for her, these days. A surreal thought crosses her mind, that it is good that all parts of the body age at the same rate; good, in other words, that her heart is old and baggy because if it was young and pert the banging it would be capable of would surely crack her powdery ribs.

'Hello?' she says.

'Are you decent?' comes back Mandy's voice.

Violet wonders what the answer to this is. There is something indecent about the way she is lying, something that in a younger woman might be thought of as sexual, so therefore, she assumes, will look on her twisted and grotesque. And there is something indecent about the thought that being found like this may mean that she will never get to dress herself again.

'You've got a visitor,' says Mandy.

'My sister?' she says. Why would she come at this time? And without telephoning first?

'No. A lady.'

Violet blinks at the ceiling of her room. It is like a blank screen on which she tries to project who this might be. Only Valerie ever comes to see her. Only Valerie has ever come to visit her at Redcliffe House. The shock of it being someone else, in fact, gives her system a jolt, enabling her to sit upright on the bed just as Mandy, taking her silence as acquiescence, opens the door. She smiles at Violet – also somewhat unusual – and then steps aside, allowing a woman into the room.

'Hello,' says the woman, and then, noticing Violet's feet: 'Oh, sorry, were you just getting dressed?'

'Um … I was, yes, but it's fine.' She does not know who this woman is, but visits, especially from young people, are currency in Redcliffe House, raising the receiver of the visit in everyone's estimation. Besides, something about her suggests that she has good reason to be here. Violet feels a trickle in her mind of what it might be about. She looks to Mandy, who is perched nosily at the door. 'Thank you, Mandy,' she says. Mandy's smile fades as she goes.

'Do sit down,' Violet says, standing. She puts her feet into her slippers and gestures towards her chair. 'Can I get you a cup of tea?'

'Um. Yes. But, please: I'll make it. Through here?'

'I'm fine to make the tea, really.'

'OK,' says the woman, reddening. Violet has seen this shadow play before with the other residents, where a young, able-bodied visitor offers some small form of help, and then feels, once told that it is unnecessary, that they should not have offered it, and that what they had thought was kindness may have been interpreted as condescension.

'Don't worry, please,' she says, 'I would have been just as happy for you to make it. But I know where everything is. Sugar? Or perhaps you'd like coffee?'

'No, tea is fine. And no sugar, thank you.' She sits down. How old can she be? Forty, even? She is slim, and her face is finely framed by much curling reddish hair. Violet wonders when last this amount of hair, hair with life like this, was in this room. As the woman's body makes its first contact with the chair, Violet feels suddenly self-conscious about her surroundings. It must seem all so musty to her, she thinks. Will the seat still be warm from when she sat in it this morning, naked, trying to build up the energy to put her clothes on? Will this warmth disgust her?

'Tea with no sugar it is then,' she says, and turns towards the kitchenette.

'Violet,' says the woman. She turns back. 'It is Violet, isn't it? Violet Gold?'

'Yes …?'

'I'm so sorry, I haven't introduced myself. My name is Stella. Stella Marsten.'

'Right. Well, it's lovely to meet you, Stella.'

'Yes. I mean … it's lovely to meet you, too. My husband's name is Gold. Harvey Gold.'

The trickle in Violet's mind swells. 'Let me make that tea,' she says.

*　*　*

In the hung moment, while this tea is being made in London, Harvey Gold takes one more call before he leaves America. Due to an air traffic build-up, his flight has been delayed on the tarmac for over an hour. He has taken the phone out to turn it off, or maybe just switch it to aeroplane mode, although he is not sure about this, as it may power down somewhere across the Atlantic, leaving him bereft at Heathrow. The stewardess, who is doing the safety demonstration, is right by him – every time her arms stretch out in front of her in another section of her pointless life-saving mime, her bright red hip judders in the corner of his vision. Distracted, he has begun the process of changing his home screen from an image of the earth to one of Stella and Jamie, but flicking through his photo library he so far cannot find a perfect one – either Stella does not look quite as he would like, or Jamie is making one of the weird faces he tends to make when being photographed, or he himself is in the picture, which seems somehow inappropriate. The nearest is one of his wife and son from a family holiday a couple of years ago in Spain, standing outside a restaurant on the Cap de Creus, the unearthly rock formation that crumbles along the coast two hours north of Barcelona. Stella looks nice – it is sunset, and the deep red light throws her light tan into good relief – and Jamie is looking away across the sea, which means his face is still. And the restaurant, Harvey remembers, was called the Restaurant at the End of the World, which seems right, if he is going to replace the world with this picture. But then, looking at it again, widening it and closing up on it by splaying his fingers across the screen, he has become unsure, and instead has started playing chess again, when the phone rings.

'Dizzy,' he says. 'I'm on a plane.'

'I see.'

'I'm coming back to London.'

'Ah …'

Harvey looks across the two other passengers in his row – an old couple, the woman reading, the man staring into space – to the window. All he can see are aeroplanes coming in, trundling on the tarmac towards their gates. Nothing seems to be heading out apart from them.

'You're not going to comment about that? About what it might mean about my father?'

'Harvey, we're not in a session now. We can talk about that when we are.'

'Yeah. Well. Sorry, Dizzy, I should have said this earlier, but I'm not planning to come back.'

'Really? I see.'

Harvey had expected that his decision would induce no shattering of Dizzy's smugness, but is still disappointed with this response: there is not even the tiniest crack in his therapist's voice.

'Yes, I'm planning to do without therapy. For a while at least. See how it goes.'

'As you wish, of course. Meanwhile, you have missed eight sessions, including the one you're now going to miss tomorrow. I calculate, at a hundred and thirty pounds a session, that that means you owe me one thousand and forty pounds.'

'You're not actually going to charge me that, are you?'

'These are my rules, I'm afraid. Shall we say a thousand?'

'Yeah, but …' He thinks about saying all the stuff he normally says – about how his dad was dying, about how Dizzy could have a heart, about how, although something may have shifted in him in the last few weeks and he hopes to God it has, this has fuck-all to do with Dizzy and his fucking mantras. But all this would be, he realizes suddenly, just hacking a chanik. The stewardess takes off her life jacket and concludes the demonstration.

'Dizzy.'

'Yes, Harvey.'

'Here's the thing. I'm not going to pay you the money.'

'You're not.'

'No. But next time you feel the need to call me about that money, or maybe just next time it makes you really cross that I haven't paid it, why don't you just think: *I'd really, really like to have that thousand quid; but if I never get it, it's not the end of the world.*'

There is a small muffled cough at the other end of the line. It is not the comic-book spluttering and the 'but … but … but …' that Harvey would have liked, but it will have to do. And it just gives him the time to say, before Dizzy starts talking of lawyers and letters and whatever else, 'Goodbye, Dizzy.'

'Please now switch off all mobile phones and other electronic devices, as we are starting our run-up towards takeoff.'

He switches the iPhone to aeroplane mode. Quickly, he installs the photograph of Stella and Jamie in Spain as his home screen. It looks nice there. It looks like it should be there. He goes back to his chess game. They begin to taxi towards takeoff. As the plane moves faster and the sound of the engine rises, he notices, out of the corner of his eye, the old woman, without looking up from her book, place her hand onto the hand of her husband, who remains staring into space. The plane gets faster. Its wheels leave the ground. Harvey Gold feels good; he feels his life is on an upswing; and so he feels that he should finally beat Deep Green at chess. He plays urgently. Bishop to King 3. Rook to Queen's Knight 4. Queen to King's Rook 2. Pawn to Queen 7. Queen to King's Bishop 5. *Ting!* It goes. *Checkmate. Tiny wins.*

∗ ∗ ∗

Stella drinks her tea almost as soon as it comes, gulping it down quickly, a mannish action at odds with her deeply feminine appearance.

'You don't need to hurry,' says Violet, thinking that she is ill at ease in her company and wants to get it over with.

415

'No,' she says. 'I'm not hurrying. I always like to drink hot drinks when they're really hot. I never let them cool down. I'm sure it's really bad for my insides.'

'Oh, well. Everything's bad for your insides these days.' And as she says it, she has a strange feeling, one she has not had for many years: this is a cliché. She shouldn't say it, at least not in front of someone married to a Gold.

Stella smiles, though, sympathetically. Violet puts her mouth to her own tea, a small, cautious sip.

'Violet …' says Stella. Violet hears the note of gravity and significance, and suddenly wants to put off what it portends for one moment longer.

'How did you find me?'

'Oh. I'm a lawyer. We have people-finding software, databases, everything like that, on our computers. I'm afraid most information about you or anyone else is findable that way. These days.'

She seems, to Violet, to echo the phrase as a way of saying that using it, that speaking like ordinary people do, is all right.

'But there must be other Violet Golds?'

'Of course. But not that many with the correct date of birth. And only one with the correct date of birth and the supporting informa-tion, m dot – that means married – E. Gold, 1944–54.'

'That's on some computer somewhere?'

'Yes. Well, on some database. Which also gave me your last address – Cricklewood?' Violet nods. 'And a phone number. The people living there now knew where you were …'

So this information exists, easily accessible. Somewhere out there her life has been pinned and mounted around this central fact: her marriage to Eli Gold.

'Anyway …' says Stella. She looks uncomfortable. Violet wishes to spare her sensitivities, but cannot quite stop her, yet, even though she knows by now what she is going to say. There is something she needs to hear.

'That's why I've come to see you. Because of Eli.'

And that is it: his name, said by someone else in this room, with reference – with respect – to her.

'He's dead?'

'Yes. This morning … I didn't want you to hear it on the news.'

She feels it as a huge rush of relief, of a type that she thought had been lost to her. Relief as it is for the young – the blast of ecstasy that is a beer poured down a thirsty throat, or the sound of a lover's voice on the telephone, or orgasm – that had gone, long ago, replaced by more sedate forms of release: sitting down after standing for some time; passing water after an urgent dash to the toilet; taking off waist-biting support tights. But this felt like relief used to: it felt like the sea, dived into on the hottest day of the year.

'Are you all right?' said Stella. Violet looks up. Her face, she realizes, is wet. She must have been crying. She is a little amazed at herself – not that such a reaction has been provoked, but that she can still cry. The last time she remembers doing so was when Neville and Valerie tried to force her to sell *Solomon's Testament*, and that was so many years ago. She has assumed that the ducts must have dried up. She is surprised that her body has enough juice left in it to produce tears.

'Yes, yes. I'm fine.'

From the wrist area of her sleeve – she is, after all, an old lady – Violet produces a tissue, and dabs at her cheeks with it.

'Would you like me to get the nurse to come back?'

'No, no. I'm perfectly well, really.' She feels again something she has not felt for a long time: a concerned touch. It is Stella's hand on hers. Her skin is cool and soft. She looks up. This is what she wanted, the slow telling. She does not really understand why this woman has gone out of her way to provide her with it, but she feels deeply thankful to her. Backed by the grey light falling from the window, she sees Stella's beautiful face, full of what seems to be sympathy, real sympathy, and, despite her arthritis, Violet has an absurd and ridiculous desire to get down on her knees in front of this angel of mercy, even if it might mean never getting up again. She does not, of course. Instead, she just says:

'Thank you, Stella. Thank you so much for coming. What a nice thing to do.'

'Really, it was nothing.'

417

'I'm sure it wasn't. Do you live nearby?'

'Well …'

'No. Well, as I say. Harvey – is that what you said? – he is a very lucky man.'

Stella shakes her head at this with a self-deprecating smile, as the custom dictates, although there is something else behind it, some complexity, which the older woman cannot quite make out, but which moves her to say, again:

'A very lucky man.'

It is another cliché: she knows it as she says it. The younger woman nods, accepting the compliment, a little, as she must, ironically. For a second, nothing in particular happens. An aeroplane banks in the air, the sheets are cleaned in a hospital bed, a lock is turned in a prison cell, a child is comforted by its mother, and the world turns, like a dumb dog chasing its own tail.

'Is there anything else I can do for you?' says Stella, eventually.

Violet blinks at her. 'Would you mind helping me put on this sock?' she says.

ACKNOWLEDGEMENTS

I'd like to thank, for all their help in various ways towards this book, John Bond, Nicholas Pearson, Mark Richards, Georgia Garrett, Zadie Smith, Frank Skinner and Ben Liston.